The Islesman

Nigel Tranter

The Islesman

Hodder & Stoughton

First published in Great Britain in 2003 by Hodder and Stoughton
A division of Hodder Headline

The right of Nigel Tranter to be identified
as the Author of the Work has been asserted in accordance
with the Copyright, Designs and Patents Act 1988.

2 4 6 8 10 9 7 5 3 1

A CIP catalogue record for this title
is available from the British Library

ISBN 0 340 77018 X

Typeset in Sabon by Hewer Text Ltd, Edinburgh
Printed and bound in Great Britain by
Mackays of Chatham plc, Chatham, Kent

Hodder and Stoughton
A division of Hodder Headline
338 Euston Road
London NW1 3BH

Principal Characters in order of appearance

Angus Og mac Donald: Son of Alexander, Lord of Islay.

Angus Mor mac Donald, 4th Lord of the Isles: Grandfather of above.

Ewan MacLean, Younger of Kinlochaline: Friend of Angus Og.

Alexander mac Donald, Lord of Islay: Father of Angus Og.

Alastair mac Donald, Lord of Kintyre: Brother of Angus Mor.

Seona nic Alastair: Daughter of above.

Eithne nic Alastair: Sister of above.

Roderick mac Alan: Son of governor of the Isle of Man, known as Rory.

Abbot Fergus of Saddell Abbey: Important Kintyre churchman.

MacDonald of Gigha: Isles chieftain.

Gillemoir MacLean of Duart: Powerful chief.

MacDuffie of Colonsay: Isles chieftain.

MacIan of Ardnamurchan: Powerful chief of that mainland peninsula.

Malcolm Tormod MacLeod: Skye chief.

Alastair MacDougall of Lorn: Great mainland chief.

Ian Cameron of Locheil: Important mainland chief.

Duncan Mackintosh of Moy: Chief of Clan Chattan.

Sir Andrew Moray, Lord of Bothwell and Moray: Supporter of William Wallace.

Guy O'Cahan, Lord of Derry: Great Ulster nobleman.

Ainea O'Cahan: Daughter of above.

Richard de Burgh, Earl of Ulster: English commander.

Mackinnon of Strath: Skye chieftain.

Finguala nic Angus: Daughter of Angus Og and Ainea.

Edward the First, King of England: Known as Longshanks.

Edward, Prince of Wales: Later Edward the Second.

Nigel MacNeill of Barra: Potent Outer Isles chief.

Lord John of Brittany, Earl of Richmond: Supporter of King Edward.

John mac Angus MacDonald: Son of Angus Og.

Sir William Wallace: Scots hero.

Andrew, Bishop of the Isles: Prelate.

Sir John Comyn, The Red: A competitor for the crown of Scotland.

Aymer de Vallance, Earl of Pembroke: One of Edward's greatest commanders.

Hugh, Master of Ross: Son and heir of the Earl of Ross.

Sir Neil Campbell of Lochawe: Strong Bruce supporter.

Robert Bruce, King of Scots: Former Earl of Carrick.

Sir James Douglas: Bruce friend, known as the Good.

Lady Christina MacRuarie of Carmoran: Heiress of Clanranald.

Edward Bruce, Earl of Carrick: The Bruce's brother.

Malcolm, Earl of Lennox: Great Scots noble.

Sir Thomas Randolph: Bruce's nephew, later Earl of Moray.

John, Son of MacDougall of Lorn: Known as Ian Bacach, or John the Lame.

Sir Gilbert Hay of Erroll: Bruce supporter. High Constable.

Bishop William Lamberton of St Andrews: Primate of the Scots Church.

Master Bernard de Linton, Abbot of Arbroath: Bruce's secretary.

Sir Robert Keith: Knight Marischal.

Magnus, Earl of Orkney: Also a jarl of Norway.

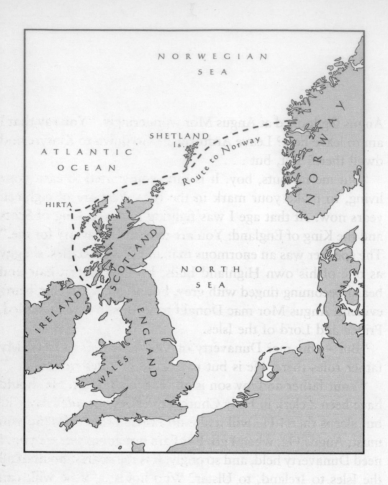

NORWEGIAN
SEA

ATLANTIC
OCEAN

SHETLAND
Is.

Route to Norway

HIRTA

NORWAY

SCOTLAND

NORTH
SEA

IRELAND

ENGLAND

WALES

Angus Og looked at Angus Mor wonderingly. "You say that I am to leave here? Leave Ardtornish? Go down to Kintyre and dwell there? But, but . . ."

"But me no buts, boy. It is time you started to earn your living, to make your mark in the Isles. You are of eighteen years now. At that age I was fighting both the King of Scots and the King of England: You are to hold Dunaverty for me." The speaker was an enormous man in his early sixties, shaggy as one of his own Highland bulls, his long flaxen hair and beard becoming tinged with grey, but no hint of ageing being evident: Angus Mor mac Donald mac Ranald mac Somerled, Prince and Lord of the Isles.

"But – why me? Dunaverty of Kintyre is near to Islay. My father rules there. He is but two score of miles from it . . ."

"Your father and my son is an idler, a dreamer. He should have been a clerk in Holy Church! He does not *rule* Islay – he but sleeps there! He will make no Prince of the Isles. So you must, Angus Og, when I go. But I am not going yet, see you. I need Dunaverty held, and strongly. It is the nearest point of all the Isles to Ireland, to Ulster. Who holds it, if he will, can control the narrow seas and the Ulster coast. And with this proud Edward Plantagenet of England dominating the Welsh and seeking to do the same over the Irish, Ulster must be denied him. He has few ships, compared with myself – or he might think to try to dominate *me*! So, Dunaverty for you. Men you shall have. And longships and birlinns. But that firth and channel must be held."

Angus Og wagged his dark head. He was of a very different

physical make from his grandsire, of only medium height, although broad of shoulder, all but swarthy instead of fair, but nowise lacking in characterful appearance. He shook that head, but shrugged.

"If I must," he said. None disobeyed Angus Mor in the Isles. "What am I to do there all the time? Apart from watching the Irish coast thirty miles off?"

"You will find a sufficiency to occupy you, if I know you, lad! And now and again you can sail over to Islay and stir up that father of yours! I will keep you informed as to my wishes, never fear."

The pair of them were standing on the parapet-walk of Ardtornish Castle in Morvern, looking southwards down the narrow sea loch of Aline to the Sound of Mull, that so important waterway of the Western Highlands, dividing the mainland from the great Isle of Mull. This was the favourite seat of the Lord of the Isles, or Prince thereof as he preferred to be named, however many other castles and strengths he held over many hundreds of miles of coastline and islands, from the foot of Kintyre to the south – if the Isle of Man was not counted – north past Rhum and Eigg and Skye and the Summer Isles to Cape Wrath itself, the very final tip of Scotland before the isles of Orkney and Shetland, which even he did not claim to rule, and westwards to all the long line of the Outer Hebrides, Lewis and Harris, the Uists and Barra and the rest, a sea-girt and island empire indeed. But here, at Ardtornish, Angus Og had been born and reared, here he had his friends and interests, however often he had sailed the rest. And now he was to leave his home and start a new life, it seemed, one hundred and fifty miles away.

"When must I go?"

"I go to Skye within the week. I would see you away south before that, lad."

"I will take Ewan MacLean with me."

"Take whom you will . . ."

Angus Og followed his grandfather down the narrow, twisting stairway to the withdrawing-room off the hall on the first floor, but himself went on further, down and out, to cross to the stables in the courtyard, where he collected his sturdy garron, long of mane and tail if short of leg. Mounting, he rode down the castle hill and across the ford of the River Aline, to turn down this southwards to the head of the loch where, at the entry of a minor stream from the west, a steep crag rose above the junction of waters. And perched on top of this was a small fortalice, a square parapeted tower, the little MacLean castle of Kinlochaline, modest compared with Ardtornish but sufficiently strongly sited. He rode up the zigzag track to this.

A hail from above welcomed him, and down came a young man of similar age to himself, clad as was Angus in saffron kilt and goatskin doublet, although his shirt was not of silk as was his friend's.

"I saw you coming, Angus," he greeted. "What's to do?" Normally Ewan MacLean was sent for rather than having the other come for him.

"Much is to do!" he was told. "We are to leave here. Or I am. And I would have you to come with me. To Kintyre."

"Kintyre! We visit Kintyre? I have never been there. A long way, is it not? Far south."

"Not to visit. To stay! To Dunaverty, on the Mull of Kintyre. I am to hold a castle there with men and ships. My grandsire orders it."

"Sakes! What is this?"

"I am to earn my living, he says. Act the chief there. What think you of that!"

On the way up to the tower Angus explained the situation. He found his friend since boyhood nowise upset or dejected by the prospect of leaving home, seeing it as an adventure rather; and in so doing raising Angus's own anticipation over the prospect. It might be none so ill a mission, although something of a responsibility, to become guardian of the narrows of the Irish Sea.

MacLean of Kinlochaline, a kinsman of Duart's across the Sound of Mull, and his wife raised their eyebrows over their young lord's tidings, but could not, of course, oppose the Prince of the Isles's wishes on this or on other matters. Ewan's young brother, Hector, wished that he could have gone also.

The two friends went fishing thereafter in a boat on Loch Aline, a favourite activity. They found much to discuss and anticipate. If Angus was going to act leader of armed men for the patrolling of the North Channel, and keeper of a strong castle, then they were going to need armour and weaponry, helmets and shields, clothing for especial occasions. And they would have to practise and improve their skills with swords and crossbows, battle-axes and lances. The more they talked, the more exciting and appealing the project grew for them.

Angus Mor set in motion all the necessary preparations without delay, for he wanted to see his grandson gone before he himself departed in the opposite direction, for Skye. So a busy four days followed, with men being summoned and longships gathered and readied. He recruited a seasoned warrior, one MacInnes of Uladail, to act as mentor to his grandson, especially in the deployment of numbers of ships to best effect; but left this worthy in no doubt as to who was in command. Needless to say, he himself gave the young man much guidance as to what was required of him, strategies to be employed, and who could be relied upon to aid him and who not to trust. Angus Og was duly impressed.

The great day dawned. At the head of the loch, below Kinlochaline Castle, no fewer than twenty longships were waiting, each with sixteen long oars or sweeps, three men to each, with a single mast and square sail. One of the long, low vessels was a dragonship, so called because of its high beaked prow in the shape of a rearing monster, this for Angus himself. His grandsire had come down to see them off. It was St Marnock's Eve, 17 August 1292.

"Look, boy, on your way to Dunaverty you have two calls to make. One on your father on Islay, to inform him of your task. Aye, and you can be mentioning to him that *he* ought to be doing it himself! The other on my brother Alastair, who is holding Kintyre for me, in the name at least! Why am I plagued with feeble weakling kin, son and brother? Two years younger than myself, Alastair acts the greybeard, seldoms stirs from his house, he who ought to be guarding the seas there. He bides over at Saddell on the east side of Kintyre, on Kilbrannan Sound, not on the west-facing coast at all. Tell him that I need action, better support. And you are to provide it, in my name."

Angus Og blinked. "Will, will they heed *me*? At my age? My father and grand-uncle!"

"They had better. See you." He turned to the man standing behind him, and took from him the great weapon he carried. This he handed to his grandson. "Here is my war-axe. All know it. All my days I have wielded it. You have seen this times a-many. On its haft are notches for every battle I have won. It is yours meantime. Wield it worthily. It is your warrant."

With something like awe the young man took the famous axe, weighty, long of shaft, this scored by many indentations, regularly cut. How many men had this slain?

"So now – off with you. And do not fail me, as these others have done, I charge you. You speak, and act, with my authority so long as you hold this axe. Go!"

Angus Og, clutching the war-axe, bowed. He turned away, followed by Ewan MacLean and MacInnes of Uladail. They strode for the dragonship, to the cheers of the many watchers. Angus had to march into the water for some splashing yards to reach the craft, all its sixteen oars upraised in salutation. He hoisted himself over the side, at the stern, in accustomed fashion, kilt up, ignoring the helmsman's outstretched hand,

Ewan following suit, although MacInnes, a middle-aged man, accepted the assistance.

Standing there at the stern beside the long, broad-bladed steering-oar, Angus raised an arm in final gesture, then waved to the helmsman, who banged down his baton on the gong hanging there, three loud clangs sounding out, to echo from the enclosing hillsides. And on all the other nineteen longships waiting there, fully manned, the gongs clashed, and sweeps were lowered to the water. With a westerly breeze the single square sails, painted with the Galley of the Isles, could not yet be hoisted. Led by the dragonship the fleet of the greyhounds of the sea, as they were known, moved off southwards in a long line, to the rhythmic beat of a score of gongs timing exact oar-pulling. Angus's helmsman, deep-voiced, started the chant, which all the others took up, in time with the gongs. And so, in typical Islesman style, the flotilla drove on down Loch Aline.

Grinning at Ewan, Angus laid down the war-axe on the stern bench, and, sitting, joined the oarsmen at their panting chanting.

They had two miles of the loch to cover before the narrows at the Kyle of the Point. There they emerged into the wide Sound of Mull, that great island's ranked mountains ahead of them, purple slashed with black against the blue and white of the sky, the waters reflecting the colourful scene.

South by east they swung now, past Ardtornish Point, then the wide bay of Innesmore, the longships behind now lining up three abreast, the grunting, regular chant maintained. For the two young men at the head of it all it made a rousing experience.

Presently, on the west, they were passing Duart Point, with its MacLean chief's castle perched on its topmost spur. Four of the longships following were Duart's. Then on due south now, down to the Firth of Lorn, heading for the open Sea of the Hebrides.

They had already rowed some twenty-five miles by the time they reached the long ocean swells, to bear south by west now in the direction of the lesser Isle of Colonsay, of the MacDuffies. They rounded the north point of this, one-time hermitage of St Oran, to row south sixteen miles skirting the west coast of long Jura, past the notorious whirlpools of the Corryvreckan, whose continual roaring temporarily drowned the chanting. Presently they were passing the strange sea loch of Tarbert, which almost cut Jura in two; and then they were under the renowned twin mountains, the Paps, these dominating the scene in suitable fashion. Islay ahead of them.

They entered the narrows of the sound.

This large island of Islay, not quite so big as Mull, and very different in character and significance, was highly important in the watery world of the Hebrides; for here was the caput of the lordship of the Isles, the seat of justice and assembly-place of chiefs, this the most populous isle of the hundreds, all but thousands, far to the south of most as it was. Yet Angus Mor had never chosen to dwell here, preferring the more central situation and more dramatic scenery. For Islay was a comparatively flat territory, although fertile compared with most, possessing only hills, not mountains, but with good grazing and tilth although poorer for deer-stalking and other sports. He had placed his elder son Alexander here, so called to distinguish him from brother Alastair, although they were the same name in reality, judging that the scene would match his temperament.

Halfway down the sound, where it narrowed still further, so that Islay and Jura all but met, Angus had his fleet pull in at the haven of Askaig, from which a ferry plied across to the other and so different island. It had taken them eight hours of vehement rowing to cover those ninety miles, part aided by wind and tides, part the reverse. So it was now evening, and the rowers deserved rest, and, their throats thirsty from chanting, lubricating with uisge-beatha, the water of life, whisky. Leaving them to the hospitality of the Port Askaig people, Angus, Ewan and MacInnes borrowed garrons to take them up to their immediate destination.

They had no great distance to go to Loch Finlaggan. It seemed a strange location to site the lordship's caput, a rather dull sheet of water set in heathery hillocks, with two islets in the midst. On one of these rose the castle, and on the other a chapel where were buried successive lords and their families, and a walled enclosure which was, in fact, the judgment seat of the Isles, and assembly-place of the chiefs. A tall standing stone rose at the head of the loch, indicating some ancient pre-Christian significance for this place.

Being now evening, Alexander of Islay would be at home – not that he was apt to be away from the castle frequently, for he was a man of mental rather than physical energy, preferring study to outdoor activities and pursuits, unlike *his* father.

Another large gong at the lochside, where there was a little pier and a cottage, brought a boat over from the castle for the visitors.

Angus found his father at his meal, as more or less expected, alone at it, his wife long dead. Even thus he was poring over paper and files.

The callers were eyed less than welcomingly until Alexander recognised his son, whom he had not seen for some time. He then smiled. And oddly perhaps, he had a warm, pleasing smile, however seldom it was demonstrated.

"Angus! Angus!" he exclaimed. "How good to see you. It is long since I did. Here is a surprise."

"Yes, Father. It is some time. When was I here last? You never come to Ardtornish."

"I am no great traveller, my son. What brings you at this time? But – sit. And your friends. There will be no feast, but some fare you shall have." He rang a bell on the table for a servant. "You look well, lad. How is my father? He grows old now. Is he still the active one? Ever sailing the Isles. Making his

8

authority accepted, whether acceptable or no!" That brought out the smile again.

"He is well, yes," Angus said. "He sends you his good wishes." That was something of an exaggeration, but probably called for, especially in front of these others.

They sat, and it was explained that Angus had been sent to take over Dunaverty Castle on the Mull of Kintyre, and to patrol the narrow seas and the Irish coasts, the threat of King Edward of England ever growing. This had the older man shaking his head, but not in any way over himself being expected to see to it all, but over the need for such precautions, and the follics of men.

Thereafter the converse lapsed somewhat, father and son having but little in common to discuss. Angus was glad when the provender arrived, simple but sufficient.

Presently Alexander did tell his son of a matter after his own heart, which Angus should see to since he was going to Kintyre. "It is this of Kilkerran," he said. "At Dunruadhan. The chapel there. You will know of it, to be sure. St Ciaran's chapel, near his cave. He was one of Columba's disciples, and brought Christianity to Kintyre. And Dunruadhan was where Somerled first founded his lordship. The chapel, I am told, has become in poor state. We must keep it in better order. My father, I judge, cares little for such. But *I* do. So go you to Dunruadhan, none so far from Dunaverty, and have the chapel put to rights. See that the cave, Ciaran's diseart, where he communed with his Maker, is kept tended also."

Angus nodded. Those Irish saints had been busy along these coasts, Oran and Ciaran and others. But that was for the Celtic Columban Church. Now they had the Roman one, brought by the Hungarian Margaret, called a saint also. He was none so sure of the difference, but his father would be. He would see to this.

Alexander was early at retiring to bed, so his visitors did likewise.

9

In the morning they were not long in taking their leave. What Ewan and MacInnes thought of Alexander of Islay they kept to themselves.

They had a fifty-mile sail, although it was mainly oar-work again, down into the Irish Sea, to the Mull of Kintyre at the southern tip of this so lengthy peninsula, the longest in all Scotland, some sixty miles of it. They skirted the islands of Gigha and Cara, and thereafter pulled down the seemingly unending and fairly featureless coastline, eyed no doubt warily from the many small fishing-boats they passed, out from the little shoreline communities. At length, in late afternoon, they at last reached the southernmost point of Sron Uamha, the Point of the Caves, and could then turn eastwards along the Mull, sails able to be hoisted at last, with the westerly wind giving the oarsmen a well-earned rest.

It was a rocky and precipitous coast now, the hills coming down close to the sea, and the long Atlantic rollers pounding the reefs and skerries in clouds of spray, a very exposed seaboard, the very toe of Scotland, as it were, kicking out towards Ireland.

Some seven miles along this, with the isle of Sanda ahead, they came at last to Dunaverty, this at least easily recognisable, with its bay, and headland beyond rising high, and on its crown the castle that was to be Angus's new home. The bay, open to the south and west, was not the best place to shelter a fleet, all there recognised, with the prevailing winds and tides as they were. But no doubt a better haven could be found for most of the longships, keeping only two or three under the lee of the headland.

The actual harbour below the castle was small, and Angus could see why Alastair mac Donald chose to live elsewhere. Disembarking, and waving in friendly fashion to the alarmed fisherfolk, he led his captains up the steep climb to the castle with its square keep and high curtain walls, a sea eagle's nest of a place indeed.

The keeper, an elderly man named Rory MacIan, unbarred the gates for them only doubtfully, looking questioningly at so young a leader of armed men, however many longships he had brought with him. But his wife, Morag, a motherly soul with a brood of her own, proved more welcoming, and said that she was proud to have Angus Og, grandson of their lord, come to bide with them. Perhaps her husband saw himself being displaced.

Angus found the bare and gaunt castle scarcely to his taste, however strongly sited and dominant, although he could improve on this accommodation. But it had magnificent views, far and wide, exposed to winter storms as it would be. From its parapet he could see Ulster, less than a score of miles away, its north shores in especial, but southwards also, down the North Channel of the Irish Sea to the tip of Galloway, and eastwards across the wide Firth of Clyde to the far Ayrshire coast and the soaring rock of Ailsa Craig. And, of course, endlessly out to the Atlantic, past Rathlin Isle. This was all to be watched over and guarded by his longships, Angus Mor had ordered, to keep Edward Plantagenet from his attempts to take it over and threaten Scotland from there.

The position of Ireland was complex. The Norman Planta-genets had started to conquer that a century before, when Henry the Second had sent Richard de Clare, Earl of Pem-broke, Strongbow as he was termed, to subdue the many quarrelling kinglets. Successful, the Anglo-Normans were able to control most of the land, so that the High King, O'Connor, had come to accept Henry as overlord, and thereafter reduced his own title to merely King of Connaught. Only Ulster, the most northerly Irish kingdom, remained more or less inde-pendent, although Hubert de Burgh was created Earl of Ulster, this without gaining more than a toehold there. He had been succeeded by his son Walter and grandson Richard de Burgh, who was a successful commander and close to Edward. He would seek to gain control of all Ulster undoubtedly, and so allow Edward to use it as a flanking threat to Scotland. Hence Angus Mor's anxiety. But the English had no warlike fleets compared with the Islesmen's longships and birlinns, so this was advantageous, meaning that all efforts against Ulster would have to be by land, from the south.

Enquiries as to a suitable anchorage to base their longship flotilla elicited from Rory MacIan the fact that Sanda Island, less than four miles off, was the obvious place, better than any of the south- and west-facing bays of the Mull itself, for it had a protected northerly harbour, quite large, where the ships could lie, and from which they could be summoned by beacons lit on Dunaverty's towers and readily seen. And there they were still nearer to the Ulster shores, and scouting vessels could patrol the channel all the time.

So far, so good.

Angus did not forget that he had orders to go and see his grand-uncle Alastair, to inform him of the position regarding Kintyre in general and this new development, at his chosen seat of Saddell, halfway up the eastern coast of the peninsula, almost thirty miles away. So, two days later, leaving MacInnes in charge at Dunaverty, he set sail in the dragonship with Ewan eastwards and then north. He took that war-axe along with him, just in case his authority was questioned.

They sailed round the eastern tip of the Mull, new territory for Angus, towards the Ayrshire coast, and then up into the Kilbrannan Sound, with the great island of Arran on their right, this larger than Islay and almost as long as Jura, and as mountainous. By comparison the Kintyre shore was distinctly tame, although when they passed the small isle of Davaar, a major bay opened, at the head of which was Dalruaidhan, where Somerled had first set up his Isles capital. Angus decided to leave that to be explored later, with the Kilkerran chapel thereabouts to be dealt with for his father.

Saddell, really Saghadail, was still a further ten miles on. It seemed strange that Angus Mor's brother should have elected to make his abode in this fairly remote spot, although it was admittedly sheltered, and secure from any likely assault. Alastair MacDonald must be a very different sort of man.

When they reached the place, it was to find it much more interesting than they had anticipated, and in picturesque wooded and hilly country, at the mouth of a quite deep glen of that name. There was a large abbey here, imposing, where Somerled had commenced to built a monastery, and his son Ranald had completed and enlarged it into an abbey in memory of his father, whose body was buried here, along with many other chiefs and prominent folk, this one hundred and forty years earlier. Nearby was a fairly modest castle, their destination.

The Lord of Kintyre proved to be a genial, portly man, with a much younger wife and two daughters, forming a very domestic and homely family, as far removed from the lordship of the Isles in character as in environment. Alastair's surprise at seeing his grand-nephew was evident, but he greeted him kindly, although clearly wondering what brought him there.

Angus liked him and his wife, the daughters also, and in explaining his mission did not really indicate his grandsire's criticism of the other's lack of urgency and militancy on the lordship's behalf, although Alastair may have guessed at it.

Their host, although he did not speak much about the Isles situation, had however interesting information to impart as to national affairs, he being that much nearer placed to such developments. Angus knew that there had been many claimants for the Scottish crown following the deaths of Alexander the Third and his niece, the Maid of Norway, but not much more than that. Now he learned that these, the Claimants for the Throne as they were called, had all but come to blows with each other over their ambitions. And, the folly of it, they had called upon Edward of England to act the arbiter, the adjudicator, as an allegedly honest and neutral assessor. And he had carefully selected the weakest of them all, and by no means the most senior, John Balliol, to be King of Scots, himself reserving the style of Lord Paramount of Scotland, to the anger of the others. These were all descendants through the female lines of King David, the youngest of the Margaretsons. This Balliol was the son of one of them, Devorgilla of Galloway who had married John de Balliol of Barnard Castle, an English lord. Now he was King of Scots, in name at least. Others, Scots, such as Comyn, Lord of Badenoch, and Bruce, Earl of Carrick, were rejected, and furious. Yet Edward made them sign a document pledging support for his choice, their rival, this being called the Ragman Roll. Alastair declared that there would undoubtedly be trouble over this new reign. Whether it would affect the Isles or not remained to be seen.

All this interested Angus, needless to say. Edward Plantagenet appeared to have gained an ascendency over Scotland without actually having to go to war. Would it make him the more free to assail Ulster, and so threaten the Isles?

He and Ewan spent a couple of nights at Saddell, enjoying the company, Angus attracted to the two daughters, the elder much of an age with himself, a lively creature, full of laughter.

Then back to Dunaverty, and duty. He had not had to produce that war-axe.

2

Angus felt that he should not delay in making his presence felt over in Ulster. He had had his longships ranging up and down that coast from the start in twos and threes, showing themselves. But something more was required. So he decided that he should proceed with his whole fleet, calling at various significant points on that seaboard, to demonstrate that the Lord of the Isles was very much aware of the danger from Edward of England, and was prepared to counter him.

Shortly after his return from Saddell therefore, he marshalled all his craft and set sail across the North Channel, his dragonship flying the Banner of the Isles, in fine style. They passed Rathlin Island, to reach Fair Head, the most northeasterly tip of Ireland, and rowed westwards from there, close inshore, the Atlantic winds against them.

It was a fairly level coastline, although the spectacular rock formation of the Giant's Causeway stood out impressively before their first call, this at Portrush in Antrim, where Angus went ashore with some of his captains, to make his name known and to declare that Angus Mor was guarding all these shores from any attempts by the English to invade Ulster. This was well received by the local folk, who cursed Edward Plantagenet and all his minions.

They proceeded on to Magilligan Point, and turned into the narrows of Lough Foyle, which separated Coleraine and Inishowen, a long arm of the sea, at the head of which they came to Derry, where was a monastery founded by St Columba before he came to Scotland. Here was a sizeable town, where the people tended to look askance at the helmeted warriors from the longships; but their leaders were more appreciative of the Islesmen's protection. They passed the night in their ships, there.

They headed on westwards next day, through the Inishtrahull Sound to pass Malin Head and so into Lough Swilly. It was all none so very different from their own seaboard, save that there were no large islands and indeed few small ones; after all, Islay was only forty miles away.

Swilly, another south-probing sea loch, was fully thirty miles long and narrowly winding and twisting. It brought them to Letterkenny of Donegal, where Angus was fortunate to meet the O'Donnell kinglet, and was able to reassure him that although English Edward had achieved, by craft, some sway over Scotland meantime, the Isles and Western Highlands remained, as always, independent, with Angus Mor staunchly supportive of Ulster and Donegal. They were hospitably entertained that night at Letterkenny.

Up the long loch to the sea again in the morning, it was still west for them, past more lochs and deep inlets, backed by mountains now, as far as sight of the isolated Tory Island and the Bloody Foreland, which represented the end of the north coast of Ulster, with a call at Dunfanaghy, the last harbour of Donegal, where Angus decided that they could turn back. Southwards was really no concern of his. They had come a long way, over one hundred miles as the sea eagle flew from Fair Head, and three times that distance, with all the sea lochs to head into and out of. Enough to demonstrate their favour and succour, surely.

At least they had the wind behind them, to hoist sails and speed home, duty done for the nonce.

Angus had not forgotten his promise to his father regarding St Ciaran's chapel and cave. Besides, he wanted to see Dalruadhan, the original seat of the lordship.

It was only about a dozen miles' sail to the north, to enter the large, all but enclosed and sheltered bay of Kildalloig opening behind Davaar Island, this making an excellent anchorage, at the head of which the community lay, now somewhat decayed but with indications that it had been much larger once, and populous. There was a ruined fort and the remains of three chapels, but although presumably all were founded by St Ciaran, these were not what his father had been concerned about. Kilkerran, it seemed, the saint's own church, lay over a mile to the south.

Thither the visitors went. They found it actually smaller than those at Dalruadhan, a humble little sanctuary indeed, oblong, low of roof, with some of this fallen in, but with a handsome carved standing stone outside. The local belief was that this marked Ciaran's burial-place, where he had died nearly seven hundred years ago. There was little to see inside the chapel, it being little more than a cottage, but with an aumbry at the east end for the reservation of the communion bread and wine, and a holy-water stoup in the walling at the other side, these having flanked the altar site.

There was not much that could be done here to any worthwhile effect, save to have the roof repaired, and perhaps a wooden door provided to keep out the rubbish and dead leaves that had accumulated. Orders would be given for this to be done.

The saint's cave was almost three miles further south, on the coast. All these Celtic missionaries had their disearts, as they were called, remote hermitages where they could go, alone to commune with their Maker every so often, renew their vows and regain spiritual strength.

It turned out that there were many caves on the cliffs along that coast, but Angus found a cottager to take them to the desired one. It proved to be halfway down a precipice, reachable only by a dizzy-making narrow track. Ciaran must have had a good head for heights as well as for missionary zeal.

The cavern, when they reached it, seemed to be full of rock

doves, which flew out at their entry, buffeting them with their wings. Within, it was found to be a sort of L-shaped tunnel in the cliff, with many little ledges on the walls providing room for nests innumerable, the flooring deep-carpeted in bird droppings. Round the bend there was a much wider ledge or shelf, at seat height, with nearby a crack in the roof, this smoke-blackened. Clearly the fissure had served as a chimney for a fire; and no doubt the saint had slept on the bench-like ledge, scarcely comfortable quarters – but then comfort would not be what he had come here for. The birds did not seem to venture round that bend, so there were no droppings. No doubt Ciaran had looked on the fowl as friends, representing the sacred dove of the Holy Spirit.

Again there was nothing they could do usefully about this odd sanctuary, which would have few visitors indeed. Angus imagined that it was all very much as the missionary had left it all those centuries before. So he would tell his father.

They could return to Dunaverty satisfied.

With Morag MacIan's help, he and Ewan and MacInnes had been making that castle a somewhat more kindly place to live in, at least *their* quarters therein. And reasonable accommodation had to be seen to for the longships' crews, some down at the harbour cottages but much more over on Sanda Island. Winter was none so far off, and this would be a cold, blustery and stormy coast to dwell upon.

Shortly thereafter a sally was made, with the fleet, down the eastfacing coast of Ulster, just to make their presence known there also, this along the Antrim shore by Garron Point, Glenarm and Larne, these backed by a long line of hills, to Island Magee – which was not really an island at all, but a backwards-curling narrow peninsula at the month of Belfast Lough. This, some forty miles, was as far as they went, making only brief calls. So far, it seemed, the English Earls of Ulster had not made any real impact on the province, the present one, Richard de Burgh, being known to be King Edward's closest companion.

Back from this expedition, Angus was not very sure what he was supposed to do with his time, other than keep his long-ships patrolling the North Channel and Irish coasts. Presumably he should be doing something useful, not just roosting in Dunaverty Castle. There were deer in the hills to be stalked, wildfowl, ducks and geese to shoot with crossbows, salmon and trout to fish for. But was that what he was there for? He decided that a visit first to his father on Islay and then to Ardtornish for further instructions was probably called for.

So presently, leaving MacInnes in charge, he and Ewan set off northwards in the dragonship.

At Finlaggan, Alexander interrupted his studies to greet them. He was glad to hear about Kilkerran, the chapel repairs and the unspoiled state of the cave. He was also reasonably interested to learn about his Uncle Alastair and family at Saddell, whom he had not seen for years. He judged him a sensible man to live where he did, even if Angus Mor did not think so.

Then it was on again, much further north, to the Sound of Mull and Ardtornish, dropping off Ewan at Kinlochaline to join his family.

His grandfather was absent, apparently off to Coll and Tiree, to ensure that these quite sizeable islands, midway between Jura and the Outer Hebrides, were in good order and doing their bit for the lordship, Tiree in especial. This was known as the Garden of the Isles, the most fertile of them all, low-lying and fair, and because it had no mountains to catch the clouds escaping much of the rain which was so much a feature of that seaboard, hence the excellent crops and produce; indeed the name, Tir-ith meant Land of Corn.

Angus Mor arrived back the next day, to raise his eyebrows at the sight of his grandson, whom he clearly judged should be elsewhere.

Angus Og delivered his report on his activities, and the conditions prevailing in Kintyre, telling of his visits to Alexander and Alastair, which had the old man shaking his head. His grandsire was interested, however, in the reactions of the Ulster chieftains, and O'Donnell of Donegal, and told Angus Og to keep in touch with these.

"Also, boy, I require you to act in regard to that other Alastair, calling himself MacDougall, Alastair mac Ewan mac Duncan, Lord of Lorn, none so far distant kin of ours, but misbehaving. Or, at least, his son is. A fool, Alastair married a sister of the Black Comyn of Badenoch, in Strathspey in the eastern Highlands, all but an Englishman, a Norman. His son, the Red Comyn, was one of the competitors for the crown of Scotland passed over by Edward Plantagenet. Now this son of that marriage, Ian Bacach, is leaguing with this Comyn. I will not have any of my Islesmen linking with the like. It could weaken us. My brother, Alastair of Kintyre, should be seeing to this. Your father is nearer to Lorn, but he will do nothing. So go you to Alastair at Saddell and tell him to move, yourself urging and if necessary aiding him. You have it?"

"To do what?" Angus asked.

"Ian Bacach, the son, I am told, is even now in Badenoch with the Comyn. This must stop. On my orders. This Ian to be summoned home to Dunollie, the MacDougall castle on the Oban bay, in the Firth of Lorn. I will not have that young man meddling with Comyns, or any other mainland barons, especially ones who claimed the throne there. See you to it. You will be passing Dunollie on your way back to Dunaverty. But best that you do not see the MacDougalls first. My brother Alastair is Lord of Kintyre, and the duty is his. But you may need to spur him."

Not particularly looking forward to this of involvement in family dissensions and squabbling, Angus Og sailed off again, southwards, with Ewan picked up.

A dozen or so miles on their way, and into the Firth of Lorn, they came to the island of Kerrera, which screened off the Oban bay from the west, and Angus elected to enter the narrows between this island and the mainland to see this Dunollie, not to visit, just to observe. He had never been there before.

They had no difficulty locating the castle, prominent on a headland a mile or so north of the township and harbour, not unlike Dunaverty but larger, a massive square keep within curtain walls, the seat of his far-out kin. They had another seat, further north still, Dunstaffnage, he had been told. Angus wondered how this Alastair MacDougall had met and wed one of the Badenoch Comyns, who had come to Scotland with King David, so far away?

Was his grandsire over-suspicious and assertive? Presumably it was necessary, to maintain the unity and strength of the lordship. This of being Prince of the Isles was as demanding a position as it was prestigious. And one day he himself would be so styled!

3

Following his grandsire's instructions, Angus carried on north past Dunaverty to Saddell to talk with his grand-uncle. He liked Alastair MacDonald and family, especially the young women, although he was not over-eager to emphasise to their father Angus Mor's instructions regarding the MacDougalls.

In the event, Alastair heard him out patiently and, shrugging, said that he would go and see these remote relations, although what this would achieve he was uncertain. Why did his brother not go himself to this Dunollie? It was none so far from Ardtornish. Angus Og could only suggest that the vast spread of the Hebrides, to north and west, demanded almost all their lord's time and attention.

His grand-uncle had more news to tell of affairs in mainland Scotland. He learned of such from the mendicant friars who came to visit the Cistercian abbey nearby, great purveyors of information and gossip. It seemed that King John Balliol was scarcely happy on his new throne. The other passed-by claimants thereto were proving to be less than co-operative, especially the Red Comyn. And King Edward was demanding strict obedience to his wishes, which were many and humiliating. The realm was almost hopelessly divided, and Balliol was no stalwart hero – or Edward would not have selected him. He was apparently being called the Toom Tabard, which meant Empty Tunic. The King of England was, in fact, distributing land, properties and even pensions to whomsoever he wished in Scotland, without consultation with the puppet monarch; he had even given the prestigious earldom of Fife, the hereditary coroner's title, he who had the privilege of placing the crown on the head of each new king, to other than the true MacDuff heir.

But the most significant aspect of it all, as far as the Isles were concerned, was that, in a move to bolster Balliol's rule, and therefore his own, Edward had "given" the Isle of Man to Scotland, this, the most southerly part of the lordship of the Isles. Angus Mor's reaction to this would be dire indeed, that was certain.

Much disturbed as he was, Angus Og allowed himself to be just slightly distracted, on this occasion, by Alastair's two daughters, Seona and Eithne. They made very good company for the young men, they probably seeing no great numbers of the like, with the monks from the abbey not quite the same. They were, of course, related to Angus however distantly, so possibly felt safe with him. They were keen horsewomen, it seemed, and offered to take their visitors round some interesting places when next they called.

Angus sent Ewan back to Ardtornish, or wherever he could find his grandsire, to inform him of this dire challenge.

It was not long before his friend was back, having found Angus Mor at Tobermory, the Well of St Mary, on Mull. His instructions were typically positive. Angus Og was to sail his fleet forthwith down the Irish Sea to Man, and make it plain to Alan mac Roderick, lord there, and other chiefs, that no mainland rule, either from Scotland or England, was to be tolerated; and that the Prince of the Isles himself would come in strength to establish his authority if anything such was attempted. The weak John Balliol was unlikely be so inclined, or indeed feel able to do so; but the Plantagenet might.

Angus knew of the Manx situation. It had been Norse dominated, like the Hebrides themselves, from the time of the early Viking invasions, but handed over to Somerled, along with the rest, over a century before. Since then Man had been part of the Isles lordship, and must remain so.

It was November, and scarcely the best time of year to make

23

seaborne sallies, but his grandfather's orders had to be obeyed. And the bulk of Ireland would help protect their ships from the westerly gales almost all the way.

There was no delay. The fleet sailed from Sanda, to go much further southwards than heretofore.

They had some sixty-five miles to the northern tip of Man, and a further score of miles down its east coast to Douglas, the chief town. In rough conditions, but occasionally able to use their sails, they ought to reach the island in one long day, and be at Douglas by next day's noon.

The first part of their journey was familiar to them, down as far as Belfast Lough on the west and the Mull of Galloway on the east. But after that it was new waters for them, although MacInnes had been to Man some years before. It seemed odd to be sailing thus close to the English Cumbrian coast, after the Solway Firth, considerably closer than to the Irish one. It was strange that the English had not themselves conquered and taken over the island effectively long ago, but their lack of any fleet of warships to challenge the Islesmen's longships had prevented this. They must see that this continued.

It was a windy dusk before weary oarsmen saw the Point of Ayre, and thereafter pulled into the sheltered Ramsey Bay, on the east side of Man, thankfully. With full crews of rowers, the score of ships made up a large company, too many, Angus decided, to burden themselves on the local folk for the night. So they all just wrapped themselves in their plaids, fortified themselves with whisky and oaten cakes, and lay down in tight-huddled proximity on their vessels' timbers. Fortunately it was not raining.

In the morning, sailing down the coast, they were interested to see that the island was very hilly, with a central mountain chain dominated by a soaring peak which MacInnes said was called Snaefell, an English-sounding name. Indeed other names he mentioned, such as Ramsey itself, Maughold, Laxey, Foxdale, even Douglas, their destination, had little of their

Isles tongue about them, more of Scots and English. Yet this had been very much a Norse appendage once. The Vikings did not seem to have left many traces. Douglas presumably did not get its name from the line of south-western Scots nobles, who were not likely to have any links here, but from the original derivation of the name, Dubh Glas, or Dark Water, which was Gaelic enough.

At that town, quite large, all were able to go ashore, and glad to do so, to sustain themselves with more substantial food than they had brought with them from Sanda, however doubtfully they were eyed by the populace there, with their winged helmets and chest armour. Angus, Ewan and MacInnes made their way up to the castle.

They found Alan mac Roderick, governor of Man, very much aware of their arrival, indeed expecting to have to welcome Angus Mor himself, instead of Og, from all these longships. He was an elderly distant kinsman, like so many in authority in the Isles, his predecessors having called themselves Kings of Man, although Angus Mor did not approve of that, descended from Reginald or Ranald, a son of Somerled, he who had founded Saddell Abbey. He declared that he was glad to see this sign of concern from the north, for he had not failed to hear of this nonsense of Man being gifted to Scotland by the scoundrelly Plantagenet, and was all too well aware that his island was over-near both Scottish and English shores to feel comfortably secure. Was Angus Og going to base himself and his ships at Douglas?

He was told that this was not envisaged meantime, but this present visit was in the nature of a showing of the Isles banner, and demonstrating their lord's support. If the man Balliol, or others, showed any signs of seeking to take over Man, that would be different, and a strong Isles presence would be forthcoming. But Balliol had a sufficiency of troubles nearer home, and it seemed unlikely that he would be greatly interested in this possibly little-wanted gift. Whether any of his powerful subjects would look in this direction was doubtful, the Comyns being more interested in north-eastern Scotland and the Bruces of Carrick always having to keep an eye on the Galloway chiefs to the south and the Douglases, who could be aggressive. Neither was likely to be interested in Man.

Alan supposed that all this might be so, and agreed that few if any of the Scots lords would have sufficient shipping to pose any real threat to his island, unless they combined, which seemed improbable. And he himself could rally a fair defensive force, if necessary.

He wanted to know what was Angus's intention now, and was told that his visitors would sail right round Man, up the west coast, to make their presence evident to all. And then return to Sanda and Dunaverty, to await further instructions. From there they could be back in a day, if necessary.

Alan said that they should make a call at Peel, one-third of the way up on the west, the main community on that side, facing Ireland, where his own deputy, actually his son Roderick, was based.

They spent the night with Alan, assured that their crews were well cared for down in the town – although those characters would themselves be apt to see to that.

Next day they made no early start, for it was raining and the winds strong, and there was no great haste. But by noon the sky had cleared, although the westerly gusts were less than kindly, and the seas running steep. So it was oar-work again, the waves making synchronised rowing difficult.

They had only about nine miles to go southwards to round the final point, and could turn westwards, to pass the Calf of Man islet, and so up the Ulster-facing coast. That southern tip of Man was spectacular as to scenery, tremendous cliffs and headlands.

They were surprised to find at Peel not only a great castle, larger than that at Douglas, but actually a cathedral church dedicated to St Germain, hardly to be expected on the island.

Roderick mac Alan mac Roderick proved to be a cheerfully outgoing youngish man whom Angus could identify with rather better than with his father. He agreed that it was not very probable that there would be any attempt to take over Man by Balliol; but King Edward might well be using this ruse to hide his own intentions at grasping it for England. He was a wily and insatiable robber-king at heart, even though he had once been proclaimed as the First Knight of Christendom: poor Christendom, in that case! This of handing over, in name, Man to Balliol might well be but a means of allaying fears and preparedness here, prior to his own descent upon them from England.

Angus had not thought of this, but was ready to believe almost anything of Edward Plantagenet. On consideration, he saw that this was a distinct possibility. He said that he would pass on the apprehension to his grandsire.

Liking this Roderick, he remained for a couple of days at Peel, his men also well content there. Then it was back to Kintyre, with the hopes that they would be spared more winter voyaging. These seas, narrow as they were, could turn into tide-races, and not the best for open longships in wild conditions.

4

Angus himself went up to Ardtornish on this occasion, to report and to pass on Roderick mac Alan's fears about King Edward's reasons for seeming to make a present of Man to Scotland, while planning a take-over himself. His grandfather admitted that he too had not thought of this, but saw that it might well be a possibility with that devious character. Indeed the more he thought about it, the more feasible it became. The Plantagenet was obsessed with increasing his power, influence and domination of territories. He all but had Scotland in his grip now, was seeking to control all Ireland, Wales was his also, and he was fighting in France to take over Aquitaine and Gascony. It must be galling for him to have the Isle of Man so near to his own shores and yet not his. Why seem to hand it over to John Balliol, then, his puppet?

Angus Mor came to a decision on this. Man was only a day's sail from Kintyre, and as near to the Ulster coasts as was Dunaverty. His grandson and his fleet would be as well based there meantime, probably at Peel rather than at Douglas, this facing Ireland, and from there making continual sallies up and down the English as well as the Ulster seaboards, to keep Edward aware that he, Angus, Prince of the Isles, was watching, ready, and could sail a couple of hundred longships and birlinns down there should there be any attempt to invade Man.

Angus Og did not contest this, calculating that he and his men would be a lot more comfortable based on Peel than on Dunaverty and Sanda, and in good company. It all made sense. And he could keep in touch with Alastair MacDonald equally well from there. Man would make an infinitely more convenient and interesting station for him and his, and keep his men in better morale probably.

Given no lack of instructions, he took his leave.

He decided that, instead of sending a messenger, it would be proper to go himself to inform Alan mac Roderick and his son of the intended coming of the Isles fleet to be based on Man, and of the decision to make his headquarters at Peel; he would have to be tactful about this, although he found the son's company much more to his taste than the father's.

With only one other vessel to escort the dragonship, he and Ewan sailed down to Douglas first, for Alan was governor of the island. There he announced Angus Mor's command to make Man the fleet's focus-point meantime, because of this of possible English invasion; and saying that it was considered best that they should harbour at Peel, on the west coast, for the English might well seek to make any assault from Ireland, as less to be expected. Alan looked sceptical at this, but since it came from the Lord of the Isles, accepted.

So, pleased, Angus made his way round to Peel, where he found a warm welcome from Roderick, and satisfaction expressed that the Isles ships were to be based at his community. He would see to it that the crews were found suitable quarters. Angus himself, of course, would lodge with him at the castle. He intimated that his friends called him Rory.

So it was all very satisfactory.

Angus sailed back to Kintyre, saying that they would return within the month.

At Dunaverty he thought that Alastair mac Donald ought to be apprised of this move, and a visit was called for. It might well have its satisfactions also.

At Saddell he was, in fact, reproached by the mother and daughters for having been so long in coming, a pleasing reaction.

Alastair said that he had been to Dunollie, and made Angus

29

Mor's wishes known. He believed that there would be improved relations with the MacDougalls, and his Comyn warnings heeded. He also said that the Red Comyn might well be kept busy, for it seemed that Edward was demanding Scots military aid, the assumption being that this was for his French campaigning. But when Angus informed of this fear that the Plantagenet might be planning an attack on Man, that put a different aspect on it all, and a worrying one, with that island too near to Kintyre for comfort if in English hands. Alastair certainly wished Angus well in his efforts to prevent anything such.

His daughters had not forgotten their suggestion that a ride round some places of interest nearby would be pleasing, the visitor by no means objecting. So garrons were saddled, and the three of them rode off, Angus not having brought Ewan with him on this occasion.

The two young women were very different, although both good-looking, Seona, the elder, being fair and lively but warm, and Eithne dark, quieter but far from subdued. There were only two years between them. Angus was attracted to them both, but Seona was the more challenging, not provocative but forthcoming.

They took him first to see the abbey, where they were on very friendly terms with the monks. Especially they went to see Somerled's grave, with its handsome tall stone monument, carved with an effigy of the first real Lord of the Isles, sword at side, surrounded by strange lean animals and interlaced Celtic decoration. Angus was quite moved to view this of his ancestor, a great man. God willing, one day he would be Somerled's sixth successor.

The abbot took them round the establishment, and all was duly admired. Angus mentioned that he had been surprised to find a cathedral on Man, this dedicated to St Germain. Who was Germain? It did not sound an Irish nor Celtic name. He was told that he was Bishop of Auxerre, in Burgundy, sent by the Vatican eight hundred years before to quell heresy developing in areas converted to Christianity by St Ninian. He was also called Germans, or even Hermon, and he had been very active in Wales, where many places were called after him. Presumably he had reached the Isle of Man.

Thereafter the young people rode on northwards up the Saddell Water for some three miles into hilly territory, making for a mountain, modest compared with many in the Isles but the highest point in Kintyre, the girls alleged, this named Beinn an Tuirc, the Hill of the Wild Boar. The view from its summit was quite superb he was assured, well worth the seeing.

Their garrons, short-legged, sturdy and sure-footed, were clearly used to this climbing, and picked their way up over heather and outcropping rock and screes without guidance, this to the chatter of the young women, Angus much enjoying the company and the freedom from the cares of leadership which not infrequently distinctly weighed upon him. He wondered whether they were likely to see any wild boars here, but his companions admitted that they had never seen any on this hill, although their father hunted them on the lower ground.

At the summit, when he helped first Seona down from her saddle, he won a squeeze of the arm for his service, which allowed him to hold on to her for a little longer. When he turned to do the same for Eithne he found her already dismounted. She made a face at him, and then smiled – and when she smiled deep dimples in her cheeks held their own fascination for him.

That young man was perhaps more interested in his present companions than in the views they had brought him to see. But these were certainly magnificent in every direction: west to Islay, Jura and Mull; south to Ulster and the Rhinns of Galloway, and indeed Man; east to all the peaks of Arran, with glimpses of the southern Ayrshire mainland, and north to Cowal, Argyll, Loch Fyne and the Lorn coast. The prospect was breathtaking in its immensity, and Angus had to admit, although he knew it all, that he had never before seen it laid out for view thus.

Clearly proud of it, the girls led him on down, eastwards now, for the coast, by a stream growing ever larger, which they called the Torrisdale Water, leading on some three miles to Torrisdale Bay, this in the hopes of seeing the wild white goats which apparently haunted this area; apparent being not quite the right word in the circumstances, for although there were allegedly many, they only managed to glimpse a pair up on a spur of rock, these promptly vanishing. Angus asked how these creatures survived if there were wild boars in the neighbourhood, but was informed that it was because of their ability to leap from rock to rock nimbly, which the boars could not do, that they were able to survive. Seona added that these Campbells, ever growing more dominant in the area of Cowal and Argyll, should include a goat's head on their banner to rival the boar crest they used to remind all that their possibly legendary ancestor Diarmid had, dismounted, slain a particularly notorious wild boar hereabouts. Diarmid was one of the heroes of the Fingalian tradition, with Fionn CacCoul, or Cuchalain, from Ireland, after whom the Cuillin Mountains of Skye were named, with Deirdre and her lover Naoise. Angus had heard this story before, but now he was given it more fully – and all because of a couple of goats.

At the shore he had pointed out to him the great basin of Carradale Bay to the north, with its mighty headland and ancient grass-grown fort at the point, with more of the Fingalian legend. Head swimming with all the tales told to him by these high-spirited and interesting sisters, he was taken back to Saddell, after a dozen-mile ride.

He was conducted to his bedchamber that evening by the pair of them, with goodnight kisses bestowed.

He left the castle in the morning reluctantly.

*   *   *

The move to Peel, on Man, was made shortly thereafter, with the seas becoming less fierce as spring advanced, although they were never calm in these areas of Atlantic tides, channels and sounds narrowing them, underwater hills, overfalls and down-draughts from flanking mountains. The crews were used to all this, to be sure, but that did not mean that they were any less of a challenge and hazard.

Rory mac Alan greeted Angus cordially, and said that he had arranged ample accommodation for his men reasonably nearby. He was allotted his own rooms in that large castle, and congratulated himself on his change of dwelling, and the friendly association. Ewan was able to share his quarters, MacInnes being given his own cot-house near the crews' various lodgings.

They settled in.

A rota of longship duties was established, in pairs, groups or sometimes the entire fleet, to patrol and manifest their presence along the English and Irish coasts to leave no doubts that these waters were theirs to command. When Angus was not himself out with them, he was taken by Rory to see interesting places on the Manx scene, the Tynwald, near at hand, where Man's council assembled; what was left of the very ancient Norse castle of Rushen, and the abbey nearby, at Ballasalla; the many harbours, with their salt-pans and smoke-houses for the preserving of fish and meat, the net manufactures, and other sources of local prosperity. They also visited Alan mac Roderick, who seemed quite content to leave Angus in his son's company.

So the months of that summer and early autumn went in, without any major event, but with no lack of activity. That is, until in September a major event did indeed shake not only Angus Og, the Isle of Man, but all the Isles lordship, and beyond. Angus Mor was dead.

It was MacLean of Kinlochaline, Ewan's father, who brought the dire tidings in his birlinn. The Prince of the Isles had been found dead in his bed one morning, presumably having suffered a heart attack – no dramatic end for him who had ruled his sea-girt empire for so long with a strong hand; but a fair way to go to a better realm nevertheless. He was of a good age, but had not been heard complaining of sickness nor hurt.

Angus Og was stunned, appalled. He had been reared by his grandsire, and they had inevitably been close, even though that man had not been of a notably affectionate nature. Now – gone! It was hardly to be taken in, accepted. The Isles without Angus Mor!

What now? Alexander, his father, would be Lord of the Isles, utterly unsuited for the position and responsibility as he was, all but a hermit on Islay. Angus realised very well that the responsibilities would fall on his own shoulders, young as he was. And undoubtedly Angus Mor would have had it so. There would be no choice in the matter. His life was going to change, entirely.

Even Rory mac Alan stared at him, in a sort of wonder.

It fell to Angus to act, and at once. Priorities? A message to Saddell to inform his grand-uncle. Then north to Islay to see his father. Then to Ardtornish, to make the necessary arrangements.

Leaving MacInnes in charge of the longship fleet, with MacLean sent to Alastair mac Donald, he and Ewan sailed for Islay without delay.

At Finlaggan he found his father already informed, and much distressed – not so much at the loss of his parent, from whom he had long been distanced in more than miles, but over his own situation. The last thing he desired was to have to act Lord of the Isles. Indeed he *could* not. In name he might be that, but only in name. His son must see to it, nothing else was conceivable. Angus would be the lord himself one day. He would have to be that in fact, now.

His son was prepared for this attitude, expecting none

34

other. But he was surprised when his father declared that he would not be coming to his father's funeral. He just was not able, he asserted. Angus must see to it, as to all else.

Shaking his head over his parent, who should have been a monk perhaps, brilliant at studies and translations of the Scriptures, Latin and other writings, the son had no option but to take over. At least he had no doubts as to the next step. Angus Mor must be taken to Saddell Abbey, and interred beside his ancestor Somerled. Then . . .

His dragonship took him, with Ewan who was a great help and support in all this, up to Ardtornish, where they found a large number of chieftains already assembled to pay their last respects to their lord, all saluting Angus Og with esteem, he noting that none asked where his father was. Angus Mor's body he found laid out, wrapped in a shroud, the features looking calm, entirely peaceful. His grandson did not actually weep over him, but knelt beside the bed and said a disjointed and incoherent prayer, and so remained for some time.

Then it was all arrangements for the morrow's journey to Saddell, with a large convoy.

In the morning all made an early start, for it was going to be a long voyage. Angus Og reckoned that it was fully one hundred and fifty miles to Saddell, two very full days' sailing and rowing. They would halt overnight at Gigha, almost halfway. Gigha's chief, MacNeill, was here with them. He sent his son ahead, there and then, to prepare for the company's reception. The dead lord was piped down to the lochside in great style.

It made an impressive sight, with fully two score of galleys, birlinns and longships of the chieftains thereafter following Angus's dragonship with the corpse, under the flapping standard of the Isles. These had come from the Outer Hebrides, from Skye and as far north as the Summer Isles, as well as Rhum, Muck, Eigg, Tiree, Col, Mull, Iona, Colonsay, Oronsay and Jura, as well as lesser isles, many of them carrying far-out kin, and proud of it, although some claimed even earlier descent, from the early Norse invaders, before Somerled, such as the MacLeods, Sons of Liotr, and the MacAulays, Sons of Olaf.

Fortunately the weather was not unkind, and they made good time of it southwards, Angus very much aware of the body he sat beside, and that he should be leading this illustrious banner-bearing procession, the like of which he had never before seen. He supposed that it might be a foretaste of things to come, and for which he was by no means eager.

They made Gigha by dusk, and their welcome at Ardminish resembled a celebration rather than a funerary cortège, Mac-Neill concerned to demonstrate his hospitality. It was not far off feasting that night. Angus supposed that the interment of the departed should not really be an occasion for gloom and grief, for had they not gone on to a better and fuller life nearer their Maker, and perhaps should be envied rather than mourned?

Rain rather damped spirits next morning, but by the time they were passing Dunaverty and rounding the Mull of Kintyre it had cleared and they were able to enter the Kilbrannan sound, the wind behind them, almost with a flourish.

Their piper thereafter, in the late afternoon, played them into Saddell Bay, giving Alastair mac Donald due warning to meet them at the shore, to greet his brother, great-nephew and kinsmen and fellow-chieftains. He had the Abbot Fergus with him. With much ceremony they took Angus Mor's body to lie in the abbey church meanwhile, to a quite stirring bagpipe lament.

The actual entombment would take place next day. So all fell to be housed and entertained overnight, the chiefs in the castle, the crews in the monastic quarters of the abbey. Alastair's wife, Anna, and her daughters were kept busy coping with all the visitors, so that Angus had but little opportunity for converse with them. But he did offer, and receive, kindly glances not a few. He shared a bedchamber with Ewan and his father and MacLean of Duart.

The burial was not delayed in the forenoon, for most there had long journeys to make to get home. Rory mac Alan from Peel arrived just in time.

The service in the church was simple but effective, the abbot emphasising the worth of their late lord, and the eternity of love and bliss to which he had moved on, also all the good company he would meet with in Paradise. Then, led by the piper again, all followed the body, borne on a stretcher by eight chieftains, Angus alone immediately behind, this out to the God's-acres where the grave had been dug alongside that of Somerled and his monument. Angus would have a suitable slab carved to mark the spot.

So they said farewell, meantime, to Angus Mor mac Donald mac Ranald mac Somerled, with shouts of praise after the benediction.

Departures followed after final drinks, thanks to their host and salutations to the successor of their late lord, none making any comment on the fact that Angus was not yet Lord of the Isles, however necessary it was for him to fill that prestigious but demanding position.

That young man himself would have liked to stay on at Saddell Castle for a while, but felt that this was not the occasion. He would be back, he declared.

It was Dunaverty for him now, while he decided on which duties, tasks and obligations he was to tackle first.

5

Due consideration left Angus in no doubt but that, after a
return to Ardtornish to settle unfinished affairs there, and
some plans made for a fairly comprehensive tour of the Isles to
show himself to their folk, this no minor undertaking, the Isle
of Man situation was his most immediate priority, with the
threat of English assault, none of the rest of his father's
territories being in any likely danger. Edward Plantagenet's
alleged donation of that island to Balliol, so unexpected and
seemingly pointless, must have some reason behind it. So there
he must concentrate his attentions. But Man, the most southerly point of the lordship, was hardly the place for the acting
lord of all to dwell, too remote from all else. He decided that
Kintyre was the best location to base himself; and this
Dunaverty be his seat meantime. The lordship had many
castles and houses all over the Hebrides and the West Highland seaboard, but these did not demand any presence, meantime, while this southern area did.

But now that he was having to play the part of leader of it
all, there would inevitably be much coming and going of chiefs
and representatives. Therefore more accommodation on the
rock-top fortalice was called for. He would have masons and
carpenters sent down from Islay to enlarge the hold, and
improve it in other ways, as his home for some time.

Ardtornish first, then, calling in at Islay on the way, then
down to Man, to instal Rory mac Alan as his deputy in
command of the fleet there, with a spell of duty for himself,
to supervise and encourage the crews, and to check on the
Ulster situation. Then, if there was no indication of enemy

activity, his tour of the Isles. On that cruising, he would wish to interview sundry of the chiefs, to choose, as it were, suitable and reliable lieutenants, active men on whose shoulders he could place some of the burdens and concerns of his new authority. He felt young for all the weight suddenly landed upon him.

Somewhere among all this he would find time to go up to Saddell – and not only to gain the tidings brought by those mendicant friars, so valuable.

At Ardtornish, he put MacLean of Duart in charge, a sound character in his early forties, and residing conveniently nearby. There was quite a lot to see to, left by Angus Mor's sudden demise, for him to clear up as best he might, and advice to solicit from various knowledgeable folk.

Much seen to, it was back all the long way to Peel of Man. There, blessedly, he found all in order, MacInnes seemingly competent as longships commander. Now, as acting Lord of the Isles, he did not have to gain Alan mac Roderick's agreement that his son should be appointed his deputy there, although he did visit him at Douglas in order to maintain fair relations.

Then, Rory accompanying him, he sailed with the fleet down the Cumbrian and Lancaster coasts as far as Morecombe Bay, and this close inshore, to ensure fullest observation by the population, and due warning. He saw nothing to worry him. Then across the Irish Sea, wide now, almost one hundred miles across, to Dundalk, where Ulster began, below the mountains of Mourne, to call in at Downpatrick to enquire of the Irish situation. There they learned from the Mac-Dunleary chieftain, supporter of O'Neill, that Richard de Burgh, Earl of Ulster in name, had come up from Dublin with quite a large company, and was seeking to establish some authority, but was being opposed by O'Neill's forces. This was significant news. Was it a move of Edward's to commence preliminaries to attacks on Man? And with possibly a synchronised assault from the English side? Vigilance was demanded from Rory and MacInnes. Angus promised at least two hundred longships, with extra men in plenty, to repel anything such.

In the circumstances could he risk making his Isles tour? He might be far to the north, many days of sailing away, before word could reach him of any invasion demanding his presence here. Safer not. But he could go up to Saddell meantime, not much further from Man than was Dunaverty. Who knew what news he could glean from there?

In fact, back at Peel, he found that Alastair mac Donald had acted first. A messenger had arrived from him to say that he had learned, from the usual sources, that a major revolt against English rule had broken out in Wales, this at the same time as Edward's forces in France had suffered a serious reverse. So the Plantagenet was presumably very much preoccupied, and unlikely to be considering any attack on Man meantime.

Here was welcome intelligence – even though it did rather rule out any need for a prompt visit to Saddell. Angus could hardly go up demanding further details. It seemed to be the obvious time and opportunity to make his cruise around his father's lordship, and show himself as leader, such as he was.

Where to begin? The area to be considered, if by no means all to be covered in a single excursion, was vast, perhaps three hundred miles long by up to eighty wide, comprising hundreds, all but thousands, of islands, and unnumbered mainland peninsulas and reaches, divided by sealochs. Most clearly he could not in any one journey visit anything like it all. The major isles, locations and areas, or as many of them as was possible, must be his first targets, with brief calls at lesser places in the by-going.

At least he did not have to do anything much about those near at hand, where already he and his situation were well known: Kintyre, Gigha, Jura, Islay and much of Mull, with

Knapdale and Lorn and Argyll on the east. The chiefs from there had nearly all been at his grandsire's funeral. But there were outlying parts of even these which he ought to visit: the long Ross of Mull, for instance, at that great isle's far south-west extremity, itself some sixty miles in length, and with the sacred isle of Iona at its tip. He had been taken to Iona as a youth, but had not been there since. He would make a start at Colonsay and Oronsay, then, and so on to the Ross and Iona. Then out to Tiree and Coll and north to the great Ardna-murchan peninsula. It would be best to have one or more of the greater chiefs with him, to emphasise his authority. He could take Gillemoir MacLean of Duart, so near to Ardtor-nish, and possibly pick up others such as MacNeill of Coll or MacDonnell of Jura on the way. It all demanded much thought and planning, and he must always be reachable, his progress roughly known, in case of word of serious trouble in the south.

So he would start from Ardtornish, with Ewan and his father, collect Duart, then sail south by west round Mull for the Ross peninsula.

Duart came in his own dragonship, quite as fine as Angus's, with two accompanying longships; so they started off with five vessels. How many more would they collect as they went on? Down the Firth of Lorn, and along Mull's south coast, they came to their first call, Lochbuie, where the old MacFadzean chief lived, on a part of the great island coveted by the MacLeans. This small clan dominated the Ross, to Duart's annoyance. Angus recognised that he would have to walk warily here, as probably in many other places in his lordship.

Then it was on along the islet-dotted coast: Angus counted no fewer than forty-four of these, not including mere atolls and sizeable skerries, many of them clearly inhabited; which gave him some conception of what being Lord of the Isles really meant. This before they turned the headland of the Ross and into the Sound of Iona, with Soa Isle on their left.

The sacred island, burial-place of Scotland's kings, was indeed a jewel, only three miles long by one wide, and very beautiful. Its original name was simply I, which indicated its unique importance as *the* isle. Here Columba had established his missionary base, from Ireland, and from which he in time converted almost all Scotland. The name had become for a while Icolmkill, the site of Columba's church. Its successor, the abbey, was still there, enlarged by Ranald mac Somerled, near the little mountain of Dun I, the highest point of the isle. The abbey's Reelig Oran chapel and burial-enclosure were where the kings were interred – and not only the kings of Dalriada and of Scots but four from Ireland, eight from distant Norway, even one from France, so holy was the place deemed. Kenneth mac Alpin, who had united Picts and Scots, lay here, as did Duncan the First and MacBeth who brought about his death. And then Malcolm Canmore married the Hungarian Margaret Atheling, who brought the Roman Church to Scotland, putting down the Columban one, of which this was the supreme sanctuary. Then did the custom cease, although other great ones, not the kings, continued to be brought here to lie in a lovely atmosphere of peace. The sheer beauty of the island helped to enhance its holiness, the white cockleshell sands of its bays and inlets gleaming through the clear waters, with the colourful seaweeds helping, and the yellowish-green marble of its rocks a further attraction.

Angus was much moved by Iona, and vowed that he would come back here before overlong, just to steep himself in its aura of loveliness and peace.

The clansfolk here were MacKinnons, but in fact the abbot was the accepted leader of the isle. His blessing was assured. They all stayed overnight in his hospitable monastic quarters.

South to Colonsay was the morning's sail, just under a score of miles, with its linked isle of Oronsay. The MacDuffie chiefs here were hereditary Recorders to the Lords of the Isles, and required little introduction to Angus. He duly admired the allegedly miraculous coloured staff of St Oran, on which, it was claimed, the fate of the MacDuffies rested.

Then on to Tiree, forty miles north-west towards the Outer Hebrides. Having been here fairly recently. Angus made merely a brief call on this, the most populous, for its size, of all the Inner Isles.

Coll lay only a mile or so north of Tiree, less flat with low hills, but about the same size, with notably fewer inhabitants. It was another MacLean isle, so no lingering was necessary here. They were taken from Breachacha Castle to see the notable Pictish souterrain, or earth-house, at Arnabost, with its long underground gallery, about which there were many stories, Angus much intrigued.

It was at this stage that he began to realise that his ideas of a comprehensive tour of the Isles had been far too ambitious. He had only so far visited a few of his intended destinations, and it was all taking much longer than he had contemplated. He had meant to go on from Coll northwards to Muck, Eigg and Rhum, the first some thirty miles away; but those three were best done together, and would undoubtedly take days, after the example of the places already visited. He just must not be away from his base for overlong, in case of important developments demanding his attention. So these must wait.

It was only a score of miles from Coll to the great mainland peninsula of Ardnamurchan, of the MacIans. He would go there now, and get that over, and then back to Dunaverty. His companions expressed themselves as thankful for his decision.

They had to skirt the northernmost shores of Mull and across the mouth of its sound to Ardnamurchan Point. As it happened this was the most westerly tip of all mainland Scotland, oddly enough even further west than England's Land's end or indeed Belfast and Dublin in Ireland. North of it the Isles were called the Nordreys, and southwards the Sudreys, right down to Man. The peninsula was a lengthy and important territory, between the sea lochs of Sunart and Shiel, almost forty miles of it. Angus had never visited it, but Duart said that its principal townships were all on its south side, Kilchoan near its tip, Glenbeg, Glenborrodale, Salen and finally Strontian. The MacIan chief could be at any of these, but most likely at Mingary Castle, near Kilchoan, his favoured seat, commanding the mouth of the Sound of Mull. Angus, concerned about timing, hoped indeed that they would not have to go seeking him along those forty more miles.

So they were thankful to find the MacIan at Mingary, a strongly placed castle isolated on a rock, not unlike Dunaverty. Angus had met the chief briefly at the funeral, but did not really know him. He was a short, stocky man of middle years, with a cast in one eye, but affable and pleased to welcome his visitor. Indeed he wanted to take them on a progress round his domain, to show him to all and present his leading folk, this right to Strontian. But Angus pleaded demands on his time elsewhere. Another occasion, perhaps? They spent only the one night at Mingary, after being taken to see the rare feature of the Rocking Stone on a hillside nearby.

Then it was south again, down the sound to Ardtornish, thirty miles, where they dropped off Duart and Ewan's father, and proceeded on to Dunaverty. Angus reckoned that, although he had done only a very small proportion of his planned itinerary, they had covered about three hundred miles of sailing, in round-about fashion.

At Dunaverty no urgent tidings awaited him, thankfully. Perhaps he ought to go up to Saddell, just in case there was news there on the wider front.

Alastair had indeed word for him, for events in Scots national affairs were taking place at no modest pace. At the urgings of his nobles, John Balliol had renounced allegiance to King Edward, however apprehensively, taking advantage of the English preoccupation with Wales and France. And a man called Wallace, son of a laird near to Paisley in Renfrewshire, had personally risen against the oppressions of the enemy governor there, and had indeed slain him, and others. Once the Plantagenet got to hear of this . . . !

Seona and Eithne did not fail in their entertaining duties, indeed asking the reasons for his delay in visiting them, for he had not been there since that funeral. They had planned another excursion, this time southwards, he far from discouraging. Their mother and father shook heads over the daughters.

The trio rode down the shore for a couple of miles to a fishing village named Ugadale, under a headland on which rose the ramparts of a Pictish dun, or fort, which they went to examine, typical grass-grown ramparts and ditches. Then round a mile-wide bay beyond, Kildonald they called this, to another headland and its companion dun, with a small isle off. But these forts were not what the young women were taking Angus to see. It was further south still, to Glen Lussa, that long valley of the Lussa Water coming from a loch, this the largest in Kintyre, apparently seven miles inland among the hills. But only a mile or two of this, and well above the glen floor they climbed to their objective, a great chambered cairn.

Never had Angus seen the like, a vast burial-mound of stones, larger than any castle, in length if not in height, with two tall stone monoliths at the east end indicating the entrance. Dismounting, he was led within. The girls had brought candles with them, and lighting these with flint and steel they picked their way into the great central chamber with a vaulted roof, four lesser apartments opening off it, Seona holding Angus's hand as they went, and whispering that these were interment-places, for whom was unknown, but they must have been very great folk of the early Picts, possibly even ancestors of their own. It was reported that a large wedge of solid gold had been found in one of them. No bones nor remains of any sort were to be found herein now.

It was altogether a ghostly sort of place, drips from the stones of the roof, although it was not raining, making the

45

only sound. But eerie as it was, it did not prevent the young man from reaching out to hold both of his companions close to him – and all but getting his hair burned by the candles in consequence, no objections raised. They wondered why this great tomb had been set here, on a fairly high shelf of the hill but not on its summit? What had these far-back people been up to here?

A return to Saddell, then, chatter succeeding awe-struck hush.

Conducted to his bedchamber later by both sisters, as usual, Angus asked himself whether he would have preferred just one to see him settled for the night. And indeed, which one? On earlier visits he would have chosen Seona, but now he was not so sure. Those dimples . . . !

It was back to Dunaverty in the morning. That news of uprisings against Edward's dominance of Scotland was interesting and significant. Let it continue. And this man . . . Wallace, was it? The name he recognised meant Welsh-speaking, as distinct from the Gaelic. But Celtic, nevertheless. And this one no great noble, it seemed, an encouraging sign. If the lesser folk were going to take action on their own initiative, then the Plantagenet could be in the greater trouble undoubtedly . . .

6

Autumn passed into winter, with Angus spending much time on Man, fearing invasion from Ireland, Edward having ruthlessly put down the Welsh uprising, with savage reprisals. Admittedly winter was not the favoured time for warlike ventures, but with the Plantagenet anything was possible. And Richard de Burgh was making his presence felt in Ulster, he who was known as Edward's right-hand man.

The year 1296 dawned without invasion, which was scarcely a wonder, for it was the wildest late winter in memory, with storms all but continuous, the air in all these coastal areas filled with spray and spume from the mountainous waves smashing against skerries and cliffs, no conditions for seagoing in open vessels. Angus latterly found himself all but roosting in Dunaverty, with even that eagle's eyrie of a hold seeming to rock in the gales.

After a couple of weeks of this, wearying, Angus felt that he had to get out of this place somehow, even though not in his ship, this moored under the shelter of the lofty headland. By land, then? It was, possibly, strange that the Islesmen seldom considered travel by land, by horse; water, the sea, constituted their world, sounds, channels and lochs their roads. But those daughters of Alastair covered the miles in their saddles. He would do the same. A garron from one of the nearby farmers, and what was to prevent him from riding up through Kintyre's hills to Saddell? How far would it be, by valleys and passes? A score of miles, as the eagle flew, but half that again, probably, ahoof, by the way he would have to go. He was no great rider, he recognised, although he had done a little of it when out hawking; but surely he could manage that journey in a day?

So leaving Ewan in charge at the castle in case any urgent call came for him, unlikely in this weather, he borrowed a garron and set off northwards into the windy hills.

He had a fairly simple and easy start, at least, up the Conieglen Water, a quite sizeable river, which entered the sea just east of Dunaverty, and would take him north for some six miles by Dunglas Mill and Dalmore and Killellan chapel, a reasonably straight course although with many minor twists and bends needless to say, no real problems other than having to negotiate and ford the innumerable tributary burns that entered the river. But up at Killellan the river, much reduced in flow now, swung off westwards, while he wanted to proceed on north, and this through hilly country, not mountainous but demanding much circling and diversions. Land travel was infinitely more devious than was water.

In time he came to the area he knew, Dalruadhain, Somerled's first base in these parts, and from where he had gone to visit that Kilkerran chapel at his father's behest. He had to ride through this community in order to round its great bay, for he judged that it would be easier going now to follow the coast northwards rather than pick his way through the ever higher-growing hills; after all, he knew this coast well enough, seen from the Kilbrannan Sound.

It proved to be much more kindly on his mount, and he made good time of it now, despite battling against the spray from the waves breaking, this blown on the wind. Soon he was on the shore of Ardnacross Bay, to reach the mouth of Glen Lussa, where he had come with the young women on their excursion to the chambered cairn. On past Ugadale village, he came, wet with spume and battered by the gusts, to Saddell, another couple of miles.

Great was the excitement, from the females at least, at this so unexpected arrival, welcome all but rapturous, the girls in

48

especial having been fretting at being kept housebound by the storms. Now boredom was to be banished.

Alastair was glad to see their guest also, for he had news to report, those wandering friars apparently not put off by the weather in their peregrinations – Angus never very sure what their objectives were in all this travelling around. At any rate they had recently brought no lack of news, and terrible news. Edward was back in Scotland, or at least on the south-east edge of it; and to show his fury at Balliol's renunciation of fealty, and the activities of the man Wallace and his adherents, had sacked the important town and port of Berwick-upon-Tweed, and deliberately slain no fewer than seventeen thousand men, women and children, and ordered their bodies to be left lying in the streets, unburied, this in order that the stink should warn the Scots what it cost to offend the Plantagenet.

Appalled by this, Angus demanded what this monster of a monarch expected to gain by such an enormity. He was told that Edward had vowed to wipe out all traces and symbols of Scottish sovereignty, destroy all national records, and remove the identity of the land as a separate nation. And he had the power to do it, the English ten times as many in numbers as the Scots. What chance had the latter to defy this evil man successfully?

Angus shook his head in distress.

All these sorry tidings inevitably cast a shadow on the visit to Saddell, even though it did not directly affect the Isles people. And the weather did not encourage outdoor activities. But the young people were not to be depressed into gloom and moping. The girls devised pastimes and entertainments, and even if Angus did not find them all wholly absorbing, at least they engendered proximity and togetherness, and sometimes opportunity for affectionate demonstrations, especially when they could be alone in some chamber. Seona was distinctly the more forthcoming in this, but to his earlier appreciation. Now Eithne's quieter, less evident warmth was ever reaching deeper into his awareness. He did not seek to judge between these two, but . . .

It was during one of their diversions, wherein they were playing the game of making up nonsensical verses regarding each other and members of their families that Seona, skirling a laugh, said that they must fashion one about aunts and nephews.

"Are not you, in fact, Angus, *our* nephew? We your aunts! Here is an oddity, surely. Aunts and nephew. I am some months younger than are you. And Eithne a score of months. Yet we are your aunts, no? Your grand-uncle's daughters! Have you thought of this?"

He blinked. Such, indeed, had never occurred to him.

"Aunt is not the right word, I think," Eithne said. "An aunt is the sister of an uncle. Or the wife. We are not that. Just what we are, I know not. In cousinship, yes – but not aunts."

Strangely, the thought of this relationship rather worried Angus. Hitherto he had just looked on these two as pleasing and attractive friends with whom he felt close, with an especial degree of intimacy – but not the closeness of kindred. Yet there was truth in it. Somehow the notion changed matters in some way.

The nonsense verses rather waned with him, after that.

Despite the conditions outside, the young women insisted on accompanying their favourite guest some way on his return ride next morning, for they were a hardy pair. Seona asked why he had to leave always after too short a stay. He tried to explain something of the duties, responsibilities and problems of an acting Lord of the Isles. He realised that these two had no conception of the complexities of seeking to govern, keep order and protect such a vast area of islands and peninsulas and their clans, the rivalry, the feuding, the difficulties posed by the seas, the danger of attack, to Man in especial. Eithne asked him whether he wished that he had never taken it all on. After all, his father had refused to do so. And *their* father did not allow his concerns as Lord of Kintyre to take over much of his life. Angus said that, no, he did not regret it, saw the challenge of it all as worthy. Somebody had to do it, and he was in the direct line of descent, born to it, whatever his father felt, even if he had come to it earlier in life than was usual or than he would have chosen.

"Would you take us with you, one day, in your dragon-ship?" Seona asked. "To show us something of the Isles. We know Kintyre, but that is all. I would like to see more. Our father never takes us. What we have seen from the top of Beinn an Tuirc is all that we know of it."

"Angus has more to do than sail two females round his kingdom," Eithne said.

"One day . . ." they were told.

This talk was quite difficult for folk on horseback in that blustery gale, gaspingly, jerkily conducted. More than once Angus urged his companions to turn back, these no conditions for pleasant riding. But they continued on with him as far as Glen Lussa before, kisses exchanged, they parted, fond advice given on both sides. Angus rode on, wondering, wondering.

The wild weather continued for a further week or so. And even when at last the winds dropped, the seas did not for some time. So it was only after quite lengthy absence that Angus was able to sail down to Man and his concerns there, feeling almost guilty. However, at least he had fairly good tidings to impart, in that he judged that there was unlikely to be any invasion of their island in the near future, with Edward in Scotland, and much to preoccupy him there.

Rory mac Alan was glad to see him, as was MacInnes. The fleet had been more or less harbour-bound for long, patrolling all but impossible, boredom prevailing among the crews. All they could console themselves with was that the same condi-tions and restraints applied to their enemies as to themselves. But now resumption of activity had commenced, and men could be men again, not just squabbling idlers and nuisances for the local womenfolk.

Angus sympathised, and accompanied the patrols in person for a few days to demonstrate his fellow-feeling.

He was interested to learn that, in the interim, Rory had decided to marry. Like so many of those prominent in the islands, the chosen had almost inevitably to be far-out kin, such communities being thus limited. This lady was the daughter of MacDowall of Ramsey, named Ailie. Angus was taken to meet her, and found her pleasing. He was able to congratulate his friend, and was asked when *he* was going to find a wife. He could only say that he had other matters on his mind meanwhile.

After a very full week on Man, with the weather now seemingly fairly settled, and the seas beginning to sink to nearly normal, Angus reckoned that this would be as good a time as any to resume his tour of the Isles. It came to him frequently that he must seem, to many, to be almost wholly based upon the far south of his lordship and neglecting the vast northern parts. Take Skye, for instance. It was the largest island of all the Inner Hebrides, and with the greatest population, fifty miles of it from south to north and of varying width, with a host of subsidiary islands. It was sufficiently famous, but he had never been there in his life. It did occur to him to wonder whether this would be an opportunity to take those two young women with him, as they would wish; but their father and mother might think otherwise. Also, it probably would not be the right occasion, with his objective of showing himself as acting lord.

Before he left for the north he gained more news, and from an unexpected quarter. Mendicants came to Rushen's Benedictine abbey, as they did to Saddell's Cistercian one, but these usually came from Cumbria or Lancashire, in fishing-boats, and were not particularly knowledgeable as to Scots affairs. However, one pair from St Bees brought word of a famous victory for King Edward. He had defeated a Scots army at Dunbar, in Lothian, with great slaughter, ten thousand dead it was said, this under the command of the Earls of Atholl, Menteith and Ross, Balliol himself not present, he being no warrior. Edward was now master of all Lowland Scotland, the rebel Wallace and his ragged followers said to be confined to the trackless Ettrick Forest.

This sorry tale sent Angus off, wondering. Would the Plantagenet seek to extend his sway north of the Lowlands and into the Highlands and the north-east? If he did, then the Isles could become involved. The thought made his planned visit to Skye and the north-west mainland the more necessary.

Angus, picking up Gillemoir MacLean at Duart, who seemed happy to accompany him after all the long confinement imposed by the storms, sailed up the Sound of Mull, to pass Mingary and the Point of Ardnamurchan, and so out into the open Sea of the Hebrides, the Sgurr of Eigg and the mountains of Rhum ahead of them. Eager as he was to visit these dramatic islands, Angus avoided them meantime. They carried only small numbers of folk, and it was the greater populated areas he sought, Skye in especial. Due east of Rhum, a mere ten miles, was the Point of Sleat, the most southerly tip of Skye. Thence they steered, the dragonship, Duart's birlinn and four longships all showing the banners and painted sails of the Galley of the Isles.

Duart was more knowledgeable than was Angus as to these areas. He said that Skye was known, in the north, as the Great Whale, from its shape, the snout and great body to the north-west, this long Sleat peninsula to the south-east the forked tail. He warned that it could take weeks to reach all of the island's six hundred square miles, with sea lochs and inlets beyond number and islets equally countless. Best to seek out only the great chiefs, and even these would not always be easy to find, with their many holds.

This Sleat was both MacDonald and MacKinnon country, the latter chief's main seat at Kyleakin, where the sound of Sleat commenced to narrow in between Skye and the mainland at Lochalsh. But he had other houses. They should sail up this eastern side of the peninsula, the protected side, where were most of the communities, and seek him out.

So up the sound they went, with mainland Knoydart on their right, wild mountain territory, to call in for the night at Ardvasar. There they learned that MacKinnon was almost certainly at Kyleakin, twenty-five miles on. And if they called in at Armadale, only a mile or so on their way, they might find MacDonald of Sleat there, in his castle.

This they did, and found an elderly chieftain who had known Angus Mor well, and assured his grandson of his fullest support. He declared, however, that he was not sure of the worthiness of Gillebride MacKinnon, and advised caution with that young man.

Duart said that this was typical feuding attitude, and ought not to be taken too seriously.

On, then, up the skerry-strewn coast to Knock Castle, a MacKinnon place, where an uncle of the MacKinnon roosted. He seemed honest enough, and informed that his nephew was a sound man, and was indeed presently at Kyleakin.

After that the scenery changed notably as the sound closed in to caols, kyles, twisting, tapering, narrow channels where the tides rushed fiercely, Kylerhea first, Kyleakin, Kyle of Lochalsh, Kylerhea especially difficult, with passage not possible against adverse tide. Warned, the oarsmen rowed hard to get through before the current changed. They were fortunate in this, at least.

They could not miss Dunakin Castle at the next kyle, on its islet, all but blocking the already narrow channel, and so able to halt any vessels that did not pay due tribute, or tolls, to the chief for onward entry to the main Inner Sound and the Sound of Raasay, and on northwards, a strategically placed hold indeed; which no doubt was why MacDonald of Armadale had been less than complimentary about the MacKinnon. However, a dragonship flying the Galley of the Isles met with no demanding reception, and the young chief promptly proclaimed his loyal duty to his prince, as he named Angus, assuring that his line had always been true bastions of the lordship, unlike some others none so far off, MacLeods and the like, even some MacDonalds. After all, the MacKinnons, really Mac Fingons, were here long before even Somerled, descended from St Fingon, one of Columba's disciples – indeed the present Abbot of Iona was his own uncle.

It was insisted that they stayed the night, despite the numbers of their crewmen. And while they were being entertained, they saw how the tribute-gathering was enforced, an underwater timber barrier being raised by means of wheel-worked chains, so that the already narrow passage was quite blocked, and a vessel from Dornie on mainland Loch Duich, on its way to the Outer Isles, could not proceed until it paid its way. The MacKinnon's unpopularity was not to be doubted.

While they were there, Angus wondered whether he should take the opportunity of heading eastwards into mainland Loch Alsh, Dornie, Loch Duich and the Kintail area, which was important, and MacRae country, that chief based on Eilean Donan Castle, but under the Isles' sway. But he came to the conclusion that this was not the time. Skye he had come to see, and he had barely started that. Already he had spent longer than he had intended. This of showing his presence was a much lengthier process than he had anticipated.

So north again next day, to Scalpay, a MacDonald isle, whose chieftain was absent, and on to Raasay, a very lengthy island, with its subsidiary of Rona, fully twenty-five miles of it although only approximately two miles wide, this lying between Skye proper and the mainland. It was MacLeod territory here, although not that clan chief's, whose hold lay far off on the west coast, at Dunvegan. They found MacLeod of

Raasay at Oskaig, and although he was a much less enthusiastic supporter than had been MacKinnon, this no doubt because of his part-Norse ancestry, he was not hostile in any way. Even the name Raasay was Scandinavian, meaning roedeer. Nevertheless the present chief's style was MacGille-Chaluim, which sounded sufficiently Celtic. He took them to see Brochel Castle, on the east side of the island, a strength which was so inaccessible that they had to go on all fours to climb up to it on its pinnacle.

From Raasay it was only a short sail across the sound to the great bay and loch of Portree, the principal community of all Skye, where Angus hoped to find his kinsman, the chief Mac-Donald, at Torvaig just to the north. But when they got there, only a mile, on foot, they discovered that MacDonald, another Angus, had gone up to a secondary seat in Trotternish, at Staffin, near the very northern tip of Skye, a score of miles at least. So staying the night at Portree, they pushed on northwards. At least this would take them eventually round to the north coast, and so to Dunvegan, the MacLeod main seat.

Angus MacDonald, at Staffin, not the island but a castle nearby, a fine-looking middle-aged man, received his visitors affably. He was full of tales about their ancestors, and of Angus Mor himself. He was obviously a great raconteur, and made excellent company. He even was able to tell Duart some details of his MacLean forebears which he had not known. He was head-shaking over Alexander, Angus's father, but praised the son for his taking on of the responsibilities.

He warned them that their reception at Dunvegan of the MacLeods might be doubtful. These descendants of Liotr the Viking were very much aware of their different background from the Somerled line, and showed it, looking on the latter almost as newcomers, incomers. After all, one Olaf had been King of Man during the Norse occupation. This Dunvegan had not attended Angus Mor's funeral, but he was not likely to be actually offensive.

Next day it was round Rubha Hunish, none so far from the Shiant Isles and Harris, and then down the much less sheltered western coast, back to Atlantic tides. MacDonald had given them a pilot, which he said they would require; and as they went southwards he pointed out the names that emphasised the Norse, not Gaelic, origins: Snizort, Ascrib, Vaternish and the like, all significant.

As well that they had this guide, for they would have gone quite far astray, down into the long Loch Snizort instead of westwards to round Vaternish Point.

At length they came to Loch Dunvegan, itself ten miles long, so that it was dusk before they reached its head and the MacLeod seat. Even so their arrival was spied, and longships came out to inspect them warily, the Isles banner and painted sails not being obvious in the failing light. They were escorted into the harbour beneath the large castle with only stiff formality. Angus wondered whether they ought to pass the night in their ships.

In the event, they were quite warmly welcomed, Tormod MacLeod surprised to see them but far from unfriendly or grudging. Despite his Viking ancestry he was a slight dark man, although with craggy features. He had a large family. There was no question of them, or their men, spending the night in their ships.

They were entertained, admittedly, with tales of Norsemen and their exploits, their odd customs and peculiar sense of humour. These included the strange celebrations of the winter solstice, dating from sun-worshipping days, of waving mistletoe boughs and rushing out of doors, naked, men and women, to greet the dawn of a new year; the careful washing of the faces and hair of victims they had slain before hanging these up on verminboards; and much else. They were shown the famous silken Fairy Flag, alleged to have been the shirt of some eastern saint, brought back from Constantinople by King Harald Haardrade of Norway five hundred years before, and often carried in warfare. Also an oxen drinking-horn, capable of holding four pints of whisky, which the heir to the MacLeods was expected to swallow at one draught to test his manhood – although this seemed improbable.

Well content with this visit, Angus decided that it should be sufficient for the meanwhile. He had spent longer than he had intended on it, and was ever very much aware of demands and responsibilities that could well be awaiting him elsewhere, especially in Man and Kintyre.

Home, then, Ewan telling him that he was getting old before his time with it all.

7

Word from Alastair of Kintyre was awaiting Angus at Dunaverty. Edward of England was showing his mastery of Scotland in no uncertain fashion, even by marching his army as far north as Elgin, in Moray, where John Comyn, Earl of Buchan, had welcomed him and offered fealty. This was significant to Angus, for Moray was getting close to Inverness, at the eastern end of the Great Glen of Scotland, and the Isles' sway extended to the western end and indeed quite a way up it. So the Plantagenet was getting over-near. And, of course, the Comyn links with the awkward MacDougalls were not to be overlooked. And the Earl of Buchan had lands in Galloway, none so far from Kintyre and Man. Altogether Scotland's national affairs were beginning to encroach on the island lordship as they had never done before.

There was no word from Man, but Angus thought he had better pay a visit there to see how MacInnes and his crews fared, and to check with Rory mac Alan.

At Peel he found Rory a worried man, despite the joys of new marriage. Edward's successes in Scotland were alarming. And with de Burgh's advances in Ulster, Man, sandwiched between the two, could well be down for the next assault. And he had had a disturbing, thought-provoking development. John Comyn, Earl of Buchan, had applied to Alan for permission to mine for lead on the Calf of Man, this allegedly to provide roofing for the new castle he was building in Galloway. Admittedly there was lead on the Calf, much used on the island. But there were plenty of other lead-mining areas on the mainland of Scotland. And why was the Comyn so concerning himself with Galloway? Was it all something to do with King Edward? A means of spying out the land perhaps? Getting a toehold on Man?

Angus recognised the possibilities, and the need for vigilance. It all added to his own apprehensions. But he felt that Rory, or Alan, could hardly refuse permission for the lead-mining. This would seem provocative, and that certainly was not advisable.

All this of Comyn involvement with Edward and with Moray seemed to indicate another call on Alastair mac Donald, for discussion on the MacDougall situation, which that man had been asked to deal with, linked as these were with the Comyns. Angus wanted no back-door entry into the Isles, by way of Dunollie.

So it was back to Saddell with him, never an unwelcome prospect.

There Alastair mac Donald was able to tell him that the other Alastair, MacDougall, had indeed summoned his son Ian Bacach back from Badenoch, as commanded, but unwillingly, because of his Comyn wife. He had left him in no doubt as to Angus Mor's wishes. But they were a thrawn lot, these MacDougalls, always had been, and if they judged that they could be advantaged over their association with the Comyns, he for one did not question but that they would seek to develop it. In this issue of Comyn co-operation with Edward Plantagenet, they might well see possibilities in their favour. Their Lorn was a wide lordship, reaching as far east as Kinlochleven, Breadalbane and Rannoch Moor, none so far from the Comyn lands. If they could extend their properties into that territory, it could serve them well . . .

This worried Angus, who felt that something must be done about it. He himself would go to Dunollie. But best to have Alastair mac Donald with him, who had dealt with the MacDougalls before, as Lord of Lorn. And, it occurred to him, here would be the opportunity to take the young women on the dragonship cruise they had craved – and they might even have their uses at Dunollie, with that Comyn woman there. They could sail in *his* vessel while their father went in his own birlinn, and so could bring them home thereafter. It would be a two-day sail up to the Oban; but they could halt for the night at the Isle of Gigha, where there was a small monastery to house them.

This suggestion was greeted with acclaim by the girls, and no objections from their father. His wife did not desire to accompany them.

That evening there was much chatter and excitement over what to wear suitable for the occasion, what was to be done about natural and bodily functions for women in a boatload of men, and how they would fare at the Gigha monastery. Would the monks be used to having women there?

At bed-going, it was Angus's turn to enter the sisters' bedchamber, to be consulted in some detail, problems pointed out to him, and shown clothing that might be appropriate. It had never occurred to him that there would be all this ado about a two-day sail. Nevertheless, he was in no hurry to depart for his own room, sitting on females' beds, and examining and selecting their garments being quite to his taste.

In the morning, dragonship and birlinn made an early start, the former's crew not a little stimulated by having two attractive young women aboard, and necessarily so close. Angus carefully erected a spare sail as screen at the stern for required privacy, although the helmsman at the great steering-oar would presumably have to move, on occasion.

So, to the resounding beat of the gong, the dragonship led off down the Kilbrannan Sound.

The sisters were quite used to travelling in their father's vessel; but this of the dragonship was different, more dramatic, the craft more slender, elongated, lower in the water, fierce of prow, three men to each sweep instead of two, the birlinn being more of a barge than a hound of the sea. It went much faster, to the grunting, chanting of the oarsmen in time with the gong. The girls soon were also beating time with clapping hands.

When, in time, they rounded the Mull and met the Atlantic waves, with much dipping, heaving and spray from the oars, Angus found himself clutched on either side by feminine hands, to the grins of the rowers, but no objections from himself. He was able to point out Dunaverty Castle on its cliff-top, even so, and agreed that they must visit it one day.

The twenty-five-mile row up the long Kintyre west coast to Gigha, with that westerly swell, made a very rolling progress, but the passengers did not complain of feeling sick. However, although they had brought food and drink with them, they let it remain untouched.

Angus explained about Gigha. The name was a corruption of the Norse Guday, meaning holy isle; and although it was only about six miles long, and narrow, it had a number of shrines, both of pagan sun-worship and of Christianity. Its sheltered situation between Islay and Kintyre no doubt accounted for its favour. Although it was Clan Donald property now, it had no resident chieftain, the prior of the monastery being the isle's leading character. Halfway up its eastern shore, in early evening, they passed by Ardminish Bay, although it was the principal harbour and landing-place, heading further north for another three miles to East Loch Tarbert. Tarbert meant a narrow neck of land between two waters, and the West Highlands were full of such names. There was indeed a West Loch Tarbert on the other side of Gigha. But in the centre of the quarter-mile of high ground was the monastery, set between a pagan burial-chamber cairn and a tall, handsome, blue stone cross monument, carved with Christian symbols, indicative of both types of worship.

Monks were unloading fish from small boats as they drew in to the sandy shore. The dragonship's prow was driven up on to the beach, and there was competition for agile oarsmen to jump over and lift down the laughing passengers, with much kicking of skirts.

Up at the monastery the prior, Colm by name, as were so many clerics, called after Columba, although surprised indeed to see them, especially females, greeted them kindly. He found a small wing of his establishment for the sisters, saying that it had not been occupied for well over a year, when they had had a visit from some nuns from Kilchiaran on Islay.

It was a while before Alastair arrived, his birlinn being much less speedy than was the dragonship.

The visitors were excellently fed, with mutton and a variety of fish. And before they sought their couches they attended a service of evening praise called compline.

The visitors did not attend early morning prayer.

They sailed up the Sound of Jura thereafter, and then that of Scarba, passing near enough the dangerous Corryvreckan whirlpool to hear its roaring, which had the girls questioning how it came about, and were told that it was caused by a particularly deep pit in the sound's floor. Then they passed the small isles of Luing and Seil and on to that of Kerrera, in Oban Bay, where King Alexander the Second had died almost fifty years earlier in an expedition against invading Norsemen. This all made another seventy miles, so that it was again evening before they reached Dunollie Castle on the north of the bay.

Angus had wondered what sort of reception they would be accorded here. The acting Lord of the Isles could not actually be rejected, of course, but his welcome would be unlikely to be warm in the circumstances. He had his grand-uncle with him in the dragonship on this part of the journey, so that he could precede them on the way up to the castle, and warn the MacDougalls who was coming. Also that there would be women to entertain.

Probably this was no misfortune, since it might make the visit seem the more congenial, and involved the ladies of the house from the first, including of course the Comyn wife, however doubtfully Angus was eyed by the chieftain.

It quickly became apparent that the son and heir, Ian Bacach, or John the Lame – he had been born with one leg slightly shorter than the other – was not at home. Enquiries elicited the fact that he was once again gone to his uncle's territories of Badenoch – which had Angus frowning. It was a difficult situation, as had indeed been anticipated, but the more so on this account, and while being entertained as guests and their hostess a Comyn. But Angus managed to leave MacDougall in no doubt as to his feelings and policy. His grand-uncle was a major help, as was the presence of the daughters.

All were glad to bed down that night. Nothing had actually been said about the development of Comyn affairs in Galloway and the Calf of Man, although the lordship's concerns with Man were indicated.

In the morning there was no delay in departing. Angus told Alastair that he was determined to make a demonstration of his presence and strength into the great mainland areas of Wester Ross, the Great Glen, Loch Ness and Beauly, that there should be no question as to the Isles' sway extending thereto, and this fairly promptly.

So he transferred the young women to their father's birlinn, to their disappointment, for he would now go north to Ardtornish to enlist Duart's aid in mustering a sizeable force for the mainland venture, while the others returned to Kintyre.

The vessels went their different ways.

8

A total of one hundred and twenty longships, galleys and birlinns laden with men to the number of almost three thousand, ten days later followed Angus Og's dragonship up the Firth of Lorn into wide Loch Linnhe to its narrows at Onich; and so, under the mighty Beinn Nevis, the highest mountain in all Scotland, this to reach Lochiel of the Camerons, whose powerful chief was one of the Isles' most valued adherents on all the mainland. This was as far as the vessels could go eastwards. Thereafter the host must go afoot.

Angus felt almost embarrassed at thus leading so large a force, an army indeed, far greater than he had looked for. But Duart's efforts in gathering the various chiefs' support had been almost too successful, and this was the result.

He left this assembly encamped at the junction of Lochs Linnhe and Eil and proceeded up the lesser one to Fassfern, one of the seats of the Cameron. He could be there, or at Achnacarry on Loch Arkaig further north, they had been told. Fortunately they found the sixth chief, Ian of Lochiel at Fassfern, a personable youngish man, and most ready to assist in their project, offering his own quota of men, which Angus by no means required and had to say so. But he would be glad of two or three knowledgeable guides to help lead them into what was little known country to most. Lochiel declared that he himself would act the guide, an offer gladly accepted.

So it was back to the camped host for the night. The great fleet was thereafter left in the care of Cameron men, and the Islesmen formed up into a very lengthy column, to head up into Glen More, the Great Glen of Scotland, with a march of scores of miles ahead of them. Prepared for this, much basic food and drink had been brought with them, for so great a company could scarcely live on the countryside, in especial friendly terrain.

Eight miles brought them to Loch Lochy – and most complained at having to trudge up the shore of this for ten more miles when their ships could have carried them had they been able to get them thus far. These Islesmen were better sailors than marchers. Lochiel grimly pointed out that this was just the beginning of it, for there was the similar Loch Oich ahead of them, and beyond that thirty miles of Loch Ness, all in this Glen More. They must get used to footwork.

They camped again at the head of Loch Lochy, none so bad for the first day's tramping.

The second day, along Loch Oich-side, they got as far as the head of long Loch Ness, fair going; and here Angus had to decide on how he wanted to proceed, Lochiel pointed out. Did he desire to go up Ness-side right to Inverness, the Capital of the North as it was called, in which case it was straight on? Or was it better to go south-eastwards first, through Mackintosh country to the beginnings of the Badenoch areas of Speyside, Strathdearn and Abernethy?

Angus concluded that this last would be wiser. A large army descending upon Inverness was bound to create a great stir, and word of it would quickly get far and wide. The Comyn country would be warned, if they were not so already – MacDougall could have sent word. Actual warfare, on any large scale, was not the objective. It was to show strength, have the Comyns watching their backs, hindering their endeavours elsewhere on their own and English Edward's behalf.

At Kilcumein, then, they swung off due eastwards into the skirts of the Monadh Liath Mountains, unpopulated country where their presence was unlikely to be reported. Cameron recommended a meeting with the Mackintosh, head of Clan Chattan federation, the most influential chief hereabouts, and known to loathe the incoming Norman Comyns, who had taken over slices of his territory. Moy, the Mackintosh seat, was in Strathdearn near the great River Findhorn. They could best get to it by way of Loch Duntelchaig, and over the low hills north-eastwards. At Moy, with its castle on an island in a smallish loch, they were on the borders of Moray and within a dozen miles of Lochindorb, the Badenoch main stronghold.

Filing through those hills mile after mile, by deer-tracks and no tracks at all, was not popular with the Islesmen; but they got as far as Loch Duntelchaig for the night, where they managed to kill some of a herd of red deer with their cross bows, and so ate well enough.

Next day, by Farr, they reached Loch Moy, a comparatively small sheet of water after those they had had to circumnavigate, with its castle-islet near the south shore. Cameron of Lochiel was known at the lochside castleton, and a boat had him rowed out to inform Mackintosh.

The chief himself had seen the great concourse of men approaching, and came over to welcome Angus. Duncan Mackintosh was elderly but hale and of a notable presence, as befitted Mac-an-Toiseach, the head of the great Clan Chattan alliance of Macphersons, MacGillivrays, Shaws, Farquharsons, Cattanachs and others. He invited all the chiefly company present to come over to his house for the night.

He was, naturally, happy to hear of the Islesmen's campaign against the Comyns, and assured fullest co-operation. He suggested that a demonstration at Lochindorb Castle would be the most telling gesture, their mutual enemy's main residence in this area, although stolen from his own clan. It was only some ten miles away. The Red Comyn would not be there, for he was known to be keeping company with the Plantagenet in the south, or had been until recently, but some of his family would be likely to be biding there. He had other establishments, at Loch-an-Eilean in Rothiemurchus and Ruthven up Speyside, but Lochindorb was his base.

Angus agreed. He would make a call there, in strength, and hope that the message reached the Comyn in due course.

Mackintosh had been greatly concerned over King Edward's recent arrival at Elgin, none so far off. Fortunately it had been only a brief visit, something of a flourish, and had not resulted in any serious upheaval. Since then there had been word of various happenings in the south. Edward had now returned to England, leaving his governors to control much of Scotland. Dramatically he had taken away with him what he thought was the famous Stone of Destiny. He had, previously, vowed to remove all emblems and symbols of Scottish sovereignty and national identity, such as were possible so to do. He had burned all records he could lay hands on, stolen the Black Rood, or piece of Christ's cross, held at Holyrood Abbey. But this of the Lia Fail, the Coronation Stone, his especial target, had eluded him. The Abbot of Scone, custodian of the stone, the ancient seat on which the Kings of Scots had been crowned over the centuries, knowing of this intention, had removed the precious relic from before the abbey's high altar and hidden it elsewhere, substituting a lump of Scone sandstone in its place. And Edward, not knowing any better, had taken this away with him in triumph to London. It was a mere oblong block of rough stone, less than a foot high, it was said, whereas the true Lia Fail was of seat height, as required for the monarch to sit upon, highly carved and ornate, with rounded volute handles at the sides for lifting it, Scotland's Marble Chair. Just where the abbot had hidden it, none but he knew. But the Plantagenet had, for once, been outwitted, beaten, and gone off with a worthless object.

This, needless to say, much tickled Angus and the other hearers. But would Comyn, or the Earl of Buchan, know about it? If so, they could tell Edward – and he might well come back!

Next day, Mackintosh leading them, with Lochiel, the Islesmen marched eastwards, to cross Findhorn and on through the hills to Lochindorb. This proved to be a larger sheet of water than Loch Moy, set amidst lofty moorland, a couple of miles in length but fairly narrow, and with its castle-islet near its northern shore midway along. At sight of the host approaching, the folk of the castleton at the lochside fled, but left their small boats beached there.

Angus, with Duart, the Mackintosh, Lochiel and other chiefs, had two of these craft pushed out, and in them were rowed towards the quite impressive red-stone stronghold, the Banner of the Isles held high.

Well before they neared the walls they were hailed, and demanded as to who they were and what they wanted, uninvited? And to emphasise their point, a shower of arrows came over to them, to splash into the water around, the two boats.

Angus stood, clutching the banner shaft, and shouted, "I am Angus Og, son of the Lord of the Isles, come to speak with the Lord of Badenoch, he who sides with King Edward of England. If he is present, have him to hear me."

"He is not here," the voice came back. "What have you to say?"

"I say that he is in treason to the Scottish crown. And unless he renounces his support of Edward Plantagenet, he will pay for it. The Isles will see to that. To whom do I speak?"

"It is no concern of yours who speaks. Aye, and all Islesmen do not think as you do, Angus Og! Ian MacDougall is with the Lord of Badenoch!"

Another shower of arrows accompanied that, some falling very near.

Angus waved a dismissive hand. "Your welcome is noted, and will not be forgotten!" he cried. "Be you, and all Comyns, warned. I speak for my father, and all who pay him service and fealty, unlike the renegade Ian Bacach. Mind it!"

"And I, Mackintosh, add my voice," that man shouted. "Clan Chattan does not forget, either!"

Angus told the oarsmen to turn back.

Ashore, men were ordered to burn the castleton and other nearby cottages, and a small mill, this to reinforce his message. There did not seem to be anything else that they could usefully do. No point in going on to visit other Comyn houses further east and south. His threat was sufficiently clear.

Had it been worth all that lengthy marching of so many men? No sword drawn, not a drop of blood shed, only a few words exchanged, and some roofs burned. But, then, he had never sought battle. His companions all declared that it was sufficient, strength and determination shown.

Now: visit to Inverness.

Back to Moy for the night, and the Islesmen host well provided for, even if it taxed Mackintosh's resources.

It was only a dozen miles northwards to Inverness, crossing the River Nairn by a ford at Daviot, wet but refreshing for tired feet. Angus did not want the entire force to enter the town, where they would be difficult to control and keep in any sort of order, to the undoubted alarm of the citizenry. So he left them on the common land and grazings of Culcabock, a bare mile to the east, promising to have supplies of food and whisky sent out to them. He headed on with his chiefly companions. Again it was only his presence that he wanted to emphasise here, no sort of dominance. Inverness was in Moray, but on the edge of the earldom of Ross, and he sought no troubles with either. The folk would be well aware of the host camped nearby, however.

There was a fine Moray castle perched on a ridge in the town centre, above the River Ness, and thither the chiefs made their way, gazed at uncertainly by the townspeople. A word with the keeper would be wise and adequate, assuring of the Isles' goodwill as well as power. However, meeting them at the castle gatehouse was none other than the Lord of Moray himself, Sir Andrew, descendant of Freskin of Moravia who had given the province its name. He was a man of about

Angus's own age, who greeted them with fair cordiality. He said that he had heard of the large influx of Islesmen to his area, and that they had been to Moy and Lochindorb; news evidently travelled fast hereabouts, even if an army on foot did not. Moray imagined that Angus Og was present with no hostile intent since he had burned the Lochindorb castleton, which suited himself well enough.

He was assured that it was anti-Comyn sentiments that had brought them to these parts, and strong opposition to the activities of English Edward, this accepted by Moray with acclaim. He took them into the castle and regaled them more than adequately, agreeing to have supplies sent out to the waiting troops at Culcabock.

Sir Andrew was Lord of Bothwell, on the Clyde, as well as of Moray, an odd combination, so far apart, but he lived mainly at Petty nearby, and came often to Inverness. He said that through his Bothwell links he knew the young man William Wallace who was proving to be so sharp a thorn in King Edward's side; he much admired his efforts. His father, Sir Malcolm Wallace, was indeed a vassal of Bothwell. And his uncle, Sir Reginald, was Sheriff of Renfrew.

He told them that Edward Longshanks was presently having considerable problems in his own England, for sundry of his important lords were objecting to his warfare in France, and refusing to supply him with men therefore. This was good news. Anything that hindered the Plantagenet was advantageous.

In the morning, then, it was back to Culcabock and the long trudge homewards to commence, their expedition as successful as it had the potential to be. They would be thankful when they reached their ships at Loch Eil.

Back at Ardtornish, it was sad to hear that Ewan's father, MacLean of Kinlochaline, was gravely ill. Ewan would have to remain at home meantime.

71

9

After quite a long absence, Angus felt that it was time he paid a visit to Man, that endangered isle, this probably a priority. And when he arrived at Peel, it was to discover that it was as well that he had come. For there was a message awaiting him, from Ulster, an urgent message. O'Cahan, Lord of Derry, was seeking the Isles' assistance. The English de Burgh was making quite major advances in Ulster, and was getting too near Derry for comfort. Some strong and positive opposition was called for, in the Isle of Man's interests as well as Ulster's. Discussion was besought.

Angus had met O'Cahan briefly on that early visit to Lough Foyle and Donegal, when he first took on his patrolling of the Ulster coasts, and remembered him as a worthy character. He agreed that de Burgh should be halted, as did Rory mac Alan. And since the call had been awaiting him for a couple of weeks, it should be answered at once.

So, with a couple of MacInnes's longships as escort, his dragonship headed off north and then west, along the Ulster coast.

O'Cahan's seat was at Limavady apparently, near the east Lough Foyle shore, with the River Roe leading up to it, and sufficiently deep to allow the vessels to reach the castle's vicinity.

Angus found Guy O'Cahan thankful indeed to see him. He was in later middle years, stout, and of lofty ancestry, a descendant of Neil of the Nine Hostages, the famous High King of Ireland, and related to the O'Donnell kinglet of Donegal. He told that de Burgh had got as near as Magherafelt

72

and the Sperrin Mountains. And if he won through these last heights, he would have much of Derry open to him, Strabane and Lifford and all the Foyle valley. He, O'Cahan, had his men manning the passes through the hills, which was holding up the English. But de Burgh might well decide to avoid this direct approach and come up due north into the Roe valley to reach Foyle by Limavady itself. That was the danger. With winter approaching he might be content with his progress, thus far, and await the spring for further major activities. But who could tell?

Angus well recognised the situation, and accepted that it was time this threat was countered, especially as Edward Longshanks appeared to be preoccupied with unco-operative English lords.

The pair had been discussing this in the first-floor hall of the castle, when there was the clatter of hooves in the courtyard outside and a woman's voice calling to someone.

"My daughter," O'Cahan said. "She is a great horse-woman."

There was ringing laughter from below, and more cries, which sounded amusedly mocking. Then footsteps on the stone stairway.

The door was flung open, and the young woman who came striding in had Angus catching his breath. To say that she was striking would be an understatement, striking in more ways than one: lovely of features yes, lissome and gracefully vigorous of carriage, shapely, positive of personality, wide-eyed, smiling, dark hair in a tangle from windy riding, all life and very feminine spirit. She began to speak, in laughing vehemence, perceived a stranger standing beside her father, and stopped, hand thrown up to her mouth, then dipped something like a small curtsy.

"Ainea, the daughter whom I have fathered!" O'Cahan said. "She is . . . herself!"

Angus bowed. "I . . . I greet you, lady," he got out. "I am

73

. . ." He did not finish that, seeking words. "You have me . . . silent!" He had never seen such a beautiful and lively creature.

"This is Angus, Lord of Islay, son to the Lord of the Isles himself," her father introduced. "Come in welcome answer to my call."

The young woman advanced, and produced another and slightly deeper curtsy, considering the visitor interestedly but nowise humbly from those warmly brilliant eyes.

"Ainea O'Cahan," she murmured. "My lord."

He reached out to take her hand and raise it to his lips, silent.

Eyeing them amusedly, her father shook his head. "I doubt if my daughter knows how great is your father's lordship," he declared. "Or should it be principality? Or even kingdom? My father used to speak of Somerled, King of the Isles."

"We no longer name it so," Angus admitted. "But it is still the same, and all ours."

"I have heard of you," the daughter said. "You do what your father should be doing, no?"

O'Cahan shook his head. "My daughter is outspoken. But she has her virtues!"

"That I can see!" Angus agreed.

"Is speaking truth so ill?" Ainea asked. "But, I go to tidy and order myself. Or, leastways, my appearance." And flicking a hand towards her father, she left them.

"I can do little with her," O'Cahan said, but not with any sort of gloom or exasperation. "Her mother was much the same."

"She is a beauty. Like, like the sun shining on a white rose!"

"Ha – a poet, as well as all else! Rose, eh? Ah, yes – with its thorns, to be sure!"

Angus had never thought of himself as poetic in any way. "You must be proud of her," he said.

The other did not deny it.

They resumed their discussion on dealing with de Burgh.

Angus wanted to know what the other Ulster lords were doing about it, in Donegal and Antrim, and was told that they were contributing to the defence, but that their men were in much demand elsewhere as well, for the English attempt to take over Ireland was not confined to de Burgh, and that Down, Armagh, Monaghan and Tyrone were also under attack, apart altogether from further south. Defences were stretched to the utmost. Hence this call on the Islesmen.

When, after an interval, Ainea came to summon them to the evening's repast in a lesser hall, her appearance had changed, in that she was now excellently clad, her hair combed and ordered, her figure the more evident, her beauty enhanced if that was possible. She was also somewhat less positive in attitude, certainly not retiring but gentler, milder. Angus was the more smitten.

They did not talk of warfare and battle over the meal. The young woman asked much about the Isles lordship, its extent and people, the clans and families, how many large islands there were, and relations with the rest of Scotland, her interest more than merely polite. Angus, answering, was bold enough to suggest that, one day, she must come and see it all, her father also, of course.

After eating, they returned to the larger hall to sit at its fireside, with wine. Ainea entertained the men with singing, accompanying herself on a harp, and proving to have a voice to match her looks. She asked if Angus was a singer, and making no claims to be, he did offer a ballad dealing with Fionn MacCoul, after whom the Cuillin Mountains of Skye were named, and his passing to the Land of the Ever Young. The young woman quickly picked up the rhythm of it, and plucking the harp strings in tuneful harmony, caused her father to beat his knee in time, to the crackle of the burning logs.

When it came to retiring for the night, Ainea led their visitor upstairs, and Angus was almost guiltily reminded of similar occasions at Saddell and the kind attentions of two other females who had appealed to him. What was it about this one which caused these to seem less stirring to him? They also were good-looking and spirited, but . . .

He was shown his bed, the steaming water to wash in, the garderobe; but there was no goodnight kissing, although he was patted on the arm and told to have pleasant dreams on being left at the door.

In fact, it was long before he slept that night, his mind and feelings busy indeed – and not about matters military.

In the morning, although invited to remain at Limavady longer, and tempted so to do, he recognised that the sooner he could get back to the Isles and muster the required force to assist O'Cahan the better, and the sooner he could return, and for longer. Before being escorted down to his vessel, he was shown Ainea's fine horse, a tall, head-tossing animal very different from the rough garrons they made do with at home. However, his dragonship was much admired, its fiercely rearing and snarling prow a challenge indeed, and unlike anything O'Cahan had to show.

Farewells were said, Angus promising to be back with a sizeable force before long, and hoping that winter storms would not delay them, however helpful these might be towards restraining de Burgh's efforts.

Ainea said that she would ride, and wave to him from the point where the River Roe entered Lough Foyle.

It was none so long a sail back across the North Channel, especially with a westerly breeze behind them, and they made Rathlin Isle by nightfall, and so were at Dunaverty the following midday. But that was not the place to raise manpower, so Angus went on to Ardtornish, halting at Gigha as usual, and then proceeding to Duart, to have Gillemoir MacLean raise the Mull, Jura and Islay men while he himself summoned them from Morvern and sent word to MacIan of Ardnamurchan.

It all took time, of course, even though the host required was not so large as for the Badenoch and Moray expedition. Fifteen hundred men, he judged, would serve, and if more proved necessary he could get some sent from Man fairly speedily.

Two weeks after leaving Limavady he was on his way back, at the head of a fleet of thirty longships. Fortunately or otherwise the weather was fairly calm for the time of year, although it did mean that de Burgh's attacks would not be held up either. So more than any mere embattled waiting would be called for in Ulster.

Angus sought to prepare himself for fighting leadership such as was required of him – but that was not his principal anticipation, as perhaps it should have been.

At Limavady it had to be all very different from his previous visit. Now he had with him numerous chiefs, Duart, MacIan, MacLaine, MacDuffie, and their lieutenants, so that O'Cahan's castle and castleton were crowded, and closeness such as Angus would have preferred was not possible, even though Ainea offered him a kindly welcome. O'Cahan was much heartened by the reinforcements, saying that de Burgh had managed to advance in these two weeks as far as Kilrea on the River Bann, and his own force, under his son Liam, had fallen back on Garvagh, where there was a good defence-point at a spur of the mountains. They must join Liam there, at the soonest.

So there was no lingering at Limavady for the newcomers. Ainea said that she wished that she could accompany them all eastwards, but her father would not hear of it. Angus was urged to take care.

It was marching again, then, for the Islesmen, through pastoral country, then ever becoming more hilly, with many rivers, great and small. Then the hills grew higher and steeper, no mountains by Isles standards although named so here, these forming a barrier between east and west, Coleraine and

Derry, for almost one hundred miles, a useful defence zone. Passes there were through them, admittedly, and these were now being manned. De Burgh had to get his men across, ripe for ambushes as they were, or else go north for a score of miles right to the coast, to get round the final heights of Downhill by a very narrow strip, this to be guarded also. O'Cahan's main force was at the widest of the passes between the quite high hills of Craiggore and Benbradagh. De Burgh might well choose a narrower one on the other side of Craiggore, between that long ridge and one called Boyd's Mountain. It was suggested that Angus send half his strength to reinforce this, while the rest went in their longships to the northern shelf of land above the sea, in case the enemy attempted that. And if they saw no sign of the English, to march due south to assail De Burgh in flank or rear.

This all made sense to Angus, O'Cahan drawing a rough map of the hill barrier and the passes. It was decided to send MacIan and MacDuffie, with seven hundred, to help at the narrower pass at Boyd's Mountain, while Angus himself went with his ships up to the coast, to block that passage. If not involved there, he would leave his vessels and move south to form a threat from behind.

So it was back to the ships, and down Lough Foyle again, and eastwards along the shoreline beyond.

There was no difficulty in finding their advised destination, for about five miles on from Magilligan Point the hills came almost right down to the sea, with only a high and narrow way round from east to west. Disembarking, the Islesmen, another seven hundred of them, ranged themselves there, to hold that cliff-top shelf. At this stage, it seemed a distinctly passive sort of warfare.

How long to wait? Presumably if De Burgh decided to come this way, or some part of his force, it would not be long delayed, if it was to be an effective move. Three days? Four?

78

Scouts were posted up on the hillsides, to report. The rest of them could remain meantime at their vessels.

Four days and nights and no sign of the enemy. So, leaving only a small guard with the longships, Angus led his men due southwards among the Coleraine foothills.

According to the chart O'Cahan had made for him, it was just over a dozen miles to the first of the passes, the narrow one behind Boyd's Mountain. In due course, reaching the entrance to this, they saw no signs of any army thereabouts or in passage, and since de Burgh would almost certainly be using horsed knights and cavalry, horse droppings there would have been. Proceeding some way up the defile, they came to scouts of their own people, MacIan's, left there watchful. They said that O'Cahan had been sent word by his son that the English were in fact seeking to force their way through the wider pass below Craiggore, and he had gone, with most of the company, to aid Liam, leaving only these guards.

It seemed obvious, then, that Angus's course was to head on southwards and get behind the English, to attack their rear. If they had indeed managed to win through the pass, and out into open country beyond, O'Cahan and MacIan retreating before them, then a threat at the enemy backs would be valuable.

They turned back then, with another half-dozen miles to go around Craiggore's skirts. And at the south of the hill, where the river emerged from the pass, there they found horse droppings in plenty.

Now for probable action. Was de Burgh held in the pass, or had he won through it? Angus sent his scouts on ahead, to learn what they could. Then he divided his people, Duart leading on the left of the river, himself on the right: horse droppings were evident on both sides. They began to move slowly up.

Scouts came back to say that there was battle going on almost a mile up the pass, a confused and scattered affray extending over quite a distance on the floor of the valley on either side of the river, also some way up the hillsides, horse and foot.

This was what Angus wanted, needed to hear. There was a part for his people to play here. Horsemen would be disadvantaged on those slopes, and on the narrow riverside levels. He ordered his men to move higher up the hillsides as they headed east, the higher the better meantime.

They heard the clash before they saw anything of it, the valley having bends in it. So they were readied, battle-axes, swords and dirks drawn. There was no real need for instructions, obvious what his men should do. They would spread along the upper slopes, and then hurl themselves upon the drawn-out conflict below. There ought to be no difficulty in distinguishing friend from foe.

When they did round a shoulder of Craiggore, there they saw the fighting ahead of them, stretching out of sight around another bend of the glen. Duart's men were able to see it first. They waved, shouted and pointed. On both flanks, the Islesmen broke into a run, an irregular, uneven run, for it was over rough ground.

In fact, they were able to achieve complete surprise, for the battlers below were all too much involved in their life-or-death struggle to be looking up the higher hillsides. Angus waved to his followers to spread themselves, so that they could make a quite extended front. Duart, across the river, an old campaigner, would do the same.

His men flung themselves downhill somewhat erratically, inevitably, but that was not of vital importance on so wide a front, and with that bend in the valley. Upon the smiting, yelling turmoil, they descended, adding to it of course, but in a very positive way.

For his own part, Angus could not now give any sort of lead. It was every man for himself in that wild disarray of rearing, kicking horses, flashing steel, tumbling bodies, made the worse by the bodies to fall over, men and beasts already down. The tactics, for foot against cavalry, were to attack each horseman on two sides at once, and while one was seeking to dodge the lance or sword aimed at him, the other stooping to slash upward with his dirk at the unfortunate animal's belly, ripping. This either had the horse down, or sent it rearing off in its agony, usually unseating the rider. Hundreds of the new Islesmen acting thus had an enormous impact on the already desperate mêlée, and swiftly.

The Englishmen, individually, wide-scattered as they were, did not take long to recognise that they were in a hopeless situation here; there could be no real leadership on their side either. Those who could began to turn back eastwards, where it was possible in the press, or else spurring some little way up the slopes on either flank to do so. Where de Burgh might be who could tell, if he was present at all. Unhorsed troopers fought bravely enough, though all but hopelessly.

How long it took for victory to be perceived to be won, Angus did not know, time unaccountable in the circumstances. He had fallen over sundry bodies, slipped on blood, received a glancing blow on one shoulder from a lance, but scarcely heeded it in the frenzy, so far escaping any serious injury. Battle was like that, all uncertainty for those taking part. Commanders might lead heroically from the front; but more success was to be achieved by standing back, surveying, and giving effective directions and orders.

When the smiting seemed to be all but over, and the cries and moans of the wounded and dying replaced all the wild shouting, Angus was able to look about him. One of Mac-Ian's men whom he found near him said that his chief was further forward, westwards. He did not know where O'Cahan was.

Seeking to assess how his own men had fared, he gathered that there were comparatively few casualties among them, some wounded but only two reported to him as slain. The toll was much worse among MacIan's people, he was sorry to learn.

When he had established some sort of order among his folk, he went off westwards, picking his way through that horrible scene, all but sickened by what he saw. Round the bend in the valley he came on O'Cahan and MacIan and their lieutenants considering the position, Duart now with them. O'Cahan was loud in his praise of Angus's efforts, which he said had turned the tide. He was grateful indeed.

The tidying up after battle always took time, the caring for the wounded, the piling of the dead in heaps for burial, identifying and counting, all distinctly incoherent after all the tension and excitement. So it was late in the day before any move could be made westwards, for Limavady, and scarcely in triumph, more in thankfulness, at least as far as Angus was concerned.

Seeing his men encamped by the Roe riverside, and being provided with local women to tend wounds and provide food, he at length found his way up to the castle. There he discovered Ainea equally busy. But she did not fail to spot his arrival, and noting the way he was carrying himself, realised that he had received some hurt. Although he sought to make light of it, she handed over her immediate task to another, and leading him into an antechamber, sat him down.

"You are wounded?" she demanded. "What is it? Where? You walk but ill. You are in pain . . ."

"It is nothing. A blow on my shoulder, that is all . . ."

Shaking her head over him, she helped him to remove his doublet and shirt, and noted his jerked indrawn breaths. Looking at his extensively bruised shoulder and two red lacerations, she pursed her lips.

"Why say that it is nothing! You are sore hurt, Angus. Wait you. Sit there."

She went to fetch warmed water to bathe it all.

The young woman's subsequent stoopings over him, so

close, and her gentle attentions were sufficiently pleasing to the sufferer to all but counter the pain, although he did jerk once or twice as she dabbed at the broken skin. She was very thorough about it, but with soothing murmurs. The sound of her voice was in itself as good as any ointment.

"Now you must rest yourself," she declared. "It is an early bed for you this night. See you, no need to put on your clothing again, nor come down to table. I will bring up food and drink for you to your bedchamber. Come you there . . ."

She led him upstairs to the room he had previously shared with Duart and MacIan, but Ainea was having none of that now. They would be installed elsewhere. His hostess acted the authoritative nurse.

She left him sitting on the bed while she went for provender. He made no demurs.

When she came back it was with a maid with hot water for the washing-tub, herself with the food. When the girl had gone, Ainea said that he should wash first, then eat in comfort in the bed.

"Off with these clothes," she ordered, and when he said that he could do that for himself she dismissed that and promptly helped him to disrobe. Naked, she led him to the bath-tub, there to be heedfully washed and sponged, the man not a little embarrassed by his own manhood, pained shoulder or none. Then dried with care, and back to bed. When settled in, first he was given honey wine to sip, then offered the food, which he accepted obediently.

Angus was still at this when O'Cahan entered the room, saying that he had not known that his friend was wounded, and was grieved to hear of it. The so-carefully tended casualty denied that it was really a wound, merely a blow struck, this to Ainea's tut-tuts. Her father observed that at any rate he was obviously in good hands, and departed.

Feeding over, finally the young woman straightened the blankets, told him not to rise until she came in the morning to examine that shoulder. Then, stooping to kiss his brow, she told him to sleep soundly, and not to think of strife and stress and pain. Then she left him.

He obeyed this last, at least, although he was barely in a soporific state of mind, his thoughts concerned with his nurse, not with himself. He was almost thankful for that damaged shoulder.

Nevertheless, he was not going to obey that injunction about not rising in the morning before Ainea came back.

In time, he slept.

Angus's next conscious awareness was of being patted on the cheek, and he woke to find Ainea at his bedside, despite his contrary decision, this and fresh hot water steaming in the tub. He sat up, apologising, and had his shoulder examined. He was told that the swelling had gone down, but that it was all still much discoloured and the cuts dry. Asked how he felt, he declared that he was more or less himself again, which had her wagging her head over him, and saying not to be foolish and tempt fate. Would she bring his breakfast to him, or would he come down for it?

He would most certainly do the latter, he declared.

He remained sitting up in bed. She asked whether he could dress himself, and when told so, in no uncertain terms, smiled, and left the room. The man had no mind to go over to the tub naked again, before her. If *she* had been unclothed also, of course, it would have been different, before breakfast as it was, but . . .

Downstairs, he found the other visitors at various stages of breaking their fast. He was able to announce that he was in no great pain, and fortunate to have escaped so lightly, even though none of these had been injured at all.

The previous day's doings were discussed, and what was to be done now, this while Ainea played the hostess.

Her father told them that he had his scouts out well beyond

84

the mountains to keep watch on the enemy. He judged that de Burgh would probably retire to Kilrea, which had been his base recently, there to "lick his wounds". But they could not be sure of this. He might not even have been present at this contest in the pass, his whole strength not involved. So there could be repercussions, a striking back. He was not the man to be easily discouraged. Until they were assured that the menace was on hold over the next months of sterner winter, he would be grateful if the Islesmen would remain for a little longer.

Angus, after glancing at Duart, MacIan and the others, nodded.

O'Cahan thought that the best way they could help, meantime, especially with their great fleet of longships, was to make their continued presence very evident to the enemy. De Burgh just might attempt a move into Derry by the northern coastal approach, around Downhill Point. So, some of the ships and a company of men holding that position could discourage anything such. And if the rest of the fleet was to sail on round the coast eastwards to show itself, not far offshore, this could be an effective deterrant. If they went as far as Portrush along the Coleraine seaboard, the word would soon get inland up the River Bann as far as Kilrea.

This was agreed. How soon? The sooner the better, they were told.

Ainea had been listening to all this. Now, she asked her father whether she might be allowed to sail in one of the longships on this little voyage. She had never been in one, and would like to do so. He had not allowed her to go with him into the pass conflict, but this of the ships would spell no danger, surely.

Looking over at Angus, O'Cahan said that was for the Lord of Islay to decide. And did he feel sufficiently fit to be going himself?

That man asserted so, definitely. This looked like the sort of action he could enjoy. He saw no hazards in it. The Lady Ainea would be welcome.

85

So without undue delay the Islesmen were readied to embark, and all were interested to see a young woman accompanying their lord, she wearing a cloak against the chill winds, something new for the crews. Their passenger professed herself as coming with them mainly to ensure that Angus did nothing to worsen the state of his shoulder.

Needless to say she went in the dragonship, sitting at the stern beside Angus and the helmsman, and smiling at all the watchful rowers. Angus did not fail to recollect the other occasion when he had taken females on his vessel, on their request, and the need for erecting that spare sail at the stern for reasons of privacy.

It was not long before the young woman was singing, in time with the gong and grunting chant of the oarsmen.

Once they had won out of Lough Foyle and into the Atlantic waves, the singing inevitably became somewhat irregular, as the vessels plunged and lurched. Ainea wondered how the rowers managed to keep up any sort of coherent pulling and dipping of their lengthy sweeps which, because of the tossing and swinging, were often high in the air when they should have been in the water. Angus agreed that it was difficult, but the crews were very practised, and were watchful of their neighbours' strokes on the other side of the boat. There was an art in it.

It made a quite rough passage along to that Downhill Point, beyond which they pulled in, and left some of the vessels and crews to land, and hold that position once more. Ainea, when asked if she had had enough of this uncomfortable cruising, said that, no, she would be happy to sail on. She was clearly exhilarated by the experience.

The main fleet drove onwards, past the Bann-mouth and the Portrush haven, where they turned in for a while to make sure that their presence was entirely evident. Then on a few miles to near Benbane Head, where the dramatic feature known as the Giant's Causeway drew all eyes. Ainea was much interested in this. She had seen it before, to be sure, in her father's vessel, but never in rough seas and winter weather, with the great waves and the clouds of spray emphasising its challenge. She told Angus that it was supposed to represent the beginning of a mighty road, of those columns and rocks, to link Ireland and Scotland, built by giants of ancient days but never completed, the stacks rising high and stretching out for almost three hundred yards. Angus supposed that Rathlin Isle, some way across the North Channel, represented an outcropping of the same rock formation.

On, to pass the precipitous Fair Head, and dusk beginning to descend upon them, it was decided that, the seas here turbulent indeed, they would be better to lie up for the night out at Rathlin itself, six miles, rather than seek some sheltered corner of that wild coast.

It was almost dark when they reached that island, crescent-shaped, some six miles long by two wide, not really hilly but with high cliffs, and quite fertile. Angus knew it well, for it was considered to be part of the Isles lordship, although much nearer to Ireland than to Scotland. It was quite populous. Its small castle would provide overnight accommodation for Ainea and some others, and food for the crews, who would remain to sleep, wrapped in their plaids, on their ships.

The keeper of the castle, taken by surprise as he was, found some sort of quarters for the unexpected visitors, his wife actually taking Ainea to share her own bed in place of her husband. Angus had his shoulder examined and rebound, however, before he bedded down elsewhere, the wife assisting in this also.

The chiefs had to share crowded rooms.

They were told that St Columba had established a church here, from Iona.

In the morning it was back to the Irish coast again, heading southwards now, to show themselves as far as Garron Point, Cushendun and Cushendall's Bay. Here they were only a score

87

of miles from Kilrea, de Burgh's alleged base; so almost certainly he would not fail to be informed of their nearness.

They turned back here, reckoning that this was as close to the enemy as they could get, with the Antrim hills between. And thereafter, having to turn west at Fair Head, they had the winds in their faces, making for still rougher and slower progress. Ainea made no complaint, a good voyager. She was entirely frank about nature's calls, behind her sail-screen, and did not pretend to be embarrassed at the like male needs being more publicly met, all part of sea travel.

This delayed headway against wind and tide meant that they got only just beyond the Giant's Causeway before darkness fell, and there was no convenient haven for overnight accommodation. So it was a matter of bedding down in the ships, in such sheltered waters as was possible, under cliffs. Angus, concerned for Ainea's comfort behind her sail, finding her plaiding to add to her cloak, said that he would be not far away if she required any help.

"Do not be foolish," she declared. "We would be as well to lie side by side, and help to keep each other warm, surely."

Needless to say, this suggestion was received with much approval. Soon they were in each other's arms under the plaids, and generating heat in more ways than one, at least as far as the man was concerned. He had never dared to contemplate anything such as this, much as he favoured closeness. Sleep, he decided, would be a stupid waste of opportunity and pleasure in the circumstances, for himself.

After a few murmurings and bodily adjustings, in the event, the young woman was soon breathing deeply in seemingly blissful slumber, that stirring of rounded and warm person producing considerably more conscious bliss in the man. He decided that he could not remember anything he had enjoyed so much in all his life.

Despite his attempts to remain awake, however, to savour it

all, Angus fell asleep all too soon, and thereafter slept all too soundly.

In fact it was Ainea who awakened him in the morning, kneeling at his side, informing him that the men were stirring, and preparing their food and drink, such as was available, and it was time to be up and doing.

"You sleep soundly!" she said. "And make a warm . . . companion. Although you do jerk, on occasion!"

"I am sorry," he got out. "I, I thank you. Thank you indeed!" That seemed quite inadequate for the occasion. But what was he to say?

"As my nights have passed, thus far, it was unusual!" she observed, as he rose and helped her to her feet also, in that swaying boat.

They ate and drank among the men, who obviously approved of their female passenger, whatever they thought of her passing of the night.

Then it was on westwards into the winds, for Lough Foyle and Limavady.

O'Cahan welcomed them back, eyeing his daughter enquiringly. He said that his scouts had reported no attempts by the English to re-enter the passes; and was glad to learn that there had been no sign of an enemy move by the northern coastwise approach. It looked as though de Burgh was accepting stalemate meantime.

Angus hoped that this was so – and that King Edward's friend would not see an assault on Man as an alternative activity in the circumstances. The fleet's appearance in Manx waters might be advisable. And it was time that he and his chiefs got back to their Isles anyway, responsibilities there not to be neglected for overlong. So, although he, Angus, would have liked to linger at Limavady, he had to recognise facts and duties. They would be off next day, then.

How much Ainea told her father of her sea-going experiences was not to be known. But she reverted to acting the hostess, to the satisfaction of her many guests, especially Angus, the more so when she declared that that shoulder of his ought to have one last inspection before he departed. He did not object, nor claim that it was unnecessary.

She escorted him up to his bedchamber again that night, and he went through the partial disrobing process and examination, she announcing that the wound, as she called it, appeared to be much bettered.

Angus, enjoying her ministrations again, decided to take a chance. He reached out to hold the arm so close to him, and kissed it.

"You are so good, so kind, so beautiful!" he said, in something of a rush. "The fairest that I have ever known! How can I thank you? Sufficiently."

"Need you?"

"I need to, yes. I need to, greatly. You have made me very happy, lass." He had never called her that before. "Grateful. But happy also." He still held her arm, and kissed it again.

"You are very . . . approving," she said.

"Can you wonder at it? After all that you have done for me, cared for me, accompanied me. And, and last night!"

"Last night was well spent, yes. Even if you did give me jerks! We warmed each other."

"I felt warm enough towards you, Ainea, without that!"

"Did you? Why, I wonder?"

"Why? Lord, can you not understand? I am longing for you." And he kissed that arm for the third time.

"Poor Angus! Wanting Ainea O'Cahan."

"Is that so strange? Who could be more desirable? In every way."

"Ah! A man's desire for a woman?"

"Not any woman. *You*! And more than any desire – *need*, I said. Long for. Ever since I first saw you. And the need has grown with each day, each hour." He shook his head. "Could I ever hope that you might . . . might gain some feeling for me?"

"Think you that I would ever have gone sailing in your ship if I had no liking for you, foolish one? Much less lie down beside you overnight."

"Liking! So, so I may hope? That one day perhaps . . ."

"I could not prevent you hoping, my lord of Islay, even if I would. Your hopes are your own. As to mine . . . ? We shall see." She straightened up. "Now – sleep for you. And for me. Differently from last night!" And she stooped again, to kiss his cheek, not his brow this time. Angus was left to his tumultuous thoughts.

In the morning the fleet sailed, having played its part meantime, O'Cahan loud in his praise and gratitude to the Islesmen, with Angus promising to be back, if required – and in his own mind, even if he was *not* required, and after no lengthy interval. He got a kiss from Ainea, this time on the lips, although not any lingering one, before climbing into his dragonship. She had not backed away from his hug of farewell.

10

It was Man for the fleet, before returning to their home isles, one hundred and fifty miles. So it was behind Isle Magee, off the Antrim coast for that night, more than halfway, with the wind behind them and sails up.

Next day, at Peel, Rory mac Alan had important news for them. MacDunleary, from Down in Ulster, had sent word two days before that de Burgh had left Ireland to return to England. Whether this was on account of his defeat at Craiggore, and discouragement, or that he had been sent for by King Edward was not known. But at least he was gone meanwhile, to all Ulstermen's relief.

Much pleased at these tidings, Angus and his people could return northwards for home waters.

And at Dunaverty there was further heartening intelligence, sent from Saddell. The warrior Wallace, with the help of none other than that Sir Andrew Moray whom they had met at Inverness, had won a great victory over the English occupying forces at Stirling Bridge, these under Warenne, Earl of Surrey, Edward's governor, and the cleric Cressingham, his treasurer. The site of the battle, carefully chosen, was a long, narrow wooden bridge over the River Forth, before it reached the salt waters of the firth, with swamp and marshland on either side. This had enabled the Scots foot utterly to defeat the English cavalry, these able to ride only two abreast over the bridge. The timbers of this, cut in half by the undermining of hidden guards at the strategic moment, had severed the English front from the rear, so that the northern part of the army, driven into the soft ground where the horses were bogged down, was massacred, while the rest had fled. And word of this victory had convinced Robert Bruce, Earl of Carrick, grandson of one of the Competitors for the Crown, to rise in arms to assist Wallace, although he had formerly been friendly towards English Edward. This would give a lead to other Scots nobles who had been tardy in aiding Wallace.

Now Angus thought he knew why de Burgh had gone back to England. The Plantagenet would be greatly shocked and angered, and would be going to muster all his strength, French and Irish wars notwithstanding, to re-establish his grip on Scotland.

At Ardtornish Angus learned that his friend's father had died, and Ewan was now MacLean of Kinlochaline. This would mean that, with the responsibilities that went with the position, he would not be able to be so much of a companion as formerly, however friendly they remained.

There was much of the Isles lordship which Angus had not yet visited, north of Skye up to Cape Wrath and west to the Outer Hebrides, Lewis, Harris, Barra and the rest, largely MacLeod country. But this was not the time of year to attempt anything such. One visit he could make, of course, and must, even though he now felt somewhat reluctant to do so – and blamed himself therefor. To Saddell he must go. Why did he find himself somehow blameworthy over those two young women there? He had been fond of them, and still was – but this of Ainca changed all. He could still, surely, feel and act kindly towards them. Should he tell them of his new yearning and fervour for O'Cahan's daughter, make the situation clear? And what *was* the situation? He was in love, yes; but was Ainea likely to respond to his passion? She was fond of him, she had admitted and demonstrated. But that might well be as far as it went with her. He could by no means assume that the need was mutual. Better to say nothing about it, at this stage, to Eithne and Seona, nor indeed their father and mother. Was that feeble and unworthy, when he would have to say much about O'Cahan himself and the Ulster situation?

93

It was all very difficult.

At Saddell, Angus was greeted, as ever, warmly by all the family, with demands as to why he had been so long again in coming, the young women especially reproachful – which did not help. He plunged into the Ulster developments, de Burgh, and O'Cahan, not mentioning Ainea however. There was much interest, of course, but no particularly deep questioning.

His grand-uncle had further information for him, brought as ever by the monks. William Wallace had actually carried out a retaliatory raid into England, in November, reaching as far south as Newcastle-upon-Tyne and even Durham. But he and his men had no siege-machinery, and could not capture the great castles there. They had come home with much plunder. But Wallace, it seemed, was not seeking to set himself up as any sort of dominant figure or Guardian; for in fact Bruce of Carrick and John Comyn of Badenoch had been appointed Joint Guardians of the Realm, an extraordinary situation, for they were known to hate and distrust each other; and while Bruce now favoured Wallace and his efforts, the Comyn was pro-Edward. Clearly this division between them could not benefit Scotland, nor long survive.

The sisters did not fail to suggest another excursion with their guest. Would he take them over this Kilbrannan Sound to the great Isle of Arran just some seven miles off, where they could hire garrons to explore some part of that terrain which so dominated their views with its high and impressive mountains?

Actually Angus was not averse to making such a visit. Arran, although on the Firth of Clyde, was almost as large as Islay, and ought to belong to the Isles lordship. It had been once, for Somerled had taken it from occupying Norsemen, together with Bute, another somewhat smaller isle to the north. And Fionn mac Coul and his Feinn had been here, his daughter allegedly buried on Arran. But, so close to mainland Scotland and the Ayrshire and Renfrewshire coasts, the line of the High Stewards had grasped both isles, and this had been confirmed by King David and his successors. So a call over there might be well worth the making.

The sound's waters were sheltered, and the dragonship crossed in less than an hour, with the girls pointing out landmarks and naming mountains. They reached a great bay called Drumadoon, the Ridge of the Fort, at the centre of which they landed, at Feorline, where the Black Water of Clauchan reached the sound, and there was a fishing-village. Here they had no difficulty in borrowing garrons from a farmer, and the three of them rode off northwards, objectives decided beforehand. They would go and inspect the Pictish dun, or fort, and then visit a renowned cave, said to have been the refuge of some king or hero of the past.

The young women made good company, full of talk and banter; and there being the two of them, there was no real competition for the man's attention. Angus tried not to keep comparing them with Ainea. He judged that he could keep them as good friends without too much difficulty, despite his preoccupation with another.

They rode up the cliff-girt coast to inspect a stone tomb of some long-ago chieftain, a cist they called it. Then on up quite a hill to the Doon, typical green ramparts covering quite a large area, with a standing stone nearby, this above a headland. Then it was on, over a mile, to a still loftier height close to the shoreline cliffs, these columnar and steep. The cave they wanted to see was part-way down. They dismounted and tethered the horses, and went to pick their way on the zigzag track, this with the girls exclaiming and holding Angus's hands, in front and behind, with much excitement.

The cave, when they got to it, proved to be only partly natural, extended internally, obviously by excavation and stone chipping, to provide shelving and benches for sleeping on. The walls bore rock-carvings of hunting scenes, deer and serpents. Who was the hero, or king, who had sheltered here was apparently uncertain, Angus wondering whether it could have been Fionn mac Coul himself, Fingal the Fairhaired Stranger. Was there any tradition of another woman than his daughter, and a great hound?

They debated this, but did not linger overlong, for it was cold in that west-facing cavern, the winds making eerie, moaning sounds.

They went to see an outstanding feature, not far off, known as the Pulpit Rock; then inland by another burial-chamber, a stone circle and cairns. Clearly this had been an important area for their Pictish ancestors. Onward they reached the Black Water valley, some way upstream, and turned back for the haven, a pleasant and interesting excursion.

That night, the guest received his usual escort and good-night kisses, and was not unduly doubtful over it all, friendship and love not being in competition, he assured himself.

In the morning, he and his were waved off, with haste-ye-backs. Angus was, even so, wondering about another haste-back excuse, this time to Limavady.

Much as he would have liked to have spent Yuletide elsewhere, Angus passed that period at Ardtornish rather than Dunaverty, with Ewan and his mother and sister, pleasingly enough. It was proving to be a very hard winter, weatherwise, and any major sea travel was not to be contemplated. Angus was planning his visit to the northern isles.

It was early March before there were further tidings sent by Alastair MacDonald. Word had come that, at Selkirk on the edge of the great Forest of Ettrick, wherein Wallace's army made its secure base, that man had actually been knighted by Bruce, Earl of Carrick and claimant to the throne, and thereafter elevated to be Guardian of Scotland. Just what was now the position of the two previous and warring Guardians, Bruce and the Red Comyn of Badenoch, was uncertain. But the new Guardian had been backed by many of the greatest in the land, however much opposed by the Comyns and their allies. The Earls of Lennox, Mar, Atholl and Strathearn had supported Bruce's proposal, with the Lords of Crawford, Maxwell, Douglas and others. So now the new Sir William had governmental authority as well as military. And this was much required, for the English were known to be massing at Newcastle, under the Earl of Surrey, to reassert Edward's dominance of the northern kingdom. That monarch had returned from Flanders, and was said to be coming north to lead this host in person.

Much concerned, Angus wondered whether there was any way in which *he* could serve the Scottish cause.

In the event he did not have to ponder this for long, nor invent any excuse to make a return to Limavady. Just as he was about to sail off on his northern visitation, a messenger came from O'Cahan, by way of Peel on Man, to say that one Thomas Bisset, from Antrim, desired to aid Wallace's fight against Edward. He was of Scots extraction himself, the Bissets being Normans brought to Scotland by William the Lion and given lands in the north, none so far from Badenoch and Moray. But his great-grandsire had slain the young Earl of Atholl at Haddington in Lothian after a tourney, in shameful circumstances; and he had been banished the realm in consequence, and exiled to Ireland. There, in Antrim, he and his descendants had settled in, and made themselves useful in supporting the petty kings in their struggles for supremacy, and thus had established themselves successfully as quite potent lords. Now this Thomas Bisset saw opportunity to regain his lost inheritance in Scotland by aiding Wallace and Bruce against Edward and the Comyns, encouraged by the great victory of Stirling Bridge. He was prepared to bring over quite a large body of gallowglasses to join the Scots army. But neither he nor O'Cahan himself had the ships required to transport such a force. Would Angus Og send a flotilla of his longships to carry them over? With the English massing for a new assault, they would be welcome, it was judged.

So there it was, most appropriate and convenient. Angus would himself take the vessels to Lough Foyle for the purpose, and see O'Cahan and his daughter in the process. The north isles cruising could wait a little longer. With no unnecessary delay, crews and ships were assembled, and the eighty-mile journey commenced, with an overnight halt at Rathlin. Needless to say, Angus would go to Limavady, not to Cushendun or some other Antrim haven, and let this Bisset and his men come to Lough Foyle for their transport.

Most encouraging was the reception accorded when the Lord of Islay came in person with his fleet, Ainea clearly pleased to see him, as was her father. The young woman seemed to him to be more beautiful and desirable than ever. Angus had not brought any of his chieftains with him on this occasion, so there was no great playing of hostess required, their single visitor gaining the more attention, the crews well looked after down at the castleton.

Asked what he had been doing since last they forgathered, apart from enduring the hard winter, and considering the situation on the mainland, Angus did mention his visit to his grand-uncle at Saddell, and the two young "aunts" he had there. This had Ainea raising her eyebrows, and wondering whether such relationship could lead to romantic complications. She was very promptly assured that no such problems arose, nor would.

With Bisset based at Ballymena in central Antrim, some thirty miles away, it would take a few days for him to be informed of the position and to get his gallowglasses through the hills to Limavady. Angus had not failed to think of this. So he ought to be able to have opportunity for time with Ainea.

That night, when she took him up to his room, to ensure that all was in order, the bed warmed and water hot, she told him that she was surprised that he had thought to come with the ships for Bisset and his men; after all, the fleet had come only for transport.

"I came because I wanted to see *you*!" he declared, he hoped not overboldly.

"A long way for an important man, acting Lord of the Isles. To see an Irishwoman," she observed. "There must be scores, hundreds, of fair young women in your own islands and clans."

"No doubt. But none to compare with Ainea O'Cahan."

"You say so? Have you made trial of them? To discover?"

"No-o-o. I did not need to. I *know* it."

"You seem very sure of yourself, my lord!"

"Of myself, I am sure. But you? I can but hope."

"You said that before, I recollect. Hope. You are a man for hoping!"

"Are my hopes . . . hopeless?"

"Who am I to say?"

"It is what *you* say that will prove whether or no."

"Dear me, what a burden you place on me!"

"A burden? You mean . . . ? You see my hopes as a burden on you?"

"Only if I have to . . . fulfil them. Such great hopes."

Angus searched those lovely features in the lamplight. "You yourself have hopes . . . otherwhere?" he asked unhappily. "A woman's hopes. There must be many men who seek O'Cahan's daughter. So beautiful, so desirable, so spirited, so . . . so challenging."

"Sakes – all that? Oh, yes, I have had men seeking, shall we say, favours! Not a few. But men are all like that towards women, are they not?"

"It is not favours that I seek, lass. It is more than that. It is you, yourself. All of you."

"Gracious goodness, you are demanding! Is this what comes of friendship with the Lord of Islay and the Isles? I must beware, I see. A dangerous man!" She shook her head, but

99

without any frowning. "I must get me hence, I see. For my safety! So I say goodnight. Sleep well. And do not feel . . . deprived."

She clasped him briefly to her person, and kissed him in a slightly less hurried salute from warm lips. She all but ran to the door, and out.

He gazed at that closed door for quite some time.

In the morning, O'Cahan announced that, while they waited, they might go and see his son Liam, at Dungiven, some ten miles further up the River Roe, he having expressed a desire to meet Angus Og, Ainea saying that she would accompany them.

They went on horseback along the winding riverside through hilly country, Angus remarking on their fine mounts, such as they did not have in the Isles.

Dungiven proved to be a hallhouse, no castle, although a ruined fort rose nearby. Liam O'Cahan was not present when they arrived, being out hawking. But they were welcomed by his wife, Edna, a pleasant, plumpish creature, with a baby son Brian, of whom Ainea was obviously very fond.

When Liam, a handsome man of thirty, came back from his sport, with three mallard ducks and a wild swan, he brought a companion with him, Padruig O'Donnell, a young man who was clearly much more interested in Ainea than in the other callers, paying her admiring attentions, Angus not unmindful.

The situation with regard to Thomas Bisset was discussed, Liam declaring that he did not like nor trust that man. But, if by helping the Scots against Edward he could regain his family's lost lands in Scotland, Antrim would be well quit of him, he judged.

Angus was asked about the Islesmen's attitude towards the rest of Scotland. Did they consider themselves Scotsmen at all? They seemed to be all but independent as a race. Angus said that, yes, they were Scots, their territories extending deep into the mainland Highlands; and their lords were entitled to sit in the Scots parliament, although they seldom did so. But they were largely independent and always had been, ever since the Norse occupation, Man, for instance, even having had its own kings. They were now, however, much concerned over Edward Plantagenet's efforts to make Scotland part of his realm. Although they had not been asked to involve themselves in the present warfare, he himself had been wondering what he might do to help, apart from keeping Man out of the English grip and aiding Ulster repel de Burgh.

O'Cahan encouraged Angus in this, and said that he, and others in Ulster, could possibly be of aid in the cause, Liam agreeing.

In due course they rode back to Limavady, Angus glad to have Ainea away from that Padruig O'Donnell and his gallantry.

At bed-going thereafter, the young woman only accompanied the guest as far as his bedchamber door, there wishing him pleasant dreams, and saying that she had become rather afraid to go further, in case of indiscretions, whatever that might mean. But she did give him a hug and kiss, which was something, and did not extricate herself from his arms over-urgently.

Next day it was Ainea's suggestion that Angus should be taken to see St Columba's first monastery, founded at Derry. They could go in his dragonship, which would impress the Derry folk. He ought to know more about the early days of the saint who had brought Christianity to Scotland. Her father was quite agreeable, and Angus enthusiastic.

On the sail up Lough Foyle, a dozen miles, he was told how Colm mac Felim O'Conall, prince of the Hy-Neill, the line of High Kings of Ireland, had chosen to serve God and the Irish rather than seek the throne at Tara, and became Abbot of Derry, where he built his first monastery. He had been born at Gartan, in central Donegal, in the year 521. By his high birth, vigorous character and sheer commitment to his Maker's cause, he aroused the envy and even hostility of many of his fellow-ecclesiastics. And, unfortunately, he was in Connaught when the new High King Dairmid attacked King Aed of Connaught unjustly. Dairmid had lapsed to paganism and sunworship of the Druids, and Aed had not. Colm did not take any part in the Battle of Cooldrevny, but encouraged the Christian fighters against the heathen. They won the day, Dairmid fleeing. This resulted in a group of important bishops and abbots, oddly enough, declaring Colm guilty of being involved in the death of over three thousand men. He was officially excommunicated and exiled from Ireland until he had converted to Christianity at least as many pagans as had died in the battle, an extraordinary decision. Much distressed, he left his beloved native land. He crossed to Dalriada, what was now Argyll, and began his great labour of bringing the heathen sun-worshipping Picts and lapsed Scots to Christ, settling at Iona.

It was Ainea who told Angus this long story, of which he had not known the Irish details, her father apparently less interested.

At Derry town, situated on an eminence above the River Foyle, they visited the monastery, and Angus was introduced to Columba's eventual successor as abbot, O'Cahan going off to speak with the town's leaders, in his position of Lord of Derry.

The monastery was all but an abbey now. It had been badly damaged by the Norsemen, and rebuilt; but they were able to see parts of the original church and establishment which Columba had erected nearly seven hundred and fifty years before.

Angus told Ainea that he would wish to take her to see Iona and its abbey one day.

It made a rewarding excursion, despite, for Angus, O'Cahan rejoining them with a younger man, who proved to be a distant kinsman who acted as governor of the town and district, and who made it very evident that he much admired and sought after Ainea, she seemingly on friendly terms with him. Angus was going to have to get used to this sort of situation.

That evening he coaxed Ainea back into his bedchamber by telling her that she was quite safe with him, safer probably than with others of her so many admirers; and she, with a little laugh, declaring that it was partly her own behaviour that she feared; which had him wondering indeed. Did she mean . . . ?

He thought it worth while to revert to his suggestion that he would like to take her to see Columba's Iona. Would she consider that? Would her father allow it, if he did not come with them?

"That I do not know," she said. "Why should he not be prepared to visit your Isles?"

"He has so much to occupy him here in Ulster. The English threat. De Burgh will likely be back . . ."

"So you would have me to sail off with you, alone, Angus Og! Think you that seemly?"

"It might be seemly enough if we were . . . betrothed!" He had to take a breath before he said that.

"Betrothed!" She eyed him searchingly. "Do I hear aright? Betrothed? You are seeking, seeking to wed me?"

"Have I not made it clear, for long, that this is my wish, my desire, my foremost aim? To have you for myself. None other. To marry you and make you mine. And myself yours!"

"You have never said it. Marriage."

"I have not dared!"

"But – you dare now." She walked over to the fireside, to gaze into the flickering flames.

He went to her there, and put an arm round her. "Do I offend?" he asked.

She turned in his embrace. "No. Never that. You but take me by surprise. My dear!"

"Dear! You say that – dear?" He all but shook her. "You are calling me *your* dear?"

"Why not? Have I not shown you that I cared for you, Angus? Shown sufficiently. Would I have done what I have otherwise?"

She got no further, her lips becoming sealed by his, as he pressed her closer in his ecstasy, she by no means passive in the exchange, lips wide, hands caressing his back.

So they stood by that fire for long moments, words no longer necessary, even if they had been possible.

There were no seats in that bedchamber, other than a form for clothing and a chest for blankets, so presently Angus led her over to the bed, where they could sit. And now his eager hands were busy about her rounded person, she shaking her head over him.

"I am not . . . used to this, so, so active a man!" she told him. "Give me a little time!" But she did not push him away.

He restrained himself somewhat. "I am the most joyful man alive!" he asserted. "You give me . . . heaven! Undeserving as I am."

"You will get all that you deserve, with me!" she assured him, laughing a little. "I fear that I am no shrinking maiden – or so I am told."

His hand was cupping one of her breasts. "You are an enchantment. Who wants shrinking enchantments? When shall we wed?"

"I hope no long delay, my love."

"So soon as may be, yes. If not sooner! Will your father agree to it?"

"He will, I am sure. But I am no longer under-age, my own woman. Until I am yours." As his hand slid down on her further, she gently pushed it up again to where it had been. "Which I am not quite yet, see you! Impatient one. But – almost."

Angus changed his posture and grip, to press her back to

rest on the pillow of his bed, and then got down on his knees, to lean over her and kiss her thus.

"One day, one night . . ." he got out.

"Oh, yes. But not this night, my lord! Is it my female person that is so important to you? Rather than me, myself, Ainea?"

"No, no – not that. It is *you*. All of you. But I have been denied it all, for so long."

"So long? How long have we known each other? Even if only . . . in part."

"It has seemed long, long. When I have been away from you, thinking of you, dreaming of you, aching for you . . ."

"Poor Angus. Is there not some saying that absence only heightens relish? But, not long to wait now, I promise."

They remained thus close for a time which neither of them considered nor were concerned with, until, with the man growing more urgent again, Ainea patted his bent head and sat up.

"Do not let us test ourselves overmuch, Angus," she said. "Our love is strong enough, I think, to wait a little longer. This has been a wonder and a gladness, to be treasured for always. Let us leave it so, to savour – not apart, for we shall never be apart now, but each on our own. Ere we sleep, no?"

Sighing, he nodded, and got to his feet, to help her up. "You are the stronger of us, I think!" he declared. "And probably wise, with it. But . . ."

"I am none so strong, my heart – that is why I say this. A good night indeed. We must keep it so."

At the door they kissed again, with a sort of tension which held its own especial message, before she tore herself away.

At breakfast in the morning, O'Cahan came to grip Angus's shoulder. "My daughter tells me that you have asked her to marry you, my friend. I wondered how long it would take for the pair of you to come to this!"

"You are not displeased, sir? You, you give your consent?"

"Could I withhold it? Yes, indeed. I am glad of it. And for her." He looked across at Ainea. "She has made her own choice. And it would have been mine. I am happy."

"I am grateful."

The young woman spoke. "To my father? Or to me?"

That had them all smiling and at ease, able to sup and eat all but normally.

The question of when, of course, came up, a matter for some debate, in the circumstances. The Isles situation had to be considered, and national affairs, both in Scotland and in Ulster, apt to have their impact. Angus did not have to stress that the soonest possible would be his choice. He pointed out that he intended to make a journey round his northern isles, which he had not done as yet, to show himself to the chiefs and people there, and that would be a notable occasion to take Ainea with him, she who was to become Lady of the Isles one day. The young woman all but clapped her hands over this suggestion, and her father nodded approval.

This would best be held in May or June, none so far ahead, Angus declared. So, marriage in little more than a month. Get this Bisset and his people over to Scotland, see to affairs at home, then back for the wedding?

After a moment's calculation, Ainea said that in five or six weeks would suit her woman's requirements. They would be wed at St Columba's church at Derry, this before she was taken to see his Iona.

O'Cahan said that evidently he was going to be busy. Only five or six weeks. Let them hope that there would be no troubles developing with the High King or any of his O'Neill line in their various positions, for among his other responsibilities he was Hereditary Inaugurator of the High Kings and all their O'Neill lieutenants. When Angus said that he did not know of this, he was quoted the saying: "If any take upon him be O'Neill, not named or chosen by O'Cahan, he is not to be obeyed nor taken for O'Neill. The people will not be bound to obey him." This had been the rule ever since Neill of the Nine Hostages reigned in the fifth century. The future son-in-law was much impressed.

That day Ainea took Angus riding, to see the terrain northwards and westwards, along the shores of Lough Foyle towards Magilligan Point, and the mountains there. The man could not have cared where they went, so long as they were alone together. But he approved of the mountains, for when they had reached a commanding height on one, with wide prospects over the Inishowen peninsula and right to Lough Swilly, even eastwards to Islay itself, and they dismounted, to tether their horses, Ainea indicated a comfortable hollow among heather to rest in. Angus could combine distant views with attractions much nearer, and was able to appreciate areas other than scenic, this despite the handicaps of riding clothing, the young woman amusedly remonstrating but not forbidding.

When they returned to Limavady it was to find Thomas Bisset there, with one or two of his subordinates, but not his armed force. He was a middle-aged man of burly build and florid features. Angus saw why Liam O'Cahan had not greatly liked him. And he came announcing complications. He wanted to be taken, with his men, to Man first rather than directly to Scotland, from there to send out emissaries to discover the present position with regard to Wallace and Bruce, in view of the word that King Edward was himself coming north to take over the English command from Surrey and advance over the border. He, Bisset, was not going to find himself isolated and facing the enemy, who, he had heard, was poised to advance on two fronts, up from Newcastle on the east but also from Carlisle on the west. If he was taken directly to the Firth of Clyde and the Ayrshire coasts, he might well find himself caught between two English hosts. So he had sent his men eastwards to a point nearer to Man. Angus did see the sense of this; but it did mean that his ships would have a much longer journey to collect these people, at least an extra sixty miles, and then another sixty to take them up to the Clyde.

It was farewells, then, even though not for long. Angus would pick up the Antrim men at Cushendall, send them on in the fleet to Man, but himself sail north to Dunaverty and Ardtornish to deal with whatever was the situation in the Isles, hopefully without finding anything that would delay his return to Limavady and bliss.

11

The word awaiting Angus at Dunaverty was that Wallace was retiring northwards, on account of the English threat, leaving the land behind him as inhospitable to the enemy advance as was possible, burning crops and hay, having the folk drive off their cattle and sheep into the hills, there to hide meantime, leaving nothing to feed large hosts and their horses. His aim was to get to the Stirling area, where he had won his famous victory, and again use the difficult Forth crossing there to put the invaders at a great disadvantage. Whether Bruce was with him or not was uncertain, but it was judged that he would be in his own country, in the west, to seek to counter an attack coming from Carlisle.

None of this affected Angus and the Islesmen at the moment, although it might well delay Bisset's movements.

At Ardtornish, Ewan informed him that Ian Bacach Mac-Dougall was known to be with the Red Comyn, and co-operating with Edward, whether at Newcastle or Carlisle was again uncertain.

A visit to his father on Islay followed, that strange man looking his age but apparently content with his so inactive life. Then up to Duart to confer with Gillemoir MacLean. There appeared to be no serious problems among the Isles requiring especial attention this summer, for which Angus was thankful. MacLean was congratulatory over the news of the marriage, saying that this would make a useful alliance – which was not in fact how the other looked on it.

He went on to see MacIan at Ardnamurchan, who likewise had nothing exceptional to report. Then it was back to Saddell for news, and to make the slightly uncomfortable announcement of his forthcoming nuptials. Actually, the two young women appeared to be nowise upset about it, saying that they had realised that their friend was finding some attractions over in Ulster other than military ones; and declaring that the lady was the fortunate one, and that they hoped that it would prove to be a most happy union. There was no hint of disappointment.

Their father, conveyor of all tidings thanks to those news-bearing clergy, had interesting word from another source. This was that a large company from Antrim had arrived at the nearby Isle of Arran, the word brought by fishermen from across the Kilbrannan Sound. It seemed that there had been some sort of alliance there by these incomers with James, the High Steward, who was presently occupying the isle in the name of the exiled King John Balliol. What did this portend? Presumably it was Bisset's people, although no mention had been made of any move from Man to Arran. That man was a strange and secretive character. He could only have brought his force there in Angus's ships; so these ought now to have returned to their various bases in the Isles.

The bridegroom-to-be saw nothing in all this to prevent him from heading back to Limavady in his dragonship without delay, a few days earlier than he had anticipated.

There were no complaints from Ainea or her father that he had come too soon and would disturb the evidently quite elaborate wedding arrangements, these all rather beyond Angus's experience and ideas. The Lord of Derry and Royal Inaugurator it seemed had to invite much of Ulster's nobility and prominent ones to his daughter's marriage; and the bride had her own preparations and priorities to attend to. So Angus found himself not exactly neglected, especially at night-time bed-going, but less than an essential presence at this stage. However, he proved to be useful in conveying sundry messages in his ship.

He found it difficult, of an evening, to prevent himself from seeking anticipatory wedding-night delights, although Ainea was able to assist in the necessary discipline by reminding him of her fore-calculated monthly woman's problems.

The great day dawned at last – and even at this stage there were complications. It was traditional that bride and groom did not see each other that day before they met at the altar. So Angus had to abandon his bedchamber at Limavady and go to spend his last single night in the abbot's house in the Derry monastery, not his idea of a sensible arrangement, however kindly received by the cleric who was going to marry him the next day.

Before he left, however, O'Cahan announced to him the dowery he proposed to make in his daughter's favour – and it was surely the most extraordinary jointure ever devised. He declared that he was not rich in gold and silver, but that he was in land and manpower, lord of the whole province of Derry. He could not give the land, but he could some of the men, to aid Angus. He would send him one hundred and forty men of every major surname in the O'Cahan territory, Munroes, MacYs MacMuries, MacFirbis, MacSweenys, as well as O'Donnells, O'Rourkes, even O'Cahans. They would no doubt be a help in keeping the Isles in order.

Astonished, Angus protested that it was too much, too much. How many men would that amount to?

O'Cahan shrugged. "Say ten names, probably. Fourteen hundred men. You will need to send a fleet for them!"

"But . . . this is beyond all! Men, yes, if so you would have it. But, so many!"

"The Lord of Derry can do no less for his daughter's marriage portion. She who is to be the Lady of the Isles. Can you not use them?"

"Oh, I could use them, yes, use them well. But fourteen hundred!"

At the monastery he got on well with the abbot and monks,

but did not mention that he would be responsible for them losing hundreds of their people.

Angus would have liked to have had Ewan as his groomsman, but he had not been able to leave Kinlochaline on account of more illness in the family. So Liam O'Cahan had offered to stand in for him, which was a help, since he would know all the procedures for weddings in these parts. He arrived from Dungiven in good time, Angus at least having no travelling to do for the great occasion.

The church, although quite large, was already full of folk when they were escorted there by the prior, and led up to wait at the chancel steps. Murmurs from the congregation greeted them, Angus hoping that he was dressed sufficiently well on finding Liam looking very grand. A choir of singing boys entertained them all as they waited.

And wait they did, for a seemingly unending interval, at least to the bridegroom, as the boys sang and sang. It was the bride's privilege to be late, of course, and Ainea was not the one to forgo anything such. And, to be sure, she had had a long way to come. But . . .

At last, horn-blowing and commotion outside heralded the appearance of the bridal party; and appearance was the challenging word when, with flourish of horns, O'Cahan led his daughter and her two attendants in. For Ainea, always strikingly beauteous, was today looking almost breathtakingly lovely, all beaming smiles and flashing eyes, superbly gowned, carrying herself proudly but most clearly joyfully, a sight to see, no blushing bride this but a vision of sheer and positive delight, of assured and vehement womanhood.

Angus, used as he was by now to her good looks, was almost stunned by what he saw. It was not just the striking lustre of her but her so evident joy in it all, her bearing, as she came with her father to stand beside him, eyeing him with a sparkling favour, and a brief shake of the head which seemed to say that they were each other's already, and all this only a public acknowledgment of the fact.

Not that the man was in any state to think clearly about this, or anything else. Mind in a whirl and unable to take in all that went on, joyously aware only that he was now about to be joined to his beloved for time and for eternity, he stood there in a kind of trance.

The abbot came out from the vestry and proceeded with the ceremony, and it was as well that not much was demanded of the bridegroom, Liam's guidance and Ainea's happy presence at his side performing what was necessary. Was getting married always like this for the male? Unreal-seeming?

The giving-away by the father, the ring exchange and fitting went without mishap, the celebrant's pronunciation that they were in fact man and wife, and the kneeling for a blessing and benediction, Ainea's gripping of his fingers in heart-felt pressure, finally got through to him, and he knew entire and overwhelming satisfaction.

Angus found himself walking down the aisle between the ranks of wedding guests, hand still in hand with his wife, his wife, his *wife*, made one with him somehow by this less than dramatic performance, she bowing and beaming on them all, he scarcely aware of anything but her arm and hand in his, the fulfilment process commenced and not to be halted now, or ever.

At the church door there was the inevitable multiple salutations, congratulations and felicities, all to be received and acknowledged, on Ainea's part winsomely, on Angus's with such patience as he could muster, his one urgent concern to be alone with this woman who was now his own, a man impatient.

The church was fairly close to the riverside, and the procession set off to escort the couple to the dragonship, O'Cahan's vessel, and other craft, the crews of which had been among the congregation. There, amidst much well-wishing and not a little advice, they embarked for the sail back to Limavady. There had been some discussion as to an alternative retreat for the marital night, but it had been decided that the bride's own home was to be preferred to some unaccustomed venue, especially with the required wedding feast to be provided. So quite a string of boats followed the two leading vessels out from river to loch, including the abbot's barge, with the rowers chanting, and the clash of cymbals, a celebratory journey indeed.

Angus now changed from being some sort of mere necessary figure on the scene to become himself again, positive, effective, the Lord of Islay, master of men – and husband. Ainea added her woman's voice to the chanting.

For the man, of course, the feasting that eventually followed was in the nature of an unavoidable delay, splendid repast as it was, with musical accompaniment, speech-making, and entertainment thereafter. He played his part as best he could, if without enthusiasm, despite his wife's admirable hostess responsibilities on this of all nights.

Fortunately there was no suggestion for a bedding ritual, such as not infrequently accompanied a wedding night, wherein the guests took the happy couple to their chamber, the men there undressing the bride and the women the groom, to lay them side by side on their bed, in the hope of seeing them joined together in more than name, to the onlookers' satisfaction, if not their own, often no successful development. Angus considered it a highly unsuitable custom, and he would have refused it, trusting in his own and O'Cahan's status so to do.

The eating over, although the drinking by no means so, and the entertainment proceeding, Ainea presently rose, glanced over at her husband, and without other demonstration quietly left the hall. Others had been doing the like, and coming back, at nature's calls. Angus wondered how long he should wait before following? He was sitting beside Liam, who smiled at him, and after a brief spell, nudged him. Nodding, the bridegroom raised his tankard for another sip, got to his feet, and strolled as casually as he was able for one of the hall doors, and out.

Once in the vaulted corridor however, he became a different man, all but running along to the stairfoot, and up the treads two at a time, making for his accustomed bedchamber. Therein he did find Ainea, and strode to sweep her into his arms, dancing her around.

They required no words now, however busy were their lips. Releasing herself, the woman took the man's hand and led him to the door, and out, to climb a further flight of the stairway to another bedroom. He did not need to be told that this was her own. Closing the door behind them with something of a flourish, she held out arms to him, with a potent mixture of invitation and possession.

It was high summer, and although no heating was needed, a small fire flickered on the hearth. They went over to it, and gazed down at the flames. More than birch-logs could flame, but the man told himself to savour the moment, so long awaited, taste, relish it, not gulp it down. At his side, Ainea, recognising this, turned to nibble at the lobe of his ear, stroking his hair, a strangely intimate gesture.

"Husband!" she said.

He nodded, searching her lovely features. "Who am I to have won . . . this?" he wondered.

"You are Angus mac Alastair mac Angus mac Donald mac Ranald mac Somerled," she said. "See you, I have remembered it all. And now all mine! Come!" And turning, she led him over to her great bed.

Now, restraining himself still, he commenced, in most heedful and deliberate fashion, to undress her, she beginning to assist him and then changing her mind and allowing him to proceed at his own pace. Admittedly that pace began to increase as her gown fell to the floor, her underbodice only just covering her full-rounded breasts. He stooped to kiss and fondle, pushing the cloth lower to free the prominent nipples, her deep breathing adding to the sensuous invitation of it all.

She herself initiated the discarding of her lower garment, and kicking the clothing free, with a sort of proud toss of the head, stood before him naked, in all her ravishing and superb womanly perfection.

He reached out to grasp and fondle and kiss, then thought better of it, and stood back to devour her with his eyes, all the sheer bliss of her, from lovely face and eyes and long swanlike neck, to proud bosom and rounded belly, dark triangle at loins, to shapely thighs and slender calves and ankles, a picture of perfection and desire which left him the more speechless than ever.

Smiling, she slowly turned herself round before him, to offer him her rearward view of long back and swelling buttocks, so complementary to the rounded prominences on her other side. Then she confronted him again, and laughing, launched herself forward to undo his doublet, as start to the process of comparable disrobing. She needed a little help when it came to unwrapping his saffron kilt, belted as it was, and urgent masculinity to be carefully countered.

Kicking off his brogues and removing his stockings, he stood before her as unclad as she was. Wide-eyed they considered each other for moments. Then by mutual consent they came together, to collapse on the bed, their physical need for one another fervent, man for woman, woman for man, fundamental as it was demanding, and utterly unreserved, basic, nature in command, ultimate satisfaction on the way.

But not quite ultimate, as yet. For that woman was a virgin, however desirous and desirable, and her needs had to be catered for with some male solicitude and care, however demanding the man's, and her own, ardour; and Ainea was very much an ardent woman. So Angus, aware of it, sought to control himself and aid her as much as in him lay. *He* was no virgin, having been educated by various kindly females as he had grown into manhood. Now, reining himself in, he had to apply that knowledge and experience, and with fair success, to her panting gratitude. It took a little time, and self-discipline, until, with a cry, she received him fully into herself, even if without the full satisfaction she craved, but with gratitude nevertheless.

Thereafter, to be sure, masculine climax was not to be withheld any longer, whatever the female state, and in groaning vehemence, Angus mounted to a pinnacle of completion, even though it was not the summit of his desire, since it was not matched by that of his loved one, and he only too well aware of it. Murmuring his regrets he sank down upon her yielding and so desirable person.

As they lay there, he saying to give him time, a little time, and he would serve her better, she wondering, questioning, whether she was failing in some way, not through any lack of desire but in her ability to reach the expected heights. Presently Ainea, sighing, suggested that they might as well now wash, since he was asking for time. She had assumed that they would have had their ablutions earlier, before bed-going, as was normal, but he had been in too great a hurry for that. So now they rose, neither satisfied, and went over to the tub, the water less than scalding. There they washed each other, comprehensively and with care, and in the doing of it the man at least felt ardour beginning to return. Whether his companion was equally roused by her ministrations he did not know, but certainly she was very attentive about it, and her drying of him afterwards.

Back to bed, and Angus not long in seeking possession again, but now with no driving haste, and with heed for her arousal made evident. And to good effect, for quite soon she was stirring and exclaiming and gripping him convulsively, and he was able to bring her to ecstatic consummation, and could joyfully let himself go with her, one indeed in ineffable unity and gratification.

Sinking back in each other's arms, murmuring, kissing, stroking, it was soon sleep.

Not for the remainder of the night, however. They came together again some unspecified time later, and on this occasion had little coaxing and preparation to engage in.

Their concord was established, in body as in mind.

The day following, with guests still to be entertained and seen off, there was little opportunity for the couple to celebrate their unity in other than exchanged glances and occasional brief embraces. But now they were past all uncertainties and had the future to look forward to, and so could put up with all this social activity, for Ainea was still hostess at Limavady, whatever was to happen thereafter. O'Cahan would have to find some sort of substitute, he acknowledged, and promptly, for Angus had let it be known that he and his would be off the next day. He had all the spread of the Isles to oversee, a vast area, not far off two thousand square miles, all but a kingdom, however much of it water, and with a population of scores of thousands. He had been absent therefrom overmuch recently. Ainea was far from urging delay.

That evening, the matter of the dowery manpower was discussed with her father. He said that it would certainly take some time to assemble the great company of men, although he had already informed most of their leaders and obtained their agreement, no real objections voiced. Give him a month, and then send over the fleet to pick them up. He, O'Cahan, might well sail over with them, to see his daughter settled into her new home. Liam could take charge in Derry for a while, ably enough.

This of a home to make for Ainea had been occupying Angus's mind for some time. The lordship had castles and strengths innumerable all over the Isles; but the matters of centrality and strategic worth were important preoccupations in present circumstances. It really came down to three possibilities. He was titular Lord of Islay, and that island was the caput of the lordship and its seat of justice. But his father occupied Finlaggan Castle, and would not want it to be turned into a family home, with a daughter-in-law in charge. Ardtornish was where Angus had been reared by his grandfather, and which he still looked upon as his home, fairly central among the islands. But it was a far cry from Man and Saddell, both so much to be in touch with, the former fully two hundred miles off. Dunaverty Castle was an eagle's nest of a place admittedly, but it was vitally sited as link with these last, and for communications with Ulster also. Could he plant Ainea in that cliff-top eyrie, and tell her to make a home of it? In summer it probably would be none so ill, the views spectacular, the feeling of being on top of the world, she become lady of all that she could see. But in winter, with shrieking gales, clouds of blown spray, whistling draughts! Roosting therein? No, it would not do.

Could they not have *two* homes, then? Winter at Ardtornish, summer at Dunaverty? Was that not a possibility? Would Ainea find it unacceptable, not to be considered? He would put it to her.

He did so, that night, in bliss before they slept. She said that she could see nothing against it. Two homes might even be better than one.

They left it at that. When she saw Dunaverty, she might change her mind.

Next day it was off with them, Ainea telling her father to come and see them soon, Liam likewise. Home for the dragonship's crew.

12

Ainea was all eagerness when they approached that shaken fist of the Mull of Kintyre at the wide Atlantic, and exclaimed with excitement when Dunaverty on its soaring, craggy summit was pointed out to her, epitomising in towering masonry the challenge of the entire area, the first proud feature of the Isles lordship that she had viewed.

"Is that it? Your defiance, your brandished battle-axe at the rest of God's world!" she cried. "Where you would have us to dwell?"

"Only if it would not . . . daunt you, my heart," he said. "Not if you mislike it. See it as but something of a prison-house up there on its rock."

"Never that, I think. But let us up to it. See it as it is. Then judge."

They pulled in to the landing-place and, leaving the crew to rest and stretch their legs on the beach, the couple climbed the steep and twisting track up and up and round to reach the castle's landward approach, which was somewhat more accessible from the north, but even so not easy.

"I see that once within, we might think twice before venturing out!" Ainea said.

"It is none so ill, from this side." He pointed down to the little castleton at the foot of the landward slope. "Horses left there, and we can ride free. And the ship reachable from there also. I have brought you up the more difficult way that you might judge for yourself."

Once within the hold, Angus let the place speak for itself. Rory MacIan and his Morag had indeed made great improvements in at least some of the apartments, and achieved a fair degree of comfort. Much more could be done, if so desired however, which no doubt the young woman perceived.

It was really the windows and parapet-walk and battlements that drew her, the tremendous prospect seen from there, and which had her exclaiming and pointing and questioning; as well it might, for the vision and sense of immensity and sheer freedom, a sort of liberation from mere earthly constraints which had to affect all but the most unimaginative. Lost for words, she gestured with one hand while gripping the man's arm with the other.

"It is . . . beyond all!" she got out. "Beyond and beyond! To, to infinity. A house in the heavens!"

"On a summer's day, like this, yes. But in winter's storms . . ."

"Oh, yes. But still defiance, dare, challenge, no?"

"I see that I have wed a contentious wife!" he declared. "I will have to see to my protection. I may need that battle-axe for my own preservation! But it is a vantage-point, yes. In summer."

"I have not yet seen the other. Ardtornish, is it? But can it rival this?"

"Not in this of immensity. But it is more beautiful. Mountains nearby, glens, lochs, waterfalls. And in winter a deal more comfortable."

"So. We shall see. But this . . . grips me."

"I am glad," he said.

When they returned to the keeper, Rory, he had word for Angus, grave word. William Wallace had suffered major defeat at the hands of Edward Longshanks. At Falkirk, before he could reach Stirling where he was heading, and the strategic Forth barrier. The English had caught up with him in overwhelming force, seven thousand horse it was said and no fewer than eighty thousand foot and bowmen, this against less than one-third on their own Scots side, and few cavalry and knights. Bruce, coming to join them from the west, was not present until the end, when he arrived in time to extricate Wallace himself from the slaughter and get him away into hiding in the great Tor Wood. So the Plantagenet was now supreme in Scotland, and the nation cowering beneath his iron heel.

Much upset, Angus could only shake his head.

These grievous tidings inevitably cast a shadow on the couple's evening and night at Dunaverty, although the sunset over the western ocean had Ainea rapturous. There was nothing that Angus was able to do about the situation meantime, and it was unlikely to affect the Isles greatly.

In the morning they were on their way northwards up the long shoreline of Kintyre, past Gigha and into the Sound of Jura. Angus decided to leave Islay, on their left, at present, for introducing his wife to his father. This could come later. It was Ardtornish for them, for Ainea to see the contrasts, and judge.

The entirely different scene was very evident long before they reached the Firth of Lorn and the Sound of Mull, the myriad of islands large and small, the mighty mountains rearing everywhere, the sea lochs with their white cockleshell sands, the colourful seaweeds and crystal-clear waters all having the young woman enthralled.

Turning into the narrows of Loch Aline eventually, Angus was able to point out his childhood home, a large square keep on its isolated rocky mound above the shore, larger than Dunaverty and less inconveniently sited, a prominent landmark. Ainea was eloquent in her praises of all that she saw, the fairness of the scene, and its sense of security compared with their last stop. And when, after landing, they entered the castle itself, the comforts and amenities of it could not fail greatly to please her. She questioned her husband on his growing up here, and wondered about Angus Mor and the strange development of a boy being reared by his grandsire while his father dwelled miles away on another island, his mother long dead.

But she kept harking back to Dunaverty. Clearly that skied stronghold had its hold on her. Angus saw that it was indeed going to be their summer home – which suited him very well.

Ainea met and approved of Ewan MacLean, who was captivated by her. She was taken to visit Duart, visible from Ardtornish across the sound, and made an impact on that MacLean also, Angus proud to display his prize. But he recognised that he must not further put off presenting her to his father, to whom she often referred wonderingly. So, after a few days, it had to be Islay for them.

The sixty-mile voyage, past dramatic Jura, the proud Paps duly pointed out and appreciated, brought them to the much less imposing but larger island, which gave title to Angus. After all the more impressive scenes, she had to have it explained to her that Islay was infinitely more fertile and populous than all the others, and, positioned where it was, served as a central hub for the lordship.

Docking at Port Askaig, Angus found garrons to carry them up to Loch Finlaggan, which the young woman saw as resembling one of her Ulster lochs in character, unlike the sea lochs she had seen so much of recently. They were rowed out to the castle islet in a small boat, she interested but her man less than comfortable about this interview. He often tended to feel guilty about his attitude towards his father, while not failing to remind himself that the boot should probably be on the other foot, that it was Alexander who had failed in their relationship, as in so much else. Ainea, aware of something of this, was tactful.

Each time son saw father he was shocked by the ageing process, on this occasion more so than ever. Bent, frail and trembling of person, the Lord of the Isles looked anything but that, a dispirited, vague, unimpressive old man, who did not so much greet his son and daughter-in-law as blink at them uncertainly and mutter incoherences.

Ainea found herself taking charge, distressed for them both.

She proclaimed her joy at their marriage, her pleasure at meeting her father-in-law, her admiration of all that she had seen of the lordship, and her looking forward to her life in it and making her homes at Ardtornish and Dunaverty; all of which the old man accepted without any real comment. Angus one moment felt like shaking him, the next sorry, and trying to sympathise. He much admired Ainea's command of the situation.

Alexander was well cared for, at least, by a motherly keeper's wife and her daughters. Despite getting few visitors, they catered adequately for these unexpected guests that night. At their meal, modest as it had to be, Angus thought that his father was going to fall asleep at the table, only toying with his food – and indeed he departed for his bed immediately thereafter, which was something of a relief.

None so very long afterwards, in the bed allotted to them, and after Ainea's understanding and supportive comments and soothing talk, they achieved their own satisfactions, to end a difficult day.

In the morning they did not long delay departure, seeing no advantage to be gained by any lingering, and certainly not being pressed to stay by Alexander of the Isles. Angus took his wife to see the other islet, on which was the chapel and the judgment-seat, before they returned to Port Askaig and the dragonship, duty done.

At Islay they were much nearer to Dunaverty than to Ardtornish, and Angus decided that they should return to the former, and the next day go up the Kilbrannan Sound to Saddell to make his other family introduction, and at the same time to learn further, if possible, of the situation prevailing on the mainland.

So another happy night in the eagle's nest.

Angus had told Ainea about Alastair mac Donald and his daughters, and she had wondered how she would be received by them. Had she usurped their places in his affections? He reassured her. There had never been anything other than kinship fondness, and the girls had expressed much interest in his romance. All would be well.

The new Lady of Islay could have had no complaints as to her reception at Saddell. The young women were quite enchanted with her looks and behaviour towards them; and their father congratulated his grand-nephew on his so remarkable and desirable godsend; most expedient also, in the circumstances, for the Isles. When he heard about the dowery, he was further gratified. Fourteen hundred men! He himself could do with some of them in his Kintyre, which had much good land capable of being better used and developed, and where they could be readily available for the lordship's use if required. Also, those MacDougalls . . . !

The latest news from the friars was that William Wallace had not been captured; but that he was now looked upon as a finished man, and expected to resign from his office of Guardian of the Realm. Who would succeed him was anybody's guess. Bruce's whereabouts were unknown also. Scotland was in chaos and dismay. The Comyns, Edward's supporters, would be in the ascendant. Therefore the Mac-Dougalls the more to be watched. Incidentally, it was reported that Thomas Bisset, on Arran, hearing of the Falkirk defeat, had promptly changed sides, and was now pro-English.

The visitors spent a couple of pleasant days at Saddell, despite these grim tidings, with Ainea being taken across the sound to see Arran. Ainea expressing a wish to climb a Scottish mountain, of all things, they rode for the nearest such, Ard Bheinn, and did manage to reach its summit. And from there she could see the far-off and much higher one, Goat Fell, which had the effect of arousing her challenging nature. She was told that any such attempt would have to await another occasion. Besides, there were higher mountains than Goat Fell in the Isles and their mainland territories, the highest of all rising near the head of Loch Linnhe, believed to be unsurpassed in all the four kingdoms. Let *that* be her target! Angus himself had never climbed it – but then, he had more to do with his time!

The following day they explored the northern parts of Kintyre as far as Crossaig, from which they could look across, beyond the Cock of Arran, to the Isle of Bute. Angus had to admit that this was beyond his domains, a Stewart place. But riding over Kintyre, he did see much land that could usefully be occupied and worked by the newcomers from Derry.

The sisters and Ainea got on well, which was a blessing. Then it was back to Dunaverty and Ardtornish.

13

Angus had never made his visit to the northern isles, and up to the topmost point of the land, facing Orkney; and he was eager, now, that he should take his fine wife with him and show her off to the chiefs and people. But he reckoned that they had better wait a little longer, for the dowery men to arrive, which could be arranged any day now. They might well find uses and calls for some of these on the said tour. He was just a little uncertain as to what to do with this influx of men. His granduncle wanted some; others might well do the same.

Meantime a brief visit to Man would be wise, probably. There had been no word from there for some time. Ainea had never seen that island, despite its comparative proximity to Ulster.

At Peel, they were warmly received by Rory mac Alan and his wife, these, like everyone else, much taken with Ainea, she herself fond of meeting people, and demonstrating it.

There was no word of any immediate threat to Man, Edward Longshanks probably preoccupied with consolidating his hold on Scotland for the time being. But the danger was always there, and vigilance necessary. The longship crews, under MacInnes, still kept up their patrols, having quite settled down on the isle.

After a couple of days it was back to Dunaverty, where they learned that the men from Derry were now indeed assembled and awaiting transport. Fourteen hundred men would demand a lot of shipping, so word had to be sent up to Islay, Gigha, Mull, Colonsay and Ardtornish for the muster, which would take some time. Even in summer weather only a maximum of some twenty men, beside the crews, could be carried in any longship or birlinn as passengers. So it meant at least seventy vessels. And they would have their baggage, so make it seventy-five.

With her father proposing perhaps to come over with them, Ainea elected to sail to meet him. And it was all her jointure-settlement, after all. So it was a major fleet that the dragonship led across the North Channel for Lough Foyle.

At Limavady they found all awaiting them. O'Cahan introduced Angus to the leaders of what amounted to a small army. There were ten names, each producing one hundred and forty men, all volunteers it seemed: Munroes, MacFerbes, MacYs, MacGees, MacColms, Dochertys, O'Cahans, O'Donnells, O'Rourkes and Flahertys. Angus promised them welcome in the Isles, lands and employment, well pleased with what he saw. Ainea was clearly proud of her bodyguard, as she called it.

All being ready, they set sail early next morning, O'Cahan with them. Angus discussed with his father-in-law, as they went, the men's best destinations. To deposit so many hundreds on any one island or territory would create difficulties and confusion. The newcomers would have to be dispersed throughout the Isles. And wisest probably to keep family groups together, in the main. So call first at Dunaverty, and disembark some there, possibly MacYs, for Alastair MacDonald's use. Then to Gigha, Islay and Jura. On to Mull, Ardtornish and Morvern. Leave the remainder of the Derrymen there under Duart and MacIan of Ardnamurchan, for disposal further north. This was agreed.

It was some fifty miles from Lough Foyle to the Mull of Kintyre, passing Rathlin Isle, so they were able to reach Dunaverty by early afternoon, with the wind behind them. The castle itself was no place to leave the MacYs, so the ships carrying these one hundred and forty were sent on up the Kilbrannan Sound to Saddell, their first discharge. While this was being arranged, Ainea took her father up to see her new summer-time home. Then on northwards, to reach Gigha for the night. No large island, it was fertile, and its chief, a MacDonald, was glad to have fifty MacGees. Angus, Ainea and O'Cahan were entertained in Ardminish, but the others had to sleep in barns or sheds, in their plaids.

Next day it was Islay, where Angus decided not to take wife and father-in-law to meet his father, and embarrass all concerned. So he avoided Finlaggan and led the fleet round to the long inlet of Loch Indaal and up it to Bowmore, the largest community of this populous island, where they disembarked a mixed contingent of Dochertys, MacGees and O'Rourkes, over two hundred of them. As Lord of Islay Angus had no difficulty in allotting these to various parts of the island. Unlike most of his domains, conditions here were none so different from Derry, so they ought to settle comfortably enough.

Jura was very different, next day, although so close, long, mountainous, and with no great amount of arable land and pasture, with sea-fishing the principal occupation. So no large numbers of men were left thereon, mainly fisherfolk from Lough Foyle.

They were near Colonsay and Oronsay here, so proceeded to these two islands, Angus explaining to his companions that Oronsay was considered to be a very holy place, second only to Iona in this, called after St Oran, one of Columba's disciples. It was said that Columba himself would have settled here, but when he climbed its hill he could still see the Ulster coast, and he felt that he must put Ireland out of sight and memory and went on to Iona. But he did declare Oronsay a garth, or sanctuary, for any man fleeing from his enemies, or even from justice, man's justice. He planted stone crosses here, one right out in the middle of the tidal sands, and anyone within the area of these markers was to be free from molestation. And if he remained on the isle for a year and a day, he was free for always. He established a monastery here. Also a horses' burial-ground, indicative of his belief that, love being eternal and part of God's person, any animal which a believing man loved would go on into eternity, and so deserved Christian burial.

Colonsay, only a mile off, was much larger, a seat of the MacDuffie chieftains, and also a sanctuary isle. That man was glad enough to have approximately half of the MacColm newcomers, Colm being a form of Columba, the dove.

Thus far they had had no problems in allocating the Derrymen.

The great island of Mull was next, one of the most extensive in all the Hebrides. Angus judged it best to hand over the distribution of the new settlers here to his friend Gillemoir MacLean at Duart. That man made no bones about taking on an assortment of O'Cahans, O'Donnells and Flahertys, over three hundred of them, which he said he and other MacLeans, MacLaines and MacKinnons could make use of, from Duart and Salen to Tobermory and Calgary, down to Ulva and the Ross of Mull and Iona itself.

O'Cahan was learning something of the spread of the Isles and their numberless constituents. Ainea likewise, both duly responsive.

They had now disposed of over half of the total dowerymen.

From Duart it was just across the sound to Loch Aline in Morvern, and Ardtornish, where O'Cahan was interested to be installed meantime in his daughter's winter-time home, while Angus, with Ewan's help, dealt with most of the remainder of the Derry folk. Morvern was no island, but as good as one, a vast peninsula of some one hundred and fifty square miles, all but separated from the rest of the mainland and from Ardnamurchan, Angus's own, or at least in name his father's property. He would hold more of the Munroes, MacForbes and the remainder of the MacColms for this area, and for MacIan of Ardnamurchan. Morvern itself was especially empty of population, much of it all but inaccessible. These incomers would be able greatly to improve its state.

It took Angus four days to arrange for this, with a call over at Mingary Castle to see MacIan, while Ainea and her father remained at Ardtornish.

Then, this task accomplished, it was back to Dunaverty, and O'Cahan's onward return to Derry, a man all but bewitched by the extent and sheer complexity of his daughter's new domicile. She had become a sort of princess indeed. He went home well satisfied.

Angus and Ainea had been at Dunaverty only two days when the most dire news was brought to them from Saddell, and not sent by Alastair mac Donald, for he was dead. He had been slain, up at Dunollie, while visiting the MacDougalls, murdered. He had gone to remonstrate with them over Ian Bacach's activities. Details as to his death were uncertain. Seona and Eithne were fatherless.

Angus was for Saddell forthwith, Ainea with him.

They found the tearful young women desolated, appalled, lost, quite alone now, for their mother had died the previous year. They had been helping to settle in the Derrymen, with the assistance of the abbot and brothers, when this devastation descended upon them.

It seemed that a MacDougall birlinn had arrived with the body, but no real explanation as to what had happened other than that the Lord of Kintyre had unfortunately been slain, no details nor apologies. Alastair's corpse was now at the abbey awaiting burial.

Seeking to comfort the bereaved daughters as best he and Ainea could, Angus wondered what must be done about this. As acting Lord of the Isles, action of some sort was called for from him; but any armed descent upon so powerful and important a branch of Somerled's descendants as were the MacDougalls would be unwise indeed. Such could set off what amounted to civil war in the Isles. Dougal, from whom they took their name, had been one of the three sons of Somerled, with Ranald and Angus. The line of Dougal remained close with that of Ranald of Garmoran, called the MacRuaries, after Ranald's son, and were very strong in the Outer Isles of Uist and Barra, also linked to the MacNeills by marriage. So, in this sad matter, Angus would have to tread carefully indeed.

He and Ainea waited two days at Saddell, to attend the funeral of Alastair, a sad and anxious time. What was to happen to these two young women? Angus felt a responsibility towards them. His wife was the kind and able comforter.

The interment at the abbey was a moving experience. Alastair was laid to rest beside his forebear Somerled. Afterwards Angus was assured by the abbot that he and his people would look heedfully and warmly after the two daughters. He also promised to send on to Angus any important news brought by the mendicant order of friars.

It was Ainea's suggestion that Seona and Eithne should come down with them to Dunaverty for a spell, as change from Saddell, in the circumstances probably to their advantage. The pair showed no eagerness to comply, but allowed themselves to be persuaded.

That move did prove to be a good one, the sisters soon becoming less doleful in that lofty pinnacle of a house, the sense of freedom and novelty not failing to reach them. It made a strange interlude for Angus, skied there alone with the three women in his life; and once the visitors were able to keep their distress less evident, he enjoyed the odd intimacy, Ainea actually encouraging him amusedly in his attentions to the others.

But as far as the man was concerned it had to be of fairly short duration. A visit to the MacDougalls was very much called for, and this no occasion for Ainea to accompany him. Presently he set off, leaving the women to their own devices.

It meant a sail of fully one hundred miles northwards to reach Dunollie on the Firth of Lorn. An overnight halt was made, as usual, at Gigha. There Angus picked up the MacDonald chief and four longships to accompany the dragonship, as indication of authority.

Next day, approaching the isle of Kerrera in Oban's bay, Angus, viewing Dunollie Castle on the cliffs to the north, was still wondering how best to deal with the situation ahead of him. He recognised that he would have to adjust his reactions to his reception.

His dragonship's approach, with its great square sail and banner of the Galley of the Isles, was not to be mistaken, and it brought a party down to the landing-place from the castle, headed by MacDougall himself, another Alastair, the fourth Lord of Lorn and, with the English links emphasised, appointed Sheriff of Lorn, the only such officer in all the Isles, these having their own justice jurisdictions.

He greeted the visitors, arm raised. "Hail, Angus Og, Lord of Islay!" he called. "Welcome to Dunollie. I think I know what brings you here!"

"I dare say you do, Alastair mac Ewan mac Duncan," he was answered. "I come on no joyful errand. My grand-uncle's death has to be . . . accounted for, see you."

"And it shall be, Angus Og." MacDougall was a handsome man of later middle years. "My regret for the deed is great. He was slain by a servant of my lame son, Ian Bacach. Alastair mac Donald was having words with Ian, hot words, whether deserved or otherwise. And the servant, deeming his master insulted, drew dirk and stabbed your uncle. It was ill done. The servant still hangs from my gallows-tree!"

"So-o! That was the way of it?" Angus tried not to let his relief sound in his voice. "Your son, Ian Bacach, not himself ordering it?"

"No. He was much angered at it. No blame on him. He aided at the hanging. Come you, and see the felon dangling."

Angus nodded. He introduced MacDonald of Gigha. And, MacDougall turning, they accompanied him up the track to the castle.

Release from tension was great, but must not be evidenced. No need to fear war within the Isles, a clash of the clans. This dire deed was explained. Nothing would bring back Alastair MacDonald, but no further blood need be shed over him, the murderer hanged.

"Your son, Ian Bacach – is he here?" Angus asked.

"No. He has gone. Affairs to see to . . . otherwhere."

"Aye, he aids the English. Which was why my uncle would be upbraiding him."

"He goes his own way," the father said.

On a mound outside the castle courtyard rose a scaffold, and Angus was taken to see the body hanging therefrom, swaying back and forth in the breeze. Shaking his head, he turned away.

In the castle he was introduced to the Lady of Lorn, Juliana Comyn, sister of the Black Comyn of Badenoch and step-mother of the Red, Edward's friend. She proved to be no elderly ogress, quite stately of carriage although not beautiful. She and her husband were fairly obviously uncomfortable with the visitors, but hospitality was provided and an offer to stay the night was extended. Angus, with no desire to linger, said that he could get to Ardtornish before darkness, where he had matters to see to. This was accepted promptly.

They were seen back down to the ships, the Lord of Islay, equally with the Lord of Lorn, reasonably content.

Back at Dunaverty next day, Angus wondered whether to tell Seona and Eithne the details he had heard of their father's death. Would it add to their distress, only reopen wounds? Or would it be of some comfort to them to know that there had been no fighting, that he had been murdered by an overzealous servant? And that the said murderer had been hanged? He would have to tell them something. Ainea advised a brief account, without comments. He would see how they were taking it.

In fact the two sisters took it very differently. Seona burst into tears again, gulping down incoherences, and hurried from the room. But Eithne said that it was sad that the servant had been hanged when he thought he was doing his duty towards his

134

master, however mistakenly. But it was good that there was no feuding and warfare involved. Peace of a sort the result. Let their dear father rest in the greater peace, where he was now gone.

Angus was much admiring of this reaction.

Speaking of it thereafter, with Ainea, he wondered for how long they should keep the young women at Dunaverty. It was now late August, and the long-postponed travel to the northern isles, which would occupy weeks, should not be delayed, with weather and seas to be considered. There appeared to be no major developments in the mainland Scottish situation meantime, with Longshanks consolidating his position, Wallace's tide ebbed, and Bruce and his allies presumably seeking to gather their strength. It was unlikely that there would be any assault on Man in these circumstances. So it might be a good time to sail northwards. Those far-flung parts of the lordship, extensive and important, must not see themselves as in any way neglected.

Ainea said she thought that the sisters would not suffer from being returned to Saddell. This period away had, she was sure, been of help to them, enabled them in some measure to come to terms with their position. The monks would seek to take care of them; and they would feel that they were as near to their father as it was possible to be. She thought that they could now be taken home.

So it was back to Saddell, and the handing of the bereaved ones over to the care of the abbot, promising to come and see them frequently.

While there, Angus learned highly interesting tidings, which further convinced him that this was a suitable time to sail north. Edward Plantagenet had suddenly returned to England, and not for any warlike reason but to remarry. His former queen, Eleanor of Castile, had died some time previously, and now he was going to wed the Princess Margaret of France. The Scots could heave a sigh of thankfulness, for the moment at least.

14

Ainea would have wished to start their tour by a visit to the precious Isle of Iona where her countryman had based himself for the conversion of this land to Christ. But Angus declared that this should wait a little longer. There was so much to see and experience at Iona. They did not want to rush it. But with the lengthy itinerary ahead of them, that would be apt to happen. Better to reserve it till later. They would start at Coll and Tiree, lying west of Mull, quite close to each other, both medium-sized isles, MacNeill holdings.

So thither they sailed. The first, Tiree, was unique, undoubtedly the lowest-lying of all the Hebrides, so much so that from any distance its houses seemed to be rising out of the water. Fertile, it was something of a world unto itself, highly populated but quiet and peaceful. Its lairdly situation was unusual also, for although it was MacDonald property, Mac-Neills were its keepers, dwelling in Isleburgh Castle. Thither the visitors repaired.

They were received by a son of the MacNeill who ruled at nearby Coll, and were interested to find a score of O'Cahans now domiciled here, and apparently well content to be so, although with a population of over four thousand it would seem that they were scarcely needed. Ainea went round greeting them.

They were taken to see the two Columban monasteries founded here. Also a singular feature, a great isolated dark stone, in this notably stoneless isle, reputed to have somehow come here from Rhum, where this colour of rock was to be found, and which was known as the Singing Stone because, when struck, it emitted a strange ringing sound.

The island was just over ten miles long, hammer-shaped, and littered with chapels, duns and standing stones.

Coll, only two miles away, was very different, with the islet of Gunna like a stepping-stone between, all low hills and small lochs innumerable, with comparatively little arable land, and consequently a much smaller population. But it had a great castle called Breachacha at its southern end, where MacNeill senior lived, quite distant from the place's only sizeable community at Arinagour. MacNeill accommodated them for the night, and took them to see a Pictish earth-house or souterrain, with a long underground gallery, of which he was very proud. Very few such had survived. Ainea insisted on creeping through its low passages, necessarily on hands and knees, wondering whether these early Picts had been tiny folk.

From Coll the scene to the north was dominated by the upthrusting snout of the Sgurr of Eigg, which Angus likened to the prow of his dragonship, challenging all, with the jagged mountains of Rhum beyond, heads in the clouds, remote, aloof, these not competing but seeming to ignore the Eigg Sgurr. There was a lesser isle called Muck, the Island of the Pigs nearer, but it tended to be dwarfed by its so striking neighbours. Ainea found that seascape ever drawing her gaze.

After passing the night at Breachacha, they sailed for Muck, this only three miles by two, and the property of the Abbey of Iona strangely enough, notorious for having neither trees nor peat, so fuel had to be imported for its folk, a major handicap. The travellers made only a brief call on the fisherfolk here, and moved on for Eigg, one more MacDonald holding. Their gaze was riveted on that extraordinary clenched fist of black columnar stone towering well over one thousand feet at the south end of the island, as though Eigg were turning its back on the much loftier rival isle.

At Kildonnan, where they found another MacDonald chief and were well received, this young far-distant kinsman was unknown to Angus although he had met the father at Angus

Mor's funeral. Ainea made a great impression, as she was apt to do, having indeed smilingly to protect herself from his admirations that evening. She observed to her husband that this young man obviously required a wife. How about recommending one of the Saddell sisters? They were all Mac-Donalds, after all. Angus was more concerned over having the dragonship's crewmen well looked after, this always to be considered on their journeying.

It was at Kildonnan, however, that they learned from the prior of the nearby monastery something which altered Angus's entire projected plans. Two days previously, a pair of those so determined and peripatetic traveller-friars had called, and informed, on their way to Skye, that King Edward had apparently made exceedingly light of his second marriage, for after only a week of new matrimonial felicity at York – this including holding a hasty parliament, which might be significant – had returned to Scotland on urgent business bent, and without his new queen. He had crossed to the west and entered Scotland from Cumbria, into Dumfries-shire and Galloway. This must surely represent some major design and stroke. Angus felt that, in consequence, this was no time for him to be up in these remoter areas of the lordship. He ought to be all but two hundred miles to the south, where he could hear quickly of the Plantagenet's doings and aims. If that evil man had chosen south-west Scotland, it could possibly mean the ever-feared assault on the Isle of Man, Whithorn in Galloway the nearest land thereto, less than a score of miles. So it had to be back south with them, with all speed, this to Ainea's disappointment and concern. She had been looking forward to climbing one or more of those tremendous Rhum peaks, to enter into the strange parasitical clouds MacDonald told them of. It seemed that these mountains had the unique ability somehow to create their own white and dense vapours, even when nowhere else in the sky was a cloud to be seen, presumably something to do with those unusual dark rock formations affecting the damp winds off the Atlantic. No other isle was so endowed, and the young woman was agog to explore the wonder.

Not on this occasion, her husband declared. Blame the wretched Plantagenet. Their northern visitation was ill-fated it seemed, under its own clouds. But they would be back.

Returning to Ardtornish, Angus besought Ewan and Duart, his so useful friends, to warn all chieftains on Morvern, Ardnamurchan, Islay, Mull and the lesser isles to be ready for prompt action.

Then on to Dunaverty, to see if any further news had come from Saddell. They found only the same word they had heard at Eigg awaited them. So Ainea was left at the castle, with instructions to send on any useful information coming from the abbot, while he himself sailed on to the Isle of Man, to confer with Rory mac Alan.

At Peel he found all in as great readiness as was possible for defence against invasion from Galloway, the same tidings having reached there as they had to the north. Angus had indeed encountered MacInnes's flotilla on his way, these ships sailing up and down off the Galloway coasts, to make a warlike presence known. Rory was greatly appreciative of Man having this great advantage of the Islesmen's longships to guard it, whereas any attack by the English would have to be made in small craft and fishing-boats collected locally. Edward's weakness was in shipping, such fleets as England possessed being mainly concentrated on its Channel coastline, to cope with the ongoing French campaigns.

Rory was worried, nevertheless, de Burgh reported back in Ulster, and attack on two sides possible again.

Angus remained with his friend meantime, ready to send for large-scale assistance at short notice, if necessary. His host was anxious over other matters than the military. His father was a very ill man, at Douglas, and feared to be dying. He had been a distinctly ineffective governor of Man for years; but family ties were still strong.

Angus had been a week at Peel when word from Ainea came, heartening word. Edward Longshanks was not having matters all his own aggressive way. His English barons had refused to rally to his latest call. They were becoming tired of his obsession with warfare, and the demands this made on them in men and time and money. The unending French campaigns were costly indeed, fought on three fronts, Flanders, Burgundy and Aquitaine and this of Scotland was just too much for many of them. Edward had found himself left with only some fifteen thousand foot and no large contingent of knights and cavalry, inadequate for his plans. And it was known that Bruce's forces in the Tor Wood of Stirling had managed to regain the English-occupied citadel of Stirling itself by starving the garrison out, a serious blow to invading morale. An angry and disappointed man, he had had to bow to hard facts on this occasion, and had returned meantime to York. The Comyns were reported to be much upset.

Sighs of relief rivalled the rising winds of autumn and early winter. Angus could go home.

15

However the Plantagenet felt about it, that winter was a notable one for the rest of Christendom. For it ended the year 1299 and the New Year heralded in the fourteenth century. Holy Church in particular was greatly exercised and ordered all true Christians to mark the occasion in suitable fashion. All sorts of celebrations, pageantry, processions and services were to be held, and orders to pray for the coming, the Second Coming of the Lord Christ, which He had promised, were issued, papal injunctions a-many. It is to be feared that many of the petitions offered up to the Almighty, in Scotland at least, were for the early death of Edward Longshanks.

At Ardtornish, Angus and Ainea duly observed the change of centuries suitably, this going so far as a visit to his father on Islay to wish him well. Also a donation was made to Saddell Abbey to build a memorial chapel in memory of Grand-uncle Alastair, and to make this an especial shrine for the mendicant friars who were such useful news-bearers.

It was when, with Ainea, he sailed thither, despite winter seas, to make this gesture, that he put his wife's suggestion tentatively to the two young women. Had they ever considered marriage? They surely could not just roost alone in this castle for the rest of their lives? This was no worthy future for them. Seona said that she had considered entering a nunnery, marrying the Church and devoting herself to good works. But Eithne declared that she was not averse to the notion of love and wedlock. This Saddell however suffered from a shortage of male neighbours and visitors, apart from the monks.

Ainea told her that they had come across a good-looking,

personable and amiable, but somewhat lonely-seeming, young man, Donald MacDonald of Eigg, kin of their own, however distant in more ways than one. He could do with a wife, they thought. They might invite him down to these parts, in due course, to see whether there was any mutual attraction. They realised that it was difficult for Eithne to meet suitable men. That girl looked thoughtful but not dismissive, although her sister shook her head.

They left it at that.

There were no new tidings from the abbey regarding affairs in Scotland.

It was shortly after their return to Ardtornish that Ainea announced to her beloved that she believed she was pregnant. Angus was delighted to hear of it, but questioning also. When would it be? But would she be able for it? In her health? Child-bearing could be a trial . . .

"Foolish one!" she reproached. "Women are made for it by their Creator. Think you that I am some feeble creature? Incapable of fullest womanhood? You have played *your* part, it seems, in bringing me to this! Now it will be my turn."

He was already counting months on his fingers. "September? October? Within this century-year. Our child to be born in 1300! That is good, well-timed. What shall we name him? Not another Angus, after Mor and Og! Nor Alastair – over many of these . . ."

"Why should it be a boy? I would like a daughter."

"Mmm. Perhaps. But . . . we can still, still take each other? In bed?"

"Of course we can. For long yet. And not only in bed, my fearing and ignorant spouse!"

"Then I shall not tell anyone, yet . . ." He shook his head. "You will not be able to climb those mountains."

"Why not? I still have good legs on me, as you so often declare! And nothing amiss elsewhere because of this small addition!"

She proved to him that night that there was no hindrance to love-making in this new development.

The later part of that winter proved to be very severe, right into March and April, which at least delayed military endeavours on Edward's part, as on others'. Angus did not venture far from Ardtornish, but he did cross the Sound of Mull on occasion, often with Ewan, to see Gillemoir MacLean at Duart. And on one of these visits he, in effect, made the latter his deputy in command of the forces of the Isles. He also appointed him to be hereditary keeper of the castles and lands of Cairnburgh, the Isle of Scarba, the Garvellochs and other properties, as indication of his regard and trust.

Ewan he made Lord of Knapdale, the area at the north end of Kintyre's lengthy peninsula, all but detached by West and East Lochs Tarbert. Since Alastair mac Donald's death, there was no acting Lord of Kintyre, which created a dangerous situation, especially with those MacDougalls so close, in Lorn. In theory Seona and Eithne heired the lordship, but were in no position to govern it, especially if Seona, the elder, were to become a nun. If Eithne married, her husband could rule it in her name. But meantime it was dangerously vacant of authority. However, Angus himself, from Dunaverty, could oversee most of it; but this northern Knapdale section, some twenty-five miles by ten, flanked by the Sound of Jura and Loch Fyne, was leaderless and possibly vulnerable, with the Lamonts and MacLachlans and MacEwans over in Cowal to the east squabbling as to claiming it, a source of weakness. Ewan could be Lord of Knapdale for the present, it readily enough reachable from Kinlochaline. Its Castle Sween, a mighty stronghold, could be his base.

Angus did wonder whether, in fact, he had the right to make such appointments. He was not yet Lord of the Isles, although acting as such. But his father was not interested, and such decisions had to be made by someone.

For himself, of course, Angus was anxious to continue with his interrupted northern visitations so soon as weather conditions allowed – not to mention Edward Plantagenet.

It was early May before he reckoned that a move could be made. Ainea was well, and declared herself fit and eager to go with him. She was determined to climb those Rhum mountains, or at least one of them, so dramatic of aspect with their clouds. No word of moves by the English restrained them.

Up past Ardnamurchan Point, to Muck and Eigg they sailed, in seas less rough than for so long, although with heavy swells still. At Kildonnan of Eigg, where they spent the night with Donald MacDonald, they did not fail to raise the matter of a possible match with Eithne, daughter of Alastair. The young man was not dismissive, but did not enthuse, more interested in taking them over to Rhum, where his elderly father lived at the head of Loch Scresort, with the highest of the mountains, Askival, nearby. They were glad to avail themselves of his help, even if Angus was doubtful over this climbing urge of his wife's; they could leave the issue of Saddell and matrimony until later.

It was only a ten-mile sail to the mouth of Scresort and up to Kinloch Castle, with those mighty peaks now reigning over all, their white wreaths of cloud lifting as the morning advanced, to hover above the summits like woolly haloes. Askival, pointed out to her, forthwith became Ainea's target.

They found the surprised Duncan MacDonald of Rhum much exercised to have a visit from Angus of Islay, of whom he had heard glowing accounts, but astonished that his wife wanted to climb Askival, which he admitted he himself had never attempted, although he had stalked deer on its lower slopes. But at least he would provide them with garrons to take them the three awkward miles to the foot of it.

Donald leading, they rode round the coast that they had just skirted, having to negotiate four quite impressive waterfalls on the way, Rhum being one of the wettest isles of all. They reached a small loch at the base of a great corrie scooped in the flank of the mountain. This corrie was to provide their route up for almost half the ascent.

They were able to remain mounted for quite a distance up, which Ainea complained was not really climbing, but her companions pooh-poohed. When the going got too steep for the horses, however, they had to tether them and start the task in earnest, the young woman hitching her skirt up high, uncaring of Donald's glances.

It was taxing work from the start, broken dark rock and scree to be clambered over where it could not be avoided. In the floor of the corrie they saw some deer, smaller than those they were used to, which, Donald panted, were typical of Rhum. But they could not do much looking about them, and more than commenting, because of the demanding nature of their efforts, for the higher they got the steeper it became.

The way they were led was not directly heading for the pointed top of the mountain, but some way north of this, towards a high ridge which clearly linked it to another and only slightly lower summit, which Donald named as Hallival. That ridge, once reached, would bring them to Askival by the best and most spectacular route, indeed the only practical one.

Perhaps it would, but the actual ascent to that almost mile-long escarpment itself was a test indeed. There were many pauses for breath, Ainea's bosom heaving. But no complaints were made. It produced an all but perpendicular cliff-like rise of fully one hundred feet to get up to, and over the lip of it, on to what amounted to a narrow bridge between the two mountains.

This surmounted at last, they sat, gasping. And at what they saw, as well as what their lungs required. For the prospect was as breathtaking as had been the climb. Westwards, suddenly opened a vast vista of mountaintops and deep, shadow-filled glens, savage precipices and glittering small lochs, right to the far ocean, a stern and stark world of its own which overawed mere mortals.

From contemplation of this, presently Ainea was gazing upwards, for there were the pure white parasitical clouds hovering over them, and none so far above, quite unlike other normal clouds in their rounded density. She asked how high above, but could not be told, only that with the evening they would descend again to clothe the summits.

At length, under this white canopy, they proceeded westwards along that escarpment for half a mile, having again to pick their way with great care, for the bare rock was damp, slippery and broken, and in places narrow indeed, Angus now continually urging care lest his eager wife fall, holding her arm where he could, for the views were so apt to distract their attention.

Oddly enough, they reached the final topmost peak of all Rhum hardly aware of it until they abruptly found all dropping away before them, this because the ridge had led them up almost imperceptibly.

There they sat and gazed and gazed, at a loss for words, all the Isles spread before them, from the blue Cuillin Mountains of Skye to the north, all the serried peaks and heights of Knoydart and Morar and Moidart to the east, even to the mighty bulk of Beinn Nevis itself, higher than all, and the positive plethora of islands, great and small to the south, right to Jura and Islay. Angus had never experienced such a panoramic view of the seemingly endless extent of the empire he was destined to inherit, the sight of it all making him feel somehow unworthy, even arrogant, to claim it as one day to be his.

They remained there for long, despite the chilly air of these high places.

Donald declared that, difficult as it had proved to be, they should return by the route they had come, any other being too dangerous, with sheer drops and impassable clefts and chasms. The descent would be no easier than was the coming up, and they would have to take it very slowly; but it was the only way he knew of. Ainea said that every inch of it, coming and going, was worth it.

They crept and crawled and worked their way down.

Weary but well pleased with themselves, they eventually rode back to Kinloch.

That night it was early bedding for them, with only a token marital demonstration.

In the morning, leaving Donald with his father meantime, to be picked up later and taken south with them, it was over to Skye with the dragonship.

The Cuillin Mountains, much as they attracted Ainea, were not where Angus was heading for first. It was to Sleat, one more long peninsula, separated from the mainland of Knoydart by its own sound, this a mere nine miles from Rhum, where in one of his castles they hoped to find MacKinnon of Strath, known to him only by repute. There were many chieftains of families on this enormous isle, the largest of all, but the greatest were this MacKinnon and MacLeod of Dunvegan. Skye was fully fifty miles long by as much as half that in width in places. Authority was shared, not always amicably, by these two; which was one of the issues that Angus was anxious to put right, the MacLeods proud of their semi-Norse descent from King Olaf the Black, whereas the MacKinnons were of the line of Fingon, younger son of Alpin, King of Dalriada, and therefore brother of Kenneth, who united Scots and Picts and formed Scotland, claiming to be of the kindred of St Columba. Two very different backgrounds, leading to much feuding. This clan feuding was ever a major weakness among the Islesmen, as it was indeed throughout all the Highlands.

This MacKinnon was to be looked for somewhere along the Sleat peninsula, where he had houses, but his main seat was Dunakin, on the narrows of Kyleakin, where the sound reached Loch Alsh and entered the Little Minch. Calls at

Armadale and Knock and Isleornsay did not find him, but eventually, after battling with the rush of the adverse tides in the narrows of Kyleakin, they ran him to earth, a young chief whom Angus had met on his previous visit. He had little good to say about the MacLeods, but again assured that the MacKinnons were loyal in support of the Isles lordship.

The following day they passed the lengthy narrow island of Raasay to the north, but as this was a MacLeod place and subsidiary to the clan's main seat at Dunvegan on the other, far side of Skye, Angus saw no need to call in at it, his journeying sufficiently lengthy as it was. So they had to sail right up to the northernmost tip of Skye, at Hunish, some thirty-five miles, before they could swing westwards across the wide mouth of Loch Snizort and down into Loch Dunvegan, another fifteen miles, with the Uists of the Outer Hebrides ahead of them.

Dunvegan, the largest stronghold on Skye, was highly important in Angus's scale of values, for these MacLeods were the most powerful of all the northern clans, dominating most of the Outer Isles also, their support most necessary. Indeed it was concern about these semi-independent chiefs that had been behind his continuing anxiety about making his delayed northern progress. So far they had not been involved in any of the Isles' tactical ventures. So this call was a vital one.

Tormod MacLeod welcomed Angus to his castle once more, clearly much more interested in Ainea than in her husband, she using her charms to ensure his goodwill and support, he declaring that Angus Og mac Alexander was a fortunate man, the implication being that he scarcely deserved her. That man had to keep himself under strict control with this individual, he recognised.

Angus spoke of the general problems facing his father's domains, the so scattered nature of the Isles, the need for unified action and collaboration, and especially readiness to repel any English assault on Man and Ulster, the other seeming only casually concerned. It was this reference to English Edward, however, which produced the unexpected information that the Plantagenet was in fact back in Scotland and again basing himself on the Galloway and Firth of Clyde coasts. Apparently there was a monastery quite close to Dunvegan, at Kilmuir, and these mendicant friars got as far north as this, hence their news.

This had Angus immediately worried. It would have taken these friars, on foot as they travelled, quite a long time to get this far, so their tidings necessarily would be considerably delayed. Edward could have been in Galloway for a matter of weeks, yet no word had reached them before they left Ardtornish. Was the Saddell information-source failing this time? Since it seemed to be Galloway and the south-west again, the Isle of Man might already be under prompt threat, even assault. Yet Duart, who knew of this northern tour, had not sent any messenger to inform him, if *he* was aware of it.

There must be no delay at this Dunvegan, however much Ainea appealed to the MacLeod. They must be off southwards in the morning, with no visit to the Outer Isles as envisaged. Angus ought to be three hundred miles away.

Ainea put up with some tokens of appreciation as they were escorted to their bedchamber that night.

Next day they were seen off with hooted invitations to return, Angus in no doubt as to who would be the more welcome.

The dragonship's crew had orders to sail and row at their fastest, with south-west winds not helping, only briefest overnight halts in sheltered bays and creeks. Four days to Ardtornish? Picking up MacDonald of Eigg would not delay them for long; if it seemed to do so, they would leave him meantime, especially if he seemed less than eager.

In the event, Donald MacDonald was waiting, ready to join them without delay. They headed on southwards. Fortunately the weather was kind.

16

Gillemoir MacLean had no word for them at Duart, nor had
Ewan across the sound. So they pressed on to Dunaverty. Still
no messages awaiting them. Should they sail on to Man?
Surely, if there had been any development, or indication of
imminent threat there, Rory mac Alan would have sent word
by MacInnes. Angus wondered whether he had been over-
apprehensive, fearing more urgent danger than there was. Or
perhaps those friars at Dunvegan had been misinformed; they
could not always be entirely accurate. Or conditions had
changed?

Up to Saddell with them then, therefore, to see what the
abbot had to tell them, and to introduce Donald, who had
become quite a friend, to Eithne.

The matter of presenting that young man to the sisters was
rather delicate, to be sure, slightly embarrassing. But Ainea
effected it with the minimum of discomfort to all concerned,
and the mutual appraising went on in natural but fairly easy
fashion.

Angus left them all to it, and went off to the abbey.

There he learned that what had been reported at Dunvegan
was accurate enough, but that there had been developments
since, and no immediate danger for Man was envisaged.
Robert Bruce was responsible. He had roused in arms all
his Carrick country, from Lochmaben in Dumfries-shire right
up to Renfrewshire and Glasgow, challenging the English
lords holding strengths thereabouts; and Edward, besieging
Caerlaverock Castle, on the Solway, had marched on to deal
with this. There had been confrontations, and Bruce had had

to retire in face of superior and better-equipped manpower. Where he had reached now was not clear, but he might well be heading back for that Tor Wood sanctuary and wilderness area near to Stirling. Edward was said to be based on Irvine.

These tidings did not remove the threat to Man, but did probably postpone any attack for the time being.

Back at the castle, Angus debated with himself. What could he do to help in this situation? He felt that some demonstration on his part would be a useful contribution. The Isles themselves were not threatened; although if Longshanks did manage to consolidate his hold on Scotland, who knew whether he might not turn his attention westwards towards the lordship, see it possibly as an aid in grasping Ulster and Man? The Plantagenet would never be content with his conquests, aggression personified. And Angus much approved of Bruce and Wallace and their gallant efforts, and would wish to assist them if possible. Suppose he was to take a great fleet of his longships, much greater than MacInnes's patrols, up into the Firth of Clyde and along the Ayrshire and Renfrewshire coasts, as far as, say, Bute? The English would be in no position to assail them, lacking suitable shipping. He need not do any actual fighting, but could make a warning presence felt. It might help.

Ainea was much in favour of this, for it would help her father and the Ulster folk also. So it was decided.

Meanwhile, Donald and the young women appeared to be getting on well with each other, Seona as well as Eithne. Perhaps she would reconsider her nunnery ambitions?

However, if there was to be a major Isles fleet demonstration, Eigg and Rhum would have to be involved, like all the other isles, so it must be a prompt return for them, Donald included. Let any marriage possibility simmer for a while – this all to the good.

They did not delay, then, the sisters quite evidently disappointed that the visit was such a short one. But they would be back, it was promised.

They sailed off again, this time for Ardtornish, where Duart and Ewan were to help muster the Isles fleet, and Donald sent off to deal with Coll, Colonsay, Tiree, Eigg and Rhum, while Angus himself roused Morvern and Ardnamurchan. Speed now was of the essence, for who knew what was going on with Edward and how far he had got.

Distances, and the time taken to cover them, were ever a major factor in any unified action in the lordship; so it was a full week before Angus was able to see a great assembly of longships, galleys and birlinns gathered at the mouth of Loch Aline. He was not for taking Ainea on this expedition, but she demanded why not, if there was to be no fighting? He bowed to that, without overmuch persuasion.

Fifty-two vessels duly set out for the Clyde, an impressive sight, the beating of all these helmsmen's gongs echoing from the hillsides as they went.

They anchored at Gigha for the night, where they were joined by an Islay contingent. Sanda Isle, off Dunaverty, was reached for the second night. Thereafter it was northwards up into the firth, past Ailsa Craig rock on the east and Arran on the west, and so along the Ayrshire shoreline, over sixty ships, a spectacle indeed, the Islesmen's presence sufficiently evident to foe and friend alike, no haste now, making a procession fully a mile long, Angus ordering the leaders' horns to be blown to add to the rhythmic clanging of the gongs, making their advance the more challenging. Ainea clapped her hands in time to the beat of it all, to the amusement of the oarsmen.

King Edward had been last reported at Irvine, which was a port to the north of Ayr itself. Whether he was still there was not to be known, nor where were Bruce and his allies. But the fleet sailed on very close to the shore, just in case. Local fishing-boats drew well away at sight of them, although the crewmen waved to these.

They sailed on, and put in for the night at the two offshore islands of the Cumbraes, where a certain amount of food and drink was to be obtained, much of this being required. At Millport, on the Great Cumbrae, Angus learned that the English were now said to be up at Largs, a short distance further north, this a name known to all, as where the Norse King Haakon had been so famously defeated by Alexander the Third almost forty years before. Presumably Edward was pressing the Scots ever northwards, towards their Tor Wood and Stirling.

Largs was only some six miles from Millport, so the fleet was able to be off the harbour there early next morning. They could see a great encampment on the open area just south of the town, before the hills closed in, with the smoke from cooking-fires rising. This could only be the English. So Angus led his armada just as close inshore as he dared, well aware of the danger from the deadly longbows; arrows coming winging out at them, as indeed soon was the case, but falling short. Horns and gongs at their loudest and most assertive, the ships beat up and down, back and forth, in as fair order as was possible considering their numbers, just out of bow-shot, keeping it up for long, so that there could be no doubt as to their challenge. What the enemy thought of it all there was no knowing, but Angus could see great companies and formations of men and horses, under banners, being drawn up in order, to repel any attack.

No such attempt was intended, but for perhaps an hour this demonstration was continued, back and forth, while the English waited, ready. It made a strange confrontation.

At length, Angus gave the signal to line up the ships into their former column, and then to sail off, still northwards. They would go on, with the firth narrowing, right to the great bend eastwards, off Gourock, where the estuary began to change into the river-mouth, this to emphasise that the fleet could continue much further, if necessary, up Loch Goil or the Gare Loch, and so deep into Cowal, this posing the danger of a flank attack to any English advance in that direction, or even towards Glasgow, on the way to Stirling.

Opposite Dunoon, on the Cowal shore, they lay up for a while, to rest the oarsmen who had been so busy. Then they turned back whence they had just come, this to make another parade off Largs, where the enemy remained encamped, to, as it were, drive the lesson home. And with the sun beginning to set behind the Arran mountains, it was the Cumbraes again for them, for a night in their sheltered bays.

Ainea had had her first taste of not exactly warfare but of martial tactics, however odd, and declared it a worthy demonstration of power and threat, yet not a drop of blood spilled.

In the morning it was over to Largs again for one final gesture, before turning and heading down-firth for home waters, flourish made, and no doubt leaving King Edward wondering. What was the ultimate effect of it all on the enemy, and on Bruce and his companions, was uncertain, but the latter would surely get to hear of this, and be heartened to know that they had a friend and ally willing to assist, and inimical to the Plantagenet.

Was there anything else Angus could do? He would have to think on this. Anything that he *could* do would tend to be an aid to Man and Ulster also. And it would serve to keep his own chiefs and their folk in a state of readiness for action, on their toes as it were.

Although at Dunaverty he sent off his fleet northwards to their respective isles, Angus himself next day took his dragon-ship down the extra fifty miles to the Isle of Man, to inform Rory, at Peel, of the position, Edward still none so far off. He had taken Caerlaverock Castle so was in a position to strike southwards if so intending. But he seemed to be preoccupied with the Bruce opposition, so the probability was that the Manxmen could breathe more freely meantime. The Isles, of course, would be ready to help counter any attack, without delay.

17

The summer progressed without calls upon Angus other than local and domestic ones – and some of the last were very domestic, for Ainea was now beginning to reveal her pregnant state, and this had her husband even more concerned for her, although she herself appeared to be not in the least anxious, even if she shook her head over her thickening waistline.

She calculated that it would be mid-September for the delivery.

They saw a lot of Gillemoir MacLean and his quiet wife Alicia, with her small son Malise; and the Lady of Duart proved to be very helpful with advice for Ainea over maternity matters, much conferring and cautions, which the mother-to-be could do with in Angus's opinion, for she insisted on living a normal life, and refusing to limit her activities.

No word came from Saddell, either on issues of national import or of the MacDonald sisters; and the question of Donald of Eigg's marital prospects did not fail to keep recurring to husband and wife. Ainea would have had Angus go up to Eigg to discover the position, but he refused to leave her side for more than an hour or two at this so important stage for them both, and agreed to send Ewan instead.

That man in due course came back with Donald himself, who declared that he was much taken with Eithne, but uncertain as to whether he should ask her to marry him. For now that her father was dead, and her sister talking of taking the veil, Eithne would be the female Lord of Kintyre, would she not? And as such, she could look for a possibly more lofty marriage than to himself. Angus saw it otherwise.

She would require a man to guide and advise her, yes, over Kintyre, but there had been no other suitors so far, and Donald's experience as the master of Eigg, however different a domain to manage, would be of assistance to her. And she had expressed her liking for him.

A visit, then, to Saddell, Ainea not to be denied accompanying them, although only a month off child-bearing. After all, travel in the dragonship was no hardship, and its crew were used to her demands for privacy behind that sail-screen.

At Saddell Castle Donald was welcomed warmly. They found that Seona had indeed arranged to enter the nearest nunnery, this over on Arran, St Bride's Convent at Lochranza, less than a score of miles away. So she would be able to see her sister frequently. She seemed happy enough about Donald's courtship, and Eithne certainly did not object to it, so all was well in this respect, the matchmakers happy to see it so.

The news given by the abbot was confusing. Somebody whom Angus had never heard of, a Sir John de Soulis, was the new Guardian of Scotland. He was reported to be no great lord but a Dumfries-shire laird; but it was he who had taken over Stirling Castle when the English had surrendered it. Now, with Wallace's eclipse, and Bruce and the Red Comyn in mutual enmity, he had been chosen as sole Guardian. He was a supporter of Bruce, indeed a vassal of the Carrick earldom, so it could be to the latter's advantage. Further hopeful reports were that Pope Boniface the Eighth had come out in favour of Scots independence, ordering Edward Plantagenet to cease his attacks on the northern kingdom.

On the whole, then, these tidings were hopeful.

Angus and Ainea returned home, not to Dunaverty, which he considered to be no suitable place for her confinement, but to Ardtornish, much more comfortable, and where Alicia of Duart was nearby to act, scarcely as a midwife, but as guide and helper. It would not be long now.

As well that they did make the move in good time, for the

travail and delivery started earlier than anticipated, and were less prolonged than Alicia MacLean had foretold. On the seventh day of September, the Eve of the Nativity of the Blessed Mary, a child was born safely, a girl.

Angus found himself quite delighted with the newcomer, despite his eagerness to produce a son and heir; also at Ainea's swift recovery from her ordeal, as he saw it, and her joy at the outcome. They had become a family. Bliss reigned.

They decided to call the child Finguala, this seemingly a favoured name in the O'Cahan line: Finguala nic Angus, mac Alexander, mac Angus.

For the time being the lordship of the Isles and the state of Scotland slipped back into secondary consideration. Word was sent of the so vital news to Derry.

The child was healthy, with no signs of abnormality, suckled regularly – rather too regularly for Angus, for she seemed to require nourishment at four-hourly intervals, and this at night also.

Others, of course, were preoccupied with alternative affairs. Donald of Eigg, for one, was eager for marriage, and Eithne apparently nothing loth. When could the wedding be?

Angus found himself to be very much involved in this matter. Eithne had no close male relative other than himself, so he would have to act the father and give her away, despite the young woman calling him her nephew. Clearly the nuptials should be celebrated soon, before late autumn and early winter gales made sea travel difficult. Mid-October, then, with much of the Isles leadership to be invited to Saddell Abbey for the ceremony. Finguala, or just Uala as they were calling her, would make her first public appearance.

The special chapel for the mendicant friars had been completed, beside the abbey, and Angus would open it after the wedding.

Donald's longship arrived at Ardtornish three days before the great date, with his father aboard, from Rhum. Others from the north also berthed in Loch Aline. So it would be quite a convoy that headed onwards, to halt overnight at Gigha, as usual. But Donald was not to see his bride before the wedding, so he would have to delay a day, although his father could go on with Angus and Ainea.

The October weather was cool and windy, but with only occasional showers. Uala made no complaints about the dragonship's rolling and dipping.

At Saddell they found all in readiness, Seona over from Arran for the occasion, Eithne much excited. Ainea more or less took over, Uala making her own impact.

Angus had to go to confer with Abbot Fergus as to procedure and timing; also over the chapel dedication. He found two friars mendicant duly present, the Brothers Anselm and Colin, who expressed themselves as most grateful for this shrine in their honour, something neither had experienced before. They had it explained to them that it was a small demonstration of gratitude to the Almighty for the most excellent marriage with which he had been blessed, and also to the brothers themselves for all the so valuable information they regularly brought, and on which he, like so many others, relied for knowledge of affairs on the wider scene.

The value of this last was emphasised there and then by the latest report these had to make. Edward had returned to England again, presumably on account of the papal injunction, for he had declared a truce until 21st May next year; why that date was not known, but it would be a most welcome breathing-space for the embattled Scots. Also, Bishop William Lamberton of St Andrews, the Primate, had proclaimed a blessing on this de Soulis, the new Guardian, and urged all leal and God-fearing men to support him. Good news.

Back at the castle all was bustle and activity, guests arriving by the score, the haven packed with their ships, for this marriage was recognised as important, Angus Mor's niece uniting Kintyre with Eigg and Rhum, the southern lordship with those central isles.

The latest news from the abbey was welcomed, although not all the Islesmen were as concerned as was Angus over the situation in mainland Scotland, seeing themselves as a quite different nation.

Ainea gave Eithne some extra counselling on this the last night of her single state.

Donald duly arrived in mid-forenoon, along with other late-comers, and was taken to the abbey guest-house to await events. The marriage was to be at noon.

Angus sought to marshal all at the castle, as though this were almost like some sort of military exercise, the groom's father sent to guide him, the guests in order of seniority marched off to take their places in the abbey church. Eithne, clad simply but fairly, was readied by her sister and Ainea, with Uala looked after by a serving-woman, Angus himself with the bridal group prepared to walk the short distance to the abbey when its bells rang out. This of acting father, not now only to his infant daughter, was a new challenge to him. He felt somehow responsible for the success of the occasion, his wife amused at his concerned attitude, this almost more evident than at his own wedding.

When the musical resonance of the summons eventually re-echoed from the surrounding hillsides, the short walk to the abbey commenced, Eithne on Angus's arm, Seona and Ainea just behind, and the dragonship's helmsman, with his gong, in the rear, to beat out a different rhythm from that for his oarsmen, to time a dignified and unhurried pacing, and to announce their approach.

Abbot Fergus's deputy met them at the church door, signed for the bell-ringers to halt their pulling and the choristers within to raise voice, and to this melodious chanting they were led into the crowded nave. Angus felt Eithne's grip tighten on his arm as they moved through the throng to the altar steps, with Donald and his father turning to watch their approach.

After placing bride beside groom, Angus stood back a little, and the abbot took over, the service commencing. It was the same cleric who had baptised the girls.

After all the preparations and arrangings, the actual nuptials were comparatively simple and brief, as Angus had noted at his own wedding, joining as one, in the sight of God and all witnesses, no prolonged task however enduring, not exactly anticlimactic but notably concise, however efficacious. Donald and Eithne were duly pronounced man and wife, in only a few minutes, to the triumphal singing of the choir.

Thereafter it was all hail and congratulation and good wishes outside.

As suitable feasting was being prepared, this not at the castle but in the abbey's refectory, as a kindly and appreciative gesture by the monks, Angus went over to the new chapel he was gifting to the mendicants, this for a second and indeed slightly longer ceremony, with dedication, thanks giving, prayers and sprinkling with holy water, followed by blessings and speeches of praise by the two friars on behalf of themselves and their fellow-brethren for the years to come, and predictions of future bliss for the donor – this to Angus's embarrassment.

Then all went to join the feasting.

Thereat, Angus, sitting on the bridegroom's right hand, was told that Donald proposed that he and his wife should spend their summers at Eigg and their winters at Kintyre, weather conditions making this the most suitable arrangement, so that both communities should be well cared for and directed, so very different in so many ways as they were. Angus approved.

The vital matter of where the happy couple were to spend their first night together had been something of a problem. The castle, like the abbey guest-house, was full to overflowing with all the visitors. It would take three full days for Donald's longship to take them to Eigg, and there were few very suitable places to stay on the way, apart from Dunaverty, which anyway could not be reached that evening. Oddly enough, it was Seona who suggested a convenient refuge for the pair. The nuns of her St Bride's Convent on Arran had the use of the old castle of Lochranza nearby, where they put up visiting clerics, even these mendicants. There was a keeper and his wife to care for such. Her sister and Donald could take her back to the nunnery, and lodge in the castle for the night, or longer if they so desired, and in fair comfort, heading off for Eigg in due course.

This was gladly agreed. So the guests saw the two sisters sail off together up Kilbrannan Sound, with the bridegroom, to laughter and cheers, an unlikely start to a wedding night indeed, Angus and Ainea highly amused.

18

Back at Ardtornish winter set in, another hard season. They consoled themselves that it would limit Edward's activities if he decided to renege on his proclaimed truce until May.

A peaceful and rewarding Christmastide was enjoyed, baby Finguala very central to it all, their first as a family.

Spring was slow in manifesting itself. But the weather conditions did not prevent the friars from making their accustomed journeyings. They brought news of varying sorts and importance. De Soulis, as Guardian, was having a difficult time. He was no great magnate, and the powerful nobles considered him an upstart, however good a soldier, and were less than supportive, especially the Comyns. King John Balliol was kept in papal custody in Burgundy, but requesting Boniface's permission to return to Scotland and his throne. Bruce, Earl of Carrick, looked on him as an imposter anyway, and declared his claim to the throne as false, and to be ignored. Scotland was in a continuing state of turmoil, all but anarchy.

Angus shook his head over it all.

His own affairs, happily, were in no such disorder, with no major problems demanding his attention; and of course the hard winter inevitably countered any trouble in the Isles, limiting sea transport for all but the most hardy.

It was early May before he and Ainea decided to transfer themselves to their summer residence at Dunaverty, Finguala now eight months old and developing fast, a great joy to them both.

In Kintyre they learned more of doings on the mainland. Edward Longshanks had made a surprising announcement.

He declared that John Balliol was still King of Scots, but under his *own* Lord Paramountcy. And in the state of disorder in the northern kingdom, he urged Pope Boniface to have Balliol sent back to his realm; and, with his own truce due to expire shortly, he himself would march north again, to see his puppet duly placed on the throne.

So, with both Bruce and Comyn, and possibly de Soulis, not in favour of John Balliol, that Toom Tabard, much trouble was clearly in store for Scotland.

Compared with that mainland, the Isles seemed to be a haven of peace.

It was Donald and Eithne, who had spent the winter at Saddell, clearly happy with each other, who brought the next report from the abbot on their way to Eigg, this very worrying indeed. Edward had ordered all seaports in England to send shipping to Berwick-upon-Tweed, to coincide with his and Balliol's return to Scotland. What was this for? He required no such fleet to fight the Scots opposition. The only need that Angus could think of for shipping was to attack either Ulster or Man, or both. But, if this was his intention, why assemble the vessels at Berwick, on the wrong side of the land? Unless it was to disguise his intentions? Provide no warning. Have them sail right round Scotland and down the west coast, an unexpected approach. Yet it would put them very much at the mercy of the Isles longships. That did not appear to make sense. But Edward was no fool, whatever else he was. There must be some reason behind this. Angus told Donald to inform Duart of it all, and to send warning to the chiefs to be ready to intercept any English flotilla entering their waters, just in case. And he had messengers go to both Rory mac Alan and O'Cahan, to heed this odd situation.

The truce expired on 21st May, and promptly the English marched north in force, two large armies, one on the east, one on the west, the latter under Edward, Prince of Wales, this presumably to confuse and divide the defenders. But at Berwick Edward did not embark his force, or any of it, on the miscellaneous assembly of shipping, mainly merchantmen, but left them there, as a threat perhaps, and turned his men westwards along Tweed, this to assail the royal castle of Roxburgh, in the name of King John Balliol. It was surrendered to them. Then due north, while his son marched, more or less unopposed, through the strategically wasted countryside of Dumfries-shire and Ayrshire, Bruce country.

Angus was not alone in wondering at the Plantagenet's tactics. Those ships . . . ?

The Scots were getting expert at laying waste their own land to make it difficult for the invaders to feed their armies and horses, however awkward and upsetting for the local inhabitants, who usually had to take refuge in the forests and hills, with which, of course, Scotland was well supplied. Distressing as this might be for them, it was at least better than being at the mercy of savage aggressors.

The next heard of Edward was that, after laying siege to castles in the Merse, he had eventually reached Linlithgow, on his way north to the Tor Wood, Stirling and the Forth crossing, that strategic hub of the land, this advance much delayed by the bad weather and devastated ground, as well as defensive guerrilla warfare. There he had settled into the dowery palace, and had King John Balliol issue commands for all warlike activity to cease, declaring that he was now resuming his rule, and backed by the Lord Paramount Edward.

Angus wondered how much heed would be taken of this by the defending forces and the Scots folk in general?

During all this period, despite the poor conditions, he paid his long-delayed visit to the Outer Hebrides, that more than usually detached part of the lordship, which maintained a very separate identity and which tended to take but little part in the affairs of the rest of the Isles. Yet they were a large and lengthy domain, stretching for some one hundred and fifty miles, north and south, and comprising innumerable islands, great and small, from Lewis in the north down to Barra and Mingulay in the south, mainly MacLeod, MacAulay, MacRuarie and MacNeill territory.

Ainea did not accompany him on this occasion, however much she would have wished to, Finguala demanding ever increasing attention. Angus took with him Gillemoir MacLean and MacIan of Ardnamurchan, to emphasise his authority.

The long pull brought them to start at the north end, at Stornoway on the great Lewis, the largest of all the isles, fifty miles long by as much as a score in width, with its own subsidiaries, the Shiants, the Berneras, Scarp, Taransay and the rest. Here were mainly MacLeods, who, although only a score of miles west of their Skye fellow-clansmen, seemed to have little dealings with them, typical of these outer Islesmen. Angus found them, although nowise hostile, and hospitable enough, scarcely interested in his problems, and quite unconcerned over mainland matters.

From Lewis they proceeded south to Harris, very much aware of the rocky, treeless nature of the land, although the western sides proved to be less barren, with golden bays and offshore islets; here were MacLeods again, with MacAulays and MacAskills, all of Norse descent.

Then it was on to the Uists, two quite large Isles, oddly enough separated by another called Benbecula, MacRuarie property, with more MacAulays. Used as he was to clan names, Angus found some difficulty in identifying all these lines. Again little knowledge of other than their own areas was evidenced, these folk seeming to live in a different world. Angus began to wonder whether this excursion was really worth while.

But at Barra, further south still, with its Eriskay, Vatersay, Mingulay and other appendages, it was different. MacNeills prevailed here, and showed much more concern for what went on elsewhere in the Isles, and even in the Scottish-English situation, and in that of Ulster. They did, of course, claim to be in direct descent from the renowned High King of Ireland, Niall of the Nine Hostages, declaring proudly that it was the twenty-first of that line who had come to Barra in 1049. There were MacNeills on Coll so they had links with the Inner Isles. Their chief had his seat at the castle of Kisimul, a fine place on a tidal islet, where the visitors were well entertained, and promises were given of aid, if required, especially against any invasion of Ulster and Man.

So Angus and his friends could sail back eastwards, feeling that their journey had not been profitless after all, for these MacNeills could field quite large numbers of men, and provide many ships. They even might persuade others of their neighbours to join them. Barra had proved to be quite the most fertile and populous of the Outer Isles.

Angus was glad to get back to Dunaverty and Ainea and Uala. He had been away for weeks, after all, covering those many hundreds of miles, and in unhelpful weather conditions for voyaging.

It was late autumn, and becoming time that they moved back to Ardtornish. There was no news of Edward and Balliol. Angus never thought of him as King John. Presumably if any major moves, victories or defeats had taken place, the friars would have reported it.

The year 1302 loomed. What would it bring?

19

In fact, that following year was a momentous one, almost from its beginning. Bruce, Earl of Carrick, started it. His father, a much less vehement character, who had been offered the Scots throne by Edward in place of Balliol some years before – he was the son of one of the many Competitors – and had refused it, had gone to dwell in England, more or less in obscurity, having resigned the Carrick earldom to his son. Now this Bruce made his own claim to the throne, declaring Balliol to be useless, and having forfeited the kingship by his long absence on the Continent and his lack of all activity on Scotland's behalf. And he, Bruce, declared that the realm no longer needed a Guardian therefore, and that he should be recognised as the supreme authority in the beleaguered country.

What the Plantagenet, still apparently at Linlithgow, thought of this, was anybody's guess.

Angus saw it probably as a worthy move, and capable of uniting the divided Scots against the English – save, of course, the Comyns.

That assessment suffered a shock only a couple of weeks later, when the word came that Bruce had actually joined Edward at Linlithgow, evidently throwing in his lot with Longshanks. This seemed scarcely believable at first, and great was the consternation at Ardtornish, and no doubt almost everywhere else. Was this Bruce another broken reed, a second Toom Tabard? Although, of course, he could not yet wear the tabard, not having been crowned king, only claiming to be the rightful monarch.

Ainea declared that there was more to this than met the eye. Especially as it was reported that Bruce's castle of Turnberry, in Ayrshire, where he was said to have been born, was still holding out against the Prince of Wales's siegery. Had Edward not offered the throne to Bruce's father before Balliol? Was this perhaps the reason for this odd move? Just a step nearer the crown?

Ainea was right, in at least some degree. For only a month later it was learned that Bruce had married, with Edward's consent, and none other than the daughter of Longshank's friend, Richard, Earl of Ulster, Elizabeth by name, whom Bruce was said to have long sought after.

What to make of all this? Was this man who claimed the throne a doubledyed scoundrel and turncoat and schemer?

Ainea said certainly the last. But not necessarily the scoundrel. Suppose it was the only way that he could gain his beloved. And at the same time get rid of Balliol. Out-scheme and outwit Edward. Seem to become his puppet, but only in order to gain his own ends, replace Balliol, become undisputed leader of Scotland, and then turn on Edward; this as well as win his Elizabeth de Burgh. Was that not all a possibility?

Angus reserved judgment.

Whatever Bruce's ultimate objectives, Edward was not distracted from seeking to grasp all of Scotland under his sway. He marched north, and with no Bruce to oppose him, at the Tor Wood or elsewhere, was able to reach the Forth. And now the reason for those English ships at Berwick became evident. They sailed up to that firth and along it to as near Stirling as they could get because of its shallowing, and were there in a position to ferry the English army across that so strategic barrier, and enable it to progress on northwards. In the event, Edward did not have to use them, for whether Bruce's supporters, lacking their leader, would have held the famous bridge-crossing, as Wallace had done, was uncertain; but with that fleet of ships available to carry the enemy over further east, there would be no point in it. So the English were able to cross unchallenged, to head on for Perth. The ships sailed off, no doubt for the Firth of Tay, in case there was a hold-up there.

All this became known to Angus in due course – but not what Bruce was doing or where he was. Stirling Castle was still said to be holding out against the enemy, an all but impregnable stronghold.

Those ships? The question for the Islesmen was still would they be used to assail Ulster and Man? Could Edward be heading for the far north of Scotland, there to embark his men, and sail round through the Pentland Firth, between the mainland and Orkney, and so into the Western Sea, and southwards? Those ships could not carry all his horses, that was for sure. Would the cavalry, then, be sent back by land, and only the foot transported by sea? That might be enough for the Plantagenet's purposes. It was all a great question-mark. Angus could only seek to be ready, in case.

Back at Dunaverty, they had a visit from Donald and Eithne, on their way to summer at Eigg; and that young woman was very obviously pregnant. She and Ainea conferred on matters matrimonial and maternal, while their husbands discussed the Isles' readiness for affairs military.

There was worrying news that summer. King Philip the Fair of France had been defeated at Courtrai in an extraordinary conflict being called the Battle of Spurs, this by the allied Flemish citizens of Ypres, Bruges, Ghent, Lille and other Flanders towns, the chivalry of France disastrously vanquished, and with it Philip's monarchial credit direly reduced, no doubt to the delight of Edward. This could mean an end, temporarily at least, to the effectiveness of the Auld Alliance, Scotland the worse off. Moreover, Pope Boniface promptly renounced his support for France and Scotland also, addressing the Plantagenet as his dearest son in Christ, King of England and the Scots.

What would the next potential calamity be? Vatican affairs did not greatly affect the Isles; but the Abbot of Saddell was much distressed by this papal turn-about.

Angus had his own concerns that summer. Bickering between the island chiefs was everlasting, but not usually serious. On this occasion it could become so, major clans involved, both on Mull, with trouble between the MacLeans and the MacKinnons over the MacQuarries. Gillemoir, Angus's friend, announced that he would have to take action against Gillebride MacKinnon of Kilninver and Mishnish, who shared the Isle of Mull in a lesser degree, the MacLeans holding the major, southern area, the MacKinnons the north. It seemed that the latter chief was claiming to take over the island of Gometra, off the south coast of his territory, this held by the small clan of the MacQuarries. Lachlan MacQuarrie had appealed to Duart for help.

This of course, was typical of Isles local squabbles, and Angus sighed over it all. But Gillemoir was his friend and deputy, and peace must be maintained.

The MacKinnons and the MacQuarries had been not exactly at feud for generations, yet they were of the same ancestry, but inimical. They both claimed descent from St Columba, or at least from Columba's father, the Prince Felim of Ireland, Fingon and Guarie being younger brothers of the saint. From the former came the MacKinnons, from the latter MacQuarries. The MacKinnons were much the more powerful. Now their chief, Gillebride, was claiming the others' Isle of Gometra, on what grounds was uncertain. Duart said that he would have to go, in strength, and support Lachlan MacQuarrie.

Angus, ever concerned that there should be no serious disharmony among the Isles clans, to the weakness of the lordship, urged no sort of armed conflict. Best that he himself should go, with Gillemoir, as representing his father, and seek a peaceful settlement. Duart nowise objected.

No lengthy sailing was involved, Dun Ara, the MacKinnon main seat, being on the northern tip of Mull. So it was up the sound a score of miles, past Salen and Aros and Tobermory, to round the headland of Ardmore on another three miles to Dun Ara, this perched like so many other Isles strongholds on its cliff-top above the waves, with a sheltered little bay nearby as haven for its longships and fishing-craft. They went in the dragonship, with two of Duart's birlinns.

They were observed on approach, and duly met by Gillebride MacKinnon, whom Angus knew, an elderly but stern man of massive build. He greeted them, carefully civil, eyeing Duart doubtfully.

It did not take long to come to the point of their visit. The Isle of Gometra, separated from Ulva of the MacQuarries by only the narrowest of straits, this even drying out at low tide, MacKinnon declared should be his, so near Ulva as it was, having originally been occupied by Fingon himself, who had founded a chapel there, at Torr Mor, in support of Columba's missionary efforts, the remains and burial-ground of which still existed. The MacQuarries denied this, holding that it had been the brother Guarie's foundation, and claiming the whole island. Not that Gometra was very large, a mere two miles by one. But it was fertile and populous, and the MacKinnon's claim was false. That chief announced that he could prove his right. He had in his charter-chest an ancient piece of calf-skin, on which his ancestor, Fingon, had drawn an outline of Gometra with the chapel marked on it.

Angus said that this was interesting, but that they would have to reserve judgment until they had heard MacQuarrie's case. After all, the two isles were all but joined, and it seemed strange that they should be in different possession, neither of them large.

With MacKinnon declaring that Lachlan MacQuarrie's assertions would be all lies, they left him, to proceed on their way to Ulva.

This was a sail of only some six miles south-eastwards across the wide mouth of Loch Tuath.

They came to Gometra first, but passed it by, noting the half-mile-wide gap between the two isles, and that it was all but dry. Ulva, to the east, was twice as large, and more hilly, with islets innumerable around it. Duart asserted that it was ridiculous that it and Gometra should be divided in ownership.

The main centre of population was at the extreme east end, this only separated from the mainland of Mull by another narrow strait, although it was called the Sound of Ulva. Here was Lachlan MacQuarrie's castle. But the callers found that the young chief was absent, over on Gometra oddly enough. His mother received them, and thankfully. She said that she would send a man to bring back her son, who was inspecting his cattle on the other isle. He would be back in an hour or so. Meanwhile the visitors must eat and drink, welcome guests.

Shona MacQuarrie, a woman of middle years, told them that this claim of MacKinnon's had been put forward actively only since her husband died, he seeking to take advantage of the young heir. Gometra had always been a MacQuarrie holding, from the days of Guarie, not Fingon his brother, the chapel *his* work.

When Angus mentioned the calf-skin drawing which Mac-Kinnon had spoken of, their hostess said that this had been stolen from Ulva by an earlier MacKinnon. It had been drawn by Guarie. Fingon had established a chapel, indeed two of them, but not on Gometra. These were on Inch Kenneth and Eorsa, smaller isles to south and east. She took them to a window and pointed out these none so far off, each only a couple of miles away.

Entertained well, the visitors were presently joined by the son Lachlan, a personable young man, who was clearly much flattered to have Angus Og of Islay calling on him, along with MacLean of Duart to whom he had appealed. He had nothing to add to what his mother had told them, but was vehement in his claim to Gometra.

Angus had been thinking on the position the while, and reckoned that he saw a possible solution. He referred to those other two isles, of Inch Kenneth and Eorsa pointed out to them. How important were they to the MacQuarries? As important as Gometra? No, no, he was told, nothing like that. Sheep and a couple of shepherds on Eorsa, and a score or so, largely fishers, on Inch Kenneth, both these modest of size; whereas Gometra was, as they would have seen, a fine and fertile isle, home to at least a couple of hundred MacQuarries.

Then why not offer MacKinnon these two instead of Gometra, since they had had links with his ancestor Fingon? Angus asked. Their loss would not greatly harm Ulva, would it? Exchange the two for that calf-skin drawing. Was that not a credible barter?

Mother and son eyed each other questioningly, while Duart nodded his support for the proposal. They could transfer the Inch Kenneth fisherfolk and Eorsa shepherds to Gometra, could they not, without any great difficulty or upset. And MacKinnon might be reasonably satisfied.

The MacQuarrie pair admitted that this might well be an acceptable outcome, of no grievous loss to them. If Mac-Kinnon would have it.

Angus said that he would strongly urge it, in the name of the Lord of the Isles.

They spent a comfortable night at Ulva Castle, and headed back to Dun Ara in the morning.

Gillebride MacKinnon was less than eager to accept this offer of the other two islands in exchange for his demand for Gometra; but Angus insisted that he should; and Duart added his own inducement by offering free use of the harbour of Aros on the Sound of Mull, hitherto reserved for only MacLean shipping, this of quite considerable value to MacKinnon for the transporting of his cattle to mainland markets, instead of having to sail them right round the island. That clinched it. The precious scrap of calf-skin was handed over, and hands shaken.

The Isles would be strengthened by the healing of this comparatively minor rift in its polity, for the word would undoubtedly get around among the other clans, and note be taken.

Back at Dunaverty, Ainea had more news from Saddell. The Red Comyn, in anger at Bruce's seeming alliance with Edward, had managed to get de Soulis to resign the guardianship, and had himself appointed again in his place. And in an unlikely compact with William Wallace, however temporary, had inflicted a defeat on an army of the invaders under Sir John de Segrave whom Edward had appointed Governor of Scotland, this at Roslin in Lothian; whereafter Wallace had headed westwards to his own countryside to tackle the Prince of Wales, still besieging Turnberry. That son of Longshanks, much less of a warrior than was his father, had promptly retired in the face of the renowned Wallace, to England. Now Edward, confronted with victors on two sides, Comyn on the east, Wallace on the west, had given up his northern project meantime and himself retired over the border, and taken Bruce with him.

Nothing was surer than that he would return. But, for the present, Comyn, in name at least, ruled Scotland, his reputation both enhanced and injured. For, after the victory at Roslin, with Wallace gone, he had massacred the prisoners taken, including Segrave, a deed that shocked many of his own people, including, it was said, William Wallace. That would serve Scotland but ill thereafter, most recognised. Slaying the enemy in battle, or the common folk in invasion, was one thing; but to kill surrendered prisoners-of-war, especially lofty ones, was quite another, against all notions of chivalry. What had made the Comyn do it?

Angus wondered what the MacDougalls of Lorn, and Ian Bacach, thought of this.

And where was John Balliol? No word of him, still in name King of Scots. His northern kingdom faced 1303 in its accustomed state of uncertainty, anxiety and, sadly, division.

20

The new year had barely commenced when there was a major change in circumstances for Angus Og. His weakly and long-ailing father died, on Islay, and suddenly Angus was un-doubted and accepted Lord of the Isles, instead of merely acting as such.

This happening demanded two formal and traditional de-velopments: the princely funeral of Alexander, however little real mourning was involved; and the ceremonial installation of the new Lord of the Isles at the caput of the lordship, Finlaggan on Islay, both calling for a large attendance of chiefs and prominent ones. Clearly it would be convenient for all that these should be held as nearly together as was possible.

So Angus had to go to Finlaggan Castle to collect the corpse, feeling guilty in that he had not visited his father for months, for when last he had, his welcome had been less than evident, even though granddaughter Finguala was with them. Now it was too late to chide himself.

With the frail body wrapped in a shroud under the Banner of the Isles, the dragonship led a long procession of vessels the sixty miles to Saddell, a lengthy and difficult voyage at this time of year, and daylight short. But in the circumstances waiting with the remains and that great gathering was some-how unsuitable, and with the abbot's agreement the burial was conducted at dusk, as Ainea suggested, somehow apt. Even so it was done with fullest pomp and ceremony, somewhat hypocritical as it might seem to many; and it had to be by torchlight that Alexander was finally laid to rest beside the other former lords, all of whom had been so very different from himself. Not that the abbot gave even the slightest indication of this in his service, any more than did the alleged mourners. It was the position and ancestry that they were honouring rather than the individual. Angus wondered how, when it came to be his turn to be interred there, *he* would be judged. He had had to follow Angus Mor, which was a testing indeed, and would remain so.

This over, the great company had to spend the night either at the abbey or in the castle, no atmosphere of gloom prevailing.

In the morning they made an early start, on account of the distance in getting back to Islay, this to a great beating of gongs and chanting, celebration and acclaim now the mood and reaction. With the south-westerly wind they made better time of it than the day previously.

Even so it was mid-afternoon before they reached Islay, but all agreed that they should not delay proceedings until the morrow. The ceremonial and parade would not be protracted, however important.

Nevertheless, it all greatly impressed Ainea.

The highly significant part commenced at Port Askaig, the haven for Finlaggan. There, while all the other longships, galleys and birlinns were lined up at anchor, the dragonship was not. it was dragged up on to the beach, out of the water. There smoothed tree-trunks, to act as rollers, were ready, and on to a row of these the vessel was drawn, Angus still within it, with his crew, oars held vertical, Ainea and the child also. Then the chiefs, chieftains and other notables from the fleet came, and ropes were attached for them to drag the craft, only the great ones to do this, heavy task as it was. All around them their men lit torches to escort them, but only that. Then, at a long blast from Duart's horn, the mighty labour began.

That dragonship had to be pulled on those rollers up the long slope all the way to Loch Finlaggan, two miles altogether, and by these chiefs, only them, as sign of their allegiance and strongest support for their new lord. Crewmen, bent double, could and must replace the rollers as they were passed over, carrying the ones passed to the front again to maintain the progress of the gasping draggers. The rest of the host of men, with their torches held high, marched up on either side, chanting and clanging their gongs. Thus, with Angus standing at the stern of his ship, under the banner held aloft, and the Galley of the Isles sail unfurled, the taxing ascent proceeded. Pipers played.

It was a slow, painful progress, needless to say, for the men on the ropes, very indicative of their continuing adherence to the chief of chiefs, whatever the cost, as the dragonship crept up the hill. It was all based on the renowned exploit of Magnus Barefoot, King of Norway, who in 1098 had his galley dragged over the hilly ground between West and East Lochs Tarbert, this in order to claim the entire further forty miles of the mainland peninsula of Kintyre as one of the isles he had conquered, because he could sail his ship around it, this extraordinary deed adopted by Somerled and his successors as sign of their authority.

Angus, very much aware of the strain on his friends and adherents, felt highly concerned to be standing there idle the while, but recognised that was his present part. Ainea did seek to show her sympathy and appreciation by adding her higher-pitched woman's chanting to that of all the crewmen, the only female involved in the performance.

At length, exhausted, the draggers got the dragonship up on to comparatively level ground, this near the hamlet of Keills, where they could pause for a rest, with whisky passed round to revive. But there was still over a mile to go to the head of Loch Finlaggan, this over undulating pasture, a deal less demanding. By this time it was almost dark, but the torches lit up the scene in a ruddy glow. The procession resumed. But it was still a slow progress, added to by the patches of damp and boggy land where the roller-logs tended to sink in. So that it was almost another hour before the chiefs were able to dispose of their burden and push the vessel out into the water, and the oarsmen could lower their upraised sweeps and row out to the castle island.

The many small boats used on the loch now had to bring out the leading men – not the great mass of the others, who were to encamp around the shore for the night.

On the castle island, the larger of the two, the performance was not yet over. At the great open council circle of standing stones, there from sun-worship days, this the actual caput of the lordship, in the torchlight the chiefs formed themselves into the Council of the Isles. Flanked by Gillemoir of Duart, MacIan of Ardnamurchan and Rory mac Alan of Man, Angus stood in the centre, and was proclaimed High and Mighty Lord, who bowed the knee to none save God Almighty, this to ringing cheers.

Then, hand held high, Angus swore, by the same Almighty, to rule and protect the Isles and all therein aright as long as his heart did beat, and to yield no inch of territory to another, while respecting the rights and privileges of every chief and clan, great and small.

That proclaimed, each chief, in due order of precedence, came forward to clasp Angus's arms, which were now upraised, sword in one hand, battle-axe in the other, thus to swear allegiance.

The Lord of the Isles's arms were almost as weary as were those of his ship-draggers before all was over, and they could move over to the castle for feasting, food and drink meanwhile having been sent out for the encamped men on the loch-shore. Ainea acted hostess with her usual flair; and Ewan of Kinlochaline played the part of sennachie, recounting the exploits of previous lords and their ancestors back into semi-mythical times, this for entertainment. There was more of the bagpipes.

Weary thereafter, all sought belated couches, a memorable day over.

Before they slept, Ainea was informed by Angus that he had no intention of residing at Finlaggan, save on especial occasions, Ardtornish and Dunaverty continuing to be their homes, this to her satisfaction.

The news from the mainland reaching them that spring was confusing. Edward was back in Scotland, but Bruce and his wife no longer seemed to be with him. Comyn, however, had yielded to him, abandoning his brief alliance with William Wallace. Scotland had now no Guardian therefore. But Stirling Castle, under Oliphant, still held out against the invaders.

A scarcely believable report came that Edward had actually held a parliament, at St Andrews, in Fife, an *English* parliament, at which all Scottish lords had been commanded to appear. How many had done so was unclear. But the main decision taken was that Scotland had no longer any monarch but Edward himself, the two realms declared one.

What did Bruce of Carrick think of this, he who had claimed the throne? Presumably he was there. And did the announcement presage any effort to bring the Isles under the Plantagenet's authority, on the assumption that they were part of Scotland? He would find that no easy task to ensure, Angus declared.

But the safety of Ulster and Man was still a worry. It was almost certainly only a matter of time before Longshanks turned his attention thither, whether or not he coveted the rest of the Isles. Readiness must be maintained for swift assembly and action.

Eithne had produced a son. Ainea said that she must do as much for *her* husband. The Lord of the Isles required a male heir. A Lady of the Isles would not serve.

They were back at Dunaverty for the summer when Donald, as well as bringing Eithne and her baby son Calum to show them, brought word from the abbot. Bruce and Comyn, both bowing before Edward, while both apparently retaining their claims to the Scots throne despite that parliament's decision at St Andrews, had made some sort of bargain with each other. If one of them proclaimed his intention to mount the throne, his lands would undoubtedly be forfeited by Longshanks. So which was it to be? Both had great estates. Comyn cherished his evidently more than did his rival. He would hold on to his properties, and Bruce could still claim the crown – if he dared. Lands were a more sure and lasting asset than any questionable regalia and sceptre – and which had to be fought for. Whether Edward knew of this compact was uncertain; but if the mendicant friars did, the probability was that he had learned of it also. Bruce would have to watch the delicate and uneasy steps he was taking on a dangerous path.

However, it seemed that the Plantagenet had other matters on his acquisitive mind at this stage. A powerful group of English nobles, led by the Earls of Gloucester and Essex, had become tired of providing men and arms and moneys for their monarch's aggressions in Scotland, Ireland, France and Flanders, and had reached the stage of refusing to co-operate any further. This came to light when Longshanks had sent south for a supply of great and effective siege-engines, ballistas, quarrells, sows, battering-rams and the like, this to endeavour to reduce Stirling Castle held by Oliphant – and these had been refused. This infuriated the monarch. Leaving his troops to control all southern Scotland, save for Wallace's Ettrick Forest sanctuary, and appointing the Earl of Richmond as governor, he forthwith headed back to London, taking both Bruce and Comyn with him, an uneasy trio indeed.

So went the account. Presumably it would be only a temporary absence. Edward would still command the great majority of the English lords, and have his way. Whether, of course, all these monkish tidings were entirely accurate was always a question. Details might often be erroneous, mere hearsay; but probably the major events recounted were true enough.

21

That late summer Angus received an unexpected visit, a repercussion of his tour of the Outer Isles. MacNeill of Barra came to him with a request, little as that potent chief was apt to be seen in these southern parts. He wanted the office of Constable of Castle Sween, in Knapdale, restored to him, as he put it, from the keepership of MacNeill of Gigha.

"Traditionally it has been held by my line, and was wrongly granted to these other MacNeills about eighty years ago by the father of Angus Mor, Donald of the Isles. I would have it back. Originally we held all Knapdale, until it was won from us by your Somerled's descendants."

Angus blinked. He was scarcely apt to be addressed in this fashion. He knew of Castle Sween, one of the greatest strong-holds of all the Isles, on Loch Sween of Knapdale, the northern part of Kintyre. It was a lordship fortress, but from early times held by MacNeills as hereditary keepers. It was now held by Torquil MacNeill of Gigha, his friend, who so often acted as host, to and from Dunaverty and Ardtornish.

Here was a difficult and complex matter. He certainly did not want to offend Gigha, one of whose sons was acting as keeper at Castle Sween. But Nigellus MacNeill of Barra was very powerful, in men and ships, and could much influence other Outer Isles chiefs. He must be kept in loyal support if at all possible. This of Constable of Sween was merely an honorary title, carrying prestige, yes, but no actual authority and sway. These two MacNeill lines, Barra and Gigha, were descended from brothers, Gigha from the younger. Here was a problem.

"You are eager for this?" he asked. "Have it taken from your kinsman, Torquil of Gigha?"

"Far-out kin, indeed! It should be mine. I head the senior line."

"I needs must think on this," Angus said. "Hear Gigha's mind on it."

"He will not wish it. But that is not of great import. It will right a wrong."

"We shall see . . ."

As it happened, this Barra chief was on his way to Man, to take part in a celebration of five hundred years' reign of the ancient Manx kings, from whom the MacNeills claimed descent, as did Rory mac Alan; for that matter, so could Angus himself as well as many others, for Somerled's wife had been Ragnhild, daughter of King Olaf the Morsel. He had not thought to attend this festivity, with more urgent affairs on his mind, although wishing it well. He sent the MacNeill on his way, with kindly regards to Rory mac Alan and his wife.

So he must go and see Torquil MacNeill of Gigha.

That man listened to his account, nodding his head. Nigel of Barra, or Nigellus as he preferred to be called, had not called on him on his way south, related as they might be. Indeed they had only met twice, at Isles functions, little love lost between the two septs of the clan. But Torquil did know that the other coveted the Castle Sween keepership, as symbol that the MacNeills had once held all Knapdale.

"Barra is important in the Isles polity, friend Torquil," he was told. "Not only for the strength he can provide but for the pressure he can bring to bear on the MacLeods, MacRuaries, MacAulays and others in the Outer Isles. And I need such active support."

"You wish me to yield up Castle Sween to Nigellus, then?"

"It would be helpful if you would, yes. But it is not my wish to cause you hurt or loss, far from it. You have always aided me, given me much hospitality. And Barra has not! But this of the constableship seems to be important to him. And I would hold his goodwill the more strongly, if I could."

"You are Lord of the Isles, Angus Og. And your will has to be mine."

"That is not the way I would have it, friend. Is there aught that I could gain for you, in exchange for this?"

The other looked away. "I scarcely can ask for it. But . . . there is the matter of Boisdale."

"Boisdale? That is an isle, a small isle, of the Uists, is it not?"

"Yes. Not really an isle but almost one. A tongue of land, all but detached. It lies at the foot of South Uist. No large promontory. Some five miles by two, lying seven or eight miles from the tip of Barra. It used to be owned by my forebears, their only toehold in the Outer Isles. But the Barra line got it, and by less than fair means."

"And you would wish it yours?"

"It would much please me, yes."

"Does it mean much to Barra? If it is part of the Uists, not of Barra?"

"I do not know. It is good pasture. It has its own sea loch and anchorage. I am told that Nigellus uses it but little. For sheep and cattle."

"You would give up Castle Sween for Boisdale?"

"Castle Sween is *yours*, not mine. But the keepership, yes. My son would be as well suited on Boisdale, holding even a small piece of the Long Island where once we were strong."

"Then I will put it to him, to Barra. Urge him to it. If I am Lord of the Isles, and Boisdale is not on the Isle of Barra, then surely my will in the matter should carry weight? Why, think you, does this of Castle Sween mean so much to him, so far away from Barra?" He smiled. "Aye, and as Boisdale is as far away from Gigha!"

"It is because we MacNeills, descended from King Niall of the Nine Hostages, came first from Ireland to Knapdale and held it for generations. We took Castle Sween, or the Dun of

Sweyn, as it was then, from the Norsemen. So it has memories for us. But so has Boisdale."

"I see it now. I will do what I can . . ."

If it seemed a comparatively small matter to take Angus all the way to Man, when he had not been going to that celebration of the ancient kings of the most southerly of all his isles, nevertheless, if he was to be a good and effective Lord of the Isles, this was the sort of task that was demanded of him, surely? And it would be good to see Rory and his wife again. He could take Ainea and Uala with him, and make a pleasure of it. That is, unless there was some news awaiting him at Dunaverty from Abbot Fergus demanding attention.

There was not, and Ainea was happy to go, always pleased to sail off with him in the dragonship.

So it was Man for them next morning, sixty miles, a full day's sailing.

The celebrations were being held at Rushen, the ancient Norse capital at the very southern end of the island where the kings had had their residence. The commemorations were nearly over, but there was still some festivity going on, in which they could join in some measure. Rory welcomed them warmly, and his wife took charge of Uala.

They found Nigellus of Barra much involved, although he was able to claim a much more illustrious descent, from the High Kings of Ireland, than could these Norse Manx monarchs whom they were remembering. It was some time before Angus could have a quiet word with him.

"This of Castle Sween," he began, "I have been thinking it out. And more than thinking. The castle itself, of course, is mine. But you desire the constableship. At what price?"

"Price? Why price? It has always been in MacNeill hands."

"No doubt. But I could change that. I have spoken with Torquil of Gigha. He is prepared to yield up, as keeper, to myself. As indeed he must, if so I say. But he would wish a recompense."

No comment, but a wary look.

"Does Boisdale mean much to you? Compared with Castle Sween?"

"Ha – that old fable! Always they have wanted that."

"Perhaps. But still they do. The issue is, do *you* esteem it so precious? More so than the Sween constableship?"

The other paused. "No-o-o. But—"

Angus cut him short. "Then let it be so. You gain keeping of Castle Sween, Gigha gains Boisdale – both with my approval." Angus was inwardly amused at himself thus acting the lord so assertively.

"Very well. But I hope that Torquil mac Ewan will not prove any trouble there. Or I will have to correct him!"

"Any correcting between chiefs in the Isles *I* will do, Nigellus MacNeill! But I will always value your aid in the Isles cause, my friend, Constable of my castle of Sween."

Barra inclined his head. And they left it at that.

There was word from Saddell when Angus and Ainea got back to Dunaverty. Edward had returned to Scotland, as expected, and was basing himself at Dunfermline Palace and Abbey, Malcolm Canmore's ancient seat. Stirling Castle had fallen to him at last, partly from starvation aided by his siege-weaponry. Sir William Oliphant had sought to surrender on terms, but anything such had been ignored by Edward, and the one hundred and forty men who had held out for so long were taken and mocked, stripped half-naked, and with ropes round their necks forced to march barefoot to Dunfermline.

There, with all Scotland now in his grasp, save for Wallace in his Ettrick Forest, the Plantagenet had issued a command that this traitor, as he called him, be brought to him for punishment, and a notable price put on his head, whoever apprehended him assured of the Lord Paramount's favour.

That realm, save for the Isles, lay prostrate. Would the said Isles, particularly Man, be Edward's next target?

Much troubled by all this, Angus reckoned that he might need such as Barra's strong support none so far ahead. Why must they all be cursed by a man such as Edward Plantagenet? What made him thus endlessly aggressive? Why must so many others, in various lands, be the victims of his overweening lust for power?

Before they returned to Ardtornish that late autumn, Ainea cheered her husband considerably by announcing that she was pregnant again. Perhaps she would give him a son this time, a new Lord of Islay?

22

At least King Edward appeared to prefer to pass his winters in England, however much he retained his iron grip on Scotland. This time, he left John of Brittany, created Earl of Richmond, another warrior, as governor, with instructions to have Wallace apprehended at all costs. He took the two claimants to the Scots throne south with him, Bruce and Comyn. How feeble were these rivals? How typical of the Scots, who, it seemed, were ever more concerned with fighting each other than with uniting against the common foe.

Further indication of this sorry weakness was not long in forthcoming. It appeared that Comyn had sought to strengthen his own position by revealing to Edward, in London, the bargain between himself and Bruce, this that he should renounce his right to the throne and be content to regain his forfeited lands, along with his rival's, while Bruce made every effort to gain the crown as sole claimant. This, needless to say, had provoked Longshanks to wrath, and decision to take prompt and positive action. The Earl of Gloucester, who was a leading critic of Edward's aggressions, had learned of it, and had sent Bruce a warning, in the shape of a pair of spurs and a pouch of coins, indicating immediate flight; that man had wisely taken heed, and there and then, by night, ridden off northwards, with two companions, for his own land.

So went the reports.

What now? Become an open foe of the Plantagenet, what could Bruce do? Join William Wallace? After all, he had knighted that heroic character and had him appointed Guardian of the Realm those years ago. If these two could unite, act in concert . . . ? Was 1304 going to be a more hopeful year for the savaged land?

Meantime, presumably, the Red Comyn basked in Edward's favour in London.

In March Ainea was brought to bed, and duly presented Angus with a brother for Finguala amidst much rejoicing, and a fairly easy birth. They decided to name him John, one day to be Lord of the Isles.

Ainea made a swift recovery and, the newcomer hale and hearty, especially at bellowing, the couple elected to make a brief trip over to Ulster. It seemed a long time since they had seen O'Cahan. They would show him his two grandchildren.

It was while they were at Limavady, and happy to be there, with much appreciation being demonstrated all round, that reports reached them from a different source than Saddell Abbey. William Wallace had been betrayed, by a Sir John Menteith, a Stewart, just why was not declared but presumably for the reward offered. He was being sent, in chains and on foot, on the long road to London. So much for Bruce uniting the Scots.

This tragic news was confirmed when Angus and family got back to Dunaverty, with the added information that Bruce was vowing to have this wretched Menteith captured and hanged. Not that this would help Wallace, but it might serve to rouse his fellow-countrymen to some sort of united action.

While in Ulster, O'Cahan had informed them that de Burgh, the Bruce's father-in-law, was back in Ireland, which might be ominous, possibly presaging the dreaded assault on Man, or Ulster, or both.

They were not long returned to Kintyre when they received a very unexpected visitor. Angus had scarcely heard of Andrew, Bishop of Argyll, who had come to him from Saddell on horseback with one of the abbot's monks. Apparently he had the additional title of "of the Isles", which presumably gave him some sort of ecclesiastical jurisdiction over them all. A genial prelate of middle age, he declared that he had been appointed in 1299 to succeed Bishop Lawrence. Now, he thought it was time that he made himself at least acquainted with the Isles portion of his large diocese, which must be one of the largest in the land, Argyll itself having occupied his attention thus far to the exclusion of the Isles. But now here he was, to seek to remedy in some small measure his apparent neglect. Abbot Fergus at Saddell, his first call, had recommended that he came to this Dunaverty Castle to see the lord of all.

Angus could scarcely confess that he knew little or nothing about bishops and their concerns, his religious links being more or less confined to the said abbot and various monkish priests. But he was a worshipper of a sort, and recognised at least some of his Christian duties; and would be glad to help his guest in whatever way he could.

Ainea made the newcomer welcome. She was more knowledgeable about lofty clerics than was her husband, but of course Irish ones.

Bishop Andrew also made confession, this as to his woeful ignorance about the Isles' churches and chapels and institutions. He understood from Abbot Fergus that it was all very much a monastic tradition here, parishes few and scattered, as not to be wondered at in the host of islands. And monks and nuns moved but little from their own establishments, save for the mendicants; so even the abbot had been able to give him little guidance as to the situation at large, at least in any detail. He hoped that the Lord Angus could instruct him better.

That man felt inadequate. But he would do what he could.

Which, he was asked, were the main worshipping centres and ecclesiastical establishments he should visit? He realised that the Isles covered a vast area, and he could, in this first attempt, reach only a few. But it would be of great assistance to hear of some none too far off.

Angus had to point out that, although the bishop had come

on horseback, that was no practical method of Isles travel. It had to be by ship. But such, at least, he could provide. He could, to be sure, provide a little more than that, some indication of places of worship for the cleric to call upon. With Ainea's help, he listed a few, apart from in Kintyre, which the abbot would have told him of. Had he mentioned three chapels here, near to Dunaverty? There were not a few others, now no longer used, ruinous, founded by early saints. But the one where they worshipped on occasion was only a mile to the west, Keil.

"You will find many so named," he told the bishop. "Keil or Kil meaning just the cell or church of one of those Columban saints, this one called after Columba himself, Kilcolmkill. Kilblaan, to the north-east is now abandoned. Kilellan you must have passed on your ride south, likewise Kildaloag. There is one on Sanda isle nearby, St Ninian's—"

Ainea interrupted this catalogue. "Spare the good bishop, Angus!" she exclaimed. "You confuse *me*, who knows something of these! Consider him. And such are only those close at hand to Dunaverty."

Admittedly the prelate was looking somewhat bewildered. "I fear that I am very ignorant," he said, "as to all these ancient Celtic Church saints."

"Aye, they were many indeed. They needed to be, Columba's missionaries, if he was to convert this land, all Scotland indeed, from pagan sun-worship. Ninian was, of course, before him, but his mission failed. The one on Sanda is named after *him*, nevertheless. The others, Cattan, Kiaran, Brandon, Congan, Crinan, Donnan, Finnan, Kenneth, Moluag and the rest, so many more, all had cells or chapels called after them." Angus shrugged. "Where are we to begin?"

"I say that we should take Bishop Andrew, tomorrow, to see our own one where we attend. Less than we should, no doubt! Kilcolmkill. And see Columba's Footsteps."

"To be sure. But what does Bishop Andrew want? He is here

not just to see buildings, however ancient, I think? But to speak with priests and churchmen. We will take him to Kilcolmkill, yes. But there are others, all over the Isles, more important. The most holy, Oronsay, with its priory. Gigha's Kilchattan. I could name four on Islay. Another Keill on Jura. Knapdale's Kilmory. Still one more Kilcolmkill at Lochaline. Four, no five, on Mull. And Tiree's Kilkenneth and Kirapol—"

"Save us – enough! Enough!" Ainea cried. "*You*, saying that you know little of it all. You will have our friend here out of his good mind! One at a time, Angus."

Her spouse grinned. "I know the names, the places. Not how many here are to his purposes."

"I had not thought that there was so much of mission here," their visitor said. "My ignorance shames me . . ."

"*Was*, not is! This of mission," he was told. "Most of these are but small chapels, many no longer used. Or not for worship. But all with their tales and stories."

"I think we should take the bishop in your dragonship, Angus, to see some few of them. Good for *us* to visit them also. Help the good work a little. And learn. Tomorrow Keil, here – Kilcolmkill. Then, others."

That was agreed.

So in the morning they rode along the cliff-top track, westwards, to the church on its knoll and its sloping grave-yard. There was no resident priest here; he had to come on Sundays and feast-days from Ormsary, another and slightly larger chapel with quite a community round it, where they would take the bishop hereafter. This Kilcolmkill was a simple oblong building with an arched doorway and tiny windows; they all tended to be, these Columban Church shrines, their founders not going in for handsome sanctuaries, indeed doing much of their worship in the open air. But they were famed for their ornamental grave slabs, highly carved, their standing crosses and their effigies; and Kilcolmkill was no exception, well supplied with the like. But its pride was what was known as Columba's Footsteps, which Bishop Andrew was taken to see, this two carvings on an outcrop of rock nearby, of right feet, one slightly larger than the other. Although they were both called Columba's, one was judged to be infinitely older, dating from prehistoric times, no doubt linked with druidical sun-worship. But the other was said to have been carved beside it by Columba himself, who landed here from Ireland. He had chiselled out the footprint, facing north, to show his destination and determination. This of footprints in stone was an ancient tradition, to be seen elsewhere, to mark great ones' decisions.

As well as this, they took their visitor to see three caves in the red-sandstone cliffs not far off, one of these containing a druidical altar, which Columba had sworn to use as a symbol of worship, as it was, but to prove to the mistaken devotees of the sun that the Creator of the sun, and His son Jesus Christ, were infinitely more worthy of worship than sun, moon and stars, this indeed to be his life's work. He had slept in another of the caves, until proceeding on to Oronsay, from which he could still see Ulster, and so further to Iona where he could not, and so settled there.

A spring gushed from the cliff-face here and was reputed to have been drunk from and blessed by the saint, and became a holy well.

The bishop was much interested in all this, needless to say.

Then they took him on to where he was able to have a word with Brother Peter, an Augustinian monk who served as priest for this quite large area, this at Ormsay, and who was greatly exercised at thus meeting his superior. The two clerics were left to discuss matters religious, while Angus and Ainea visited the local community before taking their guest back to Dunaverty.

Next day it was to sea in the dragonship, Gigha their destination, their passenger declaring that here was a new experience for him, as he eyed the oarsmen and listened to the panting chanting and the beat of the gong, this while viewing the dramatic scenery of the Sudreys, the Southern Isles. He wondered at the rowers not tiring, with those long and heavy sweeps, three men to each; and was told that practised hands could keep it up for ten to twelve hours, and sixty or seventy miles, if the seas were not too unkind, and the whisky did not run out.

It did not take them quite as long as that to reach Gigha, where Torquil MacNeill welcomed them. He told the bishop that he was a most suitable visitor, for the original name of the island was Gudoy, meaning in Norse the Isle of God. He took them to see Kilchattan, its church with its consecration cross and its famous standing stone carved with Ogham characters, these also having links with Columba. He invited the priest there back to Ardminish with them for an evening meal and talk with the bishop. He told Angus that he was not long back from a visit to Boisdale, and of his plans for that place.

Angus did not know how much of this travel Bishop Andrew could take at one time, unused as he was to voyaging. Probably, if they called at the four main chapels on Islay that would be enough for this first visit. Jura, Oronsay, Coll, Tiree and the rest would have to wait.

Crossing the sound, on the way to Finlaggan, they stopped at Keills, near to Port Askaig, which they passed so often, the chapel tiny but having a notable grave slab carved with galley, beasts and crucifix; also nearby a cross-shaft, most decorative, rising like any standing stone. Here the priest was not present, being at his other charge of Kilmeny to the south. So they passed the night at the lordship's principal castle, Finlaggan itself, which Angus so seldom visited; and the prelate learned something of the story of the Isles over which he now had spiritual oversight.

Next day they visited Kilmeny, Kildalton, Kilchairn and Kilnave, all with their notable features, high crosses and basin fonts, with satisfactory interviews with the clerics. Then they were able to return to Dunaverty and Saddell, something achieved, the bishop grateful. They asked him about Man, but were told that this had its own bishop, one Marcusa based at Fountains Abbey.

Abbot Fergus told them he had heard that Bruce had announced from his castle of Turnberry that the throne was his to mount, and that the Primate, Bishop William Lamberton of St Andrews, gave his fullest support, and would in due course anoint him when he was crowned, this as good as a declaration of war against Edward. Was Bruce prepared for that? Were his subjects-to-be?

Bishop Andrew said that he would be back, if they would spare him more of their time. He blessed them, with assurances of the Almighty's favour.

23

The following summer they heard that the heroic William Wallace, at London, had suffered the most dire and dreadful execution by Edward, charged as a traitor. He had been bound on a wooden sled and dragged behind a horse through the cobbled streets of the city, jeered at and spat upon by the crowds. At Smithfield market he had been mocked, then hanged, and while he was still conscious, his stomach cut open and his entrails removed before his eyes, then beheaded, and his heart and other parts burned, the head hung on London Bridge, limbs sent for exhibition at Newcastle, Berwick, Stirling and Perth.

Whatever else he had done, the Plantagenet, once called the First Knight of Christendom, this deed would stain his name for all time coming, one of the greatest figures in Scotland's story so treated.

Angus Og, for one, groaned aloud.

The word of it did more to arouse the Scots towards unity of action than anything else thus far, Bruce finding many coming to his cause.

That year in the Isles, its lord completed his extensive survey of his far-flung territories, by sailing all the way north from Skye, nearly another hundred miles, by the Applecross peninsula, Loch Torridon, the Melvaig peninsula, Loch Ewe, Gruinard, Loch Broom, the Summer Isles, Coigach, Stoer, Handa and Kinlochbervie to Cape Wrath itself, the most northerly tip of all the land, only the Orkney and Shetland isles ahead of him, these no domain of his. Admittedly this vast area was less populous than further south, and its chiefs but little involved in Isles affairs, less so even than those of the Outer Hebrides; but Angus did seek to reach out to them, to bind them closer and show his concern for them.

This lengthy voyage took weeks, all but months, and Ainea was not to be prevented from accompanying him, nor was she going to be parted from their two children for so long. So the dragonship had odd passengers on this occasion.

They had heard no more from Bishop Andrew meantime.

Paying a visit to Man shortly after they got back, they heard that King Edward was ill. Far from troubled by this news, they all but prayed that his sickness would be fatal.

Scotland should be blessed with a remission, at least; for even if Longshanks sent the Prince of Wales up there in his stead, that Plantagenet was not one to rival his sire in hostile fervour.

Not only the Isles passed the early winter in comparative peace.

Then, at the end of February 1306, more highly significant tidings came. Bruce had been at Dumfries, from his Lochmaben castle, to attend a justiciar meeting there, when Comyn had arrived from London. They had met in the Minorite or Grey Friars monastery in the town. Bruce had challenged his rival over his betrayal of the secret pact between them over the Scots throne and the lands to Edward. Tempers had flared, and Bruce, in fury, had drawn his dagger and stabbed, and this before the altar of the monks' church. Whether he had actually killed his enemy was uncertain. But when he had hurried out, in a state of shock, and told one of his vassals awaiting him, Kirkpatrick of Closeburn, that he feared that he had slain the Red Comyn, Kirkpatrick had grimly announced that he would "mak siccar" that is, make sure, and had gone within to do so, sword in hand.

So now Comyn was dead, and Bruce had no real rival for the throne of Scotland. But he had created other hindrances by his impetuous action. By the killing, in a church, and before the altar of all places, this where the confrontation had occurred, he had committed the unforgivable sin in churchmen's eyes. For this, he would be excommunicated, nothing surer. The Pope would see to that. And an excommunicate could not be given any of the services of Holy Church, including the essential one of being crowned and anointed.

As this dawned on him, Bruce had calculated. It would take some three weeks for the news of his action to reach Rome, and another three weeks for the undoubted excommunication to get back from the Vatican to Scotland. Thereafter, Bishop Lamberton, Primate and head of the Church in this land, however supportive, could by no means perform the necessary coronation service – and no one else could. So he, Bruce, had six weeks, that only, to get his grasp on the throne, thanks to his ungovernable rage at his betrayer. Six weeks. Could all that was necessary to ascend the throne, at Scone, the crowning-place of the Kings of Scots, be validly arranged and executed in that short space of time? It seemed scarcely possible, and not only to Bruce.

Angus shook his head over it all, the folly of it. But he did not condemn Bruce out of hand, faced as he had been by this basest treachery, and after the secret bargain struck. In the circumstances, he could not swear that he would not have done the same himself. Many another, no doubt, felt similarly.

They waited, as did all the land.

It was a full month before the so vital information reached Ardtornish. It was done. Scotland had a king again, other than the dethroned and useless John Balliol, however precarious his grip on the crown. Well within those precious six weeks, all had been achieved. Bruce had been accepted and crowned at Scone in the traditional coronation ceremony, and with the participation of the two essential characters, the Primate and a representative of the MacDuffs, hereditary Coroners. Unfortunately the present Earl of Fife, head of the MacDuffs, had been a friend of Comyn, and was lying low; and his sister,

Isabella, was married to the Black Comyn, the Earl of Buchan. But she, a high-spirited and patriotic woman, had come herself to Scone as substitute for her brother, whether with her husband's agreement or otherwise, and had duly placed the crown on Bruce's head, while Lamberton applied the holy oil, and the cheers had rung out.

For better or for worse, Robert the First had commenced his reign, and not yet announced, in Scotland, as excommunicate. It was scarcely a promising start, but it was a new beginning for the most ancient kingdom in Christendom.

What would Edward Longshanks do now, sick man as he might be?

24

They had another visit from Bishop Andrew, and took him to some of the other isles, large Mull, Iona, Oronsay, Colonsay, Coll, Tiree, Eigg and Rhum. He was, naturally, greatly interested in Iona, all but birthplace of Christianity for so much of Scotland, and burial-place of the Kings of Scots, the abbot there esteemed the most prominent cleric of the Isles. There was so much to see here that they stayed the night with the abbot who had conducted them round in person.

Small Oronsay pleased him also, with its priory and crosses and Norse ship-burial site; and Tiree, said to be the first landing-place of the Cruithne, or Picts, on Scotland, having no fewer than fifteen chapels for its large population, one of them, Kilkenneth, having an underground gallery.

Angus and Ainea saw and learned much that they would not have done otherwise, and which they realised was good for them.

By the end of this visit, the prelate had become a friend.

He told them that he had been present, with other bishops, at Bruce's coronation, and described much of that great event, and of the situation to the east generally, of how stirred and uplifted the people were over this so important development for the nation, acclaim coming from all quarters, even from some that had not been in favour of Bruce earlier, especially among the nobility. But the governor, the Earl of Richmond, had been reinforced by the coming of the warrior Earl of Pembroke, Aymer de Vallance, sent up by Edward to bring the insolent usurper of the throne to him for punishment, this with a large army to aid in the process. So the new monarch would have to beware, and his nation's loyalty to him tested indeed.

Angus asked about the attitude towards the death of the Comyn, especially that of the churchmen, and the bishop had to admit that here was a matter of question, debate and mixed reactions. Yes, Bruce was now excommunicated by the Vatican, and in theory the Primate's anointing of him was invalid. But Lamberton and most of the other prelates were declaring that even the pontiff could make a mistake, and had done in this instance, because of wrong information. The slaying was not, in fact, murder but an act of national need, the removal of a forsworn traitor, much as if it had been done in battle for the realm's weal. This made sense to Angus, even though some ecclesiastical purists might see it otherwise.

Asking where Bruce was now, in the face of Richmond's and Pembroke's potent threat, they were told that the new monarch had based himself at Perth, from which he could flee into the Highlands if the worst came to the worst. He had summoned all leal men to rally to his standard. It was an unchancy way to start a reign, but Bruce clearly had known it would be thus.

They heard also about the new monarch's brothers, of whom they knew little, but now suddenly become important. The eldest, significantly named Edward, after the Plantagenet, by their two-way-facing father, alleged to be headstrong, with Nigel, Thomas and Alexander. They seemed to be supportive. Elizabeth de Burgh, now queen, was with her husband always, it obviously a love-match, with Isabella of Buchan presently acting as her lady-in-waiting, a curious situation, the daughter of the Earl of Ulster and the wife of a Comyn, this so close to the enemy of both men.

When they delivered the bishop back to Abbot Fergus at Saddell, they learned further that Bruce had gathered an army of sorts at Perth, and that one of his principal leaders was their own neighbour, Campbell of Lochawe, not exactly an Islesman but not far off it, another interesting affiliation. The Earls of Atholl, Lennox and Menteith had come out in favour of the new monarch.

Angus had his own problems to face at this time. William, Earl of Ross was proving to be something of a nuisance in the north-east, and encroaching on the domains of MacDonald of Clanranald, these descendants of Somerled, and owning large territories north of Skye. This earl happened to be hereditary Abbot of Applecross, in the old Columban Church polity, although he was no churchman, and was now claiming that quite substantial area in the midst of Clanranald lands, this long a source of dispute. But he, the earl, was also causing upset to the east. Ross was a name given to a vast area stretching from the Atlantic to the Norse Sea, Wester and Easter Ross, although the actual name derived from *ros*, a headland, and this referred to that great peninsula on the east coast known as the Black Isle – not that it was an island at all. This, and Cromarty, and further to the north up to the bounds of the earldoms of Sutherland and Caithness, was the Earl William's lordship – all far indeed from Applecross in *Wester* Ross. But now he was seeking to take over lands in that direction, Cameron and Mackenzie country, and these mainland clans were appealing to Clanranald for help in repelling him, asserting that the earl was indeed intending to dominate all, right to his claimed Applecross heritage. Clanranald, in turn, appealed to Angus.

Something had to be done about this; but not, if possible, armed intervention. The Isles' sway eastwards on the Highland mainland was very indeterminate as to its boundaries, and Angus certainly did not want any sort of battle with Ross, Sutherland, or even Moray earldoms further south, these verging on the lands of the Comyn Earl of Buchan, especially at a time when the new King of Scots was endeavouring to unite all his nobles and lords against the English. So, a visit to William of Ross, wherever he was, for parley and negotiation was indicated, taking as strong a line as possible, but with heed and care, for the elderly Ross's second son was married to Comyn of Badenoch's daughter, therefore connected with the MacDougalls of Lorn and Ian Bacach. This confrontation would have to be conducted apparently as from strength, but with due caution. Here was no expedition on which to take Ainea.

From Dunaverty, with Ewan, Angus sailed up to the Firth of Lorn and into the long sea loch of Linnhe, and on North by east under the towering bulk of Beinn Nevis, to Loch Eil. There he had to leave the dragonship, and borrow garrons from the Cameron chief to take him and a small escort onwards. Lochiel said that Ross was thought to be in the Cannich area, where that glen joined Strath Glass, Glen Affric and Glen Urquhart, a very strategic position, verging on the Clanranald country, and from there seeking to subdue the lesser clans of MacDonell, Mathieson and Bisset.

Cameron of Lochiel himself led Angus and Ewan ever north-wards through the mountains of his own Arkaig and Glens Garry and Moriston for almost forty difficult miles, to reach long Loch Affric, where the Mackenzie chieftain put them up, and told them that William of Ross was indeed thought to be still at Cannich, with his elder son Hugh. He was summoning all the leaders of the clans of these many glens to meet him there and accept his overlordship, on threat of armed assault. Angus declared that they would have to see about that!

Reaching Cannich at length, they found quite a large con-tingent of Rossmen encamped at the MacDonell house, these staring at the newcomers on their horses. They were taken to Ross and his son, with no sign of MacDonell, who had seemingly fled. The earl was elderly, and it was evident from the start that the dominant figure was the master, Hugh, an assertive young man, who seemed unimpressed by this visit from the Lord of the Isles, although his father was more respectful.

Angus did not beat about the bush. "I have come to ask why you have come in strength into this terrain of clans which are under the authority of Clanranald, and therefore of myself, my lord? Thus far from your own lands?"

"None so far!" It was the Master of Ross who answered. "Applecross is ours, part of Ross."

"The ancient *abbacy* of Applecross you may claim is yours by name, but that is all, sir. All the rest of that great headland, between Lochs Kishorn and Torridon and Maree, is MacDonald of Clanranald's land." It was the earl Angus addressed. "Your Ross is *Easter* Ross. This is Wester, and comes under *my* sway."

"It is far from your islands, my lord," the father said, but in a very different tone from his son's.

"As are Cowal, Argyll, Morvern, Ardnamurchan, Moidart, Morar and Knoydart, all on the mainland. What makes Applecross different? The former abbey of the Columban Church, long since gone, never laid claim to other than the small monkish settlement there, over the high hills. This reached from the sea. As *I* shall do, if need be!"

The master glared. "Are you threatening us?"

"Not threatening – warning! And not only over Applecross and Torridon and thereabouts. This Cannich and Affric and Strathglass – you should not be here with armed men. Nor in the Cameron country of Arkaig. Aye, and Glengarry of the MacDonalds."

Lochiel spoke up. "Some of my folk have suffered at your hands, my lord of Ross. It must stop."

"Hold your ill tongue, Bent Nose!" the Master jerked.

"I would advise you, my lord of Ross, to have your son hold his tongue in my presence!" Angus said. "I did not come here to bicker and argue. I came to tell you that your earldom of Ross remains *Easter*. Wester is mine. And I will ensure that it is not encroached upon."

"How will you do that?" the master asked fleeringly. "We have a sufficiency of men to enforce our claims."

"I can have two hundred longships off Applecross in one week's time, sirrah. Double that, if need be. And if that is not sufficient to halt you, they can sail right round the land and down to your eastern shores, to enter Dornoch and Cromarty and Beauly Firths. That might he more . . . effective?"

"No, no!" the Earl William exclaimed. "Not that. There must be no such warfare." He looked at his son. "Enough, Hugh – enough! We must have no strife with the Islesmen. Hear me."

Angus looked from one to the other. "See you – Applecross, the old abbey grounds, I accept as yours. And access to it, through the mountains. That I will tell Clanranald. So long as you leave all west of Glen More and Loch Ness unraided. Otherwise, I gather my longships and birlinns. Is it understood?"

The earl nodded, his son set-faced.

They parted, no love lost, but the situation clear enough.

Cameron thanked Angus warmly. They ought to get as far as his Arkaig for the night.

At Dunaverty news was awaiting Angus. The new King Robert had been forced to fight a battle at Methven, not far west of Perth, and had been sorely defeated by the vastly greater strength of Aymer de Vallance, Earl of Pembroke. He and his wife and brothers had had to flee westwards, pursued, by Strathearn and Glen Ogle and Glen Dochart, MacNab country, heading for the security of Argyll, Campbell of Lochawe's land, this in mid-June. They had got as far as Dalrigh, near to Tyndrum in Mamlorn, some sixty miles, halting at St Fillan's sanctuary. Then, unexpectedly, they were met and attacked by none other than Ian Bacach, Lame John MacDougall of Lorn, who ambushed them, with a large company, in a river gorge. The king, his shoulder injured at Methven, had been unable to wield his battle-axe to best effect, and MacDougall, singling him out and shouting that he was avenging the murdered Red Comyn, tried to unseat the new monarch from his saddle. Bruce had managed to pull away from him in the mêlée, but had had his royal lion rampant cloak and jewelled clasp torn from his shoulder. His party had suffered casualties, but fortunately the queen and Bruce's daughter Marjorie by his earlier marriage had managed to win back out of the gorge; this the second defeat, even if only a small one. Thereafter there had been a parting, his brother Nigel and the Earl of Atholl being sent north with Elizabeth and Marjorie to Kildrummy Castle in Aberdeenshire, the latter's home, and if assailed there, to go on to reach the very north of Scotland, at Caithness or the Orkneys, there to escape to friendly Norway. The king himself, with his brother Edward, the Campbell and a few others, had sought refuge in the mountains. Where they all were now was not known.

It was a sorry tale indeed that the friars had told. Angus cursed Ian Bacach, one of his own people, although half a Comyn.

What now, then? Was Bruce's brief reign already coming to an end when it had scarcely begin? Was Scotland doomed to extinction as a free nation? And if so, could the Isles remain independent?

25

It was August, two months after Bruce's defeat, before further information reached Dunaverty as to the national situation, and this by the most unexpected, indeed remarkable circumstances, hardly to be believed. A small boat sailed down from Saddell, rather crowded, carrying a group of men to land at the anchorage and climb up to the castle. This shortly before Angus was due to sail for Man, all these strangers save for one, Sir Neil Campbell of Lochawe. He, dark and swarthily good-looking, hailed Angus as he was instructing some of his longships' captains as to making a call at Rathlin Island on the way to Peel.

"Ha, my lord Angus!" the Campbell called. "We have come to you in some need, assured of your goodwill." He turned. "Sire, I would present to you Angus Og mac Donald, Lord of the Isles."

That one word Sire had Angus staring. Only a monarch could be so addressed. Of a group of seven, one took a pace forward. He was clad no differently from the others, in good but travel-stained, all but ragged, garb, a man probably in his early thirties, auburn-haired, of medium height, wide-shouldered and strong-featured. He raised a hand.

"I have heard much of you, my lord," he said. "And had not thought to thrust myself upon you thus. But beggars may not choose. And I am that this day, I fear!"

"You . . . you are the Bruce? The king? High King of Scots?" Angus got out. "The Campbell named you Sire. Can it be true . . . ?"

"Sir Neil is generous! In name, I am King of Scots, yes. But in fact, my lord, I am no more than a hunted fugitive, I fear. Brought to you for succour in my extremity."

"His Grace seeks your aid, my lord. He must leave this land. Win over to Ireland; that probably would be best. To Antrim. Or other secure haven, where he may rest for a while. Recover from his wound, from his betrayal and misfortunes. We judged that you would not fail our sovereign-lord."

"Highness, I am . . . overwhelmed!" Angus bowed, and reached out to take the royal hand and kiss it. "Here is a wonder! I am at your service. All the Isles are."

"You say so, my lord? I understood that you saw yourself as an independent prince!"

"I see the Isles as a lordship . . . apart, Sire. But with strong links with Scotland. And greet you as monarch."

"Not all do." That was Campbell again. "MacDougall of Lorn acts otherwise. I would have taken His Grace to my Argyll, but it is over-close to Lorn for his safety. So we come to you. The good abbot at Saddell assured us that you would help His Grace."

"Here is my brother Edward," the king said. "And my lord Earl of Lennox. Also Sir James Douglas, Sir Gilbert Hay and Sir William Bellenden, all of whom have sacrificed much for me."

Angus gestured towards these others. "All are welcome to Dunaverty. But, Highness, come you into my house. Honour it by your presence."

Within, an astonished Ainea was presented, and was swiftly able to cope with the situation effectively, providing food and drink and accommodation, nowise put about. The royal party was appreciative indeed for the welcome and the comfort, after all the distresses and rough living.

Round a table, presently, the hosts learned something of the circumstances that had brought these lofty fugitives to Kintyre. It seemed that after the MacDougall attack at Tyndrum, and the consequent dividing up of the company and sending

208

the queen and princess to the north, Bruce and the remainder set off southwards for the Lennox country and the Loch Lomond area. There, with MacGregor help, they had found the Earl Malcolm dispossessed of his castles and houses by the English and the Comyns, and encamped on an island at the southern end of the loch. With the enemy nearby and occupying his land, this was no place for the earl or his monarch to remain, and a move westwards for Argyll had begun. The MacGregor chief had found them boats to take them across Clyde to Bute, and from there they had headed for Kintyre, landing eventually at Ugadale, just south of Saddell. So here they were, seeking secure refuge where they could not be assailed by the English occupying forces and those who treacherously supported them. Antrim probably.

Angus was very doubtful about Antrim. The word was that de Burgh was back in Ulster and in strength, making his presence felt; that was the reason for going down to the Isle of Man to confer with Rory mac Alan.

No firm decision was taken that evening, the newcomers weary and uncertain of mind, and Bruce in pain from his shoulder.

But next day there was a further development, this the arrival at Dunaverty, via Saddell again, of a veteran supporter of the king from his own Carrick territory, Sir Robert Boyd of Noddsdale, come seeking the monarch from Ayrshire. It seemed that it had become known in the land, and to the enemy also, inevitably, that the new king had been in the Lennox country. So a large force of the invaders had assembled at Dumbarton Castle, on the Clyde, the stronghold of Sir John Stewart of Menteith, Wallace's betrayer, this under a newcomer, Sir John de Botetourt, Edward Longshank's own bastard son and a reputedly fierce character, with three thousand men. Vessels were being requisitioned from all the Clyde ports and havens to carry this host westwards towards these parts, the Sudreys or South Isles, or if necessary Man or

Ulster or wherever the fugitives were fleeing, Edward determined to capture his one-time friend.

This Boyd brought even more dire news. Nigel Bruce was dead, captured at Kildrummy Castle in Aberdeenshire by Pembroke, and taken south to be hanged, drawn and quartered. Others with him. But the Earl of Atholl, with the queen and princess, had managed to escape, and were fleeing north, hoping somehow to get ship to Norway, where one of Bruce's sisters, Isabel, was queen to King Eric.

This terrible death of his brother had the king desolated, all but prostrated, his other brother Edward also, Bruce blaming himself for bringing appalling tragedy on his family and friends by this ascent of his to the throne.

When he could bring himself and others to consider the immediate future with some coherence, two possible courses seemed to offer themselves. He could borrow one of Angus's galleys, and sail north through the Isles to reach Caithness or the Orkneys, there hopefully to join up with his Elizabeth and daughter Marjorie, and with them head for safety in Norway. Or he could linger here in the Isles themselves until he could plan some effort to recover his kingdom. This last, at least, would be a positive policy, and be seen as such. He was, after all, God's anointed King of Scots and must, surely, seek somehow to deliver his people from the iron grip of Edward Plantagenet. So be it. Bide somewhere in the Isles meantime.

Angus, faced with playing host to the hunted king, and thus incurring the wrath and enmity of Longshanks, with almost certain attack by the illegitimate son Botetourt, also Richmond and Pembroke with their thousands, had to make his own vital decisions. He would send out orders for a great mustering of his longships fleet, and this hopefully could tear apart any assemblage of the sort of vessels the enemy could gather, like a wolf among lambs. But meantime this Dunaverty was too close and easily reached from the Clyde and Bute or Arran. So he would take Bruce and his party out to Rathlin, where they would be safe, while he discovered the situation on the mainland, at Man and in Ulster, and could plan accordingly. He did not want war with England, but he must be ready for the threat of it.

Orders were sent to MacLean of Duart to muster the fleet. Then it was off to Rathlin with his dragonship and escort of longships. Angus would leave the fugitives on the island, cross over the few miles to the Antrim coast to learn the position prevailing in Ulster, then head south for Man for more information, and to warn Rory of possible danger from the Clyde. Five days, or six? He would take Ainea and the children in the dragonship, in case of attack on Dunaverty.

These visits made, situations discovered, warnings given but no major developments to report, Angus and family sailed back to Rathlin in fair September weather. They found the royal party settled comfortably enough in the small tower-house, scarcely a castle, this beside the monastery that Columba had founded, the few monks there much exercised by having the King of Scots as their guest.

Awaiting at Rathlin was Ewan from Ardtornish, sent by Gillemoir MacLean, with the message that he and the fleet would be at the island very shortly, ready for whatever action its lord required of it.

So far so good. Angus sent a longship across to Dunaverty to see whether there had been any happenings there. The report brought back was that all was unchanged around Saddell and the Mull of Kintyre.

Ainea and the youngsters were quite happily installed with the king and his group, however crowded it all made the establishment, the monks most attentive, a notable change for them as this invasion was from their normal all but hermit-like existence on this isolated isle.

The great flotilla, under Duart, arrived two days later, a vast concourse of almost two hundred longships, birlinns and galleys, this all quite astonishing Bruce and his friends by its size and air of power and authority. Angus told him that he would make a demonstration progress, this up the Kilbrannan Sound, round Arran into the Clyde estuary and the Kyles of Bute, down the Renfrewshire and Ayrshire and Galloway coasts, sail across Solway and down the Cumbrian and Lancaster shorelines, then round Man and up the Irish seaboard – this to make clear to the enemy that he could destroy any shipping gathered to transport armed forces, and so inhibit attack therefrom. Meanwhile the king could stay on at Rathlin if so he wished, or sail up through the Isles, secure. What did he foresee as his best course at this stage?

Bruce said that, in consultation with his friends here, he had come to the conclusion that he should try to contact the Earl of Ross. With Angus and his people supporting him, if he could win over Ross, then he would have all the north and west of Scotland in his favour, a vast area, from which he could plan his attempts to win back the Lowlands and the enemy-occupied south. Earl William had as yet taken little active part in the warfare, although he had fought at the sorry Battle of Dunbar. He had been a supporter of the Comyn, admittedly, his second son married to a daughter of the Black Comyn, Earl of Buchan. But if he could be persuaded to join the royal cause he could be a very valuable help. So, if he, Bruce, could sail round the land to Easter Ross, and approach the earl, great benefit might accrue. Also he could learn the situation regarding his Elizabeth and daughter Marjorie, whether they had escaped to Norway, this ever on his mind.

Angus was more than doubtful, needless to say, about William of Ross, especially as to his son, the master. But he could not deny that if these could be induced to support the king the royal situation would be greatly improved. And the anxiety over the queen was understandable. So he would aid in this as best he could. He would provide the king with one of his galleys, and he could sail northwards and then eastwards to reach the Ross domains, passing close to Orkney on the way, where his wife and daughter might have gone.

King Robert was grateful.

Angus allotted the royal group the twenty-six-oared galley under MacDonald of Kiloran, a reliable far-out kinsman, with authority, if necessary, to call on help from anyone in the Isles.

So it was parting, the great fleet to make its lengthy procession round all the coastlines, making itself very evident; and the king setting off northwards in the galley. Ainea and the children would remain with the monks on Rathlin meantime.

26

October's weather beginning to deteriorate, Angus and Ainea returned to Ardtornish for the winter months, no sort of trouble having occurred at Kintyre or elsewhere in the Sudreys, the English invaders evidently having got the message from that flourish of the Isles fleet. The family had been only a few days settled in when noteworthy news was brought to them, and by the son of MacDonald of Kiloran who had taken the king north. He came alone, his father dead.

He told that the king had never reached Easter Ross, nor indeed now intended to. He was living in the care of the Lady Christina of Garmoran, at Castle Tioram in Moidart, not far north of Ardnamurchan.

It made a strange story. The galley had been sailing northwards, and was between Eigg and the Morar coast, when ahead of them they saw three other galleys none so different from their own. As they drew nearer they saw that one of these bore the galley of the Isles on its sail, but the other two showed the red and gold of Ross – and that the two latter were chasing and attacking the former. Kiloran, of course, would not allow an Isles vessel to be assailed in Isles seas by any, especially Ross craft, and he had ordered his crew to speed to its aid.

As they closed, his father had seen that there was the outline of a great fish painted on the Isles ship's sail; this was the device of his own chief, Clanranald. King of Scots aboard or no, he was for taking a hand here.

Shouting their clan's slogan, they had driven in on the small battle, small but violent and bloody. Kiloran himself had been felled, slain, as he jumped aboard the Isles craft amidst hand-to-hand fighting. On the after-deck a woman was to be seen, standing alone. In fury the newcomers surged to avenge their leader, and after a fierce struggle, in which the king himself had wielded his battle-axe, the Rossmen gave up, scrambled back to their own vessels, such as could, and those two ships drew off and turned to head northwards.

The victors found that the woman was Christina MacRuarie of Garmoran, only child and heiress of the MacRuarie chief, of the Clanranald line, descended from Somerled. The captain of the vessel was her nephew, Ranald MacRuarie of Smirisary.

With many wounded aboard, and the dead, they had made directly for Castle Tioram, the Garmoran seat, only an hour's sail away.

It was an astonishing situation. Here the king had been making for Easter Ross to seek to enroll its earl in his cause, but instead had become involved in battle, and with the earl's ships, led by the Master of Ross, whom they had managed to drive off. It was scarcely a good introduction for any efforts of support from that character's father.

Much concerned, Angus decided that he must go up forthwith to Garmoran, to discover the position and what was to be done about it. And since a woman was involved, the Lady Christina whom he knew, he would take Ainea with him.

Without undue delay they were off. It was no lengthy journey from Ardtornish, a day's sailing up the Sound of Mull and round the Point of Ardnamucchan to Eilean Shona and Moidart, fifty miles.

Castle Tioram, a large stronghold, was quite unusually sited on a rocky half-tide islet which all but blocked the mouth of Loch Moidart, a dominant position. It was unlike Dunaverty or Ardtornish, really only a lofty perimeter wall some thirty feet high, topped by a parapet and wall walk, this following the contours of the rock, with flanking towers at angles, but no central keep. Within the irregularly shaped enclosure was all but a village, clustered round a long, low hall-house, with thatched roofs, a chapel close by, cot-houses, stables, stores and byres. Angus knew it well.

They found the king and his party being well entertained, in more comfort than they had known for many a day, Lady Christina, a highly attractive woman of much spirit, proving to be a generous hostess. But Bruce was in much distress. A wounded captive from one of the Ross ships, dying here, had revealed that Queen Elizabeth and the princess, having reached Tain in Easter Ross and taken refuge in St Duthac's renowned sanctuary, still on the way to Orkney, had been assailed there, sanctuary or none, by the Earl of Ross and his son, the Earl of Atholl slain, and the queen and princess handed over to the English.

Shocked by this shameful treachery, and condoling however inadequately with Bruce, Angus vowed to make Ross pay for this foul deed in any way he could.

They stayed two nights with Christina and her distinguished guests before leaving the king with assurance of support and goodwill. Any help he could usefully give would be forthcoming.

Angus decided that his first move against Ross should be to rouse the mainland clans to unite to push the Rosses back eastwards from the Great Glen and Loch Ness area, these the Camerons, MacDonells, Mackays, Morrisons and Mackintoshes. So he went up to Lochiel, and with the Cameron chief made a tour round the area east of Morvern, Glenfinnan, Lochaber, Glengarry, Glenmoriston, Glenaffric and Strathglass, stirring up the chieftains to positive action, forgetting their ongoing feuds with each other, and concentrating on getting rid of Ross influence, Cameron of Lochiel to be the leader, under his authority.

This endeavour, which had to be pursued on garron-back, took the rest of October and well into November. When he got back to Ardtornish, reasonably satisfied, it was to learn from Ainea that young Kiloran had brought news from Castle

Tioram. The king was still there. But he was planning action, and soon, while winter conditions inhibited Edward Long-shanks from making major armed assaults. He, Bruce, had sent his brother Edward in a borrowed MacRuarie longship down to the Galloway coast, there to reach his two other brothers, Thomas and Alexander, who were residing there and seeking to keep Annandale, Carrick and the West March of the Borderland in some sort of order. Edward was to lead his brothers in rousing all the southwest, as far as possible, to be ready to counter the Plantagenet's expected thrust northwards in the spring to reinforce Richmond and Pembroke. Long-shanks was based in the Carlisle area, and was reported to be summoning men from all his lords to rally to him there. Bruce himself intended to join his brothers shortly to lead the action.

Angus wondered how best he could aid the monarch. Hired men, gallowglasses, from Ulster? Bruce, whatever else, was wealthy, at least his great lands were, and this could be a major acquisition of strength. He could see O'Cahan about this. And a fleet of his own, taken to the Ayrshire and Galloway coasts? Would that help to deter Edward? At least it could enhearten the folk thereabouts; and the Plantagenet would be unhappy with a seaborne force getting behind him by the Solway Firth.

So it was up to Castle Tioram again with these suggestions.

He and Ainea found Bruce talking about taking his depar-ture, but clearly on very close terms with his hostess, she encouraging him in his plans to regain his throne, as well as, seemingly, encouraging him in more personal matters, a very positive female.

The king was grateful for Angus's offers of assistance, and much in favour of hiring Irish gallowglasses. He said that if he could be got to his own Carrick, and an Isles presence shown there, it would help. Angus pointed out that the Isle of Arran's east coast faced across Clyde to Carrick only some fifteen miles off. He could have Bruce on Arran in three days' sailing, even in this winter weather. This offer was accepted. But give

217

his brothers a few weeks to rouse the south-west, Yuletide over, while he himself waited to hear from Bishop David of Moray, one of the prestigious Moray family, who was in the Orkneys seeking to raise a force of the islanders and Caithnessmen to threaten Ross and so hold that wretched earl and his sons back from any attempt to aid the English. Then, after Yuletide, Arran for him.

So it was arranged. Meantime Angus would cross over to Antrim to see O'Cahan.

In due course the king's sail southwards to Arran was conducted in more spectacular style than he had anticipated. He went in one of Christina's longships – he had had some difficulty in dissuading that lady from accompanying him, this no activity for a woman – and he proceeded alongside Angus's dragonship, for that man had decided to make his demonstration down the Ayrshire and Galloway coasts immediately thereafter, to support the other Bruces' efforts and encourage the local folk to rally to their standard. The king himself would not go on to Galloway meantime, his aim first to discover what the position was in Carrick and Renfrew and the Glasgow area, much of it Stewart country, and their attitude uncertain. This to seek to discover before he actually landed in his own earldom. From Arran this ought to be ascertainable.

Not to herald the king's arrival on that isle, Angus left him in his borrowed longship to sail up the west side by the Kilbrannan sound, while he took his fleet up the Firth of Clyde as far as Bute and the south of Cowal, there to turn and head slowly down the Renfrewshire coast, by Wemyss Bay and Largs and the Cumbraes, showing themselves at all centres of population. Then on down the Ayrshire seaboard, wondering how Bruce was faring. Still onward to Galloway, a total of some one hundred and twenty miles.

At the Solway mouth he led the way north-westwards, to

cross to Antrim, then to head for Lough Foyle and Limavady, where O'Cahan ought to have a fair company of gallowglasses assembled for transport back to Galloway.

His father-in-law had not failed him, and had no fewer than four hundred Ulstermen gathered and waiting. These were taken aboard the ships, with supplies of food and drink, and next day they set sail, a laden fleet now.

They entered the long, narrow bay of Loch Ryan which all but divided the Rhinns of Galloway from the mainland, making for Stranraer, where the Bruce brothers were understood to be based. But at that quite large township Angus learned dire news indeed. The brothers they sought were no more. They had been betrayed by the Galloway clans of MacDouall and MacCann, adherents of the Comyn faction, captured and handed over to King Edward at Lanercost near Carlisle, and there had been hanged and beheaded in typical Plantagenet fashion.

Much shaken, Angus enquired as to the elder brother, Longshank's namesake, and was told that, as far as was known, he had not been taken, having gone north to Carrick to try to contact the king. How that sorely tried monarch would react to this, of now three brothers executed, could only be guessed at. Was any throne worth this?

What to do now, then? Here Angus had these hundreds of gallowglasses, and no one to hand them over to. Back up to Carrick seemed to be the only answer, to seek to find the remaining two royal brothers, who presumably would be glad to have them. It was all very much a hit or miss situation – but he had to do something.

It proved a less difficult task for Angus than he had feared. For, sailing up the Ayrshire coast and making for Ayr itself to seek information, passing the Maidenhead Point, in the sheltered haven below they saw two obviously Isles longships moored, almost certainly Christina MacRuarie's vessels. Drawing in his dragonship to these, he discovered that they were the two craft loaned to Bruce and Edward, and that these brothers were now up in Turnberry Castle nearby, which they had managed to capture, with the aid of the crews and local folk, ousting the English governor, Percy of Northumberland; after all, it was in this hold that both brothers had been born.

So it was up to the castle just to the south, where they found the king and Edward, in a state of great distress over the deaths of their brothers, however slightly encouraged by this taking of their former home, the first little victory of the reign. And glad they were to see Angus and hear of the reinforcements, hundreds of Irishmen, down at the ships. They could do with them indeed, and would pay for more.

The brothers' family woes were the worse for other tidings they had just been told. Queen Elizabeth was now imprisoned at Holderness, on the Humber. Princess Marjorie had been sent to the Tower of London, to be kept alone, to see and speak to none. The Countess of Buchan, who had helped at Bruce's coronation as a MacDuff, was actually confined in a cage hanging in the open air from the walls of Berwick Castle. And Mary Bruce, their sister, in a similar cage at Roxburgh Castle. Edward Plantagenet might be a sick man, sick in body now as well as in mind, but he had not been idle these winter months in Cumbria, waiting.

Angus could not express his horror and dismay adequately at these acts of depravity. What could he say? But, more important, what could he do further to aid the devastated brothers?

The king said that, meantime, the best way he could serve was to go back to Ulster and enrol a further contingent of gallowglasses, if he could. He had managed to gather in much of the rentals for these Carrick lands, so long unpaid, and Angus could take the necessary moneys back to his gudesire, O'Cahan. Did he think that such reinforcements would be forthcoming?

Angus deemed that they would. O'Cahan, and others no

doubt, saw these contributions in men as a means of helping to keep the Plantagenet preoccupied in Scotland, and thus limiting his efforts in Ireland. Even de Burgh was much more frequently with Edward these days than in Ulster. So this of the Irish helping the King of Scots also benefited themselves. He, Angus Og, would seek to bring more Ulstermen over. And he would continue to patrol the Scottish coasts with his ships, which, all agreed, was of much value in deterring Longshanks. When it came to actual battle, the fleet's nearby presence would be a major threat to the enemy.

So it was back to Antrim. When would Edward deem it time to strike? How long would he wait in Cumberland?

27

That question, which so preoccupied Scots minds, posed its own problem for Bruce and his supporters. Would military activity, on such scale as he was able to promote, only hasten the Plantagenet's further invasion? It could well do so. On the other hand, failure to use such forces as they were accumulating in the south-west could result in apathy and lowered morale on the Scots side. The king must be seen by his people to be a fighter, not just a waiter on events. There was little use in rallying men to arms and then leaving them to wait, idle. Some demonstration of authority and challenge had to be made that spring, at the risk of bringing Edward over the border the sooner.

The issue was more or less forced to decision by events themselves. Monthermer, Earl of Gloucester, was acting as English master of this Ayrshire and Galloway area, and allegedly being criticised by Longshanks and by Pembroke for not reacting sufficiently strongly against Bruce and his brother in Carrick. He was based on Kilmarnock, a dozen miles or so north-east of Ayr and some twenty-five miles from Turnberry. He assembled his strength and marched south.

When the king heard of this, coinciding with Angus's return with another four hundred Ulstermen, he urged that the Isles fleet should not exactly assail the fortified town of Ayr, whither Gloucester appeared to be heading, but seem to threaten it offshore. Bruce and his lieutenants had left Turnberry, as too close to Ayr, leaving a garrison under Hay to hold the castle. They were now based in the difficult and hilly country of Loch Doon and Glen Trool, on the Galloway border, fully a score of miles to the south. This of Gloucester taking Ayr was ominous, and ought to be countered, or the king could find himself wedged between two English armies, north and south. So he decided to test his strength, such as it now was, against Gloucester, who was not reputed to be any mighty warrior, however high-born, and march on Ayr.

This speedily became known to the enemy, it seemed, and with Angus's fleet blockading the port and Bruce's mixed force advancing from the south, Gloucester returned to Kilmarnock, which he could hold more readily, to the king's disappointment. But he had to tackle the English now that he had started, or his repute would suffer. He headed north by east, and sent word for Angus to bring on as many men from his ships as was possible, to help.

The Isles contingent, of some two hundred, on foot necessarily, was nearing Kilmarnock, in the Tarbolton area, when they were met by messengers from Bruce. They were not to be involved in any attack on Kilmarnock meantime. The king had heard that Pembroke, presumably doubting Gloucester's efficacy, was coming south in haste from Stirling to aid him. This altered all, a vastly greater threat. But at least any confrontation would be taking place in Carrick – and Bruce and his brother knew Carrick's land over every mile. And they believed that they could take advantage of this knowledge here and now. To reach Kilmarnock from Stirling, Pembroke, taking the obvious short route, would have to come down to the River Irvine and on through hilly country by Newmilns and Galston. Before reaching these places he would have to traverse hills and moorland below Loudoun Hill, and here it ought to be possible to, as it were, ambush him, in difficult country for a horsed force. They would not have to traverse an actual pass, but the road wound its way below the hill on one side and boggy land on the other. The cavalry would be forced hereabouts to ride only three or four abreast, and this would string out the force greatly, making it vulnerable, with leadership scarcely possible for a mile or so. The Bruce people, including the gallowglasses, were on foot, and could use these conditions to seek to cut up the enemy into small sections, partly by hurling themselves down the hillside, and partly by leaping and jumping their way through the bog and so reaching the horsemen, there either to hamstring the horses, or slit their bellies and so bring down the riders, this while their leaders were far from most of them inevitably in what could be a mile-long procession. Angus Og should bring his contingent, led by the messengers, to the southern end of this chosen ambuscade, and advance up it, to deal with any escaping cavalry, and pose an additional threat.

This suited Angus well enough, and they marched on, wondering whether Pembroke had yet got thus far, and if so whether he had scouts forward, to warn him of the dangers of this stretch of Loudoun terrain. After all, he must surely have heard of Wallace's victory here.

Apparently they still had some miles to go north-eastwards to reach this strategic area; so events might well make them arrive too late to be effective.

That this proved to be the case was demonstrated, that June afternoon, when, among low hills and with a higher peaked summit coming into sight ahead, pointed out as Loudoun Hill, suddenly half a dozen horsemen came spurring round a bend of the valley they were in. At sight of a substantial body of men blocking their way, these riders, obviously fleeing, swerved off right and left, and raced past southwards. A minute or two later three more mounted men appeared, and were equally determined not to get involved with Angus's people, pulling away, most evidently eager to get clear of the vicinity.

It looked as though the ambuscade had been a success.

Round another bend, they came to a much more open stretch, with the river running through it amidst boggy levels on one side and the hill, steeper now, on the other. And the scene ahead was one of havoc and chaos and slaughter, riderless horses milling about, many cut down, men's and beasts' bodies everywhere, moaning and yelling sounding, while men on foot, swords and dirks in hand, presumably Bruce's people, were seeking further victims and robbing the fallen. Moving in on it all, some of these, questioned, declared that the king and their other leaders were well forward, chasing the enemy as best they could, the English fleeing northwards whence they had come. It had been a great victory, the damnable invaders shattered.

Heading on through the horror of it, with casualties all the way, eventually Angus came to a knot of men, with a few horses, captured or otherwise, among whom they saw King Robert and his brother.

Hurrying forward, Angus was greeted and hailed warmly, even though he had come too late to be of any use. Bruce was clearly much exhilarated, without being boastful. The day was his, very much so. He had made the land fight for him, as Wallace had taught him to do, using that steep hillside and the wide swamp on the other side to constrain and defeat the strung-out English cavalry, his only complaint that they had failed to capture Pembroke himself and many of his fleeing knights, not having the horses to pursue them. If Turnberry had been a small victory, this was a great one. It ought to rouse the nation. But what would it do to Edward Plantagenet? And what would Gloucester do now?

Presently the victors moved back southwards to a drier and more open space, in which to camp for the night, while the wounded were cared for and the dead piled in heaps for eventual burial. Much booty in arms, armour, gear and horses was gained from the fallen, even the Islesmen allotted some, unearned as it had been. Casualties among the Scots had been minimal. The gallowglass Ulstermen who had taken part were praised for their effectiveness.

That evening, round campfires, what to do about Gloucester at Kilmarnock was discussed. It was one thing to ambush a strung-out cavalry host, and quite another to assault a

225

walled town held by a forewarned force. Should they just leave it unchallenged and return to their Glen Trool fastnesses, however feeble this might seem? Angus asked, would not the townsfolk rise to help assail the invaders if an attack was staged by the king's force? This was accepted as possible, but unarmed citizenry were not likely to make any great impact on Gloucester's troops, and would pay dearly for it.

The decision taken was that at least a challenging gesture should be made on the morrow, but probably no attempt at actual assault, unless the enemy was clearly in difficulties. Gloucester might well have heard of Pembroke's defeat, some of the escaping horsemen possibly reaching the town, and be somewhat demoralised by the situation.

Next morning, then, it was marching for Kilmarnock, some of the leaders, including Angus, now mounted on captured horses. They had a dozen miles to go. Scouts ahead, also mounted, sought to discover the situation.

These were soon back, with reports that changed the direction of Bruce's force. Gloucester must have heard of Pembroke's defeat, and had presumably decided that he was in danger at Kilmarnock, so had promptly left the town at night and headed south. Where he was going was not known, but it could well be, in that direction, to seek to join King Edward at Carlisle. They would have expected him to go north, for Edinburgh, Stirling or Perth areas, where Richmond with the English leadership commanded all. But, no – southwards it seemed. And he had a long way to go to the border, one hundred miles.

There was little question as to what to do now. Bruce had intended to head for his secure fastnesses of Glen Trool and Loch Doon anyway, to assemble more strength, if possible, to face Longshanks. Now they would pursue Gloucester, in that same direction, and see if they could add to his worries. The English force would be mounted, whereas they themselves were a foot army, so they might not be able to catch up with the enemy.

Scouts ahead, in the Sorn area fifteen miles on, came back to tell that Gloucester's force had camped for the night near there, no great distance covered, but too far for Bruce's people to reach on foot. Yet a night attack on a sleeping camp would be their best tactic, however lacking in chivalry, rather than any attempt to defeat a horsed army. They could only head on at their best pace, and hope that the English got less far ahead of them.

They marched well into the June night, to halt for only a brief rest.

Next morning scouts were able to report that Gloucester was on the move again, none so very far ahead, not having made any early start.

Could they possibly reach the English?

Bruce pressed his men on. At Auchinleck they learned that Gloucester had reached that community and raided the village and area for provisions, lingering there a while, some of the local women suffering. While sympathising, the pursuit was cheered that, it seemed, Gloucester was in no great hurry in his progress southwards, presumably not knowing that he was being followed.

The June nights were not really dark. Bruce kept up the pace, however weary his people were with all this marching. At Cumnock the word was that the enemy had camped again for the night, not far ahead, much time evidently having been spent in scouring the countryside for food. Glaisnock was their present stopping-place.

Much elated, the king declared that, God willing, they could reach there well before dawn. He knew all this Carrick intimately, and Glaisnock would serve his purpose well enough. There were no real protests from the tired marchers as they trudged on.

The night was by no means over when they were able to see ahead of them, in fairly level cattle-country, the dull red glows of smouldering campfires. There was their target. The company was lined up and instructed. They numbered about six hundred, no great host, but enough to surround that camp and descend upon the sleepers. There would be sentinels posted, to be sure, but a fair degree of surprise ought to be achieved. Bruce would blow a horn for attack. Meanwhile, silence.

Angus and his crewmen crept southwards, right-about, round the area marked by those fires. No signs nor sounds of alarm reached them. In time they met others of their force coming round from the north. The camp was encircled. They waited.

Then suddenly there were shouts. Their presence had been discovered. Promptly the high notes of a horn sounded, Bruce's signal. Swords drawn, battle-axes and dirks at the ready, the encirclers surged forward.

What followed was, on the face of it, sheerest disorder in the half-dark, no least evident pattern or discipline about it, friend and foe quickly mixed up in smiting, stabbing and shouting frenzy, half-awake men running amok, arms sought, armour being donned, horses made for, all amidst yelling and shouted commands. A sort of hell developed, Angus for one unsure whom to strike at in the mêlée of struggling humanity. He found himself being all but ridden down by a man on a horse and slashed at with a sword. Dodging this, he did not slash back in case this was one of their own folk on a captured beast. Night-time and surprise attack might be very effective strategy, but it lent itself to unavoidable error and disarray among attackers as well as attacked. Angus found himself unable to act as any sort of leader.

More and more men had evidently reached the horses and mounted, this adding to the hazards and chaos.

The noise was distracting as it was appalling, helping to make men bereft of their wits.

Time became incalculable. But, presently, high above all the din, that horn sounded again. Was the Bruce sending a signal? And if so, for what? To rally to him? It came from not far ahead of Angus. He battled in that direction.

In normal battle, commanders' standards and banners marked the leadership; but here there was nothing of the sort. It was *Edward* Bruce whom Angus perceived, and then saw his brother nearby. The King shouted something incoherent, and pointed. It was horsemen that he seemed to be indicating, and these spurring off. Did this signify some sort of victory? Flight by the enemy, those who could escape on horseback, deserting the rest?

Panting, and standing beside the royal brothers, Angus saw ever more riders heading off. It did look like despair and departure. The fighting, however, went on around them, if fighting it could be called, a medley of screaming, cursing, smiting men.

They waited, then. What else was there for them to do?

Gradually the pandemonium began to decline and die away, as men came to recognise that the day, or night, was won and lost. Bruce blew on his horn again, and this time produced some recognisable effects. Men, their own men, surged towards him, and others ran off in different directions.

It was some time before any real order was achieved in that shattered encampment, and the situation fully assessed. If the night was theirs, clearly much of the enemy leadership had escaped. According to some of their folk these had been seen heading off due westwards. That is, in the Ayr direction. This would seem likely, for Ayr was a fortified town, and in English hands. There had been much slaying of the enemy rank and file, but apparently most of the commanders and knights had managed to get away. So, although the king had now won two victories, both Gloucester and Pembroke had eluded him.

But at least Gloucester was still within reach. And Angus's fleet was still lying off Ayr port. Go and encircle the besieged town, then, while word of the victories might help to rouse more lords and their people to join the royal banner. But be ready to depart for the Galloway hills, in case Edward Plantagenet marched north from Carlisle, as was to be feared.

So Angus was to head back to his ships, and bring them to present a more immediately threatening presence towards the port, closer in, possibly even make landing forays, to have Gloucester agitated, and to encourage the townsfolk to hostility to the invaders.

The king's people rested for a while, as they certainly deserved. Fortunately they had won considerable provisioning in their conquest here at Glaisnock, this much needed.

At midday Angus and his men set off westwards for the coast. His fleet would still be lying off Ayr; but of course men could not just sit idle in their vessels day and night, so they had been told to take turns at the blockading, while others landed nearby along the coast, north and south, waiting and gathering supplies.

There was a march of a dozen miles ahead of the Islemen, by Ochiltree and Coylton, so that it was evening before they reached the shoreline in the Heads of Ayr vicinity, a couple of miles south of the town. From there they could see their ships lying off the port, and soon found others of their vessels moored in the neuks and sheltered corners below the cliffs of the coast. Down to some of these they descended, and Angus was rowed out to his dragonship, where his friend Ewan was commanding in his absence.

Thereon his coming was thankfully received, for it had been a boring period for the blockaders, with really very little to do, and the short spells ashore the favoured intervals. Ewan had nothing of importance to report, but was interested to hear of the activities on land. They had seen quite large numbers of horsemen arriving at the town from the east, but were unsure as to their identity, save that no doubt they were English.

Angus ordered a closing-in move for his ships, to emphasise their threat. No actual landing was envisaged meantime, unless it became apparent that Bruce was in fact attacking, as distinct from encircling – then they could effectively join in.

Soon they could see the king's force moving into position

half-round the town. Would Bruce risk an assault? It was a fortified place, with high walls and gatehouse towers, and the monarch had no siege-engines. So, probably not. Would it be possible to starve the enemy out? That would take time, and did Bruce have the time to spare?

Angus had an answer to that question two days later, when some of his longships intercepted and captured a vessel evidently making for Ayr, this flying the St George's cross of England. It proved to be carrying an envoy from Edward Plantagenet himself, sent to Gloucester. Under strong pressure this knight was forced to inform; possibly he saw little harm for the English cause in so doing. His monarch was much angered. Bruce was to be destroyed. He, Longshanks, would see to it. He was sending his bastard son, de Botetourt, over the border with a large army forthwith; and he himself would follow, very shortly. He was feeling better in health, and gone so far as donating his travelling-litter to the cathedral of Carlisle as a thank-offering for this improvement, and had ordered a war-horse to be selected for himself. Including Botetourt's contingent, he had a host of some two hundred thousand assembled. Let the Bruce match that!

Angus promptly took the prisoner ashore to present to the king, who received his statement with much concern, needless to say. It certainly changed the situation. If Botetourt was on his way north, then continuing to wait at Ayr was folly. The sooner that he and his men were in their Galloway hills the better, where conditions for a horsed army were difficult, and traps and ambushes could be mounted by the defenders. And hopefully the recent successes against Gloucester and Pembroke would spur the Scots people into more active support of their liege-lord. It was south for him, then. And Angus's fleet would be of more use threatening the Galloway coasts and the Solway Firth than waiting off Ayr.

So that was that, movement in order – but much anxiety behind it. Gloucester was left to his own devices.

28

It was only some fifty miles down the Ayrshire coast to that of Galloway, and there Angus based his fleet at Portpatrick midway down the Rhinns shoreline, this a convenient centre for him to be able to show himself, north and south, both to the Cairnryan and Stranraer areas, and to the Machars and the Solway.

How would Botetourt advance? Inland Galloway was notably mountainous, and he would be apt to avoid that. He might drive up further east, in the Annandale and Nithsdale parts of Dumfries-shire; but that would be to bypass Carrick and the territory Bruce would be known to be occupying. So he probably would be marching by the lower country of Wigtown and west of the Kells and Glenkens Hills, for among the latter lay Loch Doon and Glen Trool, Bruce's sanctuary. Angus could only patrol the nearer coasts to these areas from Portpatrick, hoping to be of some use to his friends.

This he did for some days, with no sign of enemy movement, nor of any friendly presence.

It became a wearisome process, and not only for the oarsmen, this beating up and down that long coastline, day after day, without any least development evident. Angus called in at Stranraer and Glenluce, Wigtown and Kirkcudbright, and, on the Solway Firth, at Kirkbean and Glencaple, near to Dumfries, even as far as Annan, which was getting close indeed to the borderline and none so far from Carlisle itself, all without any positive information gained as to the English position, nor Bruce's either. There were rumours and guesses, admittedly, but these tended to contradict each other.

At length, back at Portpatrick, he decided to sail back north by west to the Mull of Kintyre, leaving his fleet to its unsatisfactory parading, this to seek information at Saddell. The abbot there always seemed to be well apprised as to what went on, those frequently calling mendicant friars seldom failing him. If anyone knew the present situation they, and therefore probably he, would. It was only forty miles across the Clyde estuary to Kintyre, a short day's passage. Ewan could command the fleet meantime.

And at Saddell that evening he learned a sufficiency of the most significant and dramatic news. Edward Plantagenet was dead, and the entire situation changed for all concerned. It seemed that, preparing to lead his great array into Scotland, after Botetourt, he had suffered what possibly was a heart-attack – if, as Angus observed, he *had* a heart! At any rate, he had been smitten direly, and knew that he was destined for a different and final sort of departure. He had ordered a throne-like chair to be taken from Lanercost Priory to Burgh-on-Sands, on the Solway shore, where he could look across at Scotland, and there cursed that nation, its people, and especially Robert Bruce who had once been his friend. His son, the Prince of Wales at his side, had been ordered to continue the warfare to complete fulfilment. Not only that, but when he, the father, had breathed his last, the prince, abruptly become Edward the Second, was to take his body and boil it in a cauldron until all the flesh was separated from the bones. Then these bones were to be wrapped in his banner and carried onward by the son, and to remain with him, night and day, until he had totally conquered that rebellious nation and got rid of Bruce. This was his fierce and final command, announced before all his commanders and the Bishop of Carlisle. He had made the prince swear to obey. And still cursing Scotland, and declaring that it was Bruce who had slain him by those assaults on his lieutenants Pembroke and Gloucester, he had stopped breathing.

And his son, now King of England, had promptly renounced his oath, as given under a madman's pressure. He refused to do anything so absurd and undignified as boiling his father's body, and carrying the bones around; and instead had ordered that the royal corpse be taken off southwards, in regal fashion, to be suitably interred in Westminster Abbey. Then he had summoned all his barons and lords spiritual to pay him due fealty at Carlisle. After this ceremonial, he had marched north over the border with only a small part of the assembled army, but this only as far as Cumnock, where he had caught up with his half-brother, Botetourt, and ordered him to retire to Dumfries with himself. There he was presently based, none knowing what were his further intentions. He appeared to have a mind of his own, even if he was no warrior like his sire. He had been somewhat under the shadow of Botetourt hitherto, that man more like their father; but now that he was the undisputed monarch that would no longer apply.

So, not only what would this Edward do now, but what would Bruce do? How would he seek to exploit this changed situation? That is, if he even knew of it. He well might not, hidden away among those wild hills. The word of Long-shanks's death, such vital news for all, friend and foe alike, would quickly get around; but would it reach into those empty fastnesses of Trool and Doon? There were no monasteries nor nunneries in those hundreds of miles of wilderness, so no mendicants would be likely to penetrate them. It was quite possible, therefore, that the king's people would be uninformed.

Here was something that Angus could usefully do, other than just continuing with his ships at their patrolling. He could seek to reach Bruce and tell him. Anyway, he would have to learn of the king's intentions in this new situation, and what he himself could do to help now.

So it was back across Clyde to Portpatrick.

He recognised that it might be quite difficult to find and

reach his friends amidst their mountainous wilderness, into which he had never penetrated. Best, probably, to enquire at Stranraer.

His fleet rejoined, he led some of the ships into Loch Ryan. And at the town at its head he sought guidance. The folk there, he found, had heard of Longshanks's death, and rejoiced over it. They knew nothing about Bruce's whereabouts, however, but declared that if the Lord of the Isles wished to reach the Loch Doon area, he should sail up to Girvan at the southern end of the Carrick coast, and, landing, proceed due eastwards from there into the hills. In a score of difficult miles he would come, they assessed, to the great loch. As to where thereabouts they might find the king, who could tell?

It was northwards, then, for some twenty-five miles to the haven and small town of Girvan, this apparently near the Ayrshire-Galloway border.

Here Angus landed with half a dozen of his people, and managed with some difficulty to hire horses for the quite lengthy journey. No one here knew where he might find their lord and monarch. But if they were heading for Loch Doon they would be best to go up the Girvan Water, round-about as its course was, rather than plunge straight through all the hills, this until they came to the uplands community of shepherds and hillmen at Straiton, a dozen miles, thereafter to pick their way east by south through the heights as best they could for another ten miles, to get to the loch. Beyond that they could not advise him, unknown territory.

It was becoming clear to Angus why Bruce had chosen this far-out terrain as his refuge-cum-assembly-point.

By following the very winding Water of Girvan, Angus had no problems in eventually reaching Straiton, however circuitous the route. But from there they faced only endless hills. They were told that for five or six miles, as the eagles flew, double that as their horses could take them, due east, they would come to the Doon Water. Turn southwards to follow

235

this, and eventually they would reach its source in the large loch of that name, seven miles in length. There was said to be a small castle on an island in it. This was as much as was known about it.

Their devious progress maintained by twisting valleys and rushing burns, narrow passes and rocky hillsides with scattered stunted trees, not even sheep to be seen anywhere although deer were in evidence. Eventually they came to a larger stream, almost a river, crossing their route, presumably the Doon Water, and southwards along this they turned.

It was as well that it was high summer, Angus declared, with the daylight long-lasting. Would they reach the king before nightfall? If they could find him at all in these serried hills. Surely an army, even a small one, would not be too hard to find?

It was late afternoon before they saw the blue waters of Loch Doon stretching ahead of them. Was this to be their destination? Bruce had always referred to Loch Doon and Glen Trool. Was the latter somewhere adjoining? Not too far away, it was to be hoped.

They rode down the west side of the long loch, and after a mile or two, rounding a major bend on its shore, they perceived that their quest was over – at least presumably so. For ahead of them they saw an islet, with the tower of a small castle rising above it, and ashore from this was spread a great encampment, the smokes from cooking-fires rising therefrom. It could only be the king's force, surely?

Quickly they saw that they were not the only ones on the look-out, for three horsemen came spurring towards them, to demand who they were, although by their garb they could be seen to be Islesmen no doubt. When Angus announced Lord of the Isles, these were suitably surprised and impressed. Yes, they told him, His Grace the King was there at the camp, although he was biding in the castle.

So they rode on, and were swiftly recognised by the knowledgeable, including Bruce and his brother sitting at one of the campfires, who, astonished, rose and came to greet them.

"Angus! Angus Og!" the monarch cried. "Here's a wonder! *You* to come hither all this road from the sea! Seeking me?"

"Aye, Sire, seeking Your Grace. God be praised that I have found you! Hidden away as you are."

"What brings you, Angus? Here is a surprise, indeed."

"The news, Sire, the news!"

"What news, friend? We learn little news here."

"Have you not heard? Edward? *King* Edward?"

"The Plantagenet? Has he marched, at last? After his bastard?"

"Aye, he has marched! But to hell, I would judge! He is dead. Edward Longshanks has gone to face his Maker!"

"Dead? Edward dead? Do I hear aright? God save us, is it true? No tale, no hoped-for hearsay?"

"I judge not. The word brought by the friars was too particular. Telling what the Prince of Wales, now become Edward the Second, had said and done. What was done with the body. How he had ordered that Botetourt back from Cumnock. Much more. This could not all be idle chatter . . ."

"But, but . . . here is news beyond all! And I knew naught of it. When was this? Edward gone!" The king turned to his brother. "Is it to be believed? He was ailing, we knew. But said to be bettering. Dear Lord, if it is true, then, then . . ."

"Edward of Caernarvon is a very different man," the brother said. "If those friars spoke truth, then we are greatly blessed by this death."

Angus went on to recount the details given him at Saddell, this greatly heartening the king and all who heard it.

When, presently, the euphoria had died down somewhat, the discussion came to be about what was to be Bruce's course now, needless to say. He could not overlook the fact, if fact it was, that the new Edward and his half-brother were still on Scots soil, and none so far off, less than thirty miles away. So no relaxation was to be considered. Confirmation of these so important developments was to be sought. It was to be hoped that, if all was true, then this news ought to bring more and more of the doubtful lords flocking to support the royal standard. So they would remain here in the Galloway hills meantime, watchful. And if Angus Og would continue to show his fleet's presence, especially in the Solway Firth, as near to Dumfries as he could go, this would help to keep the enemy in a state of uncertainty, watching their rear.

So it was a case of marking time until the new situation revealed itself more fully and certainly.

Next day Angus took his leave, to return that long road whence he had come.

29

Angus was quite prepared to have his longships continue their patrolling of the Galloway and Solway coasts; but he had his own Isles to govern and oversee, and he had been absent therefrom for overlong already. He would continue to aid Bruce in his so admirable efforts to gain Scotland's freedom; but the king was going to remain based in these Galloway hills meantime. So he could leave most of his ships to pose their threat to the English, under Ewan, and himself get back to his own territories – and to Ainea and the youngsters.

This he arranged when he got back to Portpatrick. And when the fleet sailed off southwards for the Solway, he, with only half a dozen vessels, proceeded northwards. Ainea would be at Dunaverty for the summer.

At that sea-eagle's nest of a place he found all well, and was received home with rejoicing, his dear one declaring that she was beginning to become jealous of Robert Bruce's evident hold on her husband's attentions. She also said that Finguala was needing a father's hand, a spirited child indeed.

As to Isles affairs, she reported no dire problems, save that the Earl of Ross, or more probably his son, was making trouble in Wester Ross and Moray, and required to be taught a lesson. He was said to be in league with the Comyn Earl of Buchan, and seeking to rouse the north-east against Bruce.

Angus perceived that this would have to be a priority for his action.

He went up to see Gillemoir MacLean at Duart, taking Ainea with him, and there learned sundry details as to minor difficulties among the islands and the everlasting feuding of their chiefs, which Duart had been dealing with, but which could do with the greater authority of their lord. He was concerned over the Ross situation, and agreed that something positive should be done about this. The Master of Ross was reported to be seeking to take over the area as far west as Kinlochewe and the Applecross peninsula, which would bring them in sight of Raasay and Skye. The lack of so many of the Isles ships, away aiding Bruce, had prevented himself from doing anything effective about this.

Angus declared that there was a sufficiency of other birlinns, galleys and longships, and men to row and be carried in them, especially in Skye and the Outer Isles, not involved over Bruce, and such must be rallied to deal with the Rosses. He would see to it – but Duart should come with him.

Ainea, at Ardtornish, asserted that she also would accompany him, at least for this tour round the isles. She was not going to be parted from her husband once more, and so soon.

So a few days later the dragonship led MacLean's galleys up to Ardnamurchan, to be joined by MacIan and some of his. Both had contributed to the fleet in the south, but they were not beyond producing more, and coming with Angus onwards. By Coll and Eigg and Rhum they sailed, and had little difficulty in collecting more vessels, the objective of seeing those Easter Ross interlopers off back to their own territories commending itself to all, criticism implied, if not actually stated, of their lord not having come to effect this considerably earlier, instead of involving himself in mainland warfare which had really nothing to do with the Isles, Angus not failing to point out that the Bruce's cause was, to quite a large extent, their own also.

At Skye and Raasay, beginning to feel threatened by those Rossmen, they did very well as to recruiting, and quite a large assembly then set off across the Minch for Lewis and Harris and the rest of the Outer Hebrides. These, as ever, did not feel themselves so greatly involved in affairs to south and east, but did make token contribution to the present project, the Mac-Leods and MacAulays and MacCodrums agreeing that wretched nobodies like the folk from far-off Easter Ross ought to be despatched whence they came from, if not further and thrown into their Norse Sea. These had not known of King Edward's death, nor were greatly interested.

Well enough pleased with his efforts, Angus headed his now considerable force for the Applecross peninsula, across the Inner Sound from Skye. This was a quite extensive area, its coast isolated from the rest of the mainland by very high and steep mountains, although behind these fair enough terrain, which the Ross brothers were seeking to make their own. At the shore, Angus divided his force, one part to sail up Loch Kishorn to the south, past the Crowlin Isles, this led by MacIan; and the other, led by himself, to head up for Loch Torridon to the north, this much larger and longer, these two arms of the sea creating the peninsula of Applecross. Thus they could assail the invaders from either side. It was MacRuarie country; and at the shoreside community of Applecross itself, Angus picked up Farquhar MacRuarie, kin to Christina of Garmoran, who had been appealing for help, and took him north with them towards Torridon.

Angus had never actually visited this area, although he had passed the mouth of Loch Torridon several times. Now, as they turned into it he was much impressed, and it had Ainea exclaiming. For it was all scenically striking indeed, the loch-mouth three miles wide but quickly narrowing into a mere four hundred yards between jagged cliff-girt headlands and then widening again for another eight miles, spectacular mountains on either side, MacRuarie pointing out Beinns Alligin and Liathach to the north, Beinn Damh and Sgurr Ruadh to the south.

At the head of the loch, Torridon itself, below Beinn Damh, they disembarked. Ainea was left with the wife of the chieftain here, while he escorted Angus and his three hundred men southwards, past these great peaks and into the inner plateau-like country, still high, which formed most of the peninsula. They were told that there were about ten miles of this, fair cattle-country, before they came to Loch Kishorn, the southern boundary.

It was not long before they saw the signs of invasion, croft-houses, cottages and sheds with their thatched roofs burned, even some dead bodies. They were told that although much of this terrain was all but empty, there were small communities at inland Loch Lundie, Loch Attadale, Cuileag Sheiling and elsewhere. MacRuarie of Torridon said that the Master of Ross was reported to be basing himself at the head of Loch Lundie, roughly in the centre of the area, with his brother further south-west at Culduie near the coast. MacIan would have to look after the latter.

It required an eight-mile march to gain this Loch Lundie, with no garrons for all his men, and Angus realised that it would be evening before they could reach their hoped-for target position. But that might be all to the good, for the Rossmen could well be camped for the night, and so exposed to attack by surprise.

It took them nearly three hours to gain the head of the quite long loch and well before they reached the foot they saw the smoke of campfires rising. Angus decided to halt his party until it was well into the night. Approaching now they would be seen and the foe warned, whereas an attack when all, or most, were asleep, would be much more effective. Would the master have sentinels out? He would scarcely be anticipating attack, so might well not.

Hidden in a hollow of the hillside they waited, glad of the rest.

Around midnight they moved on, silently. No alarm was evident ahead. It was not really dark, and as they neared the encampment they could see that there were two cottages or croft-houses behind, no doubt taken over by the master.

Their assault on the invaders was all on only a minor scale compared with Bruce's night attack on that English camp. They made no attempt at encircling, merely staged a sudden dash down upon the sleeping foe, in crude and no knightly fashion. But it was successful enough, little or no resistance being forthcoming, or indeed possible in the circumstances. Men died more or less defenceless.

Angus and Duart were watching those two cottages, off and on, where the leaders were apt to be. Could they surround these, before any inmates had time to be warned and off?

In the event, they could not. For suddenly they saw three men on garrons riding out from behind the buildings and spurring off, not towards their ravaged camp but away southwards into the hills. The Master of Ross, if it was himself as seemed probable, was not going to try to rescue survivors.

Some such did escape, by running away, but few.

A lesson had been taught, and learned it was to be hoped. There was no more that the Islesmen could do that night. They settled in at the devastated camp, where they found ample food and drink left to them. They dealt with the wounded and dead as best they could. No casualties of their own.

The following morning MacRuarie led them southwards, seeking any other Rossmen, and hoping to link up with MacIan's group. They found neither. They did come across sundry local shepherds and crofters, however, one of whom told them that, the day before, he had seen Rossmen being chased by what he assumed were Islesmen. So it looked as though MacIan had also achieved some success. Where the latter and his men might be now was not to be known.

Angus decided that there was nothing for it but to return to their ships at Loch Torridon, a lengthy day's walking.

Ainea and her hostess, at their bed-going, were glad to see the men back. So a very different sort of night was passed.

Next day they sailed back for the Inner Sound, and then

southwards. And reaching Applecross itself, to deposit Farquhar MacRuarie, a grateful man, they found MacIan and his ships awaiting them. Their report was, as expected, favourable. They had surprised the other Ross brother and put him to flight, following his surviving men for some distance, although he himself had been on horseback and got away.

The Rosses would know, now, not to come straying out of their own country.

30

Back at Dunaverty, the news from Saddell was of Edward the Second leaving Dumfries and heading south for London, to establish himself on the throne and make his own appointments to office in his realm, these very different from his father's, his priorities dissimilar. He left Richmond as governor of Scotland, and Pembroke as commander of the English forces there.

Bruce, hearing of this, had wasted no time. He marched north, determined to show himself as monarch, and calling on all lords and magnates to rally to his banner, with their people, although avoiding Edinburgh, Stirling and Perth, where Richmond and Pembroke were apt to be based.

So now the Isles fleet's prolonged patrolling of the Clyde and Solway coasts could cease, and the crews thankfully return home. And Angus could concentrate on his rule and duties of looking after the lording the Isles, somewhat neglected of late.

His support for the king's cause was not entirely inactive at this stage, even so. For it was not long before he had an unexpected visitor at Dunaverty, one of the Bruce's close friends, Sir Neil Campbell of Lochawe. He came at the royal behest, his mission to seek Angus's co-operation in nullifying the efforts of MacDougall of Lorn, more especially those of his son Lame John, or Ian Bacach, who was now actively aiding the Comyn Earl of Buchan, who was seeking, with the Earl of Ross, to unite the north against the king. With the Lorn district of Argyll adjoining Campbell's own territory of Lochs Awe, Fyne and Etive, *he* was also concerned. The MacDougalls must be disciplined.

Angus agreed, and suggested that they should both go up to Dunollie and see the Lord of Lorn.

The Campbell told him that the king had now gained the active support of many of the great lords who had hitherto been less than enthusiastic in his services, notably the Earls of Lennox, Fife, Menteith, Strathearn, Atholl and Angus. This much encouraged the monarch. He was now more than ever determined to proceed on right to the north, and bring Buchan and Ross and the Comyn cause to heel, the valiant Bishop David of Moray assisting, from Orkney, Caithness and Sutherland.

With Sir Neil, then, Angus sailed his dragonship up past Gigha and through the Sound of Jura, to the Firth of Lorn and Dunollie. There he confronted MacDougall, an old man now, with his Comyn wife, but no Ian Bacach, who was more or less permanently, with a number of their clansmen, over in the north-east, aiding Buchan and the Rossmen. His two callers made it very clear that this activity against the King of Scots must cease, or Lorn would suffer; and placed as it was between the Isles on the west and the Campbell country on the east, it was very vulnerable. The old lord got the message; but whether he would, or could, recall his son and the men was another matter. But at least warning had been given. His wife did not intervene.

Angus took Sir Neil down to Ardfern, in Craignish, the nearest point to inland Loch Awe, and wished him well in his further efforts for the monarch.

Ainea, at Dunaverty, had learned that her father, O'Cahan, was ill, and she was anxious to visit him. Angus sympathised and acceded, and with their two children they set off without much delay for Lough Foyle and Limavady.

They found her father looking a deal older and distinctly frail, but recovering from what had evidently been a stroke. He was greatly pleased to see them, and much diverted by his grandchildren, of whom he did not see enough. He was interested to hear of the situation in Scotland, of which conflicting tales had reached Ulster; and like so many others, he greatly rejoiced over the demise of Edward Longshanks.

They stayed a week at Derry, and visited Ainea's brother and family before returning to Kintyre, promising that they would not be so long in making another visit, God willing.

More news awaited them. Bruce had fallen ill in Aberdeenshire on his way north, just what was the cause not reported, but it had been insufficient to prevent him from winning a battle very shortly thereafter, this against the Earl of Buchan at a place called Barra Hill, and the Comyn had been routed notably, and indeed wounded, and fled the field, making, it was said, for England. What now would be the position of Ian Bacach?

The north now looked likely to fall to the king, with Ross being isolated, all an excellent prospect.

William, Earl of Ross, with Buchan's defeat and flight, was now isolated in the north, with Bishop David of Moray rallying opposition to him. Angus perceived his opportunity to bring this troublesome earldom and family to heel, hopefully once and for all; and when this recognition was reinforced by a request, sent via the Campbell, from the king – who had now returned south after a demonstration in Moray – that the Lord of the Isles could greatly aid him by uniting all northern and Highland forces against Ross, the decision was made. A major campaign was called for.

This would be, to be sure, no simple and easy endeavour. Easter Ross was a large territory in itself, stretching from just north of Inverness right up to the Sutherland border at the Dornoch Firth, some thirty odd miles, and including what was known as the Black Isle of Cromarty; also westwards into the hill country of Strathgarve, Strathglass, Strathpeffer, Strathconon and the rest, fully forty miles inland from the Norse Sea. So the earldom could be calculated to cover at least one thousand square miles. The actual boundary with *Wester*

Ross, Isles country, was unmarked, but the clans inhabiting these inland parts were in little doubt as to whom they paid their sketchy allegiance, even though the Ross earls had long dominated much of the territory down the north side of Loch Ness and the Great Glen, however unlawfully.

Angus's problem was that so much of this vast area was only to be assailed by a land force, far inland from the coasts. Although he would send his fleet up and round to the eastern seaboard and its firths, the great inland area would demand large numbers of marching men. And if the earl was attacked in strength, he would be apt to base himself here.

It was decided that while MacLean commanded the main fleet and took it eastwards, Angus himself would lead a large host afoot up the Great Glen and into the mountains. He would sail relays of craft up Loch Linnhe to Loch Eil and the Cameron country, there to disembark and muster.

Organising this and collecting the many men from all over the farflung lordship took time; and it was not until autumn that the venture could actually start. Getting five thousand men up to Loch Eil was a prolonged process, with little room in the craft for passengers. But at length the march began, MacIan second-in-command, Cameron of Lochiel sending his scouts well ahead. It was hoped that Ross would be preoccupied with the fleet's assaults on the coastal areas, and would not anticipate any land-based advance approaching his rear at this stage.

A force of this size, in hilly country, with so many rivers and streams to cross, could not cover much more than fifteen miles in a day, especially men more used to sea travel than marching; so that the first day they got only as far as halfway up Loch Lochy; and the second to midway between Loch Oich and the head of long Loch Ness, their scouts reporting no opposition ahead. Some of these Camerons also headed east and west, to inform the clan chieftains on either side of the lengthy glen, all of whom hated and feared the Rossmen, of the force coming up and requesting reinforcements.

So, indeed, as the army went on, it was joined by MacDonells, Mackintoshes, Grants and Shaws, to Angus's satisfaction.

It was at Invermoriston, a short way up the west side of Loch Ness, that a Cameron scout brought to him two of Duart's men, on garrons, sent to inform that the fleet, menacing the coastal areas of the firths and the Black Isle, had had the desired effect of causing the Ross forces to retire into the mountains west of Dingwall to the Strathconon and Garve uplands. He, MacLean, was leading men to make a threatening presence behind them.

This was what Angus wanted to know and had hoped for. So now his further strategy was clear. He must leave the Great Glen and lead his thousands due northwards through the mountains the twenty or thirty miles, to assail Ross's force from the rear. It would be a difficult approach, because of all these rocky uplands, against the grain of the land as it were, to cross innumerable glens and east-flowing rivers, rounding mountains by the score; and this, if possible, without rousing the local folk, who might send to warn Ross. They must avoid communities. Fortunately Lochiel and his Camerons knew the country well.

Not going as far as Urquhart and Drumnadrochit, the army left Ness-side at Ruskich and headed into the hills just north of the dominant peak of Meal Fuar-Mhonaidh, wild and empty country, making for upper Glen Urquhart. Inevitably progress was very slow for such a host of men; and although it was only some six miles as the birds flew, it was double that for men who had to tramp in a strung-out and winding column, often over a mile in length itself. It took them all the late October day to reach Loch Meiklie, where they were able to descend in the evening to Balnain, and surround that scattered hamlet and pillage it for food, this while preventing any would-he escapers from heading north to warn their earl.

Next day they marched on north-west as the land allowed, through more lofty and vacant territory, making for Strathglass, which they managed to attain before dark, this in the Crochail area, avoiding the populated districts of Cannich and Aigas to west and east. They forded the River Glass there, with some difficulty, and settled for that night on the far bank. Would next day bring them to the enemy, in Strathconon reputedly? And a night attack?

Feeding five thousand men was a major preoccupation and a delaying factor. But at least there were great herds of deer on the slopes for their bowmen to seek to slay in deer-drives. And uncooked oatmeal, soaked in venison blood, made sustaining rations if scarcely appetising.

Scouts ahead reported that the enemy force was encamped at the head of Loch Achonachie, out of which flowed the River Conon. This was still almost a dozen miles off, the Camerons said, through the Erchless and Corriehallie mountains, a long day's tramp. But at least it would bring them to the Ross position at night, and hopefully unseen and unreported. The foe would presumably be keeping watch to the east, for Duart's people. And possibly wary of Bishop David's Sutherland and Caithness threat from the north. So, assault from the south and west, in darkness.

They started early in the morning, all warned of what was expected of them in the next almost score of hours; but no remonstrances expressed. Angus was becoming an expert in night attacks.

The Erchless mountains were high and challenging, and the marchers kept well to the east of the major ones, although this was a less direct route, if anything such could be envisaged. They had problems in fording again, the Rivers Goibhre and Orrin, this delaying them. It was late afternoon before they won over the latter, and could work their way round between two peaks, with Loch Achonachie reportedly only some three miles away.

Angus questioned Lochiel closely as to the details of the terrain ahead, for it seemed that he knew it fairly well. This Loch Achonachie was over a mile long and a quarter that in width, the north side and the west end flanked by open woodland, the south banks steep, bare hillside. The encampment was said to be at the head, to the west, so there would be trees around it, which could both help and complicate an attack. Danger would be apt to be looked for from the east, up the River Conon. Fortunately, as it happened, the Rossmen, to gain protection from anything such, had camped on the south side of the river just where it flowed into the loch, and this would spare the Islesmen having to find a ford across. Move in, then, from up river on the west, through the woodland, difficult as it might be in darkness to control so large a force in tree-covered ground.

Angus sent out orders accordingly, to his chieftains and lieutenants, keeping in touch, and silence, priorities.

They were able to rest for an hour or so, until midnight, this about a mile from their target. And so far no alarm had evidently been aroused.

The tactics were for the force to remain in a long column until the river's edge was reached. Then to turn eastwards and the formation changed into a crescent, to make slowly and very heedfully towards the loch-head. The camp, in such circumstances, would be fairly scattered, because of the clumps of trees and bushy areas. Just where the leadership would be based was not known, probably close to the lochside. Campfires would be dispersed but probably numerous, with ample fuel so available, and although probably dying down by now, could be a helpful guide for the widely stretched semicircle of attackers. Angus would station himself at a central point, MacIan at the riverside, and Ewan at the far east end, to move in and cut off any possible retirement down the lochside.

It was a windy and cloudy night with smirrs of rain, which

might help to keep the sentinels near the fires, and possibly reduce any active patrolling of the perimeters.

All reported to be in position, the Islesmen awaited the signal to attack. This could only be given by runners informing the half-mile crescent formation, since any horn-blowing or other noise would alert the camp.

When Angus judged all ready, he sent off his runners. Then he had to wait, in a state of some agitation needless to say, for time for the advance order to get to all the force, east and west, and a concerted move made.

Those minutes were as tense as any he could recall, as he counted the many seconds.

At last, with stirrings on his right and left, he raised his sword-arm high, and the forward movement began, men picking their way through the woodland as silently and directly as they could.

It was not long before noise ahead, shouts and yells, ended any more need for silence and cautious creeping. The Islesmen plunged forward, weapons at the ready.

Inevitably, with those trees and bushes and undergrowth, it was no very coherent and simultaneous advance and assault. But then, the camped and sleeping host itself was equally affected by the scattered woodland, and the reaction irregular. And leadership was all but non-existent.

The fighting commenced erratically, if such it could be called, it more a crazy hacking, smiting slaughter, and chasing of bewildered victims. There could be no discipline and order or system about it, among those trees and bushes in the darkness. But at least there was no doubt as to who did the slaughtering and chasing. The Rossmen were utterly surprised and demoralised. They put up no real resistance, save for the odd group or individual.

Angus himself was unable to judge the situation with any accuracy, save that the enemy were either in disarray and making no attempt at united defence, or escape their preoccupation. In it all, he had his mind on finding Ross and his sons. Where were they? If these could be reached . . .

With a small group he hacked his way towards the riverside, where they would be apt to be found. But no signs of leadership were evident there, or elsewhere. Ranging to and fro in the chaos, with his party, he could discover no trace of the men he wanted, captured foemen, questioned, no more informed than he was.

How long it took for any sort of order and decision to prevail was as uncertain as was all else, save that the Islesmen were some sort of victors, the foemen dead, wounded or dispersed and gone. Among the prisoners certainly Earl William and his sons were not to be numbered, nor, so far as could be ascertained, among the slain.

It was only when all was over that a wounded man was brought to Angus to declare that the earl and master had been seen to make early escape, with a few others, in two small boats down-river and into the loch. They were gone.

It was none so far to Dingwall, where was the earl's strong castle – no hope of catching up with him before that. And, set in the midst of the town, and with no siege really possible, there was no point in pursuing. William of Ross had escaped, although he had lost his host of men.

What now, then?

Cameron said that the king was reported presently to be at Aberdeen, but had been declaring that he must proceed up to Moray and Inverness, to seek to deal with Ross. So he might well be there by now. And Ross was in no state now successfully to oppose his liege-lord. So, head for Inverness and join the monarch, to see what the next step was to be. Send word to Duart and the fleet to join them there.

At least, Wester Ross ought now to be free from encroachment from the east for some time.

They did find Bruce at Inverness, and their ships there before them. The king was summoning all the Moray lords and lairds, and chiefs to join him, with their men, for an assault on Ross, in liaison with the Bishop David of Moray and the force from the north. When Angus gained the royal presence, it was with great surprise and satisfaction that the monarch learned that the rebel earl was already defeated, although not captured. Loud was the praise for the Lord of the Isles.

There was no question as to the next step. A march by the combined forces on Dingwall, with the Isles ships threatening from the Cromarty Firth. There presumably was nothing for it but siegery. With this great host occupying the town, for how long could the castle hold out?

The royally led thousands commenced their round-about approach, by Beauly and Muir of Ord and Conon's ford, to the capital of Easter Ross.

On the way, the king informed Angus of the situation now prevailing in the rest of the land. Although certain castles and strongholds still held out against the crown, basically it was only parts of Galloway and the Argyll area of Lorn that were now in open defiance to the royal authority, although Richmond and Pembroke held the strategic stretch from Edinburgh to Stirling and Perth. Edward the Second had gone to France, to wed Princess Isabel there, and so no royally-led English assault was to be expected for some time. But when Edward did come north again in force, not only the rebel areas would undoubtedly rally to his standard but other less than loyal and Comyn-favouring factions almost certainly would do so also. So it was vital that these should be brought into submission, and promptly. He had sent his brother Edward south to assist Sir James Douglas in assailing the MacDoualls and MacCanns in Galloway. And he himself would seek to attack Lorn. But meanwhile – Ross!

It all seemed good policy to Angus. And he would help over the MacDougalls of Lorn also. Was Ian Bacach still with Ross?

Reaching Dingwall, although occupying the town was no problem for the host, the strong castle, which had actually been built by one of Bruce's predecessors, Alexander the Second, although long occupied by the Ross earls, refused to surrender. Lacking siege-machinery, battering-rams, catapults, sows and the like, clearly only starving-out would be effective – and that could take a considerable time. Equally clearly it was unsuitable that the monarch should sit there waiting, with so much elsewhere demanding his attention. So it was decided that Bruce should return meantime, not to Inverness but to Moray, to the royal castle of Auldearn near Nairn, none so far off, where he had based himself, while the siege here continued. Angus would remain with the other besiegers. At least the lordly ones had all found comfortable quarters in the town. He offered the king a galley and escort to take him to this Auldearn, on the Moray coast, and this was gladly accepted.

The host settled to wait at Dingwall.

It was only a few days later that, heralded by a blowing of horns and a great white flag, Hugh, Master of Ross himself appeared at the castle gatehouse, to announce that William, Earl of Ross was prepared to offer a truce to Sir Robert Bruce, calling himself King of Scots, this on terms which they could discuss.

Astonished, his hearers stared at each other. A truce! This wretched earl was offering a truce to his monarch, no surrender but some sort of arrangement and accommodation as between equals. It was almost beyond belief.

When he got no response, the master reiterated. A truce. What was the Bruce's reply?

Malcolm, Earl of Lennox, who had been left in charge of the royal force, shouted back. "Fool! Dolt! Think you that any, least of all a rebel Rossman, may offer truce to the King of Scots in his own realm! Watch your words, fellow!"

"My father offers a truce, sirrah! Discuss it, or . . ." He left the rest unsaid.

"We cannot and will not discuss any such insolent folly."

"Is that the Bruce who speaks?"

"His Grace King Robert is not here. He is at Auldearn in Moray."

"Then send, and have him heed. And talk terms."

"We will do nothing of the sort."

"Then there will be no truce, no yielding. And we are well supplied in this hold. And have means of remaining so."

The king's supporters eyed each other. What was their move to be now?

Angus spoke. "Arrogant as is this of the Rosses, they are prepared to talk of yielding, whatever they may call it. Would it not be wise to humour them? Wise in the king's cause? Better than sitting here for long, waiting. Our men could be put to better use. MacDougall of Lorn is to be brought low. Idle, all for the sake of a word – this of truce!"

"I say the same," Sir Simon Fraser said.

There were other nods of agreement.

Lennox shrugged. "Very well . . ."

Angus raised voice, to call. "Master of Ross, this talk of a truce is folly. But some discussion could be to good effect. For all concerned."

"There speaks a man of some wits," came back.

"I am Angus, Lord of the Isles. We will talk."

"I talk only with Robert Bruce."

"His Grace is at Auldearn, you have heard."

"Then have him brought here."

Growls from those around Angus.

"We cannot do that. He is the king. But we could take *you* to him in one of my ships under safe-conduct. If this is to the common good."

There was silence for moments. Then the master said, "I will go speak with my father."

Lennox shook his head over it all, but most there were prepared to wait for an answer, debating the issue.

At length Hugh of Ross reappeared. "Can I trust your word, Islesman?" he demanded.

"Before all these, I give it. I will take you to the king, and return you safe."

"Be it so. I will be with you within the hour."

Shortly thereafter, in one of the longships, with two others as escort, Angus took the Master of Ross, with a cousin, Ross of Cadboll, the score of sea miles across the Moray Firth to Nairn, no companionable talk between them. Auldearn Castle was inland a couple of miles and more; but, as they landed at the town's haven, they discovered that the monarch was presently in the town itself, speaking with an assembly of local magnates, these including the Thane of Cawdor and Brodie of that Ilk. So the newcomers had only a short wait before they obtained audience.

Angus had a word on the situation with Bruce first, and found the king quite prepared to talk with the master, brushing aside the foolishness of establishing a truce as of no importance. The vital matter was that Ross was prepared to yield; and that could mean that all the north could be brought into the king's peace. That was well worth some forbearance and lenity. Words counted for little so long as deeds and facts were assured. Yes, he would speak with young Ross.

So the master and his cousin were ushered into the royal presence, and greeted without any pronounced hostility. They did not actually bow, but the master jerked his very fair head once or twice, and launched forthwith into an obviously well-prepared peroration.

"Lord Robert, Earl of Carrick, I come on behalf of my father, the Lord Earl of Ross, to offer a truce to our long enmity. He, my lord of Ross, would now be at peace with you. This on worthy terms, with an end to warfare."

"That is well," the king said easily. "Your father is the only

257

lord in all the north, now, to reject my rule. Peace in these parts is . . . welcome. So long as it is true peace, and lasting. You offer such?"

"We do, Earl of Carrick. On terms that maintain our rights and freedoms."

"First of all, Master of Ross, do not name me Earl of Carrick. My brother Edward has now that earldom. I am Robert, King of Scots, crowned and anointed. Accept that, or this audience is over."

The younger man swallowed, and hesitated. "If, if our terms are agreed," he got out. "Our earldom secure. All your armed strength removed from our lands." He glanced over at Angus. "And the Islesman's also."

"There will be no need for armed strength in Easter Ross if you join my peace," Bruce said. "But king and liege-lord you must acknowledge me. That is the heart of it."

"You will call off that sinful Bishop of Moray and his Caithnessmen? He ever troubles our borders."

"He does it in my name. So, if you are in my peace, that will cease. As with other assaults." The monarch pointed. "You must cease to assail my Lord of the Isles' lands in the west."

Silence.

"You understand? Accept?"

"I accept that this is a truce, my father's truce with you, in any fighting or enmity. For a given time. Three months. Six months. As you will. Each side to swear it. No armed conflict. Each side to yield a hostage to that effect as pledge."

Bruce's lips tightened. "Hostage?"

Hostage, yes. Pledge," was repeated. "Of good faith. My father's terms."

"He who betrayed my wife and my sister to English Edward! Your father. He talks of good faith!" Bruce restrained himself with an obvious effort. "This of hostage: what mean you?"

"A token. A truce requires such pledge."

258

"From *me*? The king? My word is my pledge, Master of Ross."

"Mmm. My cousin here, Ross of Cadboll, will so inform my father. Your pledge as hostage."

"Not yourself? Why that?"

"*I* am my father's hostage to you. I remain with you, as such, for the time. Three months, or six."

Bruce stared as did all there.

"I' faith – you! You, as a hostage?"

"Yes, sir. My father's eldest son and heir. In token of his honest intentions, that there shall be no breaking of the truce."

After moments the king shrugged, and actually produced a slight smile. "I see. You are making a somewhat strange and unbidden entry to my court, Master of Ross. But, if such is your father's desire, his pledge. Mine is otherwise. My simple royal word. The word of the King of Scots. I give no other surety to any subject, or to any man. So send your cousin to tell your father so."

The master bowed this time.

There were murmurs among the company, even Angus somewhat surprised. The monarch was more or less accepting this so-called truce.

His nephew, Sir Thomas Randolph, there present, spoke up. "Here is folly, Uncle! To heed this Ross's insolent terms!" Others muttered agreement, with head-shakings.

"Ross is one of the seven great earls of Scotland. Descendants of the *ri*. I will have them all, now, into my peace. Let it be so. It may serve him – but it also serves me. And Scotland. We shall come to a conclusion another day. Three months, then, from this present. It is agreed."

The master looked round on them all, with a strange mixture of both triumph and doubt. "Sire!" he got out, on a drawn breath.

Bruce took a step forward, and held out his hand.

The other ought to have taken that hand between both his

own palms, in symbol of fealty, and sworn the oath; but presumably he did not know of this gesture, and shook it instead.

Bruce turned. "My Lord of the Isles, see you that this cousin of Ross is returned to the earl, with my word. Thomas, take you the master into your care, meantime. This audience is at an end."

All bowing, the monarch left the chamber.

What sort of a truce had that been?

31

Angus decided to remain with the king meantime, to guide him and his armed force as to the Lorn country, although Sir Neil Campbell could do that probably better than he; but his own aid might well be helpful. And he wanted to be in at any punishment for Ian Bacach. So he sent word to Gillemuir MacLean to sail the fleet back round the northern coasts and down to the Sound of Mull and Loch Linnhe, there to wait off Kerrera, Oban Bay and Dunollie, to be ready to co-operate in however the assault on the MacDougalls developed.

The royal host marched south-westwards on their lengthy journey, by Findhorn and Strathspey, Loch Ericht and Rannoch Moor, heading for Glen Orchy and Loch Awe, almost one hundred and fifty miles through the mountains, traversing Highland Scotland. Oddly enough, in Thomas Randolph's keeping, the hostage Master of Ross came with them, not seemingly objecting.

It inevitably made a particularly slow progress, the host having to go at the pace of the heaviest-laden and least active among the tramping thousands, however impatient were the mounted men. Ten days, Angus and the Campbell reckoned, it would take them to reach the borders of Lorn.

The monarch made very good company for his close associates, and an excellent commander for the rank and file, by no means keeping aloof from the troops and standing on his royal dignity. Angus got to know him well, and enjoyed their friendship. His position was, of course, rather different from that of the others, the Isles lordship being almost independent in theory, although he never emphasised that.

A week after leaving Auldearn they were into some of the wildest country even in all Scotland, which was saying something, the Moor of Rannoch, and verging on Lorn and Argyll. Hitherto the leaders had been able to spend their nights in reasonably comfortable quarters, even if it was only in cottages and crofters' barns; but Rannoch was different, a vast tract of wilderness of moor and bog and water, lochans literally by the hundred, lying between the mountain masses south of the Great Glen and those of Breadalbane, fully one hundred and fifty square miles of it, empty save for deer, boar and wildfowl, not a house therein. Traversing it made a test indeed for any company of men, let alone an army. But at least it provided a hidden approach to lands flanking it; also sport for the impatient lords and knights on horseback, with the deer slain helpful in feeding the host.

They were here nearing territory where they had to be ready for action, MacDougall country although still far from the coast. Almost certainly their presence would be known, their coming south, that is, even if not expected over Rannoch Moor. And ahead of them were more mountains, where ambush could be attempted against any approach to Lorn. Neil Campbell knew it better than any, his lands lying just east and south of Lorn; in fact they would be entering parts of it at any time now. His scouts were leading, well ahead.

In all this travel Bruce kept anxiously considering and referring to the position in Galloway, where his brother Edward and Sir James Douglas were seeking to establish the royal authority. So near to England, it was open to enemy attack. Ought he to have been devoting his present attentions and utmost strength *there*, at this time, rather than up here in the Highlands? Yet, having Ross in hoped-for submission, only this Lorn prevented him from claiming all the north of the realm was his, vital surely. Most of his supporters agreed with him.

After two days crossing Rannoch Moor, they reached high

ground again, beyond Loch Tulla and under lofty Beinn Dorain, where they came to the River Orchy, flowing south-westwards. This the Campbell claimed was undoubtedly part of his land, although boundaries were vague in these mountains, the Orchy eventually running into Loch Awe itself, under Beinn Cruachan, the Campbell giant. After that, they would have to be cautious, entering Lorn.

It was new terrain for Angus, although he knew the sea loch of Etive, none so far ahead.

They camped that night halfway down Glen Orchy, all recognising that this might well be their last peaceable halt for some time.

In the morning, as the glen opened out, they saw the gleaming waters of the foot of Loch Awe in front, with the great mountain of Cruachan dominating the scene. "Cruachan! Cruachan!" was the war-cry of the Campbells. Would they be needing it soon?

Scouts well ahead were at their most watchful.

Under that mountain itself they camped again. Sir Neil emphasised that the next stage was the most fraught with danger. Loch Awe here tailed off into narrows where Cruachan's shoulder on the north and Creag Aonaidh on the south confined all into what became a ravine, and the loch became a river rushing through. And there was well over a mile of this, the Pass of Brander, which the army would have to thread. If the MacDougall, or Ian Bacach his son, was going to hold them, this was the obvious place to do it, a tortuous track by the brief but turbulent River Awe, and steep, almost cliff-like flanks high on either side.

A council of war was held that evening, the Campbell advising. Some of the hardiest mountain-men, with his own people, might climb high on Beinn Cruachan and win westwards up there on the awkward lofty slopes, but not enough to do more than concern the enemy below – if such there were – and hurl rocks down upon them. But if the Lord of the Isles could manage to go with them, and on thereafter down to Loch Etive, there to get a fishing-boat and sail down-loch eventually to Oban Bay where his fleet had been directed to lie off; and then have his ships to come up-loch again, these could present a major threat, with the Campbells and the mountain-men at the MacDougall rear. Angus agreed to attempt this.

It was while this was being discussed that scouts came to announce what they had all come to expect. A large force of Lorn-men were entering the pass from the Taynuilt area. Passage was blocked.

So now plans had to be translated into action. Angus would have to climb that daunting hillside, go north and west along it for almost three miles, and descend to Loch Etive, find a boat from the fisherfolk there to take him some seven miles down-loch to the sea, reach his ships and then bring the fleet back. That would take him how long? Much would depend on how far offshore his ships, under Duart, lay. Also the problem of the Falls of Lora, Campbell warned. These at the mouth of Etive, where it reached the Firth of Lorn, a strange feature, not a normal waterfall but an underwater series of rapids caused by an upthrusting rock formation of the loch bed which created great tidal disturbance and violence, so that it could only be passable for shipping for short periods at high tide. A small rowing-boat could descend this, with care, at most times; but any fleet would have to tackle the falls heedfully indeed and with only a couple of hours in each twelve making it possible. This could delay all. So, one day's journey for Angus would be insufficient. Two days the army would have to wait here, before any sort of attack. Fortunately the MacDougalls would be unlikely to leave their strong blocking position in the pass; anyway, they would be bound to have a lesser array than the king's. So the delay might not be important.

All had to accept this survey of the situation, most looking doubtfully at Angus. He nodded, tight-lipped. He would be off at first light in the morning, with a couple of Campbell guides – that and the best wishes of all.

In the half-dark of the early November dawn, Angus set off, guided by two companions, leaving MacIan in charge of his men. They went on down-river for a short distance to the edge of a cataract hurtling down from Cruachan. It was up the side of this, on a series of rock steps and ledges, that they had to climb, spray soaking them – apparently almost the only way to mount the steep mountainside. Angus was fit, and used to hill-climbing; but never had he tackled such an odd and wet ascent as this. Soon, to add to the difficulties of picking and crawling their way up, was the further impediment of low November morning cloud which had not yet lifted from the heights. It was altogether a taxing and unpleasant start to the day.

However, eventually they did win out of that prolonged waterfall in its narrow stairway and on to the open but still steep hillsides. Angus was thankful for his Campbell guides, for direction was uncertain indeed in the mist, and with the terrain broken and confusing.

It was strange to think, as they worked their way westwards, that they were actually passing above an enemy host packing the pass below.

At length, he recognised that their movement was now becoming generally downwards, which was a welcome sign. Presumably they were nearing Loch Etive.

They emerged from the low cloud, and there was the long loch, leaden grey, before them, stretching westwards. The Campbells pointed. A little way to the right, three or four cottages and sheds could be seen at the waterside, fishermen's houses. They headed down for these.

Angus, seeing three small boats at the loch's edge, wondered whether these would be Lorn people, and therefore hostile, not prepared to lend a boat. Would they have to fight for one? But he was told that, on the borders of Campbell ground, they would be unlikely to offer resistance to any who claimed to be Sir Neil Campbell's men, and who required their craft for the Lord of the Isles.

At their breakfasts, the fisherfolk proved this to be an accurate assumption. Armed men, with such a requirement, were not to be refused, and Angus promised that the boat would be returned in due course.

So the three of them clambered into one of the craft, and the two Campbells took the oars, so far, so good.

The row down the loch was a straightforward exercise, Angus insisting on taking his turn at an oar. The current with them, they made good going, and the seven miles were covered in just over the hour.

At the narrows thereafter, it all became very different, and much care had to be taken. They heard the noise of the strange turbulence of the Falls of Lora well before they reached them, a sort of surging rumble. The Campbells were not over-concerned however. They said that even at low tide the rock was fully four feet below the surface, and rough as the latter was, a shallow-draught boat like this could negotiate a passage without real danger with careful steering. It would be very different for large ships.

There proved to be about two hundred yards of the loch becoming temporarily a river, and the water fast-running and in turmoil. The oarsmen were very watchful for swirls and eddies as they entered the legendary stretch, said to be named after one of the fabled characters of the Fingal story. Angus was busy eyeing it all, its depth and widths, with a view to his responsibility in bringing his longships and galleys up it hereafter, at suitable tide. They would have to come heedfully indeed, and in single file.

Once through this hazard, it was plain sailing, or rowing, for quickly the loch opened out again and they could see its mouth widening into the Firth of Lorn in a mere mile or so.

Soon their boat was heaving and dipping in a different kind

of turbulence, sea-waters and waves, and now with no current to aid them oar-work was more strenuous.

As they swung south by west they had to pass quite close to the islanded castle of Dunstaffnage, a large stronghold of the MacDougalls, this where the celebrated Stone of Destiny had been brought from Iona, for safety from the Norse raiders, before being taken deep inland to Scone Abbey. The main MacDougall seat was Dunollie, between here and Oban, more conveniently placed for shipping, the town and trade, and nearer their island of Kerrera.

Nearing these also, they saw a mile or so off seawards the many ships of the Isles fleet, as ordered, lying off. Thankfully Angus pointed. It was still only noontide, and they had made better time than had been feared. They rowed on, out to the waiting ships.

Duart and the others were astonished to find their lord coming out to them in a small boat with only two Campbell oarsmen. But they welcomed him gladly, much interested to hear of the present situation of the royal army and the hold-up at the Pass of Brander. But concern was expressed at the notion of getting the fleet up into Loch Etive. Those falls of Lora were notorious.

Angus asserted that it was possible, as Neil Campbell had declared, for larger vessels, this only during a couple of hours at high water. And having just viewed it all, he agreed that, with care, they ought to be able to do it, even these forty ships.

Calculation as to tides, then. They would have to be timed very exactly. The November days were short, and any approach in darkness to be avoided at all costs. It was just past high water now, he was told, so no use in trying this tide. And the next would have them at the falls at midnight. So it would have to be the next forenoon.

It was good for Angus to be in his dragonship again. The morrow would demand much care and leadership on his part. But until then, rest and ease.

* * *

Next day they set sail for the mouth of Loch Etive, timing themselves to arrive at the falls about an hour before noon.

Past Dunollie and Dunstaffnage Castles they went, and wondered what the occupants there thought of this.

The long column of ships was up at the approach to the danger area well before the time to make the move through. Angus changed over into the little boat that had brought him, now towed behind his own vessel, and was rowed down the line of his fleet, to shout instructions to the captains and helmsmen, stressing the need for the utmost care and vigilance. There ought to be ample water above the rock for them in their fairly shallow-draught craft, but with the current strong against them and the surface varying, caution was of the essence. A slight scrape on rock might not be too serious, especially as with the current the said stone would be apt to be comparatively smooth; but the rush of the water could swirl a craft round, temporarily out of control. He would take the dragonship through first, and all must follow, in close file – but not so close that one ahead, in difficulties, could not be avoided. The oarsmen must be watching their helmsmen all the time, swift to obey orders. And never to forget that swirling current.

Back at his own vessel, Angus waited until an hour before noon, when he was assured that the tide was not long off its highest. Then, with a prayer, he charged all to be ready, and clanged his helmsman's gong. The oarsmen dipped their long sweeps.

Standing in the bows, anxiously watching every yard of the water's surface for dips and troughs and eddies, with the rowers pulling slowly, he had the ship edge forward on a somewhat zigzag course. Once or twice the oarsmen paused, or some did, the uneven tug of the current disconcerting them, and this resulted in the bows swinging off from the line Angus aimed for. But these falters were only minimal, and the basic direction he indicated was held to. No actual near-misses among the dips and twistings came to his notice.

It seemed to him to take a long time to cover those two hundred yards. But at length, thankfully, they were through, and into widening and more placid waters, although of course that current still against them. He had the dragonship pulled in, aside, and could look back to see how others fared.

MacDonald of Gigha's ship was next behind him, but, following carefully, appeared to be in no trouble. Further back the line was coming on slowly, by no means straight but seeking to follow each the one in front. Only one birlinn, well back, appeared to be out of place, but this was probably before the actual falls were reached and need not be significant.

Angus waited, counting, counting, counting both ships and minutes.

It seemed a lengthy wait indeed, but no doubt that was more in the mind than actuality. No disaster appeared to be occurring, all there sufficiently warned and careful.

It was with a great sigh of relief that he at last saw the final ship pass him, and, with cheers from his crew, could tell them to press on eastwards to the front, to lead the way up Loch Etive.

Whatever else was to happen that day, here was a major achievement. It would all have to be done again later, of course. He did not suppose that the like had ever been attempted before.

The row up the loch was straightforward and uneventful, taking no great time. Angus's mind was on what part his people could play in the king's struggle to win through that pass. When they reached the cottages where the borrowed boat had come from, he would send his Campbells ahead to discover the royal wishes. It would be still barely mid-afternoon.

The fleet moored, and settled in around the fishers' houses, the boat returned, with thanks.

It was a grey November day, but at least the low clouds had lifted from the hilltops. But as they awaited the Campbells' return with instructions, that mist was replaced by another, smoke, great rolling clouds of smoke on the easterly wind. What was this? It seemed to come all from the Cruachan side, not the southern. Was it fire, a deliberate part of the struggle? And if so, presumably of the royal force's doing, not the enemy's.

It did not take long for them to learn. Their two Campbells came hastening back to the lochside with their tidings and instructions. The smoke was of Sir Neil's making. On hearing of the fleet's arrival, he had set the heather and bracken alight on the high ground to confuse the enemy. The Islesmen were to assail the rear of the MacDougalls in the pass, while the king moved to attack their front, both under cover of the smoke. There was a timber bridge over the short River Awe near the west end of the pass. If that could be captured and held, it would greatly assist, and help prevent enemy escape. Action, then – all action now.

Angus did not delay. The Campbells guiding, he led his people, some six hundred of them, round the westmost shoulder of Cruachan, through the smoke clouds for something over a mile, this to the entrance of the pass. And there quickly they came to the MacDougalls' rear, and surprise complete – for the foe were all facing the other way, their concern the king's attack at the far end, that and the rocks coming bounding down from on high. In fact, those rocks, at this stage, constituted the principal hazard for Angus's men, their foes defensive but confused and less than effective, escape the preoccupation.

It proved to be not really battle at all, just driving on, wielding swords and battle-axes, and watching for rocks. There must be a great supply of loose stone up there on Cruachan.

They came to the reported bridge sooner than anticipated,

with some of those they were attacking turning to flee across it to the south bank. Leaving a group to hold and block it, Angus pressed on.

It was not long, however, before the situation changed, and it became real fighting, this because it was no longer the enemy's backs they were concerned with but their fronts. Clearly the main mass of the MacDougalls were in retreat from the royal assault forward, and now found their way barred by this second force. In that narrow pass between hillside and river, it became a yelling, smiting pandemonium in that smoke, still with rocks crashing down. Would Neil Campbell up there not realise that his missiles were endangering friend equally with foe?

Although this was no night-time affray, like those others Angus had been engaged it, the pouring smoke-clouds of the east wind made it almost equally murky and obscure, and in the melee difficult to know whom to engage, especially as the Lorn-men were Highlanders and dressed as were the Islesmen. The struggle developed into sheerest shambles. Angus came to the conclusion that it was best to turn his men back, if he could, to hold that pass at the bridge. That itself was sufficiently difficult, however much he shouted and waved, few seeming to heed him.

But at least it looked like rout for the foe, and victory of some sort for the monarch.

It was when he recognised a face confronting him as that of Sir Gilbert Hay that Angus accepted that the day was won.

With Hay he worked his way back to the bridge. There he found more chaos, with so many of the MacDougalls seeking flight across it, some even hoisting themselves under the timber supports. It had ceased to be fighting now, only the prevention of escape, where possible. The rocks ceased to fall.

Eventually the king appeared, warm in his congratulations to all concerned, particularly the Islesmen and the Campbells.

The Lorn threat was surely removed, at last? All the north under control.

What now, then? Bruce said that MacDougall prisoners declared that Alastair of Lorn, the old man, was in Dunstaffnage Castle, none so far off, not commanding here. Ian Bacach had led this force, and, as far as was known, had escaped. He could be making for Dunstaffnage also. So – to that hold. It was said to be on all but an island. So the Isles ships could help to bring it down?

Angus had to point out the tidal problems of the Falls of Lora, that and darkness. It would be the morrow's noonday before he could get his vessels through. But thereafter they could aid in this of Dunstaffnage.

The King judged that by then his army should be sufficiently rested and recovered to make the ten-mile march, and attack.

It was parting then, and back to the ships for the Islesmen, leaving Bruce's people to clear up the bloody havoc of the Pass of Brander, and to re-establish their camp at this end. Fortunately casualties were very few on their side.

In the morning it was back down the loch to face the challenge of the falls. This time, at least, the current would be with them, which would probably help.

In the event, it did – or possibly it was their previous experience that did. At any rate all managed to negotiate the awkward passage without mishap, and so out to open waters, thankfully.

Dunstaffnage Castle soared before them only a mile or so off southwards, looking as though on an island. However it was not that, but set on the rocky knoll at the tip of a long, low and narrow peninsula, this forming an inlet rather than a bay on the landward side. Angus knew it well and had been in the hold on occasion. He was well aware of its strength, its great curtain walls sixty foot in height and very thick, topped by parapet and wall-walk, and within, its odd shape, following the contours of the upthrusting bluff, a large keep and three lofty angle towers. It would not be an easy fortalice to take, although in the present circumstances it probably would not be provisioned for any long siege.

Nearing it, with his ships, he could see the royal army, far outstretched, approaching it from the east round that inlet.

Ordering his fleet to surround the castle as nearly as was possible, Angus landed on the low-lying grassy peninsula leading out to it, to await the king.

When in due course the vanguard of the royal force arrived, it was to recognise that without siege-engines it would be all but impossible to reduce this stronghold. On the other hand, its lord and occupants were in a hopeless position. Although they were in MacDougall country, their army had been defeated and dispersed, and none of their people were likely to come in any numbers to tackle the king's army and relieve the fortress. So, wait for surrender.

This was accepted by Bruce as their strategy, rather than any demonstration of attack. But the king had so many responsibilities and demands in the rest of his realm that he could not afford to sit here before this hold for any length of time. He would wait for a day or two, and then leave with part of his force, but a sufficiency to remain with the Isles fleet to ensure that eventual capitulation of Dunstaffnage was obtained.

This was agreed.

They settled in along the peninsula, most of the ships' crews landing to join the royal encampment, although the vessels themselves remained in position, moored all round the castle.

How long would it take Alastair of Lorn, and presumably Ian Bacach, to recognise their forlorn situation?

It took only one night and one day. Then white cloths were seen hanging from the castle battlements, to indicate surrender. And presently the MacDougall himself, a tall, stooping, white-haired man, came out from the gatehouse with a few companions – but no Lame John.

The group were led to the king, where Alastair made gabbled obeisance and sought the royal mercy, declaring future loyalty and service from all Lorn. When Angus demanded where was Ian Bacach he was told that he had fled during the night, whence was not known. Clearly he had perceived the position as untenable.

Well pleased, the king declared that he would now expect the most assured leal support and obedience from Lorn hereafter, or all the MacDougall lands would be forfeited to the crown. Let his traitorous son and heir take due heed.

Now, it was Galloway for the royal host. Would Angus take his fleet there also?

So back to those well-known coasts it was to be for the Islesmen. But it would take a considerable time for the king's army to march that far, well over one hundred and fifty roundabout and difficult miles probably, whereas the ships could sail it, reasonably directly, in a couple of days. So this would allow Angus to have a brief spell with Ainea and the children, at Ardtornish, less than a score of miles off. Joy for him!

32

Ainea did not fail to remind him that in her opinion, husband and father was spending over-much of his time and energies in serving Robert Bruce. And was he not tending to neglect his Isles lordship? Angus conceded that he had become more involved in the monarch's affairs than he had originally intended. But the Scottish cause was worth supporting and Bruce requiring all the help he could get. If the English managed to take over Scotland, did she think that they would leave the Isles in peace? Wester Ross, Morar, Moidart and Ardnamurchan, on the mainland, would be overrun, and it would not be long before there would be grabs at the islands, especially the important ones like Mull, Islay and Skye, readily reached. No, his aiding Bruce was not all chivalrous friendship.

His wife, not fully convinced, reported that there were matters nearer home that presently required his attention. In the absence of MacIan of Ardnamurchan, with him in all this with his men, a party of wild folk, MacDuffies it was alleged, had been raiding his lands to the north, Kentra and Acarsaid, and stealing cattle to carry back to their Eilean Shona. If this was allowed to continue, who knew where it would stop?

Angus agreed that this must be dealt with, and promptly. North Ardnamurchan and Shona were none so far from Ardtornish, reachable in a day's sailing. He reckoned that he had three or four days to spare before Bruce could reach Galloway, so it was north for him meantime, and forthwith. Ainea said that she was not going to lose him again thus soon, and she would accompany him; since no fighting and danger were to be looked for in this, just authority and order demonstrated, they could take Uala and John with them.

So in the morning it was a family excursion in the dragonship, only the one vessel involved; MacIan had been left, with MacLean and the fleet, at the Oban and Kerrera area just in case Ian Bacach sought to rouse these MacDougall parts to try to regain Dunstaffnage.

It was distinctly rough weather and seas for their sail northwards, but the youngsters enjoyed it, relishing the pitching and tossing, and adding their chanting to that of the oarsmen. Rounding Ardnamurchan Point, in especial, the most westerly headland of all the mainland, with the rollers sending up clouds of spray, they shouted their excitement.

Passing Sanna Bay, they swung eastwards for some eight miles to the great bight of Kentra Bay, five miles of the latter. This north side of Ardnamurchan was strangely detached and remote from the south side of the great peninsula, where most of the population and communities were, along Loch Sunartside, few villages and hamlets here. Kentra itself, at the head of its long inlet, was the largest of them. Here the visitors landed, to make their enquiries.

They learned from the villagers, impressed to be called upon by the Lord of the Isles himself with his lady, that, lacking most of their young men who were off with MacIan, they had been descended upon some two weeks before by scores of Macfies from Shona, to the north, who had raped some of the young women and stolen cattle and sheep, and taken these away, using not only their own boats but purloining Kentra ones to do so. It was unbearable. They must be punished, and the beasts and boats returned, with compensation given.

Angus assured them all of his support and sympathy, Ainea seeking to condole with the women.

Then it was north again into the open sea, and on to Eilean Shona.

This island was strange in character in more ways than one. It was all but part of mainland Moidart, separated therefrom by only a channel or kyle of a few hundred yards width. And it was indeed basically two isles linked by the merest strand, Shona Mhor and Shona Beag; and occupied by a clan, if that is what they could be called, only some two hundred of them, the Macfies. These were alleged to have been originally MacDuffies from Colonsay and Oronsay, but there were even doubts about that, the MacDuffie chief disclaiming any links with them. They indeed paid no allegiance to any chieftain other than their own headmen, and were all but a law unto themselves.

The island was practically cut in two by inlets opening from north and south, Mhor on the left, Beag on the right. Into the southern of these Angus steered, to reach the principal haven and township, Port Tarbert Dheas.

The arrival of the Lord of the Isles' dragonship, of course, created much of a stir on Shona. Never had the like been known. And it was scarcely welcomed, although the islanders dared not show actual hostility. Presumably they had their leaders, but such did not proclaim themselves. It was difficult for Angus to know to whom to express his authority.

In the end, he declared that there must be a meeting summoned, of most of the folk, here at this haven. The isle was only two miles long by a little less in width, so it ought, given a couple of hours, to have all to attend. There was a church-cum-meeting-hall near the harbour.

In due course by no means all turned up, but sixty or seventy did, enough for Angus's purposes. Ainea and the children were left with women in one of the houses. Some of the dragonship's crew came to back their lord, all looking very fierce and tough with their helmets and weaponry.

So, addressing the gathering, Angus did not mince his words. He told his uneasy hearers that he had come in wrath and judgment, as was his right as their overlord. By their raiding on Kentra they had broken the laws of the Isles, and caused much hurt and distress, feuding within the lordship forbidden. This must be paid for. All stolen goods, cattle, sheep and boats must be returned to the rightful owners, and compensation paid in the form of some of their own beasts and craft. And the women violated must be offered apology and given some sort of recoupment, although nothing would undo or wipe out the shame of it. This was to be done without delay. And if he, the Lord of the Isles, heard that it was not so, he would order heavy punishment, by armed men, to be laid on Shona, let there be no mistake. Was there any excuse offered for this deplorable behaviour, or reason for remission of judgment?

No voices were raised.

Angus ended by declaring that his men must be given quarters for the night – it was already darkening – in this hall, and provided with food and drink. He and his wife and children would occupy the best house in this Tarbert. Let all see to it.

There appeared to be no priest on Shona. Presumably matters religious were attended to by visiting clergy from Moidart. It seemed that the Macfies could do with divine guidance.

A reasonably comfortable night was passed. In the morning the dragonship was seen off by a silent throng of islanders.

Little as he desired to head off for Galloway thereafter, especially in this winter weather and stormy seas and short days, Angus felt that he had to meet Bruce's request, for all Ainea's disapproval. He assured her that he would not be gone for long.

As it turned out, that assurance was fulfilled even sooner than was anticipated, to his own and his crews' satisfaction. For when they arrived off their old base of Portpatrick on the Rhinns, it was to hear that there had been a battle of sorts between Edward of Carrick and Sir James Douglas, with the MacDougalls and MacCanns and their allies, near Kirkcudbright, and these heavily defeated; so that when the king had arrived with his force he had found no difficulty in enforcing the royal rule on most of the dissident and difficult province. There was no need for any action by the Isles fleet. So, after a congratulatory meeting with the monarch, Angus was able to turn his ships back whence they had come.

They could celebrate Christmas and Yuletide of 1308 in peace, and in their own fashion. And King Robert could claim that, save for the English-held areas and fortresses of that belt of central Scotland, all his realm was now under his control.

The word reached Ardtornish that the Shona Macfies had made good their due requirements.

It had been an eventful year.

33

In the early spring Angus received two calls upon his time, to challenge the family life which he most enjoyed, both unexpected. One was a summons to attend the first parliament of the new reign, to be held at the ecclesiastical capital of the kingdom, St Andrews in Fife. There had not been a Scottish parliament in session for many a long year, and now, three years into his reign, Robert Bruce was going to hold one, to emphasise his authority, as well as to seek to deal with the many issues and problems that confronted the realm and monarchy.

That a call to take part in such should have come to the Lord of the Isles was in itself a matter for consideration. Normally, as far as Angus was aware, this was unusual, the semi-independent status of the Isles precluding it. At least, he had not heard of any recent predecessor having attended one. Was this an assertion of the new monarch's claim to include the West Highland seaboard under his authority? Or was it rather a gesture of appreciation and friendship on the part of Robert Bruce, in recognition of all the so-valuable assistance given to his cause? Angus preferred to judge it the latter. But Ainea warned that it could be the former as well. Being an Irishwoman from Ulster, she was less favourably disposed towards the Kings of Scots than might be her husband, however much she might be anti-English.

Traditionally forty days' notice was always given of a parliament to be held, this in order to allow even the furthest-away commissioners to make arrangements to be present and give less excuse for non-attendance. This was now adhered to. The so significant assembly would be held on 16th March 1309.

As it happened the word of this reached Ardtornish two days after the other demand on Angus's time and responsibilities had come. This was a highly unusual one also, in that it came from both MacDonald of the Uists and from MacLeod of Lewis and Harris; and it was seldom indeed that these two rival chiefs acted in concert. It was a joint complaint to the Lord of the Isles that Orkneymen had made a descent upon Hirta, and were in fact occupying that remote isle. Something had to be done about this.

Here was an odd call indeed. Hirta, and Orkney, one almost as remote from the Outer Hebrides as the other. Hirta, or, as it was sometimes called, St Gilda's Isle, lay west of Uist and Lewis, fully forty miles out into the Atlantic, both MacDonalds and MacLeods claiming it, but in fact having little to do with the place, so distant and comparatively unimportant was it, a mere rocky islet of no great value to anyone.

Why, then, had the Orkneymen troubled to intrude on it?

Angus's knowledge of Hirta was scanty. He had never been there, nor knew anyone who had had call to be so. Apart for renown for having the highest cliffs in all Scotland, or indeed of the British Isles, and said to produce an unusual breed of sheep and be a source of some sort of oil valued by the monkish folk, that was as far as most Islesmen's awareness of the place went. Even the alternative name of St Gilda's was odd, for as far as was generally known there had never been a saint of that name.

So Angus was very unsure over doing anything about this strange invasion even though it was presumably some part of his far-flung lordship. But it did concern him that the MacDonalds and MacLeods of the Outer Isles considered it sufficiently important to make a joint appeal to him over it, something he had never known them do hitherto. Presumably he had to do something in the matter. And, fortunately he had forty days before making any attendance at this especial parliament at St Andrews.

Being a MacDonald himself, he decided to go and see MacDonald of the Uists about it all.

Much as she enjoyed sailing about the Isles with her husband, Ainea recognised that not every occasion was suitable for her and the children to accompany him, and this seemed to be of that sort. He set off north-westwards, along with two longships, in case of need.

Across the Little Minch, at Lochmaddy on North Uist, he found MacDonald thereof, who recounted the Hirta situation. Why Orkneymen should have taken over the island, so far from their own parts, he did not know. But there they were, and must be got rid of. The claims of MacLeod to the island were, of course, absurd. There were no MacLeods on Hirta or Soay, but not a few MacDonalds, Mackinnons, Macqueens and Fergusons, all of MacDonald of Uist stock.

Angus did not want to get involved in bickering between these two chiefs, but agreed that the Orkneymen had no right to be on Hirta. He would go there, and see that they were expelled. Alexander MacDonald said that he would certainly go with him, with some of own vessels.

So quite a little fleet sailed off on the forty-mile voyage next morning. After that destination there was nothing more westwards than empty ocean.

Well before they reached it, they could see that word of the strangeness of Hirta had not been exaggerated. It seemed not so much an island as a gigantic rock-stack soaring out of the sea in perpendicular cliffs, not mountains, just sheer precipitous escarpment seemingly forming an enormous plateau. There must be more to it than that, or it could be no place for human habitation thereon. But that was the impression given.

As they neared it they saw that however unsuitable it looked for man's occupation, it evidently suited bird-life, for the lofty cliff-tops were encircled by dense clouds of seafowl in their screaming thousands, making all but a solid if feathery halo.

Presently they were able to perceive that it was not quite so unbroken a rock-stack as it had seemed from a distance. Also that it was divided into two separate entities, although close together, one much larger than the other. The smaller, Mac-Donald said, would be Soay, which meant the island of sheep, the larger in the form of a gigantic letter H, having lower ground within those vast perimeter cliffs, which must rise for at least a thousand feet.

Heading their vessels in between the two, they found a haven hidden in the ingoing to the larger western isle. And here were moored no fewer than eight Viking longships, these not dissimilar to their own, save with higher sides and taller masts. Angus was thankful to see that their own craft outnumbered these two to one. There appeared to be no one actually in these. There were houses not far off.

Drawing in, they beached their flotilla. Angus ordered some of their crewmen to go and take over these Viking ships and row them out some way to make them inaccessible to their owners. Then to return in one of them.

While waiting for this to be done, they saw men hurrying down to them from those houses; and by their garb and helmets they were not the islanders. So forming up his people in a solid mass, Angus awaited them.

As they came on, fair-haired and bushily bearded men, looking tough and angrily wary at this company outnumbering themselves, and pointing out at their ships now well offshore, Angus called, but level-voiced.

"Why are you here, on Hirta? Thus far from your own islands?"

"Who are you to ask?" That was not spoken in the Norse tongue, but with a pronounced accent. "And how dare you to take our ships!"

283

"I am the Lord of the Isles. And this Hirta is part of my lordship. Are you from Orkney?"

The speaker, a burly bear of a man, looked at his companions, and did not answer for moments. Then, more carefully, he gave voice.

"We are from Stromness. We come for the oil. From the . . . how you say it Petrels? Fowlmers?"

"Fulmars? Oil? You come all this way from Orkney with these longships for bird-oil? I think not!"

"It is so. This island has more of the fowl than anywhere else in all the seas. And the oil is needed. So we come."

It was Angus's turn to glance at MacDonald and the others, unbelievingly. "Many men, coming in eight ships. For oil? And remaining here. You have been on Hirta for some time. I say that you lie to us."

"No. It is truth."

"Why is this oil of so great import to you, then?"

"It is the best oil. Better than from whales, for some needs. The churchmen would have much of it. Not only in Orkney, but in other lands. Norway, Denmark. The Hansa merchants of the Rhine—"

"So-o-o! It is wealth that you are here for! To gain the oil, to sell to others. And come in force for it!"

MacDonald tapped Angus's arm, and pointed. Men had come from the houses and were standing watching them, from a distance, obviously local folk.

With a nod, Angus waved to them, beckoning them forward. Somewhat doubtfully the islanders came.

"I am the Lord of the Isles, come to Hirta to discover what is to do here," he told them. "We heard that Orkneymen had come, and were holding the isle. Now they tell us that they but come for oil, birds' oil. Can this be truth?"

The cottagers eyed each other, hesitant. One spoke. "You, you are the Isles lord? In truth? Himself!"

"I am. And this is MacDonald of the Uists. We come to see matters aright here."

"I am Malcolm MacDonald." The speaker sounded more confident. "Here is much good, my lord. You come to aid us?"

"We do. What is the truth of this? These tell us that they are here only for the oil. It seems scarcely to be believed."

The MacDonald who acted spokesman looked from Angus to the Orkneymen, and then to his fellow-islanders uneasily. "It is the oil, yes. But they come to take over our isle. They have come to hold Hirta, St Gilda's Isle. And they would take myself and others back to their Orkney, to show them how to gain the oil from the birds, that they may make wealth from it."

"Ha! Now I see it. Wealth! Gain! Trade in the oil. So that is it. Hirta becomes important because of some need for this oil."

"Yes, lord. They say that Hirta is the greatest place known for the petrels, fulmars and shearwaters. There are thousands upon thousands of them here."

Nodding again, Angus turned back to the Orkneymen. "So there we have it. You descend on this Hirta, one of my isles, to *take* it, not just to win some oil. This oil must be very precious, much sought after, to bring you to this."

Silence.

"Very well, then. You will make due amends to these good people here, for what hurt and trouble you have given them. Then back to your Orkneys with you. If they will trade some of the oil with you, that is for them. You understand? I could hold you for punishment, but I think not. I will see you gone, and note your names. To protest to the Earl of Orkney. Your names, then?"

The invaders, seeming almost relieved, muttered together. Then their leader shrugged.

"I am Thorgils Brosi. Here is Finn Crow-foot. And Hervi the Tanner."

"Brosi, Finn, Hervi, I will remember, from Stromness. Now,

make your peace with these Hirta folk, then be gone. Repay them." Angus turned to order the Orkneymen's vessels to be brought back to the beach.

It did not take long for the Orkneymen to be off; and it was to be feared that little in the way of compensation was paid, both themselves and the islanders only thankful to be quit of each other, and free.

The Isles company lingered however, staying the night, and gratefully provided for by the cottagers. Angus had become very interested in this of the oil. If it was so valuable to the invaders it would be equally so to himself and his companions, surely? He made heedful enquiries.

It seemed that there were, among all the other thousands of seafowl that thronged those cliffs and heights, three kinds of petrels. Presumably other birds had oil in their make-up, to ensure that their feathers did not become sodden with the sea-water; but for some reason the petrels were by far the best endowed. And of the three varieties, it was not the larger ones, or the shearwaters, which produced the most oil but the young fulmars, which seemed to have their insides full of the rich fluid, just why was not known. The adults were well provided also, but the chicks were the main source of it all, and Hirta's crags and ledges crowded with their nests of seaweed. They were not good to eat, as were some of the other fowl, especially the solan geese. Not that the islanders made over-much use of the oil, esteeming it for lamps and for rubbing on sores; but seemingly elsewhere it was greatly valued, although hitherto Angus had heard little of it. If the famous Hanseatic League of Baltic traders were so concerned to obtain it, then it must be a gainful product indeed. He would certainly pursue this matter hereafter.

He learned that the oil was extracted from the birds, this by the women. The men were expert in collecting the creatures, being lowered down the enormous cliffs on ropes, and scouring the ledges, this not only for fulmars of course. It seemed a curious way of life, but presumably satisfied these folk. They also bred the sheep on Soay, and plucked not sheared the brownish wool, to be spun and woven into rough cloth and blankets. And they did manage to grow some oats and barley on the scanty patches of arable soil. Angus was interested in the little dry-stone hutments that littered the isle, built up like tiny pyramids, these to dry and store fowl and grain. He had never seen such elsewhere. Hirta was a world unto itself, it seemed, but not one he would have chosen to dwell on, subject, he was told, to great storms and tempests, and when these forbore, mist was apt to prevail.

He asked about the term St Gilda's Isle, and learned that the legend was that one of St Columba's missionaries had come here, and made it a sort of sanctuary, where he could communicate with the Almighty in wordless adoration, not a resident but a frequent visitor. If so, he must have been an expert coracle-sailor, as indeed must have been all of Columba's disciples.

Next day they left Hirta, Alexander MacDonald much concerned with the possibilities of exploiting this of the oil, to his and Angus's advantage. He hoped that MacLeod of Lewis did not get to hear of it.

On his way back to Ardtornish, Angus called in at the holy island of Oronsay, there to ask at the little priory if the monks knew about petrel oil. They said that the mendicant friars sometimes spoke of it, mentioning it as famed as a medicament, having especial healing properties. It was used for anointing, as holy, in that it came from the skies, and was much prized even at the Vatican, almost too good to use as lamp-oil save in churches. The Greek and Muscovy Churches were said much to esteem it, this no doubt the Hansa merchants' market.

So here the Isles had a possible source of wealth, which its lord had known nothing of. He would have to go into this further. And, of all places, to come from Hirta!

Nor did it fail to occur to him that there must be numberless other places in his Isles where fulmar petrels were to be found, even though not in such quantities as on Hirta, seafowl always in evidence. Practically all the hundreds of islands had their cliffs, save for Tiree, many notable: in especial he thought of Eigg and Rhum, Skye, south-west Mull and Iona; Dunaverty itself and Ardnamurchan Point and Applecross. He would tell all the chiefs to prospect their areas for the birds. This might lead to a great development, to the advantage of all.

34

Apart from enquiring further about the bird-oil at Saddell, Angus's next concern was to attend the parliament at St Andrews, going warned by Ainea not to commit himself to anything over-supportive of the king which might take him away from her and his lordship so often. She had been very interested in the Hirta situation and prospects. At the back of his mind, he had the notion that he might see John, Earl of Caithness at the assembly, who was known to be in close touch with Orkney, and might well be aware of something of this oil preoccupation there.

Angus was able to sail round Scotland in his own vessel to reach the episcopal capital, near where the Firth of Tay opened off the Norse Sea.

He found the town full to overflowing, a good sign, the abbey of St Rule, the bishop's palace, and the numberless priories, monasteries and collegiate houses packed with important visitors. He decided that he would be as well continuing to sleep under the shelter at the stern of his dragonship in the harbour as seeking accommodation in this crowded community.

He duly found John, Earl of Caithness lodging in the abbey itself. But he proved to know little or nothing about the oil. He said however that Magnus, Earl of Orkney would be able to tell him what he wanted to know, a friendly character apparently, even though having to pay a mixed allegiance to two monarchs, Norwegian as well as Scottish, jarl as well as earl; he tried to keep himself from getting overmuch involved in affairs of either.

A visit to Orkney, then.

Angus was surprised to discover how great and widespread appeared to be the support demonstrated here for the new monarch. Among the magnates represented were many who had previously withheld active commitment either because of Comyn alignment, doubts as to Bruce's rights to the throne, his abilities or just in concern for their self-protection. The fact that so many had rallied to this significant gathering was a most hopeful and auspicious sign. Also the fact that the churchmen were so well represented. Bishop William Lamberton of St Andrews, the Primate, was of course a longtime collaborator, as was Bernard de Linton, the king's secretary, who was, it seemed, to be Chancellor at this parliament. Nicholas Balmyle, Bishop of Dunblane, was to be treasurer, and practically all the other prelates were present, this remarkable indeed for a monarch who was still under the ban of excommunication from the Vatican for the slaying of the Red Comyn in a church.

As for the lords, James the High Steward had come, doubtful as his position had been; the Earls of Carrick, Lennox, Menteith, Strathearn, Caithness, even William of Ross. And many powerful barons and chiefs, as well as those who had always been loyal lieutenants: Douglas, Hay, Campbell, Seton, Boyd, Lindsay, Fleming, Irvine. Even Hugh of Ross was there.

Angus was received and welcomed by Bruce at the Primate's palace, clearly much elated and heartened by this turn-out. He declared that the continued support of the Islesmen would not be forgotten.

Presently the great procession formed up to march to the cathedral church where the parliament was to be held, led by a choir of singing-boys and to the steady beat of cymbals, these however tending to be outdone by the ringing clangour of countless church bells, particularly the cathedral's own chimes.

There they found all in readiness, especial arrangements

made. A dais had been erected at the chancel steps for the throne and the Chancellor's table, with sundry other chairs behind. Rows of benches were ranged in the nave, right and left, for the lords and commissioners; and a large free area left at the west end for onlookers, all the townsfolk invited to attend for this so especial occasion to see the King-in-Parliament.

The Lyon King of Arms and his heralds greeted the procession, and led the monarch, bishops and mitred abbots, the officers of state and the earls into the vestry, while the other lords and representatives of the towns and royal burghs went to take their seats in the nave. Angus, unsure of his position, was waved into the vestry.

When all was ready, the Lord Lyon led first the Primate, Bishop Lamberton, out into the church transept, as nominal Chancellor of the realm, to mount to the dais, singing from the choristers again resounding and the church bells stilled. Then Lyon came back for the Lords Spiritual, and these paced out. Next it was the earls' turn, and they were headed by the Earl of Carrick. Angus, gestured by the king himself, was to join this group. A little disconcerted to find himself walking alongside William of Ross, he moved out, deliberately to seat himself a little apart, on the earls' benches.

There was a pause, until the talk and the choir's chanting was stilled by a trumpet flourish by two of the Lyon's heralds, and all stood. King Robert, alone, strode up to the throne, but remained standing so all must do likewise.

Then, as the choristers resumed, the acting officers of state came in from the vestry to present to the monarch the emblems of rule and authority, the regalia. Or at least symbols thereof, for Edward Longshanks had taken the true Honours of Scotland off to London thirteen years before, where still they remained. So Hay, Douglas, Keith and Lindsay carried in Bruce's own long two-handed sword, used in many a struggle, to represent the sword of state, the crown, a mere golden circlet which the Bruce had been using, golden spurs, a silver wand in place of the sceptre, and a battle-worn red and gold lion rampant standard. Each of these the monarch touched, and they were taken and held behind him.

The king raised a hand, and the singing stopped. Briefly he spoke. "I, Robert, crowned and anointed King of Scots, hereby open this first parliament of my reign, and greet you all. I call on the Primate of Holy Church, Bishop William Lamberton, Chancellor, to open the proceedings."

He sat, and all, save the officers of state behind the throne, could do the same.

Lamberton bowed to the king, and announced that although he had been appointed Chancellor, in name, he had never had the privilege of presiding at a parliament. Now, with his other responsibilities to occupy all his time and concern, he would hereby resign this office. And His Grace the king had appointed in his place Master Bernard de Linton, the royal secretary, whom he now named to be Abbot of Arbroath.

From the clerical benches the comparatively humble country priest, whom Bruce had found so useful, rose and came to climb to the dais, where Lamberton handed him the Chancellor's gavel, to muted cheers from some of the assembly.

De Linton bowed to the throne, and beat the gavel on the table before him, where a clerk waited.

"With His Grace's royal permission, I, now Chancellor of the realm, declare this parliament to be in session," he intoned. "Let us to business."

There was a pause, as men eyed each other.

The new abbot of the most prestigious abbey in the land, Arbroath, resumed. "First, the matter of forfeitures of lands and estates, imposed by the former King John Balliol at behest of the King of England. All such to be rescinded under the new reign. Is it agreed?"

There were cheers at that, and no formal motion against.

Then de Linton added, "His Grace Robert also recommends the rescinding of the forfeitures he has imposed, on lands of the Earl of Ross, of the lordship of Lorn, and of the sheriffdom of Inverness held by Comyn of Urquhart. Also those of the Galloway lords, MacDouall and MacCann. This in his clemency."

There were gasps at this extraordinary gesture towards men who had so notably opposed the monarch. Glancing back at the throne, the new Chancellor asked, "Is the motion approved?"

"It is not!" That came from the earls' benches, and from none other than Edward of Carrick, the monarch's brother. "I say that this is folly! These are forsworn traitors. They may have yielded, but they remain the enemies of the king."

There were not a few cries of agreement.

It was not the usual custom for the monarch to intervene in a parliamentary debate, but this being Bruce's brother, he did

"My lord of Carrick," he said, raising a hand. "I say that it should be so. Let the past be past. These have submitted. I would rule a united kingdom. No more warring and struggle; there will be a sufficiency of that with the English invaders. Let this stand. Only if any of these turn against the throne, their forfeitures will be renewed."

Edward began to speak, restrained himself, and sat.

In these circumstances, no one else raised voice.

With a sigh of relief the Chancellor banged his gavel. "New appointments," he declared. "Certain are required. The Earl of Buchan, who was High Constable, has died in England. It is proposed that Sir Gilbert Hay of Errol be appointed in his stead."

There was no motion against that, he known as one of the king's closest aides. Nor against the making of another, Sir Robert Keith, as Great Marischal, and Sir James Douglas as Chief Warden of the Border Marches and keeper of the royal Forest of Ettrick. Nor were there protests when Edward of Carrick was made Lord of Galloway.

One or two other appointments and sheriffdoms were announced when Angus, interested in it all only mildly, received a shock, as the Chancellor went on.

"Angus Og mac Donald, Lord of the Isles, to be Lord High Admiral."

He was not the only one to be shaken. There were various cries throughout the great church, none of them cheers. James, the High Steward stood.

"Sire, I protest! This is—"

The king himself interrupted. "Address the Chancellor, my lord, not the throne." That was flat.

Swallowing, James Stewart bowed. "This, Chancellor, is unwise, I say. The Islesmen are serving the realm, yes. But for one to be Lord High Admiral is unsuitable. Others could worthily claim it." He did not add that he himself had a number of ships in the havens of the Clyde, Bute and Arran.

Others supported that.

Sir James Douglas spoke up. "The MacDonald has the ships," he said simply. "By the hundred. As he has shown, on the Galloway coasts and elsewhere. Has any other the like?"

No one could contest that.

Angus wondered whether to rise and refuse the honour. But that would be obviously to counter Bruce's will. This must have been what the king had meant when he said that the Islesmen's continued support would not be forgotten, that time.

After that, he was scarcely aware of the remaining proceedings, that is until the name of King Philip of France registered, and he heard that that monarch, whose daughter was now married to Edward the Second of England, was seeking to initiate a revival of the Auld Alliance, and with it peace between Scotland and England. Also he was promising to appeal to the Vatican to end support for the exiled and inactive King John Balliol, and renunciation of the sentence of excommunication on Bruce, and thereafter recognition of him as King of Scots. How successful he might be in all this, who could tell; but it made a high note on which to end the parliament.

To cheers, the Lord Lyon led the monarch out.

That evening, when Angus was one of the guests invited to dine with the king in the Primate's palace, he did find opportunity to ask Robert Bruce what being High Admiral of Scotland involved for him. He greatly doubted his suitability, as the Steward had said.

The monarch patted his shoulder. He said that if he could continue to do as well as he had been doing for some time, that would be amply sufficient.

Angus wondered what Ainea would say to this.

Next day it was back to the Isles.

35

Ainea proved to be in two minds as to this High Admiral appointment. It would commit Angus still further to Bruce's cause. On the other hand, it would give him great authority to take his ships anywhere round the coasts of Scotland and beyond, and it would be useful especially in parts where the distinction between Isles lands and others was unmarked and somewhat uncertain, as on the borders of Ross, Caithness and Sutherland.

And Orkney, her husband added. And that could have its convenience in this of the oil development, which he was beginning to see of advantage to the Isles economy.

He had been collecting much information on the subject from throughout the Isles, also from the churchmen. It was reported that there was no lack of petrels over the vast spread of his domains, even though none appeared to rival Hirta. And the culling of the birds could be organised readily enough. Nor was there any doubt that there was a large market throughout Christendom for the oil, holy as it was esteemed. He had learned that, as well as being used for anointing, church lamps and medication, it was valued for helping to preserve the bodies of the dead while awaiting interment, and for keeping certain foods fresh where salt was unsuitable. Other uses also. None of which had been known to Angus and his non-ecclesiastical associates. It all made the project of exploiting this peculiar product well worth pursuing. And all because it was seen as coming from above!

An excuse, then, for a visit to Orkney, as Lord High Admiral?

Were admiral's wives recognised in this king's service? Ainea wondered. Evidently she was intending to accompany him.

It was some weeks before affairs requiring attention nearer at hand permitted the voyage northwards; as well perhaps for, from all accounts, the seas around the Orkney Isles were to be sailed cautiously, even the Pentland Firth itself demanding respectful navigation as he knew well.

The excuse he decided upon for this venture was to assert the King of Scots' concern for the threat of piracy on the seas for merchant vessels, English assailants mainly but Norse also, even Orkneymen on occasion – as witness this of Hirta. The Earl, or Jarl, of Orkney should be apprised of this.

It meant, of course, that the dragonship could not just go alone, but must have a fair number of longships with it to give due impression of authority.

So some of MacLean's and Maclan's vessels were mustered, these chiefs amused that they were becoming part of Scotland's High Admiral's fleet. And of course this of the oil production would aid them also. Gillemoir of Duart decided to accompany them. So Angus and Ainea set off for the Orkneys on the Feast of St Columba, the ninth day of June, this with the cuckoos beginning to call from all the islands, always a welcome intimation of summer come.

Enquiries had informed that although the capital of Orkney was at Kirkwall on the east side of the great island of Pomona, the main seat of the earl was quite distant therefrom, at Birsay on the west coast, near the very tip of the island. So after passing Cape Wrath, the northernmost point of all mainland Scotland, they sailed on north still, by east, for another fifty miles, across the Pentland Firth and then on past the rocky coast of Hoy. A guide who they had brought with them, who knew Orkney well, declared that this approach would spare them many of the hazards of these waters, which they would have had to negotiate had they been bound for Kirkwall, roosts as they were called, fierce eddies and whirlpools and overfalls caused, it was said, by underwater hills and cliffs. The Islesmen were used to such in their own waters between the islands, but these were evidently much more difficult, this because of the strong Atlantic tides meeting those of the colder Norse Sea.

At any rate, although their vessels did roll and sway dramatically in the crosswise currents, to the oarsmen's testing, they encountered no other navigational problems as they worked their way up the west coast of Pomona, twenty-odd miles of it to very near the top, where they had no difficulty in locating the castle of Birsay on its bold bluff above the waves, not far from Brough Head.

What Magnus, Earl of Orkney thought of the arrival of a score of longships with their sails painted with the Galley of the Isles was anybody's guess. But he did come down the cliff-path to meet them, with some of his people, looking enquiring.

"What does the Lord of the Isles, and High Admiral of Scotland, seek of Orkney?" he greeted them. "You come in peace, I take it, since you bring a lady with you!" And he gestured towards Ainea, who smiled.

Angus was not surprised that his own identity had been guessed at, owing to that galley on the sails; but surprised that this of the admiral's appointment should have been known. Possibly James of Caithness had informed him.

"We come, my lord, in amity and goodwill," he said. "To discuss this trouble of piracy on the seas, which much exercises the Scots king and parliament. And . . . other matters."

"Ha! Is it that of Brosi of Stromness and the Hirta Isle? That was ill done, I say, and I have told him so. Although, see you, we of Orkney, or our Norse forebears, had a hold on that St Gilda's Isle once!"

"As of many of my Isles," Angus said. "*My* forebear, Somerled, had some Norse blood in his veins."

"Who was this Gilda, my lord?" Ainea asked, to ease any

tension between these two. "I had not heard of him before this of Hirta."

"We know not, lady. Save that he came to Orkney, it is said, seeking to make Christians here."

This Magnus, fifth of the name, was a fine-looking, young-ish man with a golden beard but not otherwise particularly Norse-seeming; not that this was to be wondered at, for his surname was in fact Moray, the Orkney earldom having come through marriage of a predecessor's heiress with a Moray, Earl of Angus. His successors had kept the Norse name of Magnus however, paying fealty to both Scotland and Norway.

Ainea proved to be a major help in dealing with this Magnus and his wife and only child, a young daughter, when they entered Birsay Castle.

The suggestion of a fight against piracy was dealt with amicably, with no further reference to Orkneymen's part in such, Magnus agreeing that it was a sore affliction for all who lawfully sailed the seas, the English pillagers notorious. He promised to co-operate with the Isles fleet where possible.

It did not take Angus long to get down to the subject of bird-oil. His host admitted that this was quite an important part of the Orkney revenues, the export of it being by way of the Hansa merchants of the Baltic seaboard, at Lübeck, who appeared to have a sort of monopoly of its onward distribu-tion. Petrels were numerous in the Orcades, as no doubt they were in the Hebrides, although none could rival Hirta.

If the Lord Angus was sufficiently interested in this, the Earl Magnus suggested that he should go and see a man called Bjorn Birgerssen, at Skaill, a haven some miles back down this coast, easily found on its large bay. He was much concerned with the birds and the oil, and would advise in catching the fowl, extracting the oil, and where to send it.

The visitors spent a comfortable night at Birsay, learning much about life in these northern isles, similar in some ways to their own, but very different in others, wide-scattered but with no mountains, and none reaching the size of Islay, Mull, Jura, Skye or Lewis and Harris, but actually more populous, this because of the lower ground and consequently more tillable land. The people did not seem to go in for clans, either, and so the Orkneys were spared feuding, always a problem for the Isles lords. Earl Magnus did admit difficulties in having to pay tribute and nominal allegiance to different monarchies – not that the new King of Scots had so far made any real demands on him.

They took their leave next day, Ainea saying she hoped that they could now see more of each other, she and the countess getting on well together.

It did not take them long to reach Skaill, and they found the man Bjorn Birgerssen, with two assistants, in the village there at work in a shed dealing with the previous day's harvest of fulmar chicks, or squabs as he called them. With his earl's recommendation mentioned, he was very ready to describe the entire oil project.

It seemed that most seabirds did produce oil, this to keep their feathers from getting sodden in the water; but the petrels were much the best, and it was the young ones that were the most valuable, before their large oil-glands at their rumps dispersed the oil through the rest of the body. So these squabs constituted the main source of the product. Although fulmars laid only one egg at a time, they were frequent layers, so the chicks were quickly replaced.

The oil was not difficult to drain off, but it took a lot of squabs to fill one of the small barrels they used. It had to be strained through an open-woven cloth to get rid of dirt, tiny feathers and impurities – as they were doing now.

Ainea declared it sad that so many young birds had to die, an attitude the man Bjorn shook his head over.

As to the marketing, although the oil was valued all over Christendom, and possibly beyond, it proved simplest to send it to the Hansa League, based none so far east of Danish

Jutland, these merchants paying a fair price, and able to pass the oil on, by sea and land, to churchmen in many nations, especially to the Russians, where the Greek or Orthodox Church were the greatest users, those vast territories devoid of such fowl. No doubt his lordship could find other buyers for the Isles oil, but probably Lübeck, near to Hamburg on the Elbe, would be the most convenient. And they paid at once.

Grateful for the guidance and advice, Angus presented the oil-workers with a different kind of barrelled product from his dragonship, the water of life, whisky.

The flotilla sailed off southwards again, Angus now deciding to play the admiral along the Caithness, Sutherland and Easter Ross coasts, showing a presence and declaring war on pirates, no specific visits planned. It should all serve Bruce's cause.

36

Back at Dunaverty for the summer months, Angus elected to set up his oil enterprise thereabouts, since the cliffs of the Mull of Kintyre had their own population of fulmar petrels. And with Donald MacDonald of Eigg and his wife Eithne frequently visiting Kintyre as its lord and lady, and seeing her sister Seona at St Bride's nunnery at Lochranza, with himself well supplied with the birds on Eigg's sea-cliffs, Donald seemed the obvious choice to superintend this new venture, based on this area but drawing supplies from all over the Isles. That young man was happy to take on the interesting and no doubt profitable task. He could get the monks at Saddell Abbey to help with the extracting of the oil and barrelling it for export.

So Kintyre was set to become a hive of industry, and Dunaverty the distribution centre for new wealth for the Isles.

Angus's admiral-service was sought soon thereafter, with Sir Neil Campbell bringing word from the king. Ireland was, in the main, equally anti-English with Scotland, especially Ulster, and was, it seemed, prepared to assist Bruce in his struggle, at a price. The monarch had instituted a strategy of assailing areas of Northumberland and Cumberland, even north Durham, by raiding parties over the border, to attack properties and estates. However, if the lords and squires there, and landed clerics, paid him what was called mail, they were to be spared. Considerable funds were being raised thus. And with these moneys the king was to purchase much needed arms and armour, iron, saddlery and the like, even food for his ever-growing forces. Would the Lord Angus take his ships over to transport this, with the moneys to pay for it?

This was no onerous task, at least. Derry for him and his men and ships then, and Ainea and the children able to go and see her father.

At Limavady, O'Cahan turned out to have been involved in this pro-Scottish arrangement. He took Angus to Derry town, where some of the supplies were being assembled. These, in the event, did not fill more than a score of his many vessels. So he sailed on westwards for Donegal and Ballyshannon and Sligo, where more would be awaiting him, while the already loaded craft sailed back for the Solway. Ainea remained with her father. It seemed that the Irish aid was not confined to Ulster, and when this in the north and west was dealt with, the fleet was expected to go south down the Irish Sea to Cushendun, Larne, Belfast, Strangford, Dundalk and Drogheda. So it looked like being a busy summer for the new High Admiral.

In due course, his ships laden from the west coast ports, he sailed them back across the North Channel, for Annan on the Solway Firth, where Bruce was presently based for his assaults over the border and for his efforts to subdue such of Galloway as had not yet fallen to him. Dumfries was still held by the English, as was Caerlaverock and sundry other holds.

At Annan, Angus found the king, this his own territory, for he had been Lord of Annandale as well as Earl of Carrick. He was concentrating his assaults over into Cumberland meantime, while his brother Edward was commanding in Galloway. Angus was greeted and thanked warmly.

The monarch proved to be in good heart and optimistic. But so much was to be done yet, with Edinburgh, Stirling, Perth and Dundee still in Richmond's and Pembroke's hands, these areas all able to be reinforced and supplied by sea from England. Bruce wondered whether, when Angus was finished this transporting from Ireland, he would take his ships round to the east side of Scotland and harass the English vessels bringing arms, reinforcements and supplies to the foe in that central area and parts of Lothian? At least as a gesture?

Rather doubtfully, Angus agreed to do this.

So it was back, then, to Ireland.

At Cushedun, Larne and Belfast he found sufficient freight awaiting him to fill all his vessels, these, by their long and narrow construction, not capable of carrying large cargoes among the oarsmen's benches, not really built for this sort of task.

It meant another journey therefore, to Strangford, Dundalk and Drogheda, this at least closer to the Solway. These sailings were not popular with the crewmen.

It all took time, the loading and stowing, the sailing and the unloading and consequent delivery. And the rowers required rest the while. They were not slaves.

It was August before the transporting was over, and the suggested Norse Sea sally could be contemplated. But there were Isles matters to see to; and the crews, who were all family men from their various islands, had their own lives to live, and their chiefs' needs to see to, as Angus well appreciated. And there was the harvest to deal with.

Meanwhile, Bruce, leaving his brother to cope with Galloway and the raiding policy, returned to the central area of the land not still dominated by the English, this being the Douglas territories of Lanark, Clydesdale and the great wilderness of the royal Forest of Ettrick, so much used by the late heroic William Wallace. Here he would assemble a major force, to be equipped with the new weaponry imported from Ireland, this with a view at last to tackling Richmond and Pembroke. And Angus's fleet to go and patrol the far coasts, to deter English reinforcements and threaten the enemy occupation from seawards.

Early September, then, saw the fleet reassembled and setting off for the long voyage of fully five hundred miles round Scotland, to reach the vital area near the mouths of the Firths of Tay and Forth, this their first venture towards actual warfare at sea. Angus took seventy longships. They left the new oil undertaking developing satisfactorily.

It took them five days, stopping overnight at Applecross, Thurso, Burghead and Aberdeen, to reach the estuaries, that of Tay having the town and port of Dundee, in English hands, ten miles up. Angus led his ships thither, not to land but to make their presence known to the enemy, and possibly to encourage the local population. Then back again to the open sea.

They halted for the night at St Andrews, where that parliament had been held; and they were welcomed by Bishop Lamberton. He told Angus that, quite frequently, English ships were to be seen going and coming from Dundee, usually three or four at a time, seldom more.

The Islesmen spent a comfortable night with clerical and citizenry hospitality. They would make St Andrews their base.

Next day they sailed south across the mouth of the Firth of Forth, skirting the cliff-girt Isle of May, where they noted more fulmars; and then over to the mighty Craig of Bass, where no doubt there would be petrels also, but these would be lost amidst the huge flocks of circling and diving solan geese, the white droppings of which covered the crags and precipices and ledges of that dramatic stack. Then on down the Lothian coast. They saw many fishing-boats, but no merchanters or craft that might be English.

They went as far as the border waters at Berwick-upon-Tweed, then a little beyond, this to display their might, seventy longships bound to make a major impression. Then back to St Andrews.

The day following, with no sign of any enemy vessels, they went back up Tay to Dundee, to leave the invaders there in no doubt as to the continuing menace. However, of action there was none.

St Andrews fishermen told them that the English ships were irregular in appearance, sometimes only days between arrivals, sometimes all but weeks. So it was just a matter of waiting, hopefully – and they all were most satisfactorily seated at the ecclesiastical capital. But Angus, however pleasantly quartered, did not want to be away from his Isles for overlong.

It was on their third sail southwards that, off the cliffs of St Abb's, or Ebba's, Head, not far from Berwick, they saw five large vessels heading northwards. Five. Trading craft would not sail thus, unless possibly for fear of pirates. He ordered his fleet out to intercept, all now tensed for confrontation at last.

And, at sight of the longships heading out from the shadows of the cliffs, seventy of them, the five ships turned to head south again, no doubt for Berwick at the mouth of Tweed. English, then? Angus urged all speed from his oarsmen. They did not require his orders.

It was some eight miles from St Abb's Head to the Tweed, and with the prevailing south-west wind the large vessels had to tack this way and that for their sails to give them the necessary headway. The longships had no such handicap. Sails furled, they quickly overtook their targets.

With much shouting and beating of gongs, the Islesmen surrounded the enemy, seen now to be flying the red cross on white of England. Angus hailed for them to halt.

No doubt the crews aboard had arms, and may well have been brave enough men, and could have opposed boarders from lower-levelled craft. But seventy of these against five, and the assailants with their fierce-looking helmets and brandished weapons, made any defensive demonstration out of the question. Flags were hauled down, sails also, and surrender indicated.

Angus, choosing the largest of the vessels, drew alongside, and demanded that the shipmaster came down to him. A rope-ladder was lowered, and an anxious-looking individual duly descended.

"I am the Lord of the Isles, High Admiral of Scotland," he

was told. "You are in Scottish waters, while at war with Scotland, Englishman. Whither are you bound?"

"To Dundee town, lord. We, we do no hurt."

"You will not hurt now, to be sure! But at Dundee you will be aiding the invaders. You are my captives. I could have you all slain, in war!"

"No, lord, no! A God's sake! We are but shipmen. We have yielded honourably. Not that!"

Angus had had no intention of killing them. But something had to be done with them. He issued orders for all the ships' crews, and any passengers, to descend to the longships, leaving all arms and gear behind. None was in any position to disobey.

It took considerable time for this to be completed, down those swaying rope-ladders in the heaving seas. What now? Angus decided that it would be best, and practical, to send their prisoners to Berwick. He did not want them on his hands; and at the English-held town and castle they would serve as a warning, and an indication as to what could happen to any further enemy convoys.

So he ordered them all to be packed into a dozen of his longships, over one hundred of them, to be taken the four miles or so south to the Tweed, and unloaded there at some point near the walled town, and left. MacIan was to see to this.

So now he was left with five captured vessels and their contents, as prizes. What to do with them? They were of no real use to him and his; but they could be of value to the royal cause. He could have them taken to St Andrews, but that might bring down English wrath on Lamberton and his people there when it got known at Dundee. Better to disperse the ships. Perhaps in some of the Fife harbours and havens, Crail, Earlsferry, Leven, Wemyss, Dysart, Kirkcaldy, Burntisland – one in five of these, where they would lie secure. But first remove from them anything of value to his Islemen or to the king's cause.

Aboard all the vessels they found mixed cargoes of weapons, armour, horse-harness, clothing, salted and dried meat and fish, wines; all, indeed, rather similar to the supplies that they themselves had been transporting so recently from Ireland. All this would have to be unloaded on to their own craft before the prizes were left in the Fifers' care.

Now there was the problem of getting the five vessels to their various destinations. Expert seamen as the Islesmen were, they were unused to sailing vessels of this size and type, with their many and large sails. But with the south-west wind it ought not to be too difficult. And, if necessary, they could be towed behind longships.

When MacIan arrived back from Berwick, having met with no trouble there, a start was made. Angus called for volunteers among his crews to sail the captured ships, and a sufficiency responded. They would not hoist all the sails, only the main ones, and hope that the steering would not prove too difficult. It was reckoned that they had some thirty-five miles to go to the nearest of the Fife fishing-harbours.

With the wind behind them, it proved to be a simpler proceeding than feared, once the steering was mastered, no great haste required. Surrounded by the longships, the prizes were sailed northwards, well apart in case of collisions on their somewhat erratic course, to pass the town and castle of Dunbar, whose English-favouring earl had been the previous High Admiral, and the Earl of Fife's Lothian castle of Tantallon, keeping thereafter well clear of the Craig of Bass and off the Isle of May. It took them four hours to reach the first of their harbours, Anstruther, where Angus went ahead to inform the folk there that they were going to have an English ship in their care until King Robert sent orders as to what to do with it; four other havens likewise. This news was greeted with some doubts by, in this royal burgh's case, its provost and bailies; but refusal, in the circumstances, not possible. It was hoped that no English ships, heading for Leith, the port of occupied Edinburgh on the other side of the firth, would perceive this one.

The four other prizes were handed over at Leven, Buckhaven, Wemyss and Kirkcaldy.

It was evening before all this was accomplished, and thankfully the Islesmen headed back for St Andrews, their first warlike action completed and not a drop of blood shed.

For how long should he keep up this strategy? Angus wondered. Would the English seek to retaliate? They would learn from those prisoners deposited at Berwick what had happened to their ships. Would some sort of fleet be sent up to these waters to seek vengeance? Or, with the numbers of longships reported to be involved, and posing further threat, would the reverse happen, and no more enemy craft come northwards for some time?

He could not remain hereabouts indefinitely to find out. Always the Isles called him and his men homewards. This of being the admiral must not cause him to neglect his own responsibilities and interests, as Ainea would not fail to point out.

They would give it another week. And if no more Dundee-bound ships appeared, head back for home, duty done.

It proved, in fact, to be an uneventful seven days. His crews made no complaints over their good cheer at St Andrews, but undoubtedly they would be thankful to get home. They saw no enemy craft in their patrolling. After making final demonstrations off both Dundee and Berwick-upon-Tweed, Angus offered grateful farewells to Bishop Lamberton and his folk, who would no doubt get the information to Bruce, wherever he was now.

They set sail for the Hebrides.

37

At Dunaverty, thankfully welcomed home by Ainea and the youngsters, Angus found that the first shipment of the bird-oil was ready to be exported to the Hansa merchants on its lengthy voyage. It occurred to him that, since open and narrow longships were not ideal vessels for carrying cargo, he might make use of one of those captured ships over in the Fife havens. There were shipmasters and hands in his Isles, other than his longships' crews, who could sail such vessels. He would send a crew of these round to the east coast, with an escorting group of galleys with the oil, to take across the Norse Sea to the Baltic, and so initiate the trade. Donald of Eigg's brother, Andrew, could be in charge.

The news from Saddell was that King Robert was very active, and had regained much of Lothian and the Merse and eastern Borderland from English control. The enemy was becoming increasingly isolated in their central strongholds of Edinburgh, Stirling, Perth and Dundee. He was now determined to try to get Dumfries and Galloway entirely into his hands. Shameful and almost laughable tidings were that the English had appointed Ian Bacach MacDougall to be admiral and captain of English ships based on Dublin, with the express task of subduing the Isles lordship. He had started his efforts by assailing the Isle of Man. What the situation was there now was uncertain. Angus sent a couple of ships down to discover.

There were a number of matters demanding his attention here in the Isles but no serious problems. It was now late autumn, and time to be moving his headquarters back to Ardtornish. From there he would visit various isles where his authority was called for, and wife and children would be able to accompany him, to their satisfaction.

It was good just to be sailing with them all, under no pressure and not having to command men other than his dragonship's crew – although he was concerned over the Isle of Man, if scarcely over Ian Bacach's ability to challenge his own fleet. It was good weather for late October.

When they got back to Ardtornish the reports were bad. Man had fallen to a joint attack by Lame Ian from Dublin and Piers Gaveston from Lancaster, and the latter was now in command of the island. What had happened to friend Rory was not known.

Angus wondered whether there was anything he could do about this. Would an attempt to retake the island be feasible, with England and English-dominated parts of Ireland so close on either side? That would be major war, and the odds against success. If the Ulstermen would join in . . . ?

Before the winter storms set in, Andrew MacDonald came back from Lübeck, and with more silver coin of various realms than Angus had ever seen before, and loud in his praise of the Hansa traders, who were demanding more of the oil and making very satisfactory folk to deal with. The industry should be expanded.

Angus set about distributing the moneys, and encouraging increased activity in this respect, commerce a new preoccupation for him and his Islesmen generally.

A message from the king arrived, via Sir Neil Campbell of Lochawe, as before. The monarch had heard of the successful capture of the English ships, and Primate Lamberton had passed on the useful cargoes. He was much indebted to his friend the admiral. He had another task for the Islesmen however, if they would be so good. Although most of the Clyde coasts were now firmly in his hands, the fortified town of Ayr was still in English possession, as was the royal castle of Dumbarton. Bruce knew that the winter months were not ideal for sea campaigning, but he imagined that the waters of the Clyde estuary would be fairly sheltered, behind Arran and Kintyre. So would the Lord Angus take his fleet up to Ayr and Dumbarton as soon as might be possible, to assist his own landward assaults on these two strengths?

Campbell was sent back to the king with this agreed. It was mustering his ships once more; but this was a comparatively modest enterprise, it was judged, and not far from home. Man must wait, meantime.

In mid-November then, the longship fleet was again on the move, round the Mull of Kintyre and up past the heel of Arran and over the firth to Ayr. Angus, sailing past, could see the smokes of campfires all around the walled town, indicating that it was already under siege. Leaving his ships to blockade the harbour area, he himself went, that evening, to land just south of the encampment. There he found not the king but his brother, from Galloway, who said that he was glad to see him and the Isles vessels positioned there; and believed that, in this of aid by sea, or escape, being now denied the garrison, it would not be long before surrender. He said that the king was further north, assailing Dumbarton.

So Angus went back to his people, to wait, no actual attack being asked for meantime. No lengthy delay and no assault was in fact called for. The enemy perceived that their case was hopeless, and yielded. Angus left the handing-over and dealing with the garrison to Edward, and sailed on up Clyde for Dumbarton.

This proved to be a very different task from besieging Ayr town. There was a community here also, but it lay some way inland from the castle. This dominated all this stretch of the now narrowing Clyde, on not so much a clifftop as a steep and double-summited hill, this making a difficult approach indeed. There was just no way to get siege-engines or battering-rams up to the walls, and catapults would never get within range. Nor could the besiegers reach the walls either, save by most awkward climbing, when they could be shot at by archers. So night-time assault only might be attempted, but fires were kept blazing by the defenders, so that was all but impractical also. Really, it was a case of starving out.

The king was happy to see Angus, and glad to learn that Ayr had fallen. However, he admitted that there was little indeed that the Islesmen could do here to help. It was just a question of time. Even the danger of the wretched MacDougall, from Man or Dublin, bringing ships up Clyde, would not serve the enemy greatly, for if they landed with supplies, they could be kept from getting it up to the castle by the besiegers. Patience, then, was the requirement. Angus's ships could wait there in the river, just in case Lame John came, but there was little else to be done. Bruce well realised that the Lord of the Isles had other things to be doing than lying idle there.

Angus did not deny it, especially as Bruce said that he himself could be better employed elsewhere in his realm, and was intending to leave the siege to Sir Gilbert Hay, his High Constable.

Angus said he would wait there for two or three days. He was worried about the Manx situation. Bruce shook his head over that. The fact that Edward Plantagenet had sent his lover Gaveston to act governor there meant that he would be very strongly supported from mainland England, as well as from Ireland. Man must be left in enemy hands meantime.

So, three days later, with Bruce heading off eastwards, they said farewell, and Angus and his people set sail for home, leaving Hay to the siegery.

38

Christmas and Yuletide once again came upon them at Ardtornish, and celebrated and enjoyed, whatever was the case
outwith the Isles. Ainea made a wonderful wife and mother,
her husband's many absences, however much she begrudged
them, only making her the more desirable and desirous.

Angus held a Council of the Isles at Finlaggan on Islay, the
council-seat, in the spring. He was somewhat anxious that his
people, or at least their leaders, might be becoming critical of
their lord's continuing and active support for the King of
Scots, their semi-independent status being eroded. But he was
relieved to find that this was not so, that all recognised that if
the English were allowed to control mainland Scotland, it
would not be long before these aggressive folk turned their
attentions to Isles territories. Admittedly they might not be in
any position to dominate the islands themselves, in the face of
the longships fleets; but the mainland areas of Wester Ross,
Applecross, Dornie, Knoydart, Morar, Moidart, Ardnamurchan and Morvern, down to Lorn and Argyll and Cowal,
could be open to their invasion. The chiefs thereof were
vehement over the need to support Bruce's valiant efforts.

So it was the matter of Man that really preoccupied the
council. That large island, far south as it was, had always been
considered part of the Isles lordship, at least by the Islesmen
themselves if not consistently by others. Its present state was
angrily deplored, and all agreed that something must be done
about it. But what? Angus reported Bruce's assertion that at
present it was unassailable, which was grudgingly accepted.
But in alliance with Ulster could not an assault be made? An

advance from there south towards Dublin, and a simultaneous invasion by Bruce's army through Cumbria to Lancashire could gravely menace this creature Gaveston, while the Isles ships could deal with Ian Bacach.

Angus admitted that if this could be arranged there could be hope of success. He would see what he could do. Bruce, of course, could well have other priorities.

The matter of the oil commerce was much approved of, almost all there benefiting by it. It must be extended and expanded. There was no lack of the seafowl. More men must be enrolled for the admittedly quite hazardous task of being lowered down cliffs on ropes in order to reach the ledges, and from them harvest the squabs. Caves, it was pointed out, also provided roosting-places. There probably were few, if any, better locations for this commerce than their Hebridean islands. And there seemed to be an unending market for the product.

The issue of Hirta itself was debated, and the squabbling between the MacDonald and MacLeod chiefs of the Outer Isles as to ownership, this now almost certainly to be the more vehement with the oil wealth become appreciated. It was agreed that Angus himself should go and see these two and seek to resolve the dispute, for the Hirta contribution to the entire project would be very great. After all, it was from there that the recognition of the oil's value had come, thanks to those Orkneymen. Might not some division of the harvest and proceeds be acceptable; three parts, one to MacDonald, one to MacLeod and the third to the lordship itself, which could help by sending men and ships. Angus accepted that he should go. Doing so, he pointed out that, with the offer of co-operation, and the solution of the quarrel over possession, he might be able to get the two dissident chiefs to provide added longships for the Isles fleet, over which they had long been negligent, unlike MacNeill of Barra, further south in the said Long Island, who had always contributed well.

While still on the subject of Hirta and the oil, Angus mentioned an aspect of it all that had been at the back of his mind. They had, so far, only the one vessel to transport the oil. And it took a long time for their ship to sail round Scotland and over the Norse Sea to the Kattegat and the Skagerrak to the Baltic, to reach Lübeck, to unload and return. A total of some two thousand, five hundred miles was involved, he was told. So the ship was away for lengthy periods, varying according to prevailing winds and the dangerous waters around Denmark. He had captured five English vessels that time on the east coast. He had not heard that Bruce was using any of them, so one or more might still be lying in those Fife havens. A second one could be of help by permitting two cargoes of oil to be sent each year instead of one, this as their trade expanded. He could send round to Fife to discover the situation and hopefully bring back another merchanter.

And another thought. Orkney. He had got on well with Earl Magnus there. And it was these Orkneymen who had taught them the worth of the oil. So there would be much exporting from there to Lübeck or otherwhere. An alliance in the trade with Orkney, then? Make a joint enterprise of it? That could be advantageous, he judged. In the shipping, in the price gained for the greater quantities, and also in lessening the risk of loss from English and Norse pirates. The two island lordships, co-operating, could be valuable, and possibly in more ways than just this of the oil trade.

This suggestion was well received.

Angus would pay another visit to Orkney.

The council broke up, satisfaction expressed.

Ainea, who had been listening in from a gallery, was well pleased also. She had enjoyed the previous visit to Orkney and would like to go again. And they had never been to the Shetland Isles. Might not these be worth seeing? Fifty miles or so, had they not said, to the north?

No word had come from Bruce as to need for Islesmen's

316

involvement meantime. Angus decided not to delay the Orkney excursion. They would take a couple of vessels with them to go on to Fife to discover the ship situation there.

As before, they sailed up along the west coast of Hoy for Birsay Castle. But there they found Earl Magnus absent. He was at Kirkwall apparently, the capital of these isles, attending a council or parliament, which they called a Thing. So it was onwards for them, round-about, circling Brough Head and down south-eastwards between this Pomona, or main isle, and Rousay, and on past Gairsay and Shapinsay and across what was called the wide Firth, narrow as it was by their own standards, to Kirkwall at the head of its long inlet.

The town much impressed them, with its great red-stone St Magnus Cathedral, such as they could not rival at home, its Bishop's Palace, where King Haakon had died after his disastrous defeat at Largs, its network of narrow paved streets, its fine harbour and warehouses. They had no such capital in the Hebrides, Islay not claiming this status although the caput or judgment-seat of the Isles was there; but there was no town of this size.

The Thing, held in the episcopal palace, was seemingly just over, and the earl was about to return to Birsay, so they could have spared themselves this extra journey. But Ainea at least was glad that they had not, most appreciative of Kirkwall.

The Earl Magnus greeted them in surprised but friendly fashion, and they were hospitably welcomed by the bishop.

When they got down to discussing the idea of an oil-trade co-operation, this was readily approved of, Magnus seeing it as probably beneficial to both lordships. Indeed further association in trade could be valuable, especially in timber, for the Orkneys and Shetland were all but devoid of trees – as the visitors had noted – and wood was so very necessary for the islanders, for shipbuilding in particular, and had hitherto had to be imported from Norway and Denmark. But also hides and leather, wool and woven goods, and, to be sure, the spiritous liquor, whisky, which Islay was famous for producing, and much esteemed here. These, along with their own Orkney products, would all go well at Lübeck; but also at other markets in the Scandinavian lands with which they traded, such as Bergen, Stavanger, Oslo, Gothenburg, Stockholm, Copenhagen and Bornholm. A united front, as it were, could be advantageous, market-men being susceptible when it came to pricing and larger sellers. Magnus was obviously much more trade-aware than was Angus. Also, he agreed, the matter of protection against piracy was important.

Angus saw that, in fact, he might well be in need of all those ships hidden in Fife, if they were available.

Ainea, not greatly concerned in all this, went exploring Kirkwall with the bishop, especially the cathedral, the countess accompanying them.

Later, when his wife told Magnus that the visitors would be interested to see the Shetland Isles, he offered to take them there and show them something of these northern neighbours. They did not actually belong to Orkney, being possessed by Norway, but he, Magnus, acted as King Eric's representative there, more or less. Gladly his offer was accepted. So, with their escorting longships, the two dragonships, or Magnus's version of such, left Kirkwall, Ainea on board the latter with the countess.

It made an interesting day's sail, up past Stromsay, Sanday and North Ronaldsay. Ainea asked as to this term "say" for the islands, and having it explained to her that, to some extent, they used a form of it in the Hebrides also, usually just "a" at the end of the name, or "ay", as in Islay, Colonsay, Jura, Barra, Shona and Sanda. Clearly it was all of Norse extraction.

After the last of the Orkneys proper, they passed the isolated Fair Isle before at length reaching the mighty Sumburgh Head, where the fierce tides of the Atlantic and Norse Sea met, these alleged to be the most dangerous waters of all Europe, its roosts notorious indeed. If the Norsemen so declared, probably it was true, even although elsewhere hereabouts they had to be most carefully navigated likewise. Heaving and twisting through these, the visitors were left in no doubt as to the need for care, the Isles oarsmen heedfully following their Orkney counterparts.

Up the most broken coast that Angus had ever seen they went, the land shattered by the fury of the storms and seas, great rocks hurled everywhere, lone stacks and isolated columns, called drongs apparently, marking what had once been the shore. For some fifteen miles they rowed, Earl Magnus anxious about getting to Scalloway before nightfall, although at this time of year it was never really dark in these northern latitudes.

Scalloway was the largest community of Shetland – it could scarcely be called the capital – situated in as sheltered a corner as was possible on that coast, behind three craggy islets. Its houses were perched and scattered wherever the broken nature of the ground made it possible; and over all loomed the ancient broch, a circular stronghold of former days, its thick walls honeycombed with small chambers. There were two larger houses, one Magnus's own, tucked into a narrow inlet; and the visitors saw why the earl had brought them personally on this dramatic survey. The other belonged to the priest in charge. There was no bishop here.

Despite their unannounced arrival, the illustrious callers were made reasonably comfortable for the night in the earl's house, and the crewmen in the scattered cottages, being fed on whale-meat and herring, the former being kept in ice-houses among the rocks where it could be frozen. It was not unpalatable. Ainea particularly looked upon it all as a great adventure.

In the morning they sailed up what could not be called a coastline, for there was no least stretch of unbroken shore. They kept well clear of the multitude of islets, stacks, skerries and spray-shrouded reefs. They crossed what was recognisable as the mouth of a vast bay, named after St Magnus, and on to the tip of the mainland, the Point of Fethaland. Two more large islands, Yell and Unst, lay beyond; but the earl was concerned to get down to Lunna, where it seemed there was a fair-sized house owned by one of his chiefs, who acted as magistrate for the area; also a small monastery, where the crews could find some hospitality. He would have wished to get down to Lerwick, but that was too far southwards.

So, sheltered by the isle of Whalsay, they rowed in to Lunna, and were well received by the magistrate, Karl Gustavsson, and the half-dozen monks, who were much gratified to entertain such distinguished company. There was some fertile ground along these eastern coasts, and a more varied diet was available.

They sailed on next day, after a brief attendance at an early morning service in the church, for it was Sunday. They reached Lerwick, and walked the narrow, twisting but paved main street, which followed the contours of the inevitably rocky shore, eyed with astonishment by the populace. Then it was back south to make for the comforts of Birsay Castle for the final night.

It had been a highly interesting and memorable visit, and Angus and Ainea made that very clear, with their appreciation of Magnus's and his wife's kindness and good company. They had become real friends; and undoubtedly this would be to the advantage of all concerned. They said that it must not be long until the earl and countess came south to visit *their* Isles. Meantime, to send ships down, to load timber from the forests of Wester Ross, Morar, Ardnamurchan and Morvern. And whisky from Islay, to be sure.

Farewells were taken.

Back at Ardtornish, it was to learn that the other three ships left at the Fife havens were still there, lying idle. Angus sent crews to have them brought to him. They could use them in the increasing trading ventures.

He paid a visit to Saddell Abbey, to hear what he could of Bruce's activities. He learned that Edward Plantagenet had at last concerned himself with matters military – or perhaps sought to place himself nearer his friend Gaveston? At any rate, he had crossed Solway to Dumfries and was said to be sitting in Caerlaverock Castle. This Galloway and Annandale area was a major headache for Bruce. The Isle of Man situation, so comparatively near to there, was unchanged. So far, there were no calls for the Islesmen's aid.

Angus considered that a trip to Ulster was in order, over this of Man.

They went, and found O'Cahan much concerned over Ian Bacach's activities, that man, whatever else, proving to be an effective commander of ships-of-war, and in the name of King Edward controlling much of the north-east coast of Ireland, his title of admiral being earned to Ireland's cost. Could Angus not do something about this, for Ulster was much affected?

His son-in-law's anxiety was over Man. So long as it was strongly held by England, Ian Bacach would remain in a very favourable position to dominate the Irish Sea, and from there possibly the Solway Firth. He, Angus, could take the Isles fleet down there, as a gesture; but until Bruce was ready to make the proposed descent on Cumbria and Lancashire, this was scarcely practical while King Edward was basing himself on Dumfries. So to go would only be making something of a flourish, for he could not hope, alone, to make any successful assaults on the mutually supportive Irish and Manx coasts.

O'Cahan strongly urged such a demonstration. That evil MacDougall must be shown that he was not to be master of the Irish Sea and North Channel. Ainea, needless to say, supported her father.

So it was back home, to order one more muster of the fleet.

It was September before a start could be made. And it was interesting that, to this assembly, MacLeod of Lewis and

MacDonald of Harris sent a fair contribution of vessels, unlike previously, indicative of their approval of the bird-oil industry, and of Angus's suggestion that they should share in the Hirta petrel harvest and also consider exploiting their isles' own seafowl colonies. The pair were on better terms, in consequence, than they had ever been in Angus's experience. Trade and commerce, it seemed, could do what men and swords and battle-axes often failed to do.

Angus was able to lead no fewer than one hundred and twenty longships southwards, then, a sight to see indeed, stretching in column for over a mile and making the air ring with their gong-beatings. He had made it clear that this was a gesture and not expected to result in actual warfare, Lame John being highly unlikely to risk attack on such a host of the greyhounds of the seas. So there was almost a holiday atmosphere prevailing.

They sailed along the north Ulster coastline first, just to indicate to O'Cahan and his friends that promises were being kept. Then they returned, to go down the North Channel into the Irish Sea, taking their time. Angus carefully chose sheltered bays and inlets where the ships could lie moored for the nights, and where there would be small communities able to support them with food and drink, thus avoiding large harbours where enemy vessels might be based. They did see large craft at Larne, Bangor on Belfast Lough, Carlingford and Drogheda havens, and were no doubt not unobserved from these, but no sort of move nor challenge developed. Angus did wonder whether to make at least one assault on such anchored ships, but he recognised the problems involved, whether indeed any such were Lame John's vessels, and the difficulties for armed men from low-set longships seeking to climb up high-sided craft which were being defended by men who would throw back any scaling-ropes attached to anchors, and so could beat back would-be boarders. Also he had more or less promised his people that this was all only to be a demonstration.

So the fleet proceeded down as far as nearly to Dublin, and then turned to sail northwards up between Man and the Lancashire and Cumbrian coasts. Then, for good measure, they turned up eastwards into the Solway Firth, in order that King Edward should be made aware of their presence, before turning back and making another circuit of the Isle of Man.

All this, covering perhaps eight hundred sea miles, and no haste involved, had taken them the best part of a month. It was sufficient.

They arrived back for Angus to find that he now had the five English ships for his trading. He celebrated by sending off a load of timber for Earl Magnus.

39

Although that winter proved to be a severe one, with much of storm, this greatly affecting the Isles and restricting activities by sea, it did not prevent Bruce from proceeding with his land-based efforts vigorously, although he did not call on Angus for aid. They heard that King Edward had departed for London, having had enough of campaigning; what Edward Long-shanks would have thought of his son's behaviour could be imagined. His last act before retiring was to relieve his Gaveston of the governorship of Man, and send him up to take charge at Perth.

As a result of this odd behaviour of the English monarch, his garrisons at Dumfries and Caerlaverock deserted, surrendered to Edward Bruce and Sir James Douglas, this of great cheer to all loyal Scots.

Now, in fact, apart from Dundee, Perth, Stirling, Edinburgh and certain Lothians and Merse strengths down to Berwick-upon-Tweed, and the fortified town of Ayr which the English had retaken, all Scotland was in the king's hands; and he was summoning up all his strength to try to retake these so difficult strongholds. Siegery, demanding so much of time and waiting, was not his strategy; but he could, and did, seek to organise local magnates and their people to surround, threaten and prevent supplies from reaching them, as far as was possible. Meanwhile, he himself continued with his raiding over the border, as a means of causing the English lords there to scorn and spurn their own monarch for failing to come to their aid, a useful policy, Edward's popularity ever sinking.

In it all, there was no call that spring and early summer for help from the Isles.

In late April the suggested visit from the Earl and Countess of Orkney duly materialised, just as Angus and Ainea were about to leave for their summer residence at Dunaverty, a most welcome arrival. The couple were taken round the islands, all so much more scenic and dramatic in character than were their own, they both exclaiming over the splendid mountains of Rhum and Skye, Eigg's fist-like Sgurr shaken at the heavens, the lovely white cockleshell sandy beaches, the many trees, especially what they could glimpse of the mainland forests, and altogether the great variety of prospects compared with the sameness of so much of the Orkney and Shetland scene. They even went as far as Hirta, over the oil concern.

Various trading ideas were discussed, and co-operation arranged, the matter of wood, timber, being the most important, the gaining of it from these Isles instead of from distant Scandinavian countries so much more convenient and considerably cheaper. Hitherto Magnus had imported mainly pine; but here he could get hardwoods, oak and elm, ash and birch, with their diverse uses.

Other matters were considered, one in especial of importance on a loftier level than just commerce. It was Angus's suggestion that, since Magnus paid a dual allegiance to Norway and to Scotland, would it not be a help to Bruce, in his valiant efforts, to have some sort of treaty between the two realms? England would not want to be at war with Norway, which could gravely harm its trade with eastern Europe. An alliance of the kingdoms would be beneficial. And who better to negotiate it than the Earl of Orkney?

Magnus saw the point of this, and agreed. Yes, he could pay a visit to Oslo to see King Haakon the Fifth. He had not been to Norway for some time, and such was expected of him now and again. He could advance trade matters at the same time.

Angus was pleased, and hoped that good might come of this.

Altogether it made an enjoyable and rewarding visit, and over this last issue Bruce might have cause to be thankful.

He found good uses for those five ships that summer, and saw himself becoming quite a rich man, in silver as well as in lands and men, Ainea nowise discouraging him in this. She could do with fine gowns and garb from foreign parts.

It was the beginning of autumn when one of his vessels which had taken timber to Orkney arrived back with a messenger from Earl Magnus, one Erik Haraldsson. He came to declare that his earl had been to Norway, and King Haakon would be happy to conclude a treaty between his realm and that of Robert Bruce. He brought the principal terms proposed, for the King of Scots' consideration. How was he, Haraldsson, to reach that so warlike monarch?

Angus would have to discover that. He now began to wonder when last a treaty between two nations had been thought up by two individuals who were not part of the monarch's courts and officers of state. And producing of positive results so quickly. Would Bruce see this as somehow unsuitable?

So, where to find the King of Scots? He took this Haraldsson up to Saddell Abbey, his so valuable source of information, and there they were told that the latest news of the king was that he had left most of his force at Dumfries meantime, under his brother and Douglas, and was presently up in the Perth area, surveying the possibilities of bringing down that enemy-held citadel. Perth, situated on the narrowing Tay, but where shipping could still reach it, was a central key-point in Scotland, reasonably close to Dundee and Angus on the east, to Fife on the south, to Stirling on the south-west, and this on the way to Edinburgh. If Perth, now under Piers Gaveston's command, could be taken, much might be attained.

Unfortunately, however, Perth was not an easy place for

Angus to reach with his tidings, other than by sailing right round Scotland again, and up Tay, some six hundred miles, which would take a considerable time. How could he quickly get his message to the monarch? It came to him that probably the best way would be to go to Dumfries, no great distance up Solway from Dunaverty, and seek the help of Edward Bruce and Sir James Douglas, who would certainly be in constant touch with the king, to tell of this new development and seek a meeting.

Without delay, leaving Haraldsson with Ainea, he set off in his dragonship for the two-day sail to Dumfries. There he had no difficulty in contacting Douglas, just back from a raid into Cumberland – Edward Bruce was said to be almost at Durham – and that so reliable friend of the king was much impressed to hear of a possible alliance with Norway, and agreed to send riders hot-hoof northwards up to Perth to inform the monarch; and thereafter to have word sent to Dunaverty as to Bruce's reaction. This was satisfactory.

When Angus got home, it was with some amusement that he discovered that in his absence Erik Haraldsson, a notably lively and good-looking man, had been bestowing his attentions on Ainea, who seemed nowise upset by this, and indeed declared that if her husband was so much concerned with aiding Robert Bruce and abandoned her so frequently, what could he expect when he left handsome visitors with her? She was all woman, after all, was she not? He assured her that he himself was all man, and would show her so!

It seemed that they were going to have the Orkneyman with them for some time; so it was going to be necessary to keep him occupied with other than feminine attractions. Ewan MacLean was enlisted to escort him hither and thither around the islands, although Ainea did insist on accompanying him on one or two excursions, as was surely a hostess's duty?

It took almost two weeks for the awaited word to arrive, brought by one of Sir Neil Campbell's people. The king had presently gone from Perth north to Moray and Speyside, where he was seeking to enroll further numbers of Highland clansmen, fine fighters as they were, to his standard. He would meet Angus Og at Inverness which, he deemed, would be reasonably easy of access from the Isles, up Loch Linnhe and the Great Glen, this just so soon as it was possible, for he did not want to be absent from his main army, so far off, for overlong. He was much interested in this of Norway.

So it was off northwards and then eastwards promptly, with Ainea deprived of her admirer. They sailed up Lochs Linnhe and Lochy and Oich, as far as the dragonship could take them, to borrow garrons from MacDonell of Glengarry for the lengthy ride up the Great Glen and Loch Ness-side, with Haraldsson and Ewan, both good company. They spent the night with the monks at the head of Loch Ness.

At Inverness, however, they learned that the king was presently in the Cawdor, Nairn and Brodie area, seeking to raise men thereabouts. So, rather than wait idly, thitherwards they rode, and were thankful to find Bruce at Brodie Castle. It seemed long since Angus and Bruce had forgathered.

"Ha, my good friend and admiral, Lord of the Isles," that man was greeted, the monarch clasping him around the shoulders. "This is a joy! And you so active in my cause, I hear. This is Brodie of that Ilk, who is raising more men for me in these parts. I am blessed, with my supporters and well-wishers."

Brodie, a grave-faced, slender man of middle years, declared that His Grace required all the support he could gain, in view of the nearby earldoms of Ross and Buchan, and the Comyns and other unreliable lords.

Angus agreed. "Here, Sire, is the Earl of Orkney's representative, Erik Haraldsson, who brings Your Highness the proposed terms of a treaty with King Haakon the Fifth of Norway, which Earl Magnus has . . . arranged."

Haraldsson bowed.

"Earl Magnus and *yourself*, I think, my lord Angus? Here is a wonder! Something which I myself had scarcely thought of. You and the earl's doing. I found it hard to believe when I heard of it from Douglas."

"We deemed it to your advantage, Highness. And the realm's. Here is my friend, MacLean of Kinlochaline."

Brodie led them through to a withdrawing-room off the hall where, at a table with refreshments, they sat, to consider and discuss. Haraldsson referred to King Haakon's reaction, and outlined the general terms. The details could be worked out later.

The principal proposals were simplicity itself. The two nations to declare alliance, in peace and in war. Naval help was offered to the King of Scots. Threat of armed action offered to England.

Bruce shook his head in all but disbelief. "And what do I do to repay such goodwill and succour as this?" he asked. "Battling as I am against the invaders for my throne."

"Your promised aid to Norway hereafter, Highness. When you have gained your kingdom. Increased trade. Support for Norse interests where they clash with those of England. And help for Orkney and Shetland against raiding Danes from Iceland. That land formerly belonged to Norway, but the Danes took it over, and are now ungovernable. It is a sore issue between Norway and Denmark."

"That I can promise, yes." The monarch spread his hands. "My gratitude to King Haakon. And to you all . . ."

When Angus asked as to Bruce's further plans, he was told that, if only Berwick-upon-Tweed could fall to him, then the Merse and eastern Borderland and much of Lothian, lacking English support from there, would almost certainly capitulate. And if it did, there would only remain that central belt, from Dundee to Edinburgh. And distant Ayr, to be sure. And if Dundee was taken, then Perth, further up Tay, would probably have to yield. So that only the mighty fortresses of Stirling and Edinburgh, all but impregnable sadly, would remain.

Was there anything that his Grace required from him meantime?

"My friend – Ayr!" the king said simply. "Take Ayr for me, if you possibly can. It is on the coast, so your ships can reach it. My Carrick and Kennedy people keep seeking to besiege it, but cannot gain the port, which can be sustained from England and Man and even Ireland. Ayr is like a thorn in my side, no great wound but ever paining me."

"I can try," Angus said.

There was no lingering at Brodie, with so much demanding the attention elsewhere. The leave-taking was all but emotional.

40

After despatching Erik Haraldsson off back to Orkney, with
Ainea saying that she would look forward to his next visit,
with the treaty details, Angus set about planning the suggested assault on Ayr. It was only some thirty-five miles east
of Dunaverty, across the Clyde estuary. He had lain off it
threateningly before. But this time a deal more was required. A fortified and walled town, it was proving very
difficult to take. Mere numbers of men were not what was
demanded. Attack by night? Probably that had been tried
already. Blockaded by his ships, no relief and supplies could
get through to the defenders; but they might well have
sufficient stock to let them hold out for long – and undoubtedly the townsfolk would starve before the English
invaders did. Some sort of surprise, then? Something not
hitherto tried.

The fact that the town stood at the mouth of the River Ayr,
could that be used? The walls would undoubtedly be as
protective there as elsewhere. But it would mean that the
place could be assailed from water on two sides.

Fire? Smoke? And at night? Suppose vast clouds of smoke
poured down to envelop the town? This on the prevailing
south-west wind. That could greatly confuse the defence. And
with a sufficiency of men, with ropes on scaling-hooks and
anchors, climbing the walls in such conditions, enough of
entry might be achieved to ensure victory. Angus had landed
south of the town on the previous occasion, at the Heads of
Ayr, a lofty promontory thrusting out into the firth over a mile
to the south-west. He remembered it as dotted with much

gorse and broom and scrub. If much of this was gathered and set on fire, to produce great and continuing smoke, the greenery ensuring that, they could rely on the winds off the estuary to carry it over the town. It might require oil to feed the flames, in growing brush, but they had plenty of oil, at least.

Angus decided that this was a possibility. He would go over to the Ayrshire coast, first, to see the Carrickmen on their watch on the town, and seek co-operation.

It was only a three-hour sail to the Heads of Ayr. Landing there, he had no difficulty in contacting the besiegers – although they could not really be termed that, threateners rather, encamped half a mile from the town, under Kennedy of Dunure. When he explained the proposed strategy, and said that he would be adding a thousand men if necessary to the smoke-shrouded night attack, Kennedy received it all favourably. Yes, he would have his people cut and gather huge quantities of gorse and brush, and place it in a semicircle south of the town. They could supply much of dry sticks too to help it burn. Also prepare ropes and hooks.

Satisfied, Angus said four nights hence, then, to prepare his numbers. He returned to Dunaverty.

A busy three days followed. There was no lack of enthusiasm for the sally, however hard on the lungs it might be in all the smoke. The mustering of men and ships went apace.

Angus timed his fleet to arrive at Heads of Ayr just as night was falling, so that warning would not be given to the garrison, although they presumably would have seen the stacking of the brush and gorse, and wondered. Disembarking men and gear, oil and ropes, he was greeted by the waiting Carrickmen, who announced that all was ready, enough brush and shrubbery, plus dry wood, to burn for hours and produce enough reek to last all night, they judged. Their men were ready.

MacLean of Duart was to take the ships, less most of their passengers, to the harbour entrance, and once the smoke came rolling down move in to assail the walls flanking that side. It would all be confusing for attackers as well as defenders, of course. The various assaults could scarcely be exactly co-ordinated, especially with Duart having to send some of his vessels round and into the river-mouth to aid the attackers there. The walling round a town, as distinct from a castle, would be extensive. Whether the inevitable noise of it all would give some idea as to progress and permit some unified action remained to be seen.

Up at the Carrick encampment, Angus divided the re-mainder of his men into three groups, under MacIan, Mac-Neill of Barra and himself, and arranged with Kennedy the areas of walling each was to assail. It was nearly midnight before all was ready, and the fires could be lit along that great crescent.

Some parts blazed up more quickly than others, little oil being needed, but soon the entire range of it was aflame. But because of the greenery and leafage of by far the most of it, dense smoke billowed up almost at once, this soon hiding the flames behind a rosy but flickering glow. The wind did not fail them. The thick, choking fumes enveloped all, rolling and drifting on north by east down towards the town.

Angus himself, although prepared for discomfort and sore-ness of eyes, had not realised quite how damaging to the senses the smoke would be, not only to sight, however temporarily it was to be hoped. Breath-catching, choking, dizzy-making, it had the effect of producing confusion of mind as well as of movement, in himself as well no doubt as in others. It was with a major effort that he gained control of his wits, and sought to act the leader.

At least everyone knew that their target was downhill, with the swirling smoke, although there could be no massing of ranks into disciplined units, identities being all but impossible to perceive. It was to be hoped that the same conditions would apply to the defenders.

To be sure, the further all got from the fires, the less dense became the reek, a slight easement for the leaders.

The shouting going on all around, the questioning and proclaiming, and cursing and profanity, did not help.

Amidst the stumbling, uncertain crowd, Angus presently found himself at the river's bank. This meant that they were too far to the east – that was clear at least. All had to turn left to reach the town walls. When he had decided on darkness and smoke for this attack, he had not fully realised all the problems.

However, there was this mitigation: all there, of whatever grouping, were intent on one objective, the reaching and scaling of those walls. It mattered little who was who. And there were great numbers of them. Leadership was practically impossible, but it was scarcely needed in the circumstances.

Angus, on that riverbank, was seeking to discern his longships. The smoke here was thinner, more dispersed; and in a brief gap in it, soon he did see one of the vessels. He shouted, bellowed, and was heard. The craft pulled alongside, his identity recognised. He climbed in. He realised that there was another close behind, no doubt more. He waved, and sought to get men to enter the boats. Those carrying the ropes and hooks were finding these no help, but all knew that they were of the essence this night.

The master of the craft Angus was on said that the town walls did not rise very close to the river's edge. There was ample space for men to land, fifty yards perhaps. They moved downstream.

It was with a kind of thankfulness that, despite its indication of a watchful defence, through the smoke he saw hazy lights ahead and aloft: watch-fires ablaze on the parapeting of the walls. At least they had reached their target. Landing, with such men as had joined him on these two vessels, he sent them back to bring more. He led the others over to the wall-foots.

The shouting now was not all from the would-be attackers.

Quickly more men arrived. Knotted ropes were uncoiled, and hooks and small anchors readied for the hurling. Hopefully, this would be going on all around. Throwing these quite heavy attached hooks up over the thirty or so feet of the walling was no easy task, but men had been practising it. The hooks had to catch on some of the stonework up there; but parapets and wall-walks usually provided a sufficiency of protrusions, the walkways necessarily grooved for drainage of rainwater, with spouts. Even the crenellations could serve to be caught on.

So the hurling began, the biggest, strongest men at it. Only one of the first throws held. And another, which gripped soon after, came down to them again, presumably tossed back by one of the defenders. At least these, in the smoky dark, could not shoot with crossbows.

The throwing continued, and soon there were half a dozen ropes dangling. Angus, dirk actually held between his teeth, was one of the first to start climbing, this demanding two hands.

The ropes were knotted at two-foot intervals, and the ascent was not too difficult despite the swaying. He got up to the parapet, was not challenged, and climbed over, another man already coming up behind him. In the haze he could see a struggle going on nearby on the left. Dirk now in hand, he went to the aid of his neighbour, and was able to help in hurling the unfortunate defender over the walling at the far, town, side.

The watch-fires lit along the parapet now proved to be of help to the attackers, in the gloom, enabling them to see their companions ascending, and perceive guards' positions.

Angus judged that his duty was to seek to co-ordinate the assault rather than to get involved in actual combat, although he kept his dagger in hand. There were great lengths of that walling, an entire town to surround; and this did mean that the defence had to be spread out, and there were gaps in the attack as yet.

Angus, sore-eyed like all, became aware of more than this. It was din, shouting and clash from below, on the other side, from the town. That must mean that the citizenry had recognised that their oppressors were in trouble, and were rallying to support the attack, an excellent development. It all looked hopeful.

The smoke was still rolling down.

When, despite the mirk, Angus perceived a group coming along the wall-walk towards him, not just individuals fighting, and was able to recognise the typical Isles helmets, he rejoiced to meet none other than Gillemoir MacLean. Changing his grasp of his weapon, he shook hands in congratulation. His friend was able to tell him that all the seaward side of the walling was now in their grip and, as far as they could tell, demoralisation setting in among the garrison, aided by the upheaval down in the streets and alleys. Angus reported as to his side, and they agreed that they should go on together, back whence he had come, to discover the situation beyond.

The next known figure they met proved to be Kennedy of Dunure, who was elated to announce that all was well in the section where he had led.

It was beginning to look as though the night was theirs.

They, the leaders, came to one stretch of the walling where comparatively major fighting was still going on, and here their arrival in confident strength, wielding swords and dirks and maces, had the prompt effect of making the English break off and flee – this presumably down off the walk to the streets – for soon another party advancing upon themselves turned out to be MacIan's men, equally heartened by the situation. According to him, all behind them was in the attackers' hands.

The agreement, then, was that the walls at least were theirs. But what of the town? It was in turmoil, most evidently; but that did not mean that the enemy were wholly defeated.

What now, then? Was there any strong point in the burgh itself where the English could hold out? Kennedy, who knew Ayr well, said that there had been a small castle but this had been burned by Bruce in 1298 as part of his policy of rendering strongholds unfit for enemy occupation. There had been barracks built by Edward Longshanks, but Wallace had brought these down. There was only the Tolbooth that could be defensive, but it was not large and could hold only perhaps a couple of score of men, with the jail nearby.

It was decided that the leaders would attempt to assemble their men at the main South Port gatehouse, where, if it was still held, they could assail it from the rear, and thereafter march into the centre of the town to take possession

This they proceeded to do, but it took a deal of time. Not that the gate was held against them, but gathering some proportion of their forces was difficult, the continuing smoke now a hindrance not a help. Also, convincing the townsmen that they were not part of the enemy had to be met with, in the darkness. Some of their people, especially the Carrickmen, were already patrolling the streets on their own initiative. Warfare was ever thus, Angus realised, confusion and lack of central control inevitable.

But at length a sufficiency was mustered and, with torches lit from the guard-fires, the march began through crowded narrow streets, the populace now beginning to recognise them as deliverers, men, women and even children, despite the hour, waving and cheering, dogs barking. Angus wished that he could have had some of his pipers to lead them on.

Kennedy did the leading, making for the High Street and the central market-place beside the Fish Cross and the Dominican Friary of St Catherine, where was the Tolbooth. And there they were met by a group which included the provost of his royal burgh, a somewhat confused coming together because of the gloom, only those torches helping. Some of MacIan's men were already with these.

The provost was able to announce that Sir Thomas Calthrope, the English governor, was in the Tolbooth, but was prepared to surrender without further struggle if he and his men were promised freedom to leave and return to England. He still had sixty or seventy men with him, packed into the Tolbooth and the nearby jail.

Kennedy recommended agreement to this plea. It was King Robert's policy not to burden himself with prisoners, and to send them back to their own country, where such clemency would by no means harm his reputation among those who had to do the fighting. Angus accepted. The last thing he and his wanted was to have to dispose of these captives. They had gained what they had come to do. Home for them, without further involvement.

So the provost went over to announce the decision at the Tolbooth steps. And in due course out strode Sir Thomas Calthrope and his men, their expressions not obvious in the still smoky dark, their weaponry left behind in the building.

Brought to Kennedy and Angus, the latter informed them that he was Lord of the Isles, and that it was the King of Scots' custom to send all English prisoners back whence they had so wrongously come to invade another land. He understood that they had a couple of ships lying in the harbour. Let them board these and be gone – and not ever come back again.

Bowing stiffly, Calthorpe and his people marched off to the dock area.

A few longships would see them off from Scottish waters.

So that was that, a busy but effective night's work over, however chaotic as to details in the smoke, and however sore the eyes of all concerned. The provost said that there would assuredly be food and drink in the Tolbooth, where the governor had made his headquarters; and all might well be prepared to eat, drink and rest awhile. No doubt his townsfolk would gratefully supply the soldiery.

Kennedy said that he would prefer to return to his own encampment. But Angus and his lieutenants accepted the suggestion. It must be not far off dawn by now. Some food and quiet. Then, off with them, duty done.

Bruce had his Ayr back.

41

Winter was almost upon them, and it was understood that the Isles fleet should not be called upon for those stormy months in the Sea of the Hebrides. So no calls came. But, as before, King Robert was not to be restrained from his personal military action. Before Christmastide, they heard at Ardtornish that he had gone south to make an attack, by night, on the so strong and significantly strategic castle of Berwick-upon-Tweed, but had, sadly, failed to take it, when poised to do so, and all because of the barking of a dog, which has alerted the sleeping garrison. So much for even the hero-king's bold initiative.

Angus sympathised. A mere dog . . . !

The year of 1313 arrived. The word from the mainland was of ever increasing activity on the part of Bruce, winter or none. He was besieging Perth. His brother Edward and the Douglas had at last managed to bring down the strengths of Dumfries and Caerlaverock, with MacDouall fled to England. So these two commanders could now come north to assist at Perth, this in February.

Ainea declared that it was only a question of weeks before her husband would be required to set sail again. Perth could be approached by water, could it not? Why had he ever agreed to be appointed admiral?

Actually Perth had fallen by the end of that month, a major triumph. So Dundee was now isolated. But the two greatest citadels, those of Stirling and Edinburgh, remained firmly in enemy hands.

Edward Bruce went to besiege the former, and prepared for a long stay, impatient man as he was.

Angus expected a summons to Dundee at any time now.

Then they heard of a very unexpected move by the king. Presumably he judged that, in this adverse situation for the invaders, statecraft might assist armed conflict, for he seemingly had sent one of his reliable clerics, the Abbot Maurice of Inchaffray, down to London, to propose to King Edward a truce, if not complete withdrawal from Scotland and peace, as advocated by the King of France.

The Dundee summons duly came. Four or five days to reach Tay, some four hundred miles. A co-ordinated attack was to be made by land and sea. So Angus was to wait with the fleet, lying off, until the royal army arrived, if it was not there by then. Dundee was a larger town than Ayr.

The sail round Scotland completed in four days, Angus, seeing no sign of any army around Dundee, lay off as instructed. The town stretched for almost half a mile along the levels of the north shore of Tay, with the land rising quickly behind it, in braes and hillocks, to the quite major summit of the Law.

With his experience of Ayr, Angus considered it quite likely that the population of the town could be encouraged to rise in useful co-operation with the attackers. To attain this, of course, timing would be vital, the assaults to be synchronised, lest the folk rose too soon and could be massacred by the garrison based on Dudhope Castle, this some distance behind on the higher ground. So somehow word must be got to them. It occurred to him that this might be achieved by local fishermen. The fleet had passed a number of the small boats in the estuary as they approached. These might not all come from Dundee itself, for there were other havens along that coast; but the town being the largest seat of population would attract most fishermen with their catches. So probably any one of these would serve.

Such craft had tended to draw well away from the longship flotilla, needless to say; but when Angus detached his dragonship to approach one, he had the three men aboard hastily pulling in their net, looking distinctly alarmed. But, hailing them in friendly fashion, he was able to reassure them. He learned that these were indeed Dundee men.

He told them of his project. Would they help to get the hated English ejected from their town? Would they go in, and urge the provost of the royal burgh and his bailies to get the folk to assist in the forthcoming assault? Readying them, but not to act, or seem to assemble, until a signal was given, so as not to arouse the suspicions of the garrison. Just when depended on how soon the royal force arrived; and there was no sign of this as yet, but come it would. It could well be on the morrow. Only when the town was surrounded by land and sea should they arise. As to signal, a column of smoke rising from this dragonship's stern should serve. If by night, a continuing flame. Tarred sails would burn well enough.

The fishers agreed to do this.

How to get the word of it to the royal force coming up the Carse of Gowrie from Perth, so that all was duly co-ordinated? The message from Bruce had not stipulated which day his move would be made, allowing time for the fleet to get there. Angus had rather expected to see the besieging army in position round the town, or nearby – but no. So he sent a couple of longships up-river for Perth that evening, the score of miles, to declare the position and to seek an early engagement.

These craft had only been gone a couple of hours when they came back, to announce that the army was well on the way up the carse, but had camped for the night at Errol, about halfway. It ought to arrive before noon next day.

Angus came to the conclusion that he ought to go in person to confer with Bruce over the proposed tactics, and the populace hopefully assisting, that there be no confusion over the assault. Those slopes and braes at the back of the town could be both an aid and a hindrance for an army.

At first light next day he set off in his own vessel to reach the king's force. At least he had no difficulty in finding it. The road up the carse followed fairly close to the level shore. He saw the army beginning to leave its camp. So he landed, and hurried across the grassy pastureland, to meet the vanguard. He was glad to see the royal standard flying above horsemen.

But when he reached the head of the column it was to discover not Bruce but his brother Edward, whom he had been told was away besieging Stirling. Now he learned that the king had had an attack of his sickness, a recurring blight, which he called "the finger of God laid upon him" this for the slaying of the Red Comyn before that altar at Dumfries those years before.

Edward Bruce was happy enough to fall in with the plan Angus proposed, and this of the townsfolk's hoped-for rising. An evening attack, then, at dusk? Unfortunately smoke could not be used to help here, as at Ayr, for although there were bushes and scrub on the high ground behind, the wind would carry it in the wrong direction, off north and east. But as daylight was fading would be the best time, and probably for the populace as well. Give Edward and Douglas time to get in position round the half-mile of the town's landward side, and await dusk.

Angus arranged for the royal force to light a large fire up on the flank of the Law when ready, where he could see it clearly, and he would make his own signal, and close his ships and men in on the harbour area.

Back at his fleet, they waited.

In due course they saw two fires on the high ground, for good measure. Angus promptly lit his own tarred-sail beacon. It blazed up at the dragonship's stern platform, having to be heedfully controlled, but sending up a worthy column of smoke which could not fail to be seen in the town and on the hill behind.

The oars out, the ships moved in.

Unlike Ayr, there were no lofty parapeted walls and gates here, presumably attack by sea not having been anticipated by Dundee's builders. But the presence of the fleet had, of course, been obvious for two days, and the garrison had erected barricades to block the streets and lanes which gave access from the harbour area; and these were presently manned by men-at-arms.

So the disembarked Islesmen were faced with prompt opposition and difficult fighting, crossbow-bolts coming at them and having to be shielded off as far as possible, and the barricades stormed in the face of sheltered defenders. The narrowness of the various streets, flanked by houses and harbour sheds, made it all awkward to assail, for only a few men, close-packed, could lead the advance, however much greater in numbers were the attackers than were the defenders here. Fortunately the folk in the houses could help in some measure by hurling down missiles, furniture and even buckets of water, on the Englishmen. But it made a most formidable assault to stage.

There were four of these alleyways leading into the town proper; and one proved more accessible than the others. Angus sent men up this, to get behind the enemy and assail them from their rear. Even so it was a hard-fought struggle, even though actual casualties were not large.

How long it was before noise, sheer din, came to comfort Angus and his people he knew not, this from behind, from the town's main streets. Undoubtedly it meant that the populace was indeed rising to the challenge. And very quickly this had its effect on their opponents. Recognising the danger from behind, the barricades' defenders began to withdraw, and had to hack their way through the shouting crowds of the residents they had oppressed. Dundee was in process of becoming a nightmare that night.

And not only for the English. Because of the narrowness of the streets, Angus could not control his men, or many of them, and most became strung out and divided, dispersed. And some of the citizens were apt to judge them as enemies, and further block their way in the increasing darkness.

Angus, confused himself, and out of touch with his own leaders, eventually reached a wider and crosswise street, where he found a group of men, not armed with weapons other than staves and hatchets, this at the gateway of what was seemingly a monastery or nunnery. Shouting that he was the Lord of the Isles come to free them, he was accepted, and told that they were town officers, and here was the master of the Franciscan monastery. This street was the Seagait, and the other main one was the Cowgait, just ahead, linked by the Markergait. The provost and bailies were there . . .

A sufficiency of noise was coming from ahead, presumably Edward Bruce's attack in progress. This town was not wide, although quite long, these two main streets constituting the centre of it.

Angus sought to gather his men here, some of them complaining that the militant citizens were of more danger than the Englishmen – the latter indeed now being less than evident. MacIan arrived, oddly from ahead, having come down the Marketgait after pushing further into the town, more or less unopposed. He said that he had spoken with Sir James Douglas, who had got as far as the Cowgait, from the north. He did not think that the enemy garrison was now attempting to defend the town at all, but presumably were going to concentrate on the defence of Dudhope Castle, the citadel, which stood on the higher ground to the north-west.

So it seemed that Dundee town itself was more or less in their hands, little as Angus's people seemed to have done to gain it. If Ayr had been a confused affair, this was also, although very differently.

The Isles contingent, such of it as had been re-mustered, proceeded up the Marketgait to the Cowgait.

There they found Edward Bruce, with Douglas, well pleased

with progress so far. From what they had seen of Dudhope Castle, however, before the light faded, it would be a hard nut to crack. Only a siege would bring that hold down.

Angus certainly had no wish to become involved in sitting around this citadel indefinitely, and said so. Edward had a sufficiency of men for that. He declared that it was back to his ships with him and his men, duty done. The others did not complain.

So, with good wishes for the sick monarch, leave was taken and it was the Tay for the Islesmen. Once the fighting started, it had been a comparatively brief episode. Home, then.

Ainea would be well content with that.

42

Angus had his own domain's concerns to see to on his return from Dundee, one of which arose out of his own institution of the bird-oil commerce in the Isles. This was a contest that had developed over an isolated and hitherto useless stack of rock named Dubh Heartach, out in the Sea of the Hebrides, barren and uninhabited, but which had been recognised to be home of thousands of seabirds, including petrels. It was now being claimed by two would-be owners, MacDuffie of Colonsay and the Abbot of Iona, from whose isles it was more or less equidistant, a dozen miles from each, west and south. Bad blood was being generated. The dispute would have to be settled, complicated as it was by one of the claimants being the important successor of the celebrated St Columba, one of the most renowned characters of all the Isles.

Angus's authority had to be involved. He had to think deeply before he set off to seek an acceptable solution. Something at the back of his mind nagged at him, something he was sure he had heard on this subject, long ago presumably. Who or what could he consult? He started to make enquiries.

He decided that he ought to go and see Gilchrist MacDuffie first, who had been with him at both Ayr and Dundee, a sound supporter. And in this of argument and negotiation, a woman's presence might possibly be of help. So he was glad to take Ainea with him, she nowise objecting.

It was no long sail to Colonsay from Dunaverty, up through the Sound of Islay, to follow the coast of Jura and some seven miles beyond to the MacDuffie isles, Oronsay being linked to

347

Colonsay by a narrow sandy strand, passable on foot at low tides.

At Scalasaig, the main community, they found Gilchrist, a man of about Angus's own age, with a young wife. He was proud of his name and line, MacDuffie being but a corruption and shortening of Mac Dubhshith, meaning the Dark Man of Peace, who was said to have been one of St Columba's disciples, as indeed was Oron, who gave name to the other island – although the local story was that it meant Son of the Seal-woman! He claimed that one of his ancestors had been Bishop of Dunkeld, on the mainland. The chieftain was thankful that his lord had come in person, with his lady, to see to this matter. He was highly indignant that Iona should be claiming this stack of Dubh Heartach.

"It is obvious," he declared. "Dubh Heartach, the Dark Deadly one, is but a dozen sea miles out from here. We can see it yonder, in good weather. It must be a deal further from Iona. It is part of our life here, always has been, our fishermen having to avoid its reefs. We tell our children, if they mis-behave, that they will find themselves on Dubh Heartach! *I* was so chided. Obvious, it is."

"Not quite so obvious, friend Gilchrist," Angus said. "See you, quite apart from this of Iona, *I* have a concern with that rock-stack. Before the caput of the lordship was moved to Islay, at Finlaggan, it was based here, on the sacred Isle of Oronsay. You must know of this. And all that island's links and possessions, including Dubh Heartach and Skerryvore. When Colonsay and Oronsay were handed over to your ancestor, Murdoch mac Fearchar mac Cormac, he who was the bishop, these two stacks and the Torran Rocks, further north, remained in the lordship's possession. And they still can be so claimed, for they have never been passed over to you, or other."

This was what Angus had had somewhere in his memory, and which he had gone to have confirmed and assured before he came, by the Abbot of Saddell, who was knowledgeable, and held most of the records of Somerled and his line of successors.

Ainea laughed. "For a single lump of rock out in the middle of the sea, it seems to have much interest, many claimants!"

MacDuffie stared at his lord. "You? You say that *you* own Dubh Heartach!"

"I can lay claim to it, at least, yes. If so I choose."

"But . . . this is scarcely to be believed. I mean no ill by that, Lord Angus. But always we have looked on the Dark Deadly one as ours. It is our guardian against the God of the Storms! A stone finger pointing upwards. And part of Colonsay's and Oronsay's past."

"Maybe so. But that does not mean ownership, my friend."

The other drew a deep breath, shaking his head. "So, what of Iona?"

"The same applies there, to be sure. I shall go and see the abbot. Tell him." Angus smiled, and patted the other's arm. "Gilchrist, all is not lost in this regard, for you. Or for him. I see it all as offering a compact, a trade, shall we say, in more than the bird-oil. Let us divide up this rock in the ocean. Or rocks, for there are others, none so far off from Dubh Heartach, which I certainly can claim: Skerryvore and the Torrans. Shall we say one-third to each of us, Colonsay, Iona and the lordship? In this of the oil. There will be many more petrels on these other stacks and rocks for us to share. Cull them all. How say you?"

MacDuffie looked from Angus to Ainea, wagging his head. "All these? And the Torrans! They are many."

Ainea nodded. "Your lord is good, kind, is he not? *I* frequently have found him so. But not always!" And she grimaced.

"Kind, yes. This will be a great blessing. All these others, as well as Dubh Heartach. Much to be gained . . ."

"For us all, I judge. *Your* people will no doubt have to do the collecting of the birds, the squabs, from all the ledges and cliffs and ascents on ropes. They will be busy. Especially the Torrans, for they are a multitude! But there is no lack of demand for the oil, from near and far parts, I am assured."

"It would be something of a task for monks!" Ainea put in. "I do not think that Iona's abbot will seek to rival your men at it!" She laughed again. "Can you see the holy brothers hanging down cliffs on ropes?"

MacDuffie nodded. "This is well thought on, lady. And my lord. A notable project . . ."

They spent the night with Gilchrist and his young wife, Seona, and their children. And in the morning they sailed on northwards to Iona the dozen or so miles.

At that sacred isle off the tip of the Ross of Mull, Angus, although always impressed, all but awed, by the atmosphere of serenity and peace and worship of the island, its aura of history and its impact on Scotland's long story, was never entirely sure of his own status and position thereon. It was part of his Isles; but it scarcely seemed so, giving little impression of paying allegiance to him, its concerns more lofty and remote. Its abbot was an important dignitary in his own right, not even seeming to come under the authority of the Primate-Bishop of St Andrews. No doubt its abbots had been always sufficiently God-fearing, but it always seemed as though it were Columba who was the object of worship here, the man who had brought Christ to the land. The fact that the Kings of Scots had been brought here for burial, and kings of other lands also, left in the abbots' final care, spoke for itself.

Ainea, however, did not feel much, or any, of this. To her, Iona was just a picturesque isle with an interesting background and with a large religious establishment. After all, Columba, Colm mac Neill, had been an Irishman, voyaging here from her own Ulster, of royal blood admittedly but all but banished from Ireland by his own senior clerics of their most ancient Church. *She* did not find this island in any way awesome. She told her husband to take a firm line with the abbot.

Abbot Kenneth greeted his visitors politely, but no more than that. The Lords of the Isles had Norse blood in them; and the Norsemen had ravaged Iona once, desecrated the holy sanctuaries, and necessitated the removal of the renowned Stone of Destiny to safety at far-away Scone. And the Ulster-woman was of the breed that had, out of jealousy, ejected Columba from his native land. Memories were long and dominant on this island.

In the circumstances, Angus came quickly to the point.

"I understand, my lord Abbot, that you are in dispute with MacDuffie of Colonsay over the ownership of Dubh Heart-ach, and of the bird-oil to be gained there," he said. "I think that perhaps you . . . mistake."

"I do not," he was answered coldly. "Long before the MacDuffies came to Colonsay and Oronsay, the Dark Rock was Iona's. St Columba it was who gave it its name."

"He may have done so. But that did not make it his property. The rock has belonged to my lordship ever since Somerled's time. I have come from telling Gilchrist so."

That had the abbot eyeing him tight-lipped. He was ignoring Ainea.

"But I told him something else. This. That I am prepared to share Dubh Heartach with him, and also with you. And equally. And not only that, but also the rock of Skerryvore and the Torrans, all of them. For this of the oil. How say you to that?"

The change in the other's expression was immediate and noteworthy. "The Torrans!" he exclaimed. "All of the Tor-rans?"

"All!" Angus agreed.

Well might the abbot blink. For the Torran Rocks were one of the most extraordinary features of all the Isles. Everywhere in the Hebrides the reefs and skerries and islets were legion. But there, four or five miles south of Iona, was an area which represented a menace to all shipping, some three miles by three,

351

a scatter of what might be called protuberances from the waves, presumably the tips of a submerged mountain range, jagged pinnacles, ridges, spurs, platforms of rock, almost a score of what might be called small islets, some reaching high, others barely breaking the surface, nine square but spray-filled miles of turbulence, avoided by all seafarers. But not by seafowl, that was for sure. And they belonged to no one, save, it could be assumed, the Lord of the Isles, if he claimed them.

The abbot was calculating. "These, these could make difficult culling," he said. "Could they be climbed, the birds reached?"

"Possibly not by your monks. But MacDuffie has many young men. Used to his rock-bound coasts. He could glean the harvest for us, for all three. Equally."

"That would be . . . satisfactory," the other conceded.

"I should say so. For you, my lord Abbot," Ainea observed, judicially.

She was ignored.

"He will act for us?" Angus was asked.

"His people will. The oil will be divided equally. Or the squabs will. Your monks will serve to gain the oil from them. And my ships will take it over to the foreign traders."

Abbot Kenneth appeared to be content.

So a problem was solved.

They did not stay long on Iona. They sailed round the island, for Ainea to see its various aspects, lovely as it was: the nuns' quarters over the sound at Kintra on Mull, kept well separate; Dun Y, the only real peak; the famous Spouting Cave on the west coast; and the white-sand cove where Columba had landed, with its green marble rocks, where he thankfully declared that he could no longer see Ireland.

Then it was home to Dunaverty, well satisfied.

The matter of Man much concerned Angus. But was there any point in making another sally with his fleet down there meantime? Bruce was fully preoccupied with the central belt of the land, Stirling, Edinburgh and Bothwell; and until he was prepared to make a joint assault, there was little to be gained by showing a presence in Manx waters. Was Piers Gaveston, deposed from Perth, now back governing Man? Or had he returned to his friend's side at London?

Ainea reminded Angus that there was still trouble up in Skye, this the largest of all their islands divided between the two great chiefs of MacDonald in the east and MacLeod in the west, with the smaller MacKinnon in the middle. This last, she urged, should be aided, lest he was ousted, crushed between the other two. The MacKinnons were loyal, and had small branches on Mull and even on Iona, a scattered clan. Did they not deserve help?

Her husband conceded this, but pointed out that he did not want in any way to offend their great neighbours, who were among his major supporters in his galley fleet. But a visit to Skye would be advisable, yes.

But before they set off northwards, Angus went to Saddell for information. There he learned of two important happenings. First, Toom Tabard, ex-King John Balliol, had died in France, which was news of some significance, however insignificant he had become himself. For he left a son, Edward Balliol, who was ambitious, and claimed that he was the rightful successor to the Scots throne; and this could be a source of conflict. Second, that Edward Bruce, besieging the all but impregnable castle of Stirling, and frustrated, had come to a highly unusual arrangement with the governor there, Sir Philip Moubray. If the citadel was not relieved in one year's time, not having fallen in the interim, it would be yielded up voluntarily, on condition that its garrison should have safe-conduct to England. This odd compact was said to have much angered King Robert, who saw it as delaying his complete conquest of all Scotland for another twelve months, when he had hopes that at last the tides were running in his favour. So the brothers had, to some extent, fallen out.

The subsequent visit to Skye took up a considerable time, the size of the island with its countless peninsulas, bays, islets and the numerous seats of its chiefs and chieftains demanding much coming and going. But it all proved to be a worthwhile exercise, MacDonald at Portree, Armadale and Borve, accepting Angus's urgings over the MacKinnons, and MacLeod at Dunvegan and Boreray allowing himself to be persuaded likewise when he heard of the other's agreement. So the MacKinnons here were secure meantime.

Home then, to their youngsters, now growing apace, with, hopefully, a fairly peaceful winter to look forward to in the Isles.

43

The year 1314 dawned without any signs from the heavens, nor foretellings from prophets and seers, of any especial events. News from the mainland was scarce, and the Isles remained comparatively trouble-free.

Then the worrying word came that Bruce was a sick man again. For a battling war-leader he did not enjoy good health. He was said to be greatly concerned over the fact that the unfortunate agreement between his brother Edward and Sir Philip Moubray over Stirling Castle's year of immunity expired in June; and he feared that the English would almost certainly not let this become any humiliating surrender of probably the strongest citadel in all Scotland, and that he himself would not be fit enough to deal with the situation. Whether King Edward would be greatly preoccupied by it was uncertain, but undoubtedly his earls and lords would.

The ever-growing divergence between the English monarchy and its nobility was, to be sure, in Scotland's favour. And that early spring it was all exemplified and increased in highly dramatic fashion. For Edward of Caernarvon, as he was known, had taken the unwise step of creating Piers Gaveston Earl of Cornwall, low-born as he was, and offering him high office in the realm. This infuriated the lords, and parliament also, especially the earls of royal blood, kinsmen of the king, notably Thomas of Lancaster, the most important, grandson of Henry the Third, he who also held the earldoms of Derby and Leicester and had married the heiress to those of Lincoln and Salisbury, so the most powerful lord in England. Now, with the support of the Earl of Warwick and others, he had

355

actually seized and executed Gaveston. King Edward was devastated.

The question that all were asking themselves was, how long would Edward himself survive?

In the Isles, all this was of interest and something of wonder, but not vital meantime. But Angus realised that it could have its effects on Bruce's fortunes. If Edward fell, and was succeeded by the warlike and unscrupulous Lancaster, then the campaign against Scotland could well be much intensified by a monarch of the same sort and blood as the late Edward Longshanks. Edward of Caernarvon had a young son, one more Edward, but he could likewise be swept aside.

Nearer home, meanwhile, no calls were forthcoming for Angus's aid. He learned that a Sir Henry Beaumont, another warrior type, had been appointed governor of the Isle of Man to succeed the late Gaveston, no welcome news.

This last concerned O'Cahan and the Ulster folk. De Burgh, the earl, was said to be in close touch with this Beaumont and the so-called Lords Ordainers, supporters of Thomas of Lancaster. So there might well be grave developments in the Man and Irish situation. It looked as though a much more aggressive regime was taking over in England; and Ireland, like Scotland and Wales, would be targets. It might be helpful, in the circumstances, if the Lord of the Isles and his fleet made their presence known again, down the Irish Sea and along the Cumbrian and Lancaster coasts.

Angus agreed to assemble his ships, once more, in late March, with the winter gales largely over. He was glad to see that the Skye chiefs of MacDonald and MacLeod had not reduced their contribution in vessels and men. They sailed off southwards.

As previously, they went as far down as Dublin's bay, taking their time, calling in at havens and communities, not actually making any attacks but demonstrating their ability so to do very evident. Then over to the Lancashire coast, arraying themselves before Southport, Blackpool, Fleetwood, Lancaster and Morecambe. Thomas of Lancaster himself was unlikely to be there, London and the Thames being where he would be based; but he would certainly get to hear of their presence in strength, and take note.

Then a closer circuit of Man itself was made. Enquiries from fishing-boats elicited the information that this Beaumont was basing himself on Douglas and Ramsey, on the east, English-facing, side of the island; so Angus judged that he could risk a brief call at Peel, on the west, to see his old friend Rory and family. He did not want to get him into trouble with the new governor; but one ship's landing there for an hour or so, if reported, would not be considered as any prelude to invasion, surely.

It made a pleasant visit, no matter so short, Rory delighted to see him, however sorrowful his accounts of Manx conditions. Gaveston had not been so bad, when there, not acting the tyrant, indeed being more or less inactive. But this new man was very different, arrogant, hard and officious. What were the chances of an assault on Man by King Robert?

Angus said that he had urged it, but that Bruce was all too busy over ridding central Scotland of the invaders, and he could not forecast any very early action, he feared. But he would continue to make these sallies around Man on occasion.

In fact, this promise was not truly fulfilled, not out of lack of sympathetic support but because of a new and urgent request from King Robert. He, the monarch, now having only Stirling and Edinburgh citadels to demand attention from his armed forces, was concentrating his attentions on attacks south of the border once more, this becoming a major strategy. "Attack! Attack! And with the longest stick that I have!" he declared. So his troops were to make Northumberland, Cumberland, Westmoreland and down even south of Durham a misery for the English north; this to cause the lords and people there to turn against King Edward for not supporting them, and so weaken that monarch. Also, of course, to gain therefrom goods, food, cattle, corn, arms – and money. For the Scots were making the towns and lordships pay for truces from such ravagement. Northumberland, at Hexham for instance, paid the vast sum of two thousand pounds for such relief, and other areas such as Redesdale, Coquetdale and the lower Tyne down to New-castle contributing their dues – this to such an extent that they could not afford to pay their normal taxes to the London treasury. Durham was attacked by Douglas on its market-day, and he even reached a score of miles further south, to take over Hartlepool, its mayor and leaders taking to ships from the harbour to negotiate financial terms. But there was little or no killing – those were Bruce's orders.

The north of England became all but detached from the south.

All this had its effect on the Isles. For King Robert needed arms, iron, steel, from as far away as Genoa, clothing and gear from the Low Countries, goods from France. Also to send Scotland's own exports to the merchants there, the Hansa traders in especial. And this demanded much shipping.

So to Angus came the plea. Escort for the trading-vessels. Would the Lord of the Isles provide longships and galleys to guard the merchanters on their voyages from attack by the English? This was vital.

Angus saw the point, and was prepared to co-operate. But it would be a very different sort of support for Bruce than hitherto, no great fleet showing the flag and threatening assault; but small numbers of his ships accompanying different groups of trading vessels to various destinations, some afar off indeed, to France, the Low Countries, the Baltic and the Mediterranean, a completely new conception for the Islesmen.

Arranging this took much consideration and planning. Many of these groups would be away for lengthy periods. This was not a task for chiefs and leaders with their own

358

responsibilities at home, but for men with fewer demands upon them, sons and kinsfolk, yet capable of acting with authority and decision. There would, probably, be profit in it for these, for Bruce promised reward in goods and moneys. And there would be opportunities for the Islesmen's own trade undoubtedly.

Angus had to discover the details of what was required, the whereabouts of ships to be escorted and their destinations. Bruce had advised to see the Archdeacon Keith of Glasgow, Bishop Wishart thereof being a prisoner in England. Glasgow and the Clyde ports were to be the assembly and loading-places for the shipping, safer from attack than the east coast havens, also convenient for the Islesmen's escorts. So he sailed up Clyde from Dunaverty, to reach the busy commercial hub of Scotland.

Although he had frequently been to Dumbarton, Angus had never had call to visit Glasgow itself, another dozen miles up Clyde, this now changing from an estuary to a river, but one wide enough for shipping, a busy and bustling town. He found the dock area extending for almost a mile along the riverside, with many ships moored, the great cathedral of St Mungo towering over all.

Docking his dragonship among the merchanters, to much staring, he disembarked, to make his way past the sheds and warehouses, and through the narrow crooked streets to the cathedral. There, after some delay, he was able to find the Archdeacon Keith, who, in the absence of the bishop, all but ruled Glasgow, and seemed to be almost more merchant-prince than cleric, much more important in all things, trade included, that the provost and bailies.

This busy individual had been instructed by the king on the matter of the Islesmen's escort duties, and was able to give fairly clear direction. He was in fact impatient for the first convoys to be off, having been waiting for the longships to appear. Three groups were ready to sail, one to Genoa, one to

359

Veere in the Netherlands, and one to Hamburg, consisting of four, six and three ships respectively. How soon would the Isles galleys be forthcoming?

Angus pointed out that it was not long since he had received the king's request, and making that arrangement with his people took time. But he judged that he could have the escorts here at Glasgow in a week.

The archdeacon clearly thought that this was an unfortunate delay, and Angus had to act the Lord of the Isles, and indicate that he and his Islesmen were not at the beck and call of churchmen and traders. But he agreed to get the necessary vessels up to Glasgow at the earliest possible.

On the way home, he wondered how many longships would be required to protect each of the convoys. More than one per trading-vessel? Probably. Say ten for the six, seven for the four and five for the three. That ought to be sufficient: twenty-two. And that archdeacon had said that other vessels were ready to move shortly. So the entire project was going to demand considerable numbers of men and craft, and for lengthy periods, with quite long voyages to be undertaken. His great fleet would not be involved; but there would have to be much enrolment.

In the event, he had no difficulty in assembling volunteers. This sailing to foreign parts, with probably little actual fighting called for, and the prospect of profitable dealings and rewards, appealed, especially to the younger men, chieftains' sons and the like. Angus got his first twenty-two ships off to Glasgow within the week. He sent another galley with them, to bring back word as to when the next group would be called for.

Ainea declared that, with summer approaching, she herself would quite enjoy making a voyage to warm and sunny climes, with interesting sights to view. Why not make a holiday of it, and sail with one of the convoys? Possibly to the great Middle Sea. This Genoa seemed to be an important place for weapons and armour. A sail there, then? It was none so far from Rome, was it not? Visit the Pope, perhaps?

Angus said that he would think on it. He would find that interesting, yes. But it would mean being away from his Isles for quite a long time.

He got a request from the Archdeacon Keith for another escorting force only a few days later. The summer, of course, was the season for voyaging. And Bruce was needing all the aid he could assemble, and not, seemingly, the main Isles fleet itself.

The first of the convoys from Glasgow came back to the Clyde after various periods, the Low Countries group first. They reported no attacks, although one or two English ships had shadowed them, but not risked assailing the dreaded "greyhounds of the seas" and their fierce warriors.

The Genoa group returned, heavy-laden with arms and iron and steel, the men loud in their praise of that city state, its trade and prosperity, its great buildings and its people – this making Ainea the more eager to go there. By this time she had infected her husband with something of her enthusiasm. There was another group of shipping going for more of the so necessary ironware, and they could have sailed in one of these vessels. But Angus declared that, if going they were, his dragonship would be much faster. Using it, they would be back the sooner, which was important to him. He reckoned that it would be almost three thousand miles of sailing to reach Genoa, this probably taking them about three weeks each way, depending on the winds and weather. So, a week at Genoa, and they would be away for seven weeks, longer than he would have wished. But they might possibly improve on that, especially coming back, if the south-west winds prevailed.

Ainea was less concerned about timing. Their young people were now old enough to be left in good care. But at the back of Angus's mind was the thought of Bruce's situation over the surrender of Stirling Castle. This could well have the effect of bringing up some great English army to seek to relieve the stronghold, and major conflict ensuing. The Islesmen might well be needed then. So . . .

Leaving Duart and MacIan as representatives to see to the Isles affairs, Angus and Ainea set off at the end of April, in reasonable weather conditions, their dragonship notably well stocked with food and drink, especially smoked meat and fish, and supplies of whisky, this not only for themselves and crew but to use for barter where silver might be unsuitable. Also hides, deerskins and other trade goods. Theirs was no trading venture, but such could well be useful. The crewmen were almost as interested in this voyage as were their lord and lady.

Sailing from Dunaverty, they halted at Peel for the first night, and were envied by Rory and family over their excursion. Conditions on Man were unchanged, with much coming and going from the English and Irish shores.

They made good time the next day, winning as far south as Cardigan Bay of Wales, to moor in the shelter of Bardsey Isle. But the day following they passed out from the shelter, westwards, of Ireland, into the strong winds and tides of the open Atlantic, and progress became less good, much tacking called for. So they got only as far as Lundy Isle, off the mouth of the Bristol Channel. These conditions would prevail for the next ten days at least. Angus almost prayed for an east wind, but none such was forthcoming. Now they were dependent on their own supplies of food, as they crossed the English Channel and thence into the vast Bay of Biscay, off France, squalls becoming frequent; very different conditions from the waters of their own Hebrides, but at least they were spared their prevalent down-draughts, swirling currents and overfalls. Angus consoled himself with the thought that it would be quicker coming back.

Actually when they reached the north-west tip of Spain, off Corunna, the going became somewhat less demanding, just why they did not know, but said to be something to do with North Atlantic currents striking the submerged land-table to flow along the Spanish coast. At any rate the dragonship made better time down the Portuguese shoreline, and they were able to pull in at a haven near Oporto and the Berlengas Isles.

It was a relief when they rounded Cape St Vincent and could turn eastwards, with the wind at last behind them, and their large sail greatly aiding the weary oarsmen. It would be thus, now, for hundreds of miles.

It was at least one hundred and fifty of those miles, across the Gulf of Cadiz, to the entry of the Straits of Gibraltar, but they made it in a day, so helpful were the Atlantic winds and currents, now in their favour. They landed for the night near lion-like Cape Trafalgar, and sailed past the mighty rock of Gibraltar next forenoon, into the Middle Sea.

They still had a thousand miles to go, to be sure, but in these conditions, all being well, they could cover that within the week. Basking in sunshine, relaxed, and well pleased with themselves, they sped on.

Angus had been told by the merchant shipmasters to look out for the Balearic Isles, Ibiza, Majorca and Minorca, off southern Spain, and thereafter begin to turn north by east into what was called the Ligurian Sea, this well west of Sardinia and Corsica. This would eventually bring them into the Gulf of Genoa, at the head of which was their destination.

It proved to be further up the west coast of Italy than they had anticipated. But when at last they reached Genoa they were far from disappointed.

It turned out to be a magnificent city, almost as large as London, with a great cathedral, many other handsome churches, of finer architecture than they had ever seen, an archepiscopal palace unrivalled in its splendour and size, although large and impressive mansions proliferated. The streets were regular, with many squares and market-places and gardens, statues everywhere, fountains and crosses. And the commercial areas were extensive, for this was the greatest trading and manufacturing centre of all the Mediterranean, having surpassed Pisa and even Venice. Apart from the usual warehouses and dockland buildings, there were iron-works, forges and smelteries, textile factories, brewhouses, sheds for the wine, mills, shipbuilding yards, and every kind of work-shop and craft centre. And over all, the aura of prosperity and busyness.

Behind the city, hills rose quite close, the lower slopes clothed with vineyards and olive groves. And all under sun-light and warmth.

The Isles folk felt very much wondering strangers amidst all this, but soaked it up appreciatively, Ainea almost raptur-ously.

There were monastic quarters for lodging in, these being a deal less severe than some at home, even decorated with pictures, tapestries and statues. When the prior of the one in which the visitors were guided to for accommodation learned that he had lordly guests from far-away Scotland, nothing would do but that he must go and tell Archbishop Dominic. He came back with an invitation to attend at the archepiscopal palazzo. They could scarcely refuse.

They found a gorgeously robed prelate, younger than they would have expected, in quite the most imposing and dec-orative series of halls, salons, corridors and galleries that they had ever imagined, much less seen, full of divines and bowing officials. They were greeted by the archbishop, formally at first, but soon he thawed, undoubtedly Ainea's presence and person hastening this process, he evidently a ladies' man, cleric or none. Presently he had her by the arm to conduct round the premises and show treasures, shrines, jewelled ornaments, saints' relics, paintings and the like, Angus following, mildly amused.

The prelate insisted that they must dine with him. And not only that, but that they should move from that monastery to his palace; he would have no dissent. Angus wondered, modestly clad as they were for their voyaging in an open longship, how they would fit in to this splendid establishment, he in Highland fashion; but presumably this did not worry the prelate.

They were allotted a fine chamber in a wing, this with a single bed in it, and an ante-room off with another bed, presumably this considered suitable for priestly premises. Ainea declared that there was quite enough room in the main bed for them both, whatever the customs were here.

The repast that followed was fully up to the standards of the surroundings, the dining accompanied by the singing of a choir. Ainea was the only woman present, although Angus, perhaps wrongfully, wondered whether there might not be female quarters elsewhere in this large building.

Dominic pressed delicacies and wines on Ainea, and thereafter these came on to her husband also.

After the meal, or banquet rather, they adjourned to a salon, where there was entertainment, singing boys with lovely voices, gypsy acrobats, and even a dancing bear, altogether a memorable evening. The archbishop himself escorted the visitors to their chambers, with a goodnight blessing which involved an embrace.

Angus observed that he would have to watch His Eminence, but Ainea seemed to approve of him.

In the morning they were provided with a guide to show them round the crescent-shaped city-state, or some part of it, for there was a great deal to see, all highly interesting. They learned of the Etruscan, Phoenician and Greek origins of it all, before the Romans took over. How it became involved in the Crusades, and was indeed sacked by the Saracens. Genoa recovered, and thereafter was able to extend its sway eastwards to Syria and the Byzantine areas, even as far as India and the Crimea. They brought gold from North Africa, as well as domestic slaves.

The archbishop himself took them round the churches and the cathedral the day following, the latter and many of the others largely built of black and white marble. The third day was spent on horseback, riding up into the hilly background among the great vineyards and peach orchards and other fruit-growing locations. They had not realised how close, relatively, Genoa was to the Alpine foothills, these providing a dramatic background.

That evening, Dominic showed them something of much interest to Angus, and of which he had not heard. Cartography, or map-making, had become an especial concern of the Genoese, this of great value to navigation. They saw maps of lands of which they had never so much as heard, especially eastwards and southwards, to the Russias, Turkey, Arabia, Persia, India and the Holy Land. Admittedly westwards, beyond Spain, it was all distinctly vague; and as far as Scotland was concerned, very much so. But it was to be noted that there was indication of a great land beyond the Atlantic Ocean. Whether such existed or not was an open question.

They continued with their guided touring for the next two days, by which time they were all but satiated with sights and scenes and wonders, indeed to the extent of wondering how they possibly could remember all that they had been shown.

Angus decided it was time that they departed. He kept thinking of the long voyage home, and what might be happening there, especially over Bruce's situation. Ainea could have stayed longer, but accepted her husband's concern.

When they told the archbishop that they were going, he showered them with presents, jewellery and small paintings and fine cloths for Ainea, and parchment maps for Angus, even a small pearl-handled dagger. He said that they must come back one day, they would always be welcome. And at the parting, he kissed Ainea warmly.

The dragonship's crew they found had also managed to accumulate quite a variety of gifts and mementoes.

On their outward voyage the notion had been mentioned of perhaps calling at Rome to visit the Pope. But now they both felt that they had had a sufficiency of meeting clerics and sightseeing. Also Boniface the Eighth had a reputation for grandeur and imperious behaviour; and not only that, but of demanding contributions of gold and silver from all visitors to St Peter's, the which Angus was not inclined to offer. He was said to act the emperor indeed, wore emperor's golden sandals, and always had two great swords carried before him, representing rule spiritual and temporal. He had, in fact, imprisoned his predecessor, Pope Celestine, in a noisome dungeon where he had died. So, although Saint Peter's successor he might be, and supreme Head of Holy Church, the travellers decided not to call at Rome.

The return voyage was delayed by south-westerly winds for the first half through the Mediterranean, but aided once they turned northwards up the coasts of Spain and Portugal. On the whole, then, they made better time than when coming. It was now the beginning of June, and the weather fine.

All had plenty to talk about on the way.

But when, at length, they reached the Isles, it was to find very urgent tidings. Angus's concern for the king had not been unfounded. Edward of England was known to be on his way north, with the biggest army seen since his father's invasions, this to prevent the surrender of Stirling Castle. Bruce beseeched Angus Og to come to his aid with as large a force of his Islesmen as he could possibly muster, for this was, he feared, going to be the touchstone battle of all, and against the might of English cavalry, archers and foot by the thousand. Come, and quickly, he pleaded.

And this message had been waiting, Gillemoir MacLean said, for two weeks, no less.

Angus was much disconcerted. While he had been enjoying himself in foreign parts, his friend and monarch had been in greatest need of help, and gaining no word of it. Here was shame!

Duart said he had done the best he could. He had warned most of the chiefs to have their men ready for a swift assembly, with their ships. The word was that Bruce was intending to have the English meet him south of Stirling, where the great Tor Wood came close to the marshy, narrow coastal plain of Forth, the river's meanderings through this presenting a hazard for cavalry, soft and difficult ground for horses. Somehow force the enemy down into this from the higher ground. Seek to isolate the archers . . .

Angus was already assessing the best and quickest way to reach that area with his men. There was indeed little choice. Up Clyde, and past Dumbarton, to disembark on the north bank before Glasgow. Kilpatrick? Then march. How many miles to Stirling? The Kilpatrick Hills and the Campsie Fells in between. Get to Fintry, a dozen miles? Then another dozen over to the Carse of Forth. Down-river to Stirling. Almost still another dozen. Two days marching for his people.

Three days, then, to gather his ships off Dunaverty. A day's sailing up Clyde. Two days marching through the hills. Six days at the soonest, the best that he could do.

Orders were issued. Haste!

44

The Islesmen were never very happy to leave their ships and start marching. But that June afternoon they had to do so at Kilpatrick, the name commemorating where St Patrick had been born, and which he had left, later to become the patron saint of Ireland. Here the Clyde narrowed notably, before Glasgow, under the thrust of the Kilpatrick Hills.

They marched on all that June night, six hundred men, heavily armed, north by east through the hills, by Strathblane, to rest awhile among the commencement of the Campsie Fells, reaching Killearn, short of Fintry, weary.

With dawn they were on their way again, by Balfron, through the Campsies proper, and over Kippen Muir, to reach the low ground of the Carse of Forth at Kippen itself. Now they could see, eastwards, the mighty mass of Stirling Castle on its rock rising out of the plain, but still eight miles off. Cheered by the sight of it, they trudged on, relays of pipers playing, to help footsore men. It was the Eve of the Vigil of St John, midsummer, early morning.

As they neared their destination, no sign nor sound of battle greeted them. So they were in time, after all? But, of course, the extensive Tor Wood lay immediately to the south-east of the castle rock, and the Scots army was thought to be waiting there. Where was the enemy?

The English garrison was still in the castle, at any rate, for banners bearing the leopards of England flew from its towers. Glaring up at it, the Islesmen marched round its southern flank, pipers playing the louder.

As they neared the first trees of the wood, two horsemen

came spurring out towards them, one quickly to be recognised as Sir Neil Campbell of Lochawe.

"Angus Og! Thank God, thank God, my lord!" he cried. "You come at last! We feared – His Grace feared . . . !"

"I have been afar. To the Middle Sea. Came so soon as I heard. The English? Where are they? No battle as yet?"

"Battle, no. But fighting, yes. The king himself. He has slain de Bohun, Hereford the Constable's nephew. In single combat!"

"Single combat! King Robert? Never that, surely!"

"It is true. We all saw it. Hereford and Gloucester, King Edward's nephew, led the enemy van. Edward himself, with Pembroke, are still back near to Falkirk, with their main army. But ahead, even of the vanguard, spearheading it, was this de Bohun – a young man. Bold. He saw His Grace's standard. Saw it was the king. Yelled challenge to him for single combat. And came spurring."

"And Bruce fought him? Accepted? Alone!"

"Aye. He saw it as opportunity to encourage us all. He, veteran of much warfare. The other young, lacking experience. Arrogant. So, he met him. On a garron, a nimbler horse. Veered his beast in front. Risked overthrow by the other's great destrier, that beast rearing. He crashed his battle-axe down on Bohun's helmet with great force. Cleft it. Slew him. We all saw it. One blow!"

Angus marvelled. They were walking on, side by side, Campbell's esquire leading the two horses.

"Gloucester himself, with the van, and Hereford, they were more . . . cautious. Held back, to mass their strength. But the king led his forward troop on to immediate attack. Three hundred perhaps. Charged. Struck. It became all confusion. The English outnumbered us, yes. But were unready for such sudden attack. Gloucester was unhorsed. Hereford behind. They were not well led. They scattered. Most turned back, disengaged. Back towards the main vanguard. The first field was ours!"

"Lord! What a wonder! Scarce believable. Where now? The king? And the English van?"

"We hold a vantage-point. On a knoll, at the edge of this wood. They, Gloucester and Hereford, are down at the Milton of Bannock. Where the Bannock Burn begins to drop to the carse, the marshland . . ."

They marched on, pipers still playing.

Through the wood, Campbell led them to the king's camp, there overlooking the levels of the Forth with its marshy, watery waste and the coiling meanderings of the now widening river.

King Robert rejoiced to see Angus, greeting him as a close friend, his men a most welcome addition to the Scots array, tired with their long marching as they were. With him were his brother Edward, his nephew Thomas Randolph of Moray, Lennox, the High Steward, the Douglas, Hay the Constable, Seton, Boyd, Irvine his armour-bearer, Lindsay, and the clerics Bernard de Linton, the secretary and William Lamberton, Bishop of St Andrews.

As they spoke, Sir Robert Keith, the Knight Marischal, came to report, his scouts, well forward, having informed him. The main English army was approaching, a vast host, covering all the plain between Falkirk and the Sauchie Ford, thousands of barded destrier cavalry, heavily armoured, hundreds of mounted Welsh archers, and foot behind, numberless. King Edward would be leading, in name, but undoubtedly the warrior Pembroke would be in actual command.

They were listening to Keith when a call, and pointing, had them all gazing southwards by east. There, none so far off, a force of light cavalry were to be seen advancing, not up towards this Tor Wood but turning down, heading for the low ground of the carse, banners flying.

King Robert pointed. "Those are Clifford's colours – I know them well," he exclaimed. "He who came late to battle at Loudoun Hill. Sir Robert Clifford, Lord of Brougham."

"They go into the marshland – that is strange," Sir Gilbert Hay of Erroll, the High Constable, said. "Why that? Ill ground for horses. They must be going to see if they can win round by the riverside to gain Stirling Bridge. By the flats. Get behind us."

"They must have a guide, then," Campbell suggested. "One who knows the marshes."

"Some traitor. Or one of the castle garrison, perhaps," Bruce said. "If so, he may know more than the marshes. Our positions. And the traps we have set."

"These marshes," Angus asked, yawning, despite himself. "*Can* the English get round to Stirling by the shore? If so, we must retire, no? Behind that castle rock. Or be cut off."

Bruce shook his head. "I know that ground well, soft, boggy, crossed by streamlets. Clifford may be able to go a mile or so, twisting and turning among and through them. Then he will reach the Pelstream Burn, which flows into the larger Bannock. That, the Bannock, is tidal there, with soft muddy banks. Cavalry cannot cross that. There was a bridge over the Pelstream, but we have demolished it. They will have to turn back. Foot perhaps could win round but not horses. They would sink in. And if they seek to creep round this edge below us, firmer ground, Thomas Randolph's men, at St Ninian's Kirk, will descend to halt them."

"Can you go to their aid, Sire?"

"No. We must wait here. Hold this strong position. The main English force may now well advance . . ."

They could watch from this high ground Clifford's cavalry being confronted by Randolph's foot, a strange battle, the Scots spearmen promptly forming up into a schiltrom to block the narrow way, lances bristling out like a great hedgehog all round, the enemy cavalry unable to gain sufficient firm footing to give them the charging impetus they required. Had Clifford had archers it would have been different. But he had not. The horses it was which inevitably bore the brunt of the punish-

372

ment, seeking to ride down those spears. Many fell, their mail-clad riders with them.

The watchers eyed it all, frustrated that they dared not go to Randolph's men's assistance; they also had to keep looking the other way, to where Gloucester and Hereford and the vanguard waited. Clearly they looked for the arrival of the main English host.

It all made a strange waiting strategy for both sides, for all but Clifford and Randolph. And presently it became clear to the former that he could not win there, for he began to draw off and reform, but now facing the other way, southwards again. And it looked as though he had lost about one-third of his numbers. The sounds of throaty cheering came echoing across the carseland, and was re-echoed from the other Scots positions.

"There we have seen something men will wonder at for long!" the king told his companions. "Infantry defeating a greater force of mailed cavalry in the open field. If Randolph does naught else, he has had his hour, I say! That fight is ours also."

All eyes were turned southwards now. And soon there came into view a tremendous, an all but terrifying sight, an enormous mass of men and horses crowding in over the Bannock Burn and stretching far out of sight behind. It was early evening now. Were the English going to attack? Up towards this knoll at the wood's edge? A difficult approach against determined defenders.

And then the king burst out with a mighty and wondering oath. The enemy van, under Gloucester and Hereford, so long stationary, had started to move again; but not now uphill and in battle array, but down, down into the carse, in troops and columns. And behind them came the great host, to start to do likewise, extraordinary as this seemed. Angus could scarcely believe it, a great horsed army leaving the firm ground for the soft.

373

It was the monarch who perceived the reason. "They go to spend the night in safety. No attack until the morrow. Down there they will be more secure among the pools and runnels. Scattered. We cannot assail them there by night, with effect – or so they judge. They will come out again in the morning."

Angus was not the only one to ask what was the royal strategy now?

Bruce declared that he would think on it. There must be some way that he could take advantage of this unexpected development.

The June night descended on them, never really dark, but banks of mist arising from the waterlogged ground, a myriad of small campfires gleaming through it. A short period of rest it would be, undoubtedly, but greatly needed by Angus and his men. They lay down, in their plaids, like most of the rest in the Scots brigades, but King Robert did not. They left him pacing to and fro, a man restless, seeking to make up his mind as to the action that would decide all, and whether men lived or died.

Whether Bruce got any sleep at all Angus knew not. But he himself was wakened, as were they all, by the royal command, in the dove-grey half-light soon after three hours past midnight. And, not to fight yet, but to worship and pray, at least the king's brigade. Whether the other three Scots groups did the same was not to be known.

The monarch addressed his yawning, coughing people. They would celebrate High Mass, and seek the Almighty God's guidance and blessing on this new day.

Abbot Maurice of Inchaffray, although by no means the most senior cleric there, celebrated, aided by the others, even the Primate, prayed, and passed the Sacrament round the kneeling ranks of men. The Abbot of Arbroath, Bernard de Linton, held up the famous Brecbennoch of St Columba before all, their talisman. And the Dewar of the Main, who had aided Bruce after his defeat at Methven eight years before, carried St Fillan's arm-bone, his precious relic.

374

The king addressed all, sounding sternly confident. On this, the birthday of John the Baptist, and under the guidance of the son of God Himself, St Andrew aiding them, they would have the victory. And all who fought would have pardon for any and every offence committed by them; all who fell and died, their families would have relief from every tax and duty, on the royal word.

Then he directed the clergy and all non-combatants, porters, grooms, servants, any of the populace they could find, to go and occupy the edge of the fifty-foot drop down into the carseland, massing, where they would look like a second force, reinforcements, awaiting, as seen by the enemy below, when the light grew brighter. For the rest of them, it was advance, quiet advance in a long line, all four brigades, down to the soft ground, this now, before the English stirred. Silence, then, and down, down to the wetlands. It was no place to fight a battle, but a deal worse for the foe than for themselves, with all their heavy cavalry. It was to be hoped that they did not stir over-early. It was now barely four hours after midnight.

Bruce's plan was to stretch his four brigades all along the foot of that slope, in schiltroms of spears, with the non-fighting folk up on the crest but evident. Then, when the enemy camp roused and prepared to climb back out of the carse, he would move his schiltroms forward, one at a time, the other three guarding the flanks, this to force the English to direct action. A primary concern was the Welsh archers. These could be the main menace. But bowmen needed height, to be able to see and reach their targets. And in all that spread of marshland there was only the one recognisable firm outcrop, no ridge but a sort of hogsback of rocky ground and firm soil, to the north-west. That was the place for the archers; and would have to be avoided by most of their force, at all costs.

No doubt the enemy guards were on duty, and listening, but the mists that this wet land produced would hide both sides from each other. That would lift at sun-up. So now silence was essential, difficult as it was for an army on the move. But all were warned that their lives could depend on it.

They moved forward and down. And it was very evident when they reached the slope-foot and on, with the surface becoming ever softer and soon men's feet sinking in, to muttered cursing. But, to be sure, the same would apply to the foe, and so much worse for the horses.

The king, very much in personal command, ordered his groups into position however slow and awkward the process because of the lack of vision as well as the difficult treading, the many men involved, and the silence which must be kept. He reckoned that, at this midsummer, the dawn would be about four of the clock, and sunrise an hour later. Then the mists would lift, and their presence become known to the foe. Action would follow.

Edward Bruce's brigade occupied the extreme south end of the long line. Then Randolph of Moray's. Then the king's own. Then Douglas, with the young High Steward. And finally, well to the north, Keith the Marischal, with his light cavalry, would be ready to cut off any possible English move towards Stirling, unlikely as this was; but also to threaten that hogsback where the archers would be apt to be, his men chain-mailed as some protection against arrows.

Gradually all got approximately into position, however uncomfortably in that deep mud and among the pools and streamlets. They waited.

Presently they could hear stirrings, sounds, calls, even, in the mist, the gleam of campfires being revived, although there would be little fuel for them in that terrain. Soon now.

The sky, pink with the dawn, was becoming brighter, and, facing east as the Scots were, they could see the sun beginning to make its reddish rising evident.

Quite quickly the white vapour rose, did not disperse but lifted up from ground level to hang overhead. And there, some four hundred yards ahead, were the outskirts of the English encampment, the fires, the horse-lines, the baggage, contrived shelters, the stacks of lances – and, to be sure, the staring men. For if they could be seen now, so could the Scots.

No doubt there was much to-do among the foe, as their new situation dawned on them; but Bruce and his people were equally engaged. The king gave his orders for his own group to move forward promptly, and the first so to do, flanked right and left by Randolph and Douglas, stationary still. Almost one hundred yards they advanced, to halt and form up into eight schiltroms side by side, the Islesmen, who had never done the like before, being told what to do and supplied with the necessary spears.

Each schiltrom had to form a circle of men, those on the outer perimeter kneeling, however wet the ground, spears out-pointing; the next rank crouching behind, their spears over the others' shoulders; then the taller, weapons up high and ready to thrust against riders, while the lower ones dealt with the horses. Angus found himself in the middle of one of these, the king in the next on the right.

A blast on the royal horn was the signal for Douglas to move up next.

The enemy had not been idle the while. There was much blowing of bugles, mustering of men and mounting of horses, raising of standards, this no doubt Gloucester's and Hereford's vanguard. A long line of horsemen was forming up.

Randolph's group now advanced, to settle in schiltroms on the king's right. Edward of Carrick did not wait to be signalled, but came out in flank.

Bruce had not failed, during all this, to look for those archers, gazing half-left, north-westwards. And there he saw what he had not looked to see, not bowmen gathered on the slightly higher ground of the outcrop but heavy cavalry. He stared.

"Fools!" he cried. "Mailed knights! What good can they do there? Where their bowmen should be. Sakes, here is a blessing

377

for us! Where are their archers? Still in their main camp? They must be. So we are spared them meantime. And that cavalry cannot serve them anything up there, however firm their footing. As on an island! The wonder of it! Who commands the enemy? Or fails to command! Edward of Caernarvon? Or Pembroke – who should know better?"

Angus was looking right ahead, as were most of the Scots. The English vanguard was clearly making ready to advance, however slowly they must do so. That slope down from the Tor Wood's edge was less steep in some places than in others. The enemy host had come down at one of these points, and would presumably seek to climb back whence they had come, to get to fighting-ground. But now the long line of over thirty schiltroms barred the way. Would they try archery first? Too far for effective range, at three hundred yards or so. But they could send the bowmen forward, at no risk.

They did not do so. A long trumpet-blast heralded movement – and it was the vanguard cavalry that moved, and movement was all that it could be called, however much a horsed charge would have been desired, to ride down the stationary foe. For the mounts, unable to pick their way through the bog and runnels by any choice, were sinking hock-deep into the mire, and clearly disliking it, tossing heads, snorting and sidling, however much their riders might spur. It made the slowest of advances.

The schiltroms waited, tense.

In the centre of this long and plodding progress, the standards of the Earls of Gloucester and Hereford were borne high over the mailed and helmeted leaders, their swords drawn, their men's lances couched. Fully four-deep they came, shouting.

Their advance was less than direct, and not only because of the ground. The evening before, they had come down here by a track where there had been a bridge over the Bannock Burn, this bridge demolished by the Scots previously, but its position marking a fording-place. For this the vanguard headed.

As they came to the line of the Scots, young Gloucester, playing the gallant leader, sought to show the way by urging his spirited steed forward ahead of the others, to drive between two of the schiltroms, narrow as the gap was, aiming no doubt to divide them still further. But the Scots pikemen on both flanks broke through their own kneeling ranks to assail, spears thrusting, dirks stabbing. The horses were the targets, Gloucester's and those who closely followed him. Bearing and plunging and whinnying in fear and hurt, these went down in a chaos of flailing limbs and hooves, the young earl with them, to disappear beneath his own mount.

Hereford nearby was less valiant. He rode along the line northwards, to find an entry near Angus's schiltrom where penetration had been achieved and managed to ride through.

He was one of the fortunate ones. Elsewhere along the extended line, the slaughter of horses, and many of the fallen riders, went on, these hedgehogs of spears all but impassable for dragging-hooved beasts to ride down. Lances did not reach the spearmen, although battle-axes and maces were thrown at them. However the defenders' casualties were very few compared with the enemy.

Then it was a case of slaying any unhorsed riders who could not manage to flee. Randolph shouted along the line that Gloucester was dead.

The king sought to assess and to forward the situation, chaotic as it was. Clearly they had broken the English vanguard, or it had broken itself by this action. Some had escaped, but as a force it was decimated. The main English host, however, was still there, behind, and would not, almost certainly, repeat this disastrous procedure. What, then?

Keeping the line of schiltroms intact, Bruce called that he saw no opportunity for actual attack. He shouted his commands, to be passed on from group to group on either side. Wait where they were meantime.

Then two movements became apparent among the enemy.

One was the heavy cavalry based on that hogsback, starting to leave it and make back through the marshland for the main encampment. The other was men on foot heading out from the mass to meet them. These would be the archers, to occupy the outcrop. Somebody was using his wits out there, at length.

The two groups, those on foot going faster than the horsemen, met and passed each other. So the menace of the bowmen was going to develop.

Bruce had arranged a signal for Keith and his light cavalry, away to the north: three long blasts on his horn. He blew them now. It was to be hoped that the Marischal could hear them, and ride to reach that hogsback before the archers did. And he and his men able to withstand arrows coming their way.

There was nothing more to be done about this threat meantime. But action was called for against the main enemy mass, which seemed to be preparing to move almost due southwards, on a different line from the ill-fated vanguard, presumably to ford the major burn at the Mill of Bannock. This would entail moving across a stretch of levels called the Carse of Skeoch, that name meaning blackthorns, which indicated slightly firmer ground. This move must be halted, if possible, or the enemy might indeed win out of the trap.

Bruce ordered his schiltroms to edge forward, keeping as nearly an unbroken line as they could, to seek to cut off that English advance, this behind their frieze of long pikes, whatever the state of the going.

It all made a strange contest indeed, two so very different forces moving in approximately the same direction, slowly picking their way, and the foot more effectively than the cavalry, this applying also to the enemy infantry in their thousands, these in fact drawing well ahead, to become two distinct forces. To call it a race was a contradiction in terms, so halting and devious was the progress of all concerned, but competition it was, and the horsemen getting the worst of it.

This recognition very evident, the English commanders

sought to create a diversion. A quite large detachment of their cavalry turned to face back, to confront the Scots ragged line, while the main force pressed on.

King Robert had to decide, and swiftly. To form up into compact schiltroms again, although the safest course, would not serve here. This enemy group needed only to stand still to allow their principal host, no doubt including King Edward, Pembroke and the other leaders, to follow their footmen and presently gain firmer ground. So it had to be onward, behind their banks of spears, for the Scots, to attack the stationary horsemen, pike against lances and swords. There was really no choice.

At least they were drawing ever further away from those archers, as they advanced. This would be an even greater testing than against Gloucester's vanguard, where they had formed the many schiltroms. Now it was only an uneven line, four or five deep, yes, but much more vulnerable.

Then they perceived a new development. Not a few of the waiting English cavalrymen were dismounting, recognising that their horses were but a handicap in this, and that they would do better afoot. This was a disadvantage, but had to be faced.

The Scots came close, wading, stumbling, cursing. And some of those dismounted English formed themselves up into tight little groups, their lances forward, not exactly schiltroms but something of the sort, having seen how effective these could be. Behind them the horsed men and the riderless mounts were massed.

It was those riderless horses which gave Bruce his new immediate policy. His line of men was much longer than the enemy front. If it could form into a moving crescent, all but a great U, to enclose the enemy, and his men hurl everything they could, save for the essential spears, into the mass of the waiting horsemen, axes, maces, daggers, even helmets, it might well serve. Riderless horses were readily alarmed and excited. If these could be roused, startled, there would follow major confusion among the remainder of the cavalry, and consequent turmoil among the dismounted men in front.

Bruce shouted his instructions, these to be passed along the lines, right and left. At least the slow and plodding pace of the advance gave time for the word to spread and be heeded, missiles readied for the throwing.

It was, to be sure, a very strange way into battle – but were not all the conditions sufficiently strange? As the enemy was reached, and the centre-front clashed spears with the English lances, the wings rounded forward at either side, and the tossing and hurling of weaponry began, amidst great shouting.

The result was speedy as it was effective. Not only the riderless mounts but the others also took fright at the shower of objects raining down on them, many of them sharp as well as heavy, and reared and curvetted, tossed and wheeled and sidled, to the confusion of all, including the men in front with their lances. It quickly became a chaos as the animals plunged hither and thither, riderless beasts upsetting the others. In fact the Scots themselves were endangered by the lashing, kicking rabble.

But the disorder and ferment was all in favour of the attackers who had contrived it. The enemy, such as could do so, scattered, drew aside, and became no longer a force to be reckoned with, leadership impossible. Many fled, and on foot, if so their departure could be termed. One more odd contest had been won on this so vital and decisive day for Scotland.

Whether the sight of this was the cause, or not, now the lengthy concourse of non-combatants up on the St Ninians and Tor wood escarpment decided to play their part. Down the steep slope from the high ground they came, clergy, grooms, cooks, baggage-men, local folk, even women, jumping, tripping, with staves and hatchets and kitchen-knives, shouting and cheering. It certainly did give the impression of reinforcements arriving in large numbers for the King of Scots.

And so it evidently appeared to the English leaders. This, and the last affray, however minor they both actually were, had a major effect on the entire situation. The enemy host was now not only split up and in disarray, but demoralised – at least the command evidently was. And in it all Angus, like the others, could see, and none so far off, a quite large party of horsemen filing off from the rest, along the Skeoch firmer ground, due southwards, this notably well supplied with banners, the largest of which bore the three lions passant gardant of the royal house of England. Edward of Caernarvon was on his way from that field of Bannockburn.

All but unbelieving, speechless at first, even Robert Bruce gazed. They all did. The King of England had accepted defeat, major and entire defeat, and had fled the field. And Pembroke's banner was to be seen just behind the royal one.

Was the day theirs, then? Was it? Could it be? Or did the rest of the English lords and knights and chivalry seek to fight on?

They did, but although it was fighting the Scots to some extent, it was, for their men, much more generally fighting the morass and carseland, as they sought to pick and hack and even swim their way to freedom, many failing, in this last, to do so. Those who did stand and fight sought to sell their lives dearly, especially among the knights and chivalry, but the ordinary men-at-arms and troopers were concerned mainly with escape in these circumstances, their monarch and chief commanders gone. The river drew ever increasing numbers, but swimming in any sort of armour, leather gear and heavy boots was a great handicap, and not all were expert in the water. The Forth meanders became all but choked with bodies.

One group that surrendered in a mass, and early on, was the dreaded archers. These were, of course, Welshmen, and had been pressed into service. Now, seeing their masters in disorder or fled, they yielded to Keith.

Some of the lords made a brave show of it, however handicapped by their heavy and armoured destriers. But most well understood their present situation, its hopelessness, and the accustomed usage in such defeat: ransom. Lives spared, in return for gold and silver promised. Their attackers knew it also, to be sure, and were loud in their demands in return for mercy and freedom.

It all made no very gallant proceeding, the ending and tidying up of battle, in mud and blood, self-interest, desperation, panic, vengeance and plunder. And it took a long time to conclude. It had been just after noon when King Edward had departed, but the sun was low in the sky before King Robert was able to address himself to accepting the formal surrender of many lords, nobles, knights and squires, who were lined up for him to receive and inspect; these, and the many who were brought to him borne on shields and hurdles, wounded and dead, Gloucester's body among them. This was arranged in the nearby Cambuskenneth Abbey.

Angus was there, to watch, with not a few of his chiefs. This was something that none had ever before witnessed, the procession of the defeated, alive and dead, and their captors negotiating ransom-moneys. By the Islesmen's standards it was scarcely dignified.

The Bruce, in it all, did retain his royal dignity, indeed his beneficence and actual generosity towards some of the defeated, declaring them free to go back to their own land, especially ones whom he had known of old, when he had been often at Edward the First's court. But one such, borne lying on a hurdle, he stared at, shaking his head, a man whom he had hated.

"Clifford!" he exclaimed. "Robert Clifford, 'fore God! Aye, before God at last! May He . . . have mercy. As this one seldom had! Mercy on his soul. May he rest in peace."

Angus wondered.

That night, in the refectory of the abbey, the king and his closer associates took stock of it all and what had been achieved, among which thanks were offered to the Lord of the Isles for all the help given, and not only in this battle but over the years before. It would not be forgotten. In this, Angus did bring up the subject never far from his mind: the Isle of Man. What now, in that English-occupied southernmost corner of his domains? Would His Grace now do what had been mooted for long: make, with himself, a full-scale assault on that semi-independent island polity? He was assured, yes, that would be an urgent priority. But it was not unlikely that Edward of Caernarvon would, in the circumstances, himself order an evacuation of Man. He would now be anxious to remove all subjects of dispute between the two kingdoms, lest Scotland sought to build further on the great defeat, and invade far southwards. He, Bruce, would not be surprised if Man was abandoned by the foe.

Angus rejoiced for his friend Rory. And possibly for his father-in-law O'Cahan and the Ulstermen also. That might well be another evacuation.

A bright future almost certainly shone ahead, for the Isles as for all Scotland.

EPILOGUE

Angus Og had reason to be well content thereafter, and for years to come. The Isles were at peace, as was all Scotland. The Isle of Man was secure. Trade flourished, not only the bird-oil. Relations with Orkney and Norway were rewarding. Ulster was free of the English – although not all Ireland was. Indeed King Robert himself visited there on occasion, and when he did, called in at Dunaverty for the necessary transport, and maintained pleasant association with the Islesman and his family.

Ainea remained a most satisfying, endearing and helpful wife; and the young people grew fast, Finguala clearly going to be good-looking, and John a youth of spirit – too much spirit sometimes for his father. What sort of Lord of the Isles would he make, one day?

Robert the Bruce found those years rewarding also, or most of them, although in time his health deteriorated, to his vexation; not that he was sorry for himself, but that he had sworn to make a crusade to the Holy Land if God gave him the kingdom; and his recurring ailment, which he feared was leprosy, the price he paid for the slaying of the Red Comyn in a church, was preventing him from doing anything such. He did make pilgrimages to the Isle of Whithorn, on the Solway coast of Galloway, where St Ninian had first brought Christianity to parts of Scotland before Columba came from Ireland in 563 – he once having to be carried in a litter there, like any portly priest. But that was not the same as a crusade.

Angus sympathised, and gave thanks for his own good health.

It was during one of the royal visits to Ulster, in the August of 1328, fourteen years after Bannockburn no less, that Angus was shocked at the monarch's appearance. Bruce told him that he did not think that he would survive for much longer, and he wished to setle certain matters, including this of Ulster, while still he could. His queen, Elizabeth de Burgh, had presented him with a son at last, young Robert, this four years previously; and it looked as though the lad might become King of Scots at a very early age. He would, in that eventuality, expect his friend the Lord of the Isles to aid and support the child, for he might well need all the help he could gain – for John Balliol's son, Edward, was now claiming the Scots throne, and would almost certainly take advantage of a child's succession.

Angus promised the fullest backing.

There was another matter, Bruce mentioned: this of the Stone of Destiny and its safety, on his death. This would have to be dealt with. Edward Balliol knew, if not all his English friends did, that the Coronation Stone at Westminster Abbey, which Edward Longshanks had taken south in 1296, was not the real Lia Fail, the Stone of Destiny, but only a lump of Scone sandstone which the abbot there, the custodian, had substituted for the precious crowning-seat of Scotland's monarchy. And Edward Balliol would wish to be crowned on it, and require English support to gain the Scots throne. So its safety would have to be seen to. And Angus might well be the best person to help. After all, the true Stone had come from the Isles, had it not? Iona, where it was thought to have been St Columba's portable altar. Perhaps it should go back there? Its safety would certainly have to be considered.

Angus declared that he was ready to help in this, as in all else.

It was not until June of next year, 1329, that there was any direct word from the King of Scots; and it came, as so often such had, by way of Sir Neil Campbell of Lochawe, one of the Bruce's closest associates. And it was grim news. The king was

387

almost certainly dying, at Cardross near to Dumbarton on the Clyde, the comparatively modest house which he had built recently for himself and his queen. And he desired to see the Lord of the Isles before he passed on to a greater kingdom than Scotland, if so he was blest.

So it was northwards up Clyde to just west of the royal fortress of Dumbarton, with the Campbell, a sad journey.

At Cardross, no great strength nor palace, he was received by worried-looking men, Thomas Randolph, Bruce's nephew, whom he had created Earl of Moray, Sir James Douglas, whom the king called the Good, and Bernard, Abbot of Arbroath, all in a state of gloom and anxiety. Edward Bruce was in Ireland. The child Robert was the only cheerful member of the establishment.

Bernard de Linton said that he would go and see whether His Grace was in a state to receive the visitors. He was apt to be asleep, or scarcely awake.

When the secretary came back, it was to inform that, yes, the king was heedful and in his right mind. He, in fact, desired to see not only the Lord of the Isles but them all. He, the abbot, advised that they did not remain overlong in the bedchamber, for His Grace tired quickly; but meantime, this was a royal command.

All but on tiptoe, then, the men entered the presence.

The man lying on the bed was only a shadow of what he had been, even compared with Angus's last sight of him a matter of nine months before. Bruce opened his eyes as they came in, looking, and raising a trembling hand in salute.

"Your devoted servants, Sire," de Linton said.

The royal voice began as little more than a whisper, but strengthened somewhat as, with an effort, the monarch sought to raise himself from the pillow. He failed in that but, lying back, the words came more clearly, lucidly enough.

"My friends," he said, "My good friends all. I greet you, who am . . . on my way. Not long now, I think. Bound for a

388

better place, God willing. My son you should grieve for. You must aid and guide him with all that is in you. In you all."

He paused for long moments as they gave their assurances. Then making a very evident summoning of strength, if that it could be called, the king went on.

"There will be much need of your good efforts. My son is but of five years. This of Edward Balliol, whose father was crowned king, however feeble. The son is otherwise. He will strive to replace *my* son. Rob will require a regent. For long. A strong regent. You, Thomas, his cousin, must be that. Not my brother. Who seeks to be King of Ireland. Heed it, Thomas."

Randolph bowed, but in silence.

"You all to accord him your fullest strength. This my last command to you." Bruce raised that shaking hand. "Or . . . not quite last. James, my good and true companion in so much. When I breathe my last, you are to see to it. You know of my vow to go on crusade. This you are to do. Have my breast cut open. My heart taken out. Bury the body at Dunfermline; Bernard, you see to that. But the Douglas to take the heart. Carry it against the Infidel. On the crusade which I could nowise make. The best that I can now do. You have it, James? You must act for me, friend. No light token. No gesture. Cut, and take. Or . . . I shall haunt you ever after!"

Douglas, the Good Sir James, as all knew him, bowed. "Yes, Sire."

"That is well." Another quite lengthy pause, eyes closed. But they opened again.

"And you, friend Angus of the Isles – the Stone! Your last service to me, if not to my son. I have had it brought here, the Lia Fail. From Scone Abbey. You are to take it to your Hebridean fastnesses, where it came from. And keep it secure until a worthy successor sits on my throne. Iona. Or Islay. Or wherever you will. Secure. Young Rob will be brought to be crowned on it, Thomas, in due course. Is it understood? By all of you? The Stone of Destiny. Scotland's precious symbol. Bernard, you will keep Columba's Brecbennoch safe, where you will. But the Stone goes to the Isles. Balliol, unlike the English, will not be content with the lump of stone quarried at Scone, those years ago, to deceive Longshanks. His father sat on the true Lia Fail. As did I. So, see to it . . ." The failing voice died away.

"It shall be so, Sire," Angus assured. "We shall hold it safe."

The royal eyes closed, the laboured if light breathing the only sound in that room.

They waited. Then Abbot Bernard pointed to the door, and they all backed out, bowing towards the bed.

"I will take you to the Stone, my lord Angus," de Linton said.